JESUS WEARS DOCKERS

The Gospel Conspiracy Story

I0650638

OREST STOCCO

JESUS WEARS DOCKERS

Copyright © 2013 by OREST STOCCO

ISBN 978-0-9879357-7-9

Edited by Penny Lynn Cates

Cover Design by Penny Lynn Cates

My gratitude to Padre Pio,
Roman Catholic Saint and Ascended Spiritual Master,
who encouraged me to publish this book.

"For when the master himself was asked by someone
when his kingdom would come, he said, *'When the two will be one,
and the outer like the inner, and the male with the female neither
male nor female.'*"

*"God's kingdom is spread out upon the earth,
and people do not see it."*

*"Whoever finds the interpretation of these sayings
will not taste death."*

THE UNKNOWN SAYINGS OF JESUS

Marvin Meyer

Contents

PART ONE

<u>Jesus in the Park</u>

1. *Let the World Find Its Own Way* 1

2. *You Cannot Put New Wine into Old Bottles* 7

3. *The Garden of Life Forever Needs Tending* 12

4. *In the Garden of Mystic Lovers* 18

5. *Suffer the Little Squirrels unto Us* 23

6. *The Heart of the Matter* 26

7. *Disemboweling Christianity* 30

8. *Keep Your Eye on the Ball* 38

9. *Dig for Dig* 43

10. *The Insidious Worm of Christian Conceit* 46

11. *The Divine Imminence* 50

12. *The Dual Consciousness of Man* 55

13. *Life Is a Waking Dream* 59

14. *For the Sake of the Reader* 63

15. *The I of God* 67

16. *The Way of Love* 71

17. *A Grease Monkey for God* 76

18. *Out, O Damned Spot!* 82

19. *My Sense of Life* 87

20. *The Meat of the Last Supper* 92

21. *In the Shoes of Christ's Sayings* 98

22. *The Seductive Power of the Way* 102

23. *A Tricky Question for Jesus* 107

24. *A Curious Pair of Bridge Builders* 111

25. *The Scales of Divine Justice* 115

26. *The Three Stages of the Self* 123

27. *The Sacred Mantra* 129

28. *The Confession of Jesus Christ* 134

29. *Many Are Called but Few Are Chosen* 139

30. *Savior of the Status Quo* 146

PART TWO

<u>The Sayings of Jesus Revealed</u>

31. *My Jesus Book* 153

32. *Why Me, Jesus?* 158

33. *So, What Is the Way Then?* 161

34. *Levi Virtue* 167

35. *Would You Take Out the Garbage for Me, Please?* 173

36. *Breaking the Law of Silence* 178

37. *The Greater Wisdom in My Box of Books* 182

38. *A Journey through the Consciousness of Jesus Christ* 188

39. *Who's Going to Pay My Bills, Jesus Christ?* 194

40. *Once Again, Jesus Surprised Me* 198

41. *The Shocking Truth of Christ's Message Two Thousand Years Ago* 202

42. *Leading a Horse to Water* 208

43. *The Golden Thread of God*..213

44. *Jesus Lets the Big Cat Out of the Bag* 219

45. *The Historical Duplicity of Christ's Life and Teaching* 228

46. *Letting Soul Speak* 234

47. *Frolicking With God*...237

48. *The Parable of the Sower Revealed*..242

49. *A Man of Flesh and Spirit* 255

50. *A Foil for Christ* 261

51. *The Metaphysics of Karma*..273

52. *The Incredible Technique of Letting Go and Letting God* 281

53. *The Greatest Salesman in the World*.......................................287

54. *Jesus Resolves the Paradox of His Teaching* 291

55. *The Secret of the Way* 306

56. *One of the Most Unholy Mysteries* 314

57. *The Good Shepherd Is Witness for the Prosecution*.................321

58. *I Am Soul, Therefore I Am* 328

59. *A Short Dialogue with the Inner Master* 349

60. *Stupidity Is Not a Gift of God*...352

PART THREE

<u>Jesus Comes Clean</u>

61. *Sifting the Wisdom of God from the Wisdom of Man* 358

62. *The Parable of Christ's Temptation* 364

63. *The House that Jesus Built* 372

64. *The Real Cost of Being a Christian* 391

65. *Journey into the Heart of God* 400

66. *The Living Way* 407

67. *A Bone to Pick with St. Paul* 418

68. *The Word Behind the Words of Jesus* 425

69. *The Psychology of Christ's Teaching* 438

70. *A Foretelling Dream* 444

71. *Be a Good Person, and Let the Universe Unfold as It Should* ..447

72. *Out of the Abundance of the Heart of Man* 454

73. *The Unholy Children of God* 461

74. *The Beatitudes Revealed* 469

75. *Coming Clean* 478

OTHER BOOKS BY OREST STOCCO

COMING WORKS

PART ONE

<u>JESUS IN THE PARK</u>

1. *Let the World Find Its Own Way*

I felt a gentle tap on my shoulder. I turned to look. It was Jesus. "Did you enjoy the service?" he asked, with a bright twinkle in his eyes.

"As a matter of fact, it was the most satisfying service I've attended yet," I replied, smiling with surprise. "I'm glad you appeared, because I had serious doubts about attending any more worship services."

Jesus did not say anything, but his eyes beckoned me.

"Tell me, Jesus," I said, as though talking to an old friend, "is it me, or is what I'm witnessing a clear picture of the conceit that I see in some of these High Initiates?"

"Both," replied Jesus. "You have to appreciate where they're coming from, even if they have no idea of the effect they have on people. Not all of them, of course. Just those High Initiates that have not yet resolved the deeper issues of their own vanity."

"It is a curse, isn't it?"

"What, vanity?"

"Yes."

"Tell me about it! Even on the cross I preened like a peacock!"

I burst into laughter. "You certainly fooled a lot of people," I said, still laughing at Christ's surprising candor. "But not the Living Soul Master. He saw through the vanity of your mission to save the world and called you the boldest of peacocks. But that's all water under the bridge, isn't it? So, what are you doing here now?"

"How can I put this?" Jesus said, furrowing his brow. I looked at him, smiling at the contrast the real Jesus made with the image the world has drawn of its savior. A small, slender man Jesus was still dressed in the same casuals that he had on when he appeared at our worship service at the library earlier: a warm yellow short-sleeve polo shirt and tan Dockers just like the ones Cathy had purchased for me, and sandals on his bare feet. Clean shaven, his face was broad, full jowled, and although striking it was not what one would call handsome. But it wasn't his face that my eyes fell upon first; it was his eyes. Jesus had the most striking dark eyes that shone with such clarity it felt like looking into the barrier reef of his soul, which was infinite in its beauty; and his hair was cut short in a modish style that gave him a young, professorial look. In fact, his whole presence gave me the feeling that we were old alumni of the Way taking a leisurely stroll through the campus of life. "It's time to set the record straight," he finally said, which gave me a feeling of regret that it had taken him this long to reveal the messiah secret. I had decided to walk to the park several blocks from the library to reflect on my other-worldly experience with Jesus at the service when he surprised me again. "The world has greatly misunderstood my teaching," he continued, with obvious remorse in his voice, "and you can help me to set the record straight."

I felt the strangest presentiment, like I was about to enter once more into another parallel world. I couldn't speak for a moment or two. "Why me?" I finally asked.

"Need I tell you?" Jesus said, his face lighting up with so much love that I actually felt it touching me like a strong draft of warm air.

I was compelled to smile. Suddenly I broke into a fit of giddy laughter as Holy Spirit rushed into me with such incredible force that I could not contain the electric joy of two Souls connecting with the Holy Current of God. "You don't have to tell me," I replied, feeling the strongest urge to grab Jesus and give him a big hug. "But I'd sure love to hear you say it," I quickly added, to my own amazement.

Jesus laughed. I felt embarrassed for revealing my emotions.

"Alright, O," he said, with the sweetest smile on his remarkable face. "I'll firm up your confidence for you, if you like.

You have proven to be an exceptional channel for the true spirit of my sayings that have puzzled the world far too long, and I need your help to set the record straight. Would you be interested in having a dialogue with me to explain the secret of spiritual rebirth in my gospel to the world?"

"Finally!" I exclaimed, once again to my amazement. I felt like I was so far outside myself that I wasn't even the same person; I was another me. *"What the hell took you so long?"* I instantly added, and burst into another fit of giddy laughter.

Jesus laughed also. And the more we laughed, the more light-headed I felt. "I have to sit down," I said. "I feel dizzy—"

"There's a bench," Jesus pointed, and walked over and sat down. I staggered over and flopped down. The moment I got off my feet my dizziness went away.

"What was it you asked?" I said. I still felt giddy with love. I looked at Jesus and laughed again. His energy was too much for me all at once.

"That's what divine love can do to a person when two Souls connect," Jesus said.

"Yes. I understand. I've always associated laughter with love. And yet the world has come to see you as a humorless savior. Why is that, J?" I asked, but with such surprising familiarity that it set free another bout of giddy laughter.

"These are difficult times, and the world needs more humor today," he said, with that same feeling of sympathetic camaraderie in his voice that had just overwhelmed me. "This is why I need your help to set the record straight. You have the right spirit, O."

"Set the record straight?" I said, as the most vivid image of the most crooked path in the world flashed across my mind. *"We couldn't set Christianity straight if we had the faith of a million mustard seeds!"*

Jesus broke into a fit of irrepressible laughter. He had to hold his stomach. "Probably not," he finally said, once again with the sweetest smile on his exceptional face. "But I'd sure like to try all the same, O."

3

Sobering up at the serious tone of his voice, I collected myself and replied, "It's the Way of Christ that you want to explain to the world?"

"Exactly," said Jesus.

"And what consequences can I expect for helping you?" I asked, feeling the gravity of his request. "Another malicious rebuff from the world? If you don't know it yet, J; as far as I'm concerned the world can find its own way — *and I mean that!*"

Jesus smiled. "I know you do, O. This is why I have chosen you. You are the right man for this task. You have just the right attitude to help put my gospel teaching into proper perspective. This is why Stanley Hansen has difficulty with you. And other chelas. It's your attitude, O. I love it, but it's too much for most people."

"Why is that?" I had to ask. Jesus was referring to my relationship with my spiritual community. From the day Cathy and I moved to Georgian Bay I felt an underlying tension with my fellow chelas, but I couldn't explain it.

"You chafe people, O. You have a way of pricking their vanity," Jesus explained. "Some chelas have difficulty accepting how you treat the teachings of the Light and Sound of God like any other spiritual path. It's a blow to their spiritual conceit."

"But that's only because I know that life is the Way!" I heard myself shouting at Jesus. *"O vanity of vanities, all is vanity!"* I added, feeling very defensive.

"EXACTLY!" Jesus exclaimed, to my surprise. "This is why I want to dialogue with you on my gospel teaching. We're both Initiates of the Way. With your help I can finally set the record of my gospel straight. What do you say, O? Are you up to the challenge?"

Again, sobering up at Christ's tone I felt myself suddenly centered, and replied, "By gospel, you're referring to your sayings?"

"Essentially, yes. It's in my sayings that my gospel can be found."

"And it doesn't really matter if you authored these sayings or not, does it?" I said, and suddenly broke into another fit of laughter at the image of an endless line of hunch-backed monks leaning over their Bible baffling over Christ's enigmatic sayings.

"Precisely!" Jesus burst out, with such force in his voice that it brought me back to myself. **"The gospel of Christ is the Way of Life! The Way of Life is the Way! And the Way exists in all the sayings of life, because the Way is life itself!"** Jesus added, with such intensity that I centered completely. "This is why I need your help, O. Too much has been made of who said this and who said that. What does it matter if one angel or ten billion angels can stand on the head of a pin, or if you live one life or a thousand lives? This is just another one of *Deus Deceptor's* little games to keep Soul trapped in the lower worlds. You have broken through this barrier, O. You know that life is the Way. You speak the language of the Way. And you know my teaching as well as the Gospel writers. What do you say, O; are you up to the challenge?" Jesus asked, almost like he was pleading with me.

I couldn't believe my ears. I had to chuckle to relieve the pressure of Christ's words; but I did relish the idea of helping the messiah of the world reveal his secret.

"I see where you're coming from," I said, feeling totally myself now. "As a matter of fact," I added as the memory surfaced, "I anticipated this dialogue with you fifteen years ago with a book I wanted to write. I was going to call it *The Meat of the Last Supper.*"

Jesus burst into laughter again. The infectious spirit of joy possessed me once more, and I giggled with light-headed abandon.

"What do you say, O? Are you up to the challenge of helping me to dispel the Gospel conspiracy?" Jesus asked, with just the right edge to provoke me.

"Gospel conspiracy?" I asked, puzzled. "What Gospel conspiracy?"

Jesus looked me deep in the eyes. It was the first time I saw it, but there was the most subtle hint of a playfully mischievous smile in his eyes and sweet curve on his lips that I would come to see often in the course of our talks, not unlike the mystic Mona Lisa's smile that teased my sense of reality. "You'll come to see what I mean in good time," he replied.

"What the hell!" I burst out, surprising myself. *"Why not?"*

"Good!" said Jesus, and gave me a friendly slap on the shoulder.

"You know, J," I said, feeling his love filling me up again so quickly that I could not contain it, "that's the problem with the spiritual life today — *not enough whimsy!*"

"You won't regret this, O. I promise you," Jesus said, with the biggest grin.

"Please, no promises! I couldn't stand to be disappointed in you again!" I said, and broke into another fit of irrepressibly giddy laughter.

Jesus joined me, and we laughed to our heart's content like two old friends who hadn't seen each other in many, many years.

2. *You Cannot Put New Wine into Old Bottles*

"Why now after all this time?" I asked Jesus, once we had settled down from our initial connection. I took in a deep breath and cast my gaze out.

It was a beautiful day, and people wandered in and out of the little park by the river in the heart of the city. A fortuneteller had set up his table under a shady red maple, and two or three people were waiting to have their fortunes read. I had seen him before, a little oriental man with glasses, and I thought of having my fortune read but I chose not to because I didn't dabble in the psychic realm.

"Your future lies in your present," Jesus replied to my unspoken thoughts. "You make your own future with every thought you think. Control your thoughts and you control your future."

I turned to Jesus. I wanted to say something witty, but his eyes pierced the depths of my soul and I said, "To a point. Karma dictates much of our future, does it not? I know this for a fact now since I had my seven past-life regressions. I would never have believed my life was so pre-determined by my past lives. My relationship with Cathy began as a karmic debt because of what I did to her in our past life together. We were husband and wife in Genoa, Italy and I abandoned her for my mistress whom I met when we moved to Georgian Bay. She's also a chela of the Light and Sound of God. Thank God Cathy and I were able to rebuild our relationship after we faced the karma that brought all three of us together again. Once I brought our karma to the surface with my regression, it drove a wedge between Cathy and me. Being chelas however, the Inner Master helped us resolve our karma and rebuild our relationship on karma-free love. I could not dishonor Cathy again. I had to do what was right for all three of us. It cost us dearly, but now we are free of that karmic bond. I agree with you, J; controlling our thoughts does set up conditions for our future, but our thoughts are much more colored by our past lives than we can possibly imagine."

"Our past comes back to haunt us, certainly," Jesus replied, in a soft, understanding voice. "But from the spiritual perspective we live our life in the present," he added, his voice becoming more serious. "Treat your life as one eternal moment and call it the Present. By living your life in the Present you take control of your life, because the Present includes the past and future. This concept takes getting used to. In time you will get used to it. I promise you; once you step into the Holy Now you will never again want to live your life any other way. So, do you want to have your fortune read?"

"What's the point now?" I said, and laughed.

Jesus broke into a hearty chuckle. "The world loves your sense of humor, O," he said, smiling at me. "It crosses all planes of consciousness and even takes Soul Masters by surprise. May I ask; to what do you attribute your sense of humor?"

"Pain!" I burst out, and grimaced.

Jesus laughed again. "Yes, pain will open the heart center eventually. But you heal much more quickly these days, do you not?"

"I suppose. But it doesn't get any easier, does it?"

"Yes and no. Life is life. Some days it's harder and some days it's easier. All in all, life keeps a pretty balanced account. Have you decided what to call our dialogue?"

"Why do you ask?"

"I'd love to know what spin you put on our relationship."

"Spin? How contemporary. And you think the title will reflect that?"

"Certainly. The whole is always reflected in its parts."

"And you'd like to know how I perceive the whole of Jesus Christ, is that it?" I asked, with a suspicious smile.

"The Jesus Christ that you have experienced through my sayings," Jesus replied, with a bright twinkle in his all-knowing eyes.

"Yes, of course. What other Jesus could I know?"

"The Jesus you've met on the inner planes," he responded, to my surprise. "You don't remember because the Dream Censor has kept this information from you. As we get on in these talks your memory will awaken, and you will add new and exciting textures to our dialogue. Tell me, what title do you have in mind?"

As Jesus was talking I was looking at his Dockers, which looked very comfortable on him, and then I looked at my own same tan Dockers, which I found very comfortable; and then I smiled at the thought of Jesus in a long robe, long hair, and beard.

"What? Jesus said.

"How about *Jesus Wears Dockers*?"

"I like that. And so will Sears."

"Sears?"

"Yes. Sears sells Dockers, do they not?"

"I don't know. Cathy bought my Dockers."

"Well, they do. That's where I purchased mine," Jesus said, with a big grin on his face. "It's a good title because it puts me into the present. Believe me; Christianity needs to be put into the present. It seems to be stuck in a time warp, don't you think?"

"The twilight zone's more like it," I said, and snickered.

"That's because of Christianity's greatest fear," Jesus responded, totally serious in his confident, professorial-sounding voice.

"Which is?" I asked.

"You tell me. Stop and think for a minute, O. Why do Christians refuse to get it, to use your expression?"

"My expression?" I said, intrigued.

"Yes. From your chapter 'Getting It,' in your book *The Way of Soul*."

"I haven't even transcribed that book yet," I said, my heart skipping with joy because I knew what Jesus was going to say.

"I know. But it's published on the inner planes," he said, grinning, "and it's taken a lot of people by surprise. Tell me, why do you think Christians refuse to get it?"

"Give me a minute," I said, still smiling at the confirmation of my first Soul talk book being published in the inner worlds. "Alright," I said, snapping myself out of my dream world, "why do some people get it and some don't?"

"Go on," said Jesus. "Why do some people get it and others don't?"

"Let's take me," I pondered, casting my mind inward. "Why do I get it sometimes and not others? It's all a question of consciousness. The more conscious I am, the more variables I see, and the more variables I see, the easier it will be to connect the dots. It seems that making the connections is what getting it is all about. Christianity can't make the connections because it refuses to see all the variables. Christianity is stuck in one dogmatic perspective that will not allow perception of all the necessary variables to make enough connections to get it. In a word, I would have to say that Christianity's greatest fear is the fear of consciousness."

"Bingo!" exclaimed Jesus, with a rapturous smile. "We'll talk more about this when we discourse on the fears of Christianity," he added, in his serious voice. "For now, let's just prime the pump so the waters of everlasting life can flow freely in our dialogue. If you will, O; we're just connecting in that special way that lets Soul speak."

"Thank goodness I did my three Soul talk books, then. They're not transcribed yet; but as you seem to know, they certainly opened up the channel in me for Soul to speak freely. If I may ask, J; where do you see our dialogue going?"

"Who knows? I definitely want to reveal the secret of my sayings so we can dispel the Gospel conspiracy. Why don't we talk about that now? Why do you suppose so much fuss is made about whether I authored my sayings or not?"

I thought for a moment, and said, "I've come to the conclusion that the world — the Christian world, in any event — is under the illusion that you possess a spiritual knowledge that is exclusive to you alone, and this obsession to know everything about you distorts the real picture of the Way. Once I realized that the Way is everywhere — which, I might add, did not come easily. I paid a very dear price to *get it* — then I realized that the Jesus of my Christian youth was not the Jesus of my adulthood, because I had grown enough spiritually to see that you were just a messenger of the Way and not the Way as Christianity believes; and that's the crux of the whole matter, isn't it?"

"I knew you would conceptualize it," Jesus replied, with a grin from ear to ear. "This is your gift, O. You can take the muddle out of the puddle for me. This is why you were chosen by the Way to help me dispel the Gospel conspiracy. I'm sure of it now."

Snickering at Christ's confidence in me, I replied, "Let's make it clear for the reader here that by Way we mean Holy Spirit. The world out there still doesn't know what the Way is yet."

"Yes, of course. But in due course the new will replace the old, because as I said two thousand years ago — and I did say this — *you cannot put new wine into old bottles!"*

10

JESUS WEARS DOCKERS

I laughed and laughed while Jesus just stared at me with a grin on his clean-shaven, full jowled happy face!

3. *The Garden of Life Forever Needs Tending*

"There's something I want to make clear before we get too involved in our dialogue," I said to Jesus, crossing my legs and resting my arm on the back of the bench. "I don't quite know how to put this, but I'd like your perspective. It has to do with the Bible."

"What about it?" Jesus asked, with an eagerness I didn't expect.

A beautiful blond woman in white shorts walked by, her arms swinging in rhythm with her shapely tanned long legs, and as she glanced at us I got the most peculiar sensation of being in two worlds at once. Jesus sensed this, and said, "Don't worry; you're not talking to yourself. She saw me as well. You were going to tell me something about the Bible?"

Smiling, I said, "If I touch you, you will feel solid, won't you?"

"Yes, of course," Jesus said, and patted my knee.

"That doesn't really prove anything," I said, reflecting on my experience with Jesus at the worship service where everyone experienced Jesus but only I remembered.

"I know," said Jesus, and sprang to his feet. He walked over to the hot dog vendor's cart on the sidewalk and got two hot dogs. When he returned, he handed me one and said, "I know you love onions, so I loaded yours."

"Thanks," I said, and laughed. "I think you've made your point."

"Let's eat our dogs. Then you can tell me what you want to know about the Bible," Jesus said, and took a generous bite.

. We ate our hot dogs in silence as we watched the park fill up with people. It didn't surprise me. People are always attracted to carriers of the Light and Sound of God. I first noticed this in shopping malls. I can walk into a bookstore and be the only customer and within minutes the store will be teeming with customers. The same happens when Cathy walks into a clothing or shoe store.

"It is wonderful, is it not, how people are attracted to the Holy Light and Sound of God?" Jesus mused, once again reading my thoughts.

The Light and Sound of God are the twin aspects of Divine Spirit.

"If they're so attracted to the energy of God, why do so few people take to the Way of the Eternal, then? No, don't answer that. I was being facetious. I know why."

"But do you really?" Jesus asked.

"Because it takes courage to let go of the old and embrace the new, that's why" I answered. "Is there another reason?"

"Yes. But now is not the time to discuss it."

"Why not?" I asked, eager to know.

"You were going to ask me something about the Bible?" Jesus said, deliberately avoiding my question.

I looked into Christ's eyes. "There's no messing with you, is there?"

"Nor with you. We're both cut from the same cloth, O. This is why I want to clear up this mess that Christianity has gotten itself into."

"I'm sure you will," I said, and laughed. "I'm afraid this mess has to see itself to the bitter end of this life cycle. It's much too ingrained in society."

"Yes, I know. But the seeds of spiritual clarity have to be planted to begin the process. Hopefully some will take root. *Ahhhhh,"* Jesus sighed. *"The Garden of Life forever needs tending!"*

"That's what Jacob the Elder used to say," I quickly responded. Jesus had triggered the memory of my past lifetime as Samuel the Essene.

"Yes, I know. That's who I was quoting."

"So you were there, then?"

"Of course. Why? Do you doubt it?"

"I have no way of proving it, but I'm certain I was there."

"That should be enough," Jesus said, with that same tenor of authority that I began to recognize was different from his casual voice. "For your information, O; I remember you. You asked me if I had looked into the Face of God."

13

"I did?" I said, now more intrigued than ever.

"Yes," Jesus replied, with that suspicious twinkle in his eyes.

"What did you say? That you and God were one?"

"That came later when I went out to save the world," Jesus said, with a chuckle.

I laughed also. "Did you really expect to save the world?"

"Not really," Jesus said, smiling playfully. "But I knew that I had to reveal the secret gateway into the kingdom of heaven."

"Why? Why were you so compelled to reveal the secret teaching to the world? You must have known how foolish that would be?" I asked, trying to be serious about something that really bothered me. I had a real bone to pick with Jesus.

"I just did," he said, in a different voice, sounding vulnerable. "I couldn't help myself. I was so crazy with God that I had to sow the seeds of God's kingdom. That was my destiny, O. There wasn't much I could do about it. I had to do my Father's work."

"Here's a question for you, then," I said, with complete seriousness. "Do you think the world would have been better off without your crucifixion and resurrection?"

"Let's not go there," Jesus abruptly said.

"Why not? I have a right to know. I've been haunted by this question for years, and you're the only person who can answer it. I really would like to know, J. It's important to me," I pleaded. "It's one of the few remaining puzzles of my life."

Jesus paused before answering. "The truth is, I don't know. Perhaps the world would have been better off without me. But then, Christianity has proven to be a wonderful school for Soul. Take your own life, for example. How do you feel about Christianity now?"

By turning the question back on me Jesus forced me to see that without his sayings I would not have initiated myself into the Creative Life Stream and experienced my own immortality when I did. I smiled, and said, "Speaking from the perspective of Soul, I'd have to say yes; Christianity has been a spiritual boon to the world. From the human perspective however, Christianity is—"

"Don't say it! We don't want that kind of language in our talks!"

I laughed. "I would have been polite about it."

"Polite or not, your sentiment would have been the same!"

"The thought's the thing wherein we will catch the conscience of the king," I said, playing upon Hamlet's famous line in Shakespeare's play, and burst into laughter.

Jesus smiled. "Indeed. Now, the Bible?"

"Yes. Well, I met the Living Soul Master, who founded the Way of the Eternal, one night in the inner worlds and he told me that the Christian Bible was mostly a work of dialectical fiction. That gave me a whole new perspective on Christianity."

"And for the sake of your reader, who was this Soul Master?"

"He brought the ancient spiritual teachings of the Light and Sound of God to the modern world. In the early sixties, I believe. These are the pure teachings of the Way, which he said you studied at the Katsupari Monastery in northern Tibet for three years during your so-called lost years. He called it the Way of the Eternal for the modern world. I studied the Way in three of my past lives: once with Pythagoras; another time, as you know, with Master Zadok in the Essene community at Qumran; and again in 15th Century in Persia. My name was Salaam, and I was a member of the secret Sufi Order of the White Tiger. That's why I'm so familiar with the Way," I said, smiling at the memories of my past lives.

Jesus made no comment. "What new perspective did you have on Christianity after you met the Living Soul Master?" he asked, and then quickly added, "Incidentally, where did you meet him?"

"In a dream. I don't know which plane of consciousness we were on, but it was in a library. He was the Living Soul Master before he translated."

"Translated?" Jesus queried, with a puzzled smile.

"That's the term we use in our spiritual community for dying. He's a Soul Master on the Other Side now working on his new spiritual duties and helping the current Living Soul Master; behind the scenes, as it were."

"If I may, what do you mean by Living Soul Master?" Jesus asked.

"For the sake of the reader, right?" I said, finally catching on to all his questions.

"Of course," Jesus said, and smiled contentedly.

"The Living Soul Master is the spiritual leader of the Way of the Eternal, the new religion of the Light and Sound of God. The Living Soul Master is the Living Word, the Light-giver and Way-shower of the world. He's the Way, or Divine Spirit incarnate if you will; and he is always with his chelas as the Inner Master."

"Chelas?" Jesus queried.

"In this context, a chela is a student of the Way of the Eternal."

"Okay. You were saying about the Bible?"

"Finally," I said, and laughed. "Well, I guess there's no other way of saying it, J. As I read the Bible I grew more and more suspicious that dialectical fiction was the genre used by the authors to get the message of the Way out to the world. I have a gut feeling now that it didn't really matter to the writers of the Bible that they took creative liberties with their stories, because their intent was to get the secret teaching out to the world in the best possible light; like the *Book of Job*, which reads to me now like an elaborate parable on good and evil. Am I correct in this feeling, or am I off the mark here?"

Jesus hesitated, studying my face. "You're correct to a point," he said, with a satisfied smile. "This is why we're having this dialogue. In the dynamic of our relationship we have the perfect medium for my message, and my message today is spiritual clarity. This is how you and I are going to dispel the Gospel conspiracy."

I smiled, pretending to understand what Jesus meant by Gospel conspiracy; but I hadn't made the connection yet, and I was too proud to ask.

"We can't decode your sayings without the larger context of the Divine Plan of God," I replied, with absolute confidence in my gnostic knowledge of the Way. "It will only muddle the puddle more, if I may use your expression."

"Yes, of course," Jesus said, nodding his head. "This is why we're talking. You've been initiated into the Divine Plan of God, so you can put my sayings into their proper perspective. Can we begin now?"

"No; not yet. We have to spell out the Divine Plan of God first. Let me ask you this, J. Did you intuit the Divine Plan of God, or did you experience it like I did when I had my past-life regressions?"

"I intuited it first, and then I experienced it when Master Zadok brought me to the Ocean of Love and Mercy. And then I refracted the Light of God in my gospel teaching according to the prism of my own individuality."

"Prism of my own individuality? That phrase sounds awfully familiar."

"It should. I've read everything you have published on the inner planes. In all frankness, O; I love the way you have conceptualized the secret teachings of the Way. It's a whole new thought pattern much more in keeping with the coming shift in world consciousness. If you will allow a moment's flattery, you have provided some exciting new bottles for a very old wine, and you have made it very palatable indeed!"

"But it wasn't me! It was Holy Spirit!" I exclaimed.

"Of course it was," Jesus calmly said, patting my knee. "As I said two thousand years ago, he who believeth in me out of his stomach shall flow the water of everlasting life."

"He who believeth in you?" I said, just to rub it in, and then I broke into an irrepressible chuckle. I couldn't help myself. The irony was too much to contain.

Jesus smiled, his eyes twinkling with a brilliant sparkle. "In the fullness of time, O; in the fullness of time your reader will connect all the dots..."

4. *In the Garden of Mystic Lovers*

"Here's a thought," I said to Jesus, with a snicker. "When *Jesus Wears Dockers* is in the marketplace and read by a public hungry to know the last detail of your life, what's to say that it won't be labeled a work of dialectical fiction by the skeptics?"

"That would be ironic," said Jesus, and laughed. "Alright, let's play out this scenario and get it out of the way. What does it matter? The effect your book will have on the reader will be the same if it's dialectical fiction or actual fact, because it's the content of the cups of God that is important; not the cups per say. Truth is truth, O; regardless of its medium."

"Cups of God?" I repeated. "That sounds very familiar. Where did I hear — *Jacob the Elder!*" I exclaimed again as the memory of my past lifetime as Samuel rushed to the surface. *"Cups of God were what we called the wisdom sayings in our teaching!"*

"You remember?" Jesus said, with a big grin.

"Yes, I do. Jacob told us that the wisdom sayings were like cups of God. As we lived the sayings, we dipped the cups of God into the Holy Stream of Life and filled them with the energy of everlasting life. That's how we grew in Spirit. *I remember that as clearly as if it were yesterday!*"

"Good. So you see the point, then? Whether your reader sees your book as dialectical fiction or an actual, albeit paranormal experience, it's the truth that matters."

"That's why it never really mattered to me whether you authored all the sayings that you uttered in my red-letter edition of the Bible. *I knew that the Way is the Way regardless who speaks for the Way!*"

"Absolutely," said Jesus.

"So the first thing we should clear up then before we get to the meat of the last supper—"

Jesus burst into laughter. "How you dance upon the waves of life! It would be a joy if we could sustain this levity throughout our dialogue."

"There's no reason why not — *as long as life doesn't drop a big one on me before our dialogue is completed!"* I replied, with an irrepressible snicker.

"It won't," Jesus said, in a more serious tone. "You're doing God's work now, and you will have respite for the time being."

"And then what?" I asked, as I felt the other shoe dropping.

"Life will continue as before according to your spiritual schedule. You will have your ups and downs. Just consider this as time out," Jesus replied, and smiled.

"Time out?" I said, as I felt the other shoe drop. *"That's just wonderful!"*

Still smiling, Jesus said, "Now, the meat of the last supper?"

"Okay," I said, jumping right back into the spirit of our talk. "As I was saying, we have to clear up one thing before we reveal your messianic secret. We have to be absolutely clear on this, J. You are NOT the message. You are only the messenger; right?"

"Absolutely," Jesus replied, and then broke into a private chuckle. I couldn't see what he was laughing at, so I asked him.

"What?" I said.

"Nothing. You'll see in good time. As I was saying, I have always been the messenger. Holy Spirit is the message. I, Jesus, son of Joseph and Mary, sower of the seeds of God's kingdom, want to set the record straight that I did not come to save the world. I came only to open the door to the kingdom of heaven. There, are you satisfied?"

"I've always been satisfied," I said, smiling at Christ's formal pronouncement of his true spiritual status in the world. "I came to this realization long before I worked out the Divine Plan of God. The point is, will the reader be satisfied?"

"Who knows? Some will, and some won't. That's not our problem, is it?" Jesus replied with such matter-of-fact bluntness that I burst into laughter.

"We are cut from the same cloth!" I exclaimed.

"We certainly are," Jesus said, with the biggest grin on face. "As are all those that have looked into the Face of God."

"I should have known! *'I, you, he, she, we /In the garden of mystic lovers, these are not true distinctions!'"* I burst out, unable to contain my emotions.

"Yes," said Jesus, his face just glowing with love. "Shams of Tabriz, who was the Living Soul Master of his time, went a long way to revealing this mystical union with God; as did his now famous and popular student."

"Who, Rumi?"

"Yes."

Suddenly it hit me. "Is this the reason for the strange effect that mystic lovers have on the rest of the world, even on High Initiates of the Way of the Eternal?"

Jesus laughed. "Yes. So you need not concern yourself with how your fellow chelas react to your light. Accept them for what they are."

"For how they reveal themselves, you mean?" I corrected.

"They will do that, certainly; for such is the power of the God-realized Soul to awaken the shadow personality in others. But don't fancy yourself home free yet, O. The Love of God will continue to scorch your Soul no less than theirs."

"Don't I know it?" I exclaimed. "The veins of vanity run so deep in my life that they go all the way back to my primordial lifetime as Grunt!"

Grunt was the name I had given myself when I was regressed to my first primordial human life on earth. In that lifetime I experienced the dawning of my own reflective self-consciousness, and I called myself Grunt because I was the alpha male of my clan of ten or twelve higher primates and I grunted all the time to keep them in fear of me. Jesus laughed. Then he said, "The lower self of man is made of vanity. Now would be a good time to introduce the Divine Plan of God for your reader, don't you think?"

"Yes, it would; but I'd like to clear up something else first. Now that we have acknowledged membership to this exclusive club of mystic lovers, don't you think this is going to present a problem for me when *Jesus Wears Dockers* gets published?"

"How so?" Jesus asked, trying to look puzzled.

"People will think that I'm an equal to the only Begotten Son of God and savior of the world. God only knows what the fates will have in store for me if that happens!"

"Of course they will!" Jesus exclaimed, to my astonishment. "There is only one savior for these people because they cannot fathom

a club of mystic lovers! But that's the risk that all messengers of the Way have to take. You are you and I am me, and we have both looked into the Face of God. I have my message of the Way, and you have yours; but my message was made exclusive by the Gospel writers. This is why I'm here, O. I have come to dispel this infamous conspiracy and set the record straight!"

"And the place to start would be with your crucifixion," I quickly responded, still proudly unaware of what Jesus had just revealed to me. "The world is under the illusion that God sacrificed his only Begotten Son to atone for the sins of the world—"

"*Nonsense! Absolute nonsense!* I don't know if I will ever take the muddle out of that puddle, but I'm certainly going to try. Why did you have to start with my crucifixion, O? I was hoping we could build up to my sacrifice on the cross gradually. You know, build up the reader's confidence first before revealing the real bottom line?"

I burst into laughter again. I loved this lighthearted side of Jesus so much that it actually brought tears to my eyes. And I knew in my heart that Jesus loved my sense of spiritual whimsy no less. He was right; we were cut from the same cloth!

"Why beat around the bush?" I said, milking the humor of all its goodness. "People have grown tired of being fed tiny morsels of truth. Why don't we let the reader feast on the meat of the last supper first? Then we can reveal the secrets of your sayings."

Jesus paused for moment. "Maybe you're right, O," he said, very thoughtfully. "Maybe it's best to get this out of the way first. Alright, I was crucified; but I will not reveal whether I died upon the cross or not. That is immaterial to our dialogue—"

"*Immaterial?*" I exclaimed, feigning outrage. "The crux of our whole dialogue is going to rest upon whether you staged your own death or not! That's the meat of the last supper! Was it a symbolic or an actual death, or both? *You have to tell me, J!*"

"Could you be any more blunt?" Jesus responded, in a deliberately calm voice, and with that twinkle in his eyes that I now discerned to be his whimsical side.

"No," I said, and laughed. "I'm afraid that's my nature, J. Life made me this way, and I'm not going to apologize for it. So did you stage your own death or not?"

21

"I will tell you, but not now. It's not appropriate to reveal this at this point in our dialogue."

"But you will tell me?"

"Yes."

"Promise?"

"I thought you didn't want me to make any more promises?"

"True. But I do have a few more issues with you that I want to clear up before we decode your sayings." I said, with affected indifference.

"What issues?" Jesus asked.

"Not now, J. They'll come up in the course of our dialogue," I replied, with a playful twinkle in my own eyes.

"Fair enough," Jesus said, letting me have my fun. Then he stretched his legs, folded his hands on his lap (which I noticed for the first time had the faint marks of his crucifixion, and glancing down I noticed them on his bare sandaled feet as well), and he took in all the people that had gravitated to the little oasis in the heart of Southlake. *"God's beautiful, beautiful garden."* he sighed, with the sweetest smile on his youthful face.

5. *Suffer the Little Squirrels unto Us*

It was all so natural, two men talking on a park bench fully enjoying each other's company, but a gray squirrel alerted me to the oddity of the experience. It got up on its hind legs and stared at us long enough for me to snap out of the feeling and realize what was really happening: *I was having a dialogue with Jesus Christ!*

Had I not read the Living Soul Master's dialogues with the torchbearer of the Way of the Eternal (who appeared to him in his Soul body to dictate books on the Way of the Eternal to him), and Pat Montamuri's book *Talks With Soul Masters* (who also appeared to him in their Light body), I would have been a lot more startled than I was.

Even so, realizing the full consciousness of my experience I had to get up and pace back and forth and stare at Jesus who just sat there with a big grin on his face.

Jesus looked young. Humor, laughter, and joy will keep one looking young. This is why people do a double take when they find out how old I really am. Jesus picked up on my thoughts, "Don't worry about it, O. When the floodgates open, your life will catch up to your age. Then you will be more comfortable in yourself than you have ever been."

"If only I could believe that," I said, and sat down.

The gray squirrel was now joined by two others, also standing on their hind legs, and they all stared at Jesus and me. It was cute, but very strange.

"We have an audience," said Jesus, and laughed.

"So we have," I said, trying to make light of my feelings. "Suffer the little squirrels unto us," I added, with a nervous chuckle.

"Now there's a subject that needs a lot of explaining," Jesus said, in a tone of voice that revealed the whole weight of the world.

"What, suffering?" I said.

"Yes, suffering. Christianity has taken suffering to the point of absurdity because it cannot see the natural order of God's Plan. You came to understand the spiritual purpose of suffering as you lived your mentor's teaching—"

"Who, Gurdjieff?" I interrupted.

"Yes," Jesus said.

"You know a lot about me, don't you?"

"As I said, I have read everything you have published on the Other Side, and you have more published than you realize. You're a well-read author of the Way in the inner worlds, O. Your perspective on the Divine Plan of God is so illuminating that even Soul Masters are quoting from your works now. So don't fret about not being acknowledged out here yet. It will come much more quickly than you think. And when it does come, it won't stop. Now, back to this question of suffering—"

"I just love talking with an open channel!" I jumped in, cutting Jesus off again. "Holy Spirit takes over and we just tag along!"

Jesus laughed. "How can we get the reader to see this? Holy Spirit is the guiding light of the Way. It has always been, and it will always be. How can I convince your readers that I'm only a channel for Holy Spirit? How, O?"

"Surely you jest!" I exclaimed, feigning surprise.

Jesus laughed. "You know what I mean!"

"I know exactly what you mean. But that's only because I'm a member of this exclusive club of mystic lovers. The world on the other hand has no idea that when a Soul becomes God-realized it becomes one with Holy Spirit, and being one with Spirit Soul becomes the Way. You have a real dilemma on your hands, J!"

"Don't I know it!" Jesus exclaimed.

I laughed. It felt good to experience the human side of Christ's personality. It made him so much more real and my experience with him less surreal. "That's the problem with the world's perception of you, J," I said, thinking out loud. "Everyone sees you as this serious-minded savior who died for the sins—"

"Tosh!" Jesus shouted, cutting me off.

"It may well be tosh, J; but not for Christians. You *are* their savior, and nothing will change that but a lot of good old-fashioned karmic suffering. Do you think I would have turned on you in my lifetime as the infamous *Scoundrel of Paris* had I not taken you seriously? I believed in you. I believed in the Holy Mother Church. I believed in God. But I was betrayed. That's why I spit on your crucifix and blasphemed you every chance I got. Truth be told, J; I'm still reeling from what I did to you with my whores."

"I know," Jesus sighed. "This is the dark side of Christianity that I have to face every time I'm hauled up to the High Court of Karma. How do you think I feel every time I'm asked to explain myself to the Lords of Karma?"

I burst into laughter. "Would you like to hear something funny?"

"What?" Jesus asked, surprised by my laughter.

"I have the sneaky suspicion that I'm being trained to become a Lord of Karma," I said, and laughed some more.

"Well, better to be a Lord of Karma than a fool of God!" Jesus replied.

"But J," I said, holding back my laughter; "in the garden of mystic lovers, these are not true distinctions—"

We both burst into laughter, and we laughed to our heart's content as our little fluffy-tailed audience looked on in wonder.

6. *The Heart of the Matter*

I leaned my head back and stared up at the vast pale blue sky. I watched the fluffy white cumulus clouds gently floating by, and I let my mind wander.

"Decoding your sayings won't make any sense unless we spell out the Divine Plan of God," I said, as though without thought. "Even within the context of the Divine Plan of God," I continued, in that same mode of wandering thought, "we have to convince the reader that the life experience is how God grows. This concept will present a problem to the Christian mindset, don't you think?" I asked, turning to Jesus.

"Of course it will," Jesus replied, tuning into my thoughts. "This is what killed the Holy Light in Christianity. When the Church fathers removed reincarnation from its core belief they pulled the curtain on the Light of God. The only way it can be brought back is to reinstate the principle of God's expansion of consciousness, which can only be realized through man's spiritual growth. Christians have to realize that man lives more than one lifetime, and not until this realization becomes central to Christian doctrine can there be any hope for the Light of God to awaken Christianity from its dogmatic stupor."

I laughed. I couldn't help myself. As serious as Jesus was, I knew how foolish it was to hope that Christianity would abandon its core belief that we only lived one lifetime that Jesus died on the cross to save for us. Jesus waited for an explanation.

"What you're proposing is so radical that it would transform the very nature of Christianity," I said, with fresh laughter at the absurdity. "It would cease to be Christianity and become something else entirely, and do you think the powers that be would ever allow that to happen? *Not on your life, J!*"

"No. But change begins at the grass roots," Jesus replied, with that same magical twinkle in his eyes. "After all, isn't that how Christianity began in the first place?"

"Okay, I see where you're coming from," I said, instantly catching the wave of Christ's thought. "So our dialogue is intended for the reader who has outgrown his Christian faith and is looking for a way out?"

"Exactly!" Jesus exclaimed, startling me. "Christianity inhibits Soul's growth with its doctrine of one life and one savior, and what is life for if not for the growth of Soul?"

"That's where the idiocy of Christian suffering comes into the picture, doesn't it? I said, and laughed at the absurdity of Christianity's dilemma.

Jesus laughed also. "You do see where I'm coming from. Yes, of course. When Soul needs new experiences to grow it cannot have them because it is confined by the strictures of blind Christian faith, and Soul suffers the unbearable anguish of the unfulfilled desire of life's greater experience—"

"Soul's greatest desire, you mean?" I interjected.

"Which is?" Jesus asked, for the sake of the reader.

"To be itself," I answered, feeling a surge of Holy Spirit rising within. "This is what the Divine Plan of God is all about. When the atom of God has evolved enough to become aware of itself, it wants to become more itself. This is Soul's greatest desire — *to become more itself!* And Soul cannot do this when it is confined by a belief system that will not allow it to grow into itself. That's Christianity's dilemma!

"For example," I continued, smiling at the painful memories of my own Christian conundrum, "I fell in love with a married woman once. More than once, actually. My faith forbade our love, and we both suffered the anguish of unfulfilled love. This doesn't give us license to satisfy all of our unbridled desires. That would be foolish, because the ego knows no limits when it comes to desire. This is the dilemma that all Souls face that have outgrown their Christian faith. As restraining as it may be, Christian faith does harness the life force to help the young Soul grow. That's the positive side of Christianity. No; the issue here is for those Souls that have outgrown their Christian faith. It is for those Souls mature enough to realize that moral strictures are necessary to keep one's appetites in check; but spiritual growth is all about the freedom of self-responsibility. This is

27

why Soul has to break free of these confining moral strictures and become a spiritual law unto itself; right?"

"Absolutely," said Jesus, with a beaming smile of approval. "I could not have expressed it more eloquently. This is what I hope our dialogue will do. I hope we can draw the distinction between the levels of spiritual growth so the reader will come to realize that life is a school for Soul. Once Soul has learned all it can from one grade it must move on to a higher grade until it rests in the arms of the Holy Now."

"As far as Christianity is concerned, it offers Soul the highest matriculation in the school of life with your sacrificial death upon the cross for the salvation of the world," I replied, now fully engaged with Christ's spiritual logic.

"I know!" Jesus exclaimed, startling me again. *"That's the Gospel conspiracy that I have come to dispel!"*

It was so refreshing to see Jesus display such human emotion that I had to share how I felt with him. "If only the world could see you as I do now," I said, and laughed some more to let all of that exuberant energy out. *"They wouldn't believe it!"*

"Yes, I know," said Jesus, with a wry smile. "I have been transformed into something that I am not and have never been. It's this image that I hope to break down with our dialogue. I hope to get your reader to see that I am also an atom of God on my own journey to the Higher Planes of God."

"Let's make it clear here that there is no end to God-realization consciousness or the reader will never understand what you're trying to say to him," I quickly added.

"Yes," said Jesus. "God is forever growing, and man's evolving spiritual consciousness is how God becomes more God. For man to limit the nature of God is to limit his own spiritual growth, and this is the heart of the matter; don't you think?"

"Absolutely!" I agreed, smiling that Jesus would ask for my confirmation. "And your dilemma is to reveal that Christianity has outgrown its God!"

"Yes," replied Jesus.

"That means you!" I exclaimed, and burst into laughter at the irony.

"I know," said Jesus, with a silly grin on his adorable face. "I was hoping you wouldn't make that connection. It does embarrass me, you know."

"I don't envy you your task, J!" I replied, with fresh laughter.

"Aren't I a glutton for punishment?" Jesus replied, with a rueful smile.

7. Disemboweling Christianity

"Alright," said Jesus, with a serious look on his face, "I think we can disembowel Christianity now, don't you?"

"Disembowel? That's a curious word for the Prince of Peace to use."

Jesus laughed. "Yes, I suppose it is. If the world only knew what I did for two and a half years during my silent years, people wouldn't be so starry-eyed about me. That's the problem with Christianity; it's made of me something that I have never been!"

"What did you do for those two and a half years?"

"I had to earn my keep somehow as I lived the secret teaching. In this period of my life I had to deal with the inevitable reality of death, so I slaughtered sheep. That's how I overcame my natural human fear of death."

"You slaughtered sheep? How ironic for the Good Shepherd!"

Jesus did not say anything. He just stared at me. He had his sweet smile, his eyes glistening with love, and his face radiated a goodness so pure it went to the core of my being and warmed me all over. It embarrassed me.

"And what else did you do during your silent years?" I had to ask, unable to take Christ's gaze any longer.

"That's the big mystery, isn't it?" he replied. His voice was suddenly all business. "I was directed by Master Zadok to go into the world and put the wisdom sayings to the test so I could fulfill my mission. 'Experience as much of life as you can,' he told me when I left the community. 'In the experience of life you will find the Source of life. Once you find the Source of life, you will be initiated into the holy mystery of life.' I went into the world to master as much of life as I could. I butchered sheep, I worked in vineyards, I made mud bricks, thatched, wove, did carpentry, pottery — everything I could to become master of my own life. My silent years were lived to the fullest. Not in a monastic cave where life slows down to a trickle, but in the throes of life itself where the Holy Current of God flows the swiftest and most powerful. I will tell you this, O; what the scholars call the lost years of Jesus Christ were the hardest, most rewarding years of my life. The irony of my lost years is that those were the years where Jesus found his Christ. There is no record of this in the history books, so no one will believe what I am revealing to you."

"That's when you found your way to the Katsupari Monastery in northern Tibet, isn't it?" I asked, to take advantage of Christ's surprising candor.

"Yes. I spent the last three of my silent years there learning the pure teachings of the Way from the guardian of the Golden Wisdom Temple. Mastering the power sayings that Master Zadok gave me from the Great Book of Life had transformed my consciousness enough to be pulled to the Katsupari Monastery where I received my final training from Master Fubbi Quantz before returning home to introduce the Way to the world. And for your information, O," Jesus added, with a playful twinkle in his eyes, "I also received my Second Initiation from Fubbi Quantz, as well as my spiritual name Jesus."

I smiled. I knew from one of the private chela books that the founder of the Way of the Eternal had written that Jesus, whose name was Jeshua, had received his Second Initiation at the Golden Wisdom Temple just before he began his mission, and then I broke into laughter at the thought of Stanley Hansen checking Jesus' identification card at the worship service earlier. When Stanley learned from Christ's ID card that Jesus was only a Second Initiate, Stanley's spiritual conceit was revealed by the smirk on his face, which would have kept me from attending any more services had Jesus not set me straight.

Stanley Hansen was a Sixth Initiate in the Way of the Eternal, and Jesus was only a Second. The irony of Stanley's smug smirk of spiritual superiority over Jesus Christ's lower initiation status forced me to smile, and I could not help myself; I broke into a new fit of laughter at Stanley's unimaginable arrogance. Jesus stared at me grinning.

"You know what I'm laughing at, don't you?" I said.

"Yes," Jesus replied.

"Wasn't Stanley transparent?" I said.

"He was," Jesus replied, with no judgment in his voice whatsoever. "He had to do it," Jesus added, for my benefit because

Stanley's H. I. conceit really got under my skin. "His authority was threatened by my response to his talk on love, so he propped up his vanity by checking my ID card to see my level of initiation," Jesus explained. "But let's not dwell on that, O. It's his life, and one day he will sense that hump on his back."

"What!" I exclaimed. "Don't tell me my novel is already published on the Other Side?" I asked, surprised by Christ's reference to the physical image I had created of my Stanley Hansen character's spiritual conceit in my new novel!

Jesus broke into such a mirthful chuckle that I wondered if he was playing with me. I couldn't put it past him, because he gave me back more than I put out.

"Of course it is," he replied. "And a fascinating read it was too. You were a little hard on Stanley's character, but in the context of your theme it worked very well."

I couldn't believe my ears. "No kidding? It's published already?"

"Yes. And I'll tell you, O; you're waking up a lot of Souls with the incredible story of your waking dream experience. But that's your gift, isn't it?"

"Gift alright!" I exclaimed, startling Jesus. "That's life, period! And my job is to tell it as it is! That's what wakes Soul up from its stupor — a strong dose of reality!"

"Of course," Jesus calmly replied in his soft, gentle voice. Then he paused, looked out at the people coming and going, and said, "That's what the spiritual journey is all about, waking Soul up to its divine nature. This is why Master Zadok gave me the most powerful sayings from the Great Book of Life. He knew they would quicken my Spirit. The more passionately I lived the reconciliation sayings, the more I connected with the Holy Current of God. And the more Holy Spirit flowed through me, the more possessed I became until I was so crazy with God that I had to suffer my sacrificial death upon the cross. But you understand all of this, don't you?"

"Yes, I do," I said, full of new emotion. "To be honest with you J, I had the good sense not to try to save the world when I became possessed by Holy Spirit. When I say that the world has to find its own way, I mean it. Soul is responsible for its own karma. The most I can do as a co-worker with God is serve life when Spirit calls upon me to point the Way. Life is life, and it will forever be so. There is only self-initiation into the mysteries of life, and that's the premise of my favorite maxim."

"What? Letting the world find its own way?"

"Yes."

"Good," said Jesus, his voice taking on that all-business tenor again. "This brings me back to the point. Why do you think I have initiated this dialogue with you? The Way has called upon me to disembowel Christianity and cast its guts into the Great River of Life where they will be made pure by the goodness of Holy Spirit; but I need your help."

"And by guts, you mean?"

"You know what I mean. You spelled it out in your novel with the false premises of Christianity. Let's start with Christianity's greatest hold upon Soul," Jesus said, crossing his legs and resting his slender arm on the bench so he could look at me. The look on his face was deadly serious and full of authority, but I kept glancing at his slender arm, wondering how in God's name he had managed to carry his own cross to his crucifixion.

"Greatest hold?" I said, snapping myself back to our talk.

"Eternal damnation," Jesus replied, to my relief because I honestly did not know where he was going with that thought. "Because Christianity has failed to decode my sayings it has completely distorted the message of my gospel," he continued, as though confiding in an old friend. "All of this weeping and gnashing of teeth in the Gospels of Christ is nothing more than the natural transformation of human consciousness, but who has the courage to say no to their selfish nature and deny the pleasure that the discipline of my sayings transforms? Few people have found the correct interpretation of my sayings. It is much easier to have one's cake and eat it too. Why work for your salvation when you can have it for the asking? This is what I mean by disemboweling Christianity, O. As long as man believes that he can have his cake and eat it too Christianity will never wake up to the Spiritual Laws of Karma and Reincarnation. You understand this. Your books address this issue more boldly than anything written in the literature of the Way."

"That's why I asked if the world would have been better off without Christianity," I replied. "You turned the question back on me, and I felt compelled to agree that Christianity has served a great spiritual purpose in life; but in all honesty J, I still have a nagging doubt about the role that Christianity has played in life. I still feel deep inside that the world would have been better off without Christianity. I can't help it, but that's just how I feel."

"Spell this doubt out for me, please," Jesus said, with genuine concern.

"I don't know if I can," I said, feeling a little nervous.

"Please try," Jesus said, his eyes beckoning.

I could not say no to Jesus. I paused to reflect. The thought came to me to do a silent HU to connect with the Holy Current of God. HU is one of the most secret names of God and Sound of all sounds, and it opens Soul up to the Holy Current. I chanted HU silently for a minute or so with my eyes closed, and then I repeated my secret spiritual word for a moment longer to open me up to Soul Consciousness. Jesus waited patiently.

I turned to Jesus, looked into his incredibly deep, all-knowing eyes and just let Soul speak: "I can't help but feel that for all the good Christianity has done the world, for all the invaluable experiences that it has provided for Soul to grow and learn, it is one of the world's greatest illusions. Just as Buddhism has deluded itself into believing that there is no God and that we do not have a self, so has Christianity deluded itself into believing that we only live one lifetime that you sacrificed your life upon the cross to save for us. I can't help but feel that this lie is so overwhelming that it suffocates the spiritual life of man. I can't help but feel that this is not in keeping with the Divine Plan of God, and it has to be corrected. Soul needs help to breathe, and with all due respect to Christianity it de-oxygenates the spiritual life of man. In a word, J; I can't help but feel that Kal Niranjan, the demiurgic deity of these lower planes of consciousness, is laughing at the world. He's been laughing for a long, long time. And I won't hesitate to tell you that I find his laughter insufferable now; and I'm sick of it. Tell me honestly, what do you really think?"

Without hesitation, Jesus said, "I think you have a valid point. And I think we're ready now to reveal the secret of my sayings."

Surprised by Christ's frankness, I had to chuckle to release the conflicting emotions that he had set free in me. I sat back and paused to reflect before responding. I had to center myself, so I called upon the Inner Master for guidance.

"Z," I said, in the quiet of my mind, *"is this it? Is this where my book starts?"*

"No," he replied, silently. *"Your story began long ago. Now you are about to introduce the world to a new pattern of thought on Jesus Christ and his teaching, which the world needs at this time. Trust Divine Spirit, O."*

"I will," I replied, in the quiet of my mind. Turning to Jesus, I said, "Perhaps we're ready J, but not without clearing the air first. It's not enough to decode your sayings and reveal the messiah secret to the world. The reader has to catch a glimpse of the big picture first. To do this, we have to spell out Soul's purpose in life. I've given a lot of thought to the three stages of human consciousness, and I can't help but feel that even though life evolves naturally according to the Spiritual Laws of Karma and Reincarnation, man is always given direction by spiritual teachers like you. This has led me to wonder if other worlds have not evolved in an entirely different way, without this fear of death hanging over one's head as it does on Planet Earth. Do you see where I'm going with this?"

Jesus did not reply. He looked at me with wonder in his eyes, which I felt was strange for the all-knowing Jesus. And then, to my astonishment, tears began to form in the corner of his eyes and slowly trickle down his cheeks.

I stared in awe, but said nothing. Jesus made no effort to wipe his tears. Taking a long breath and letting it out slowly, he very emotionally said, "What you say is undeniable. There are other worlds where the fear of death does not possess Soul as it does on Earth, and in many ways I am responsible for feeding man's fear of death. Life is an experiment in all the lower worlds of God, and on Planet Earth life has evolved with this fear of mortality intact because no Soul Master has been able to eradicate it. Try as I may, I will never undo what I have done to feed man's fear of death; but you can help to eradicate man's fear of death with your understanding of the Divine Plan of God. You cannot imagine how delighted we were when you

35

connected all the dots that led to your understanding of the Way in the Divine Plan of God. We all breathed a collective sigh of relief. Finally, the window on God's Plan for the atom of God had been opened to the world!"

Moved by Christ's emotions, I could not speak. Then I had to ask Jesus something that I simply could not contain. Very softly, which was unusual for me, I said, "Why wasn't it revealed? Why couldn't one of you all-knowing Masters spell out the Divine Plan of God? I've read all the great literature of the Way that I could lay my hands on, and not once did I catch a glimpse of the big picture of life. Only when the Inner Master took me to the Ocean of Love and Mercy during my fourth past-life regression did I catch a glimpse of Soul's purpose in life. Why, J? Why has it taken so long for the Divine Plan of God to be revealed to the world? I can't understand this. It boggles my mind."

Jesus smiled, his eyes shining with such love that I was overwhelmed with a feeling of comforting goodness. "As you explained to Doctor Jung in your novel," Jesus replied, "you refracted a Ray of God's Light for the Divine Plan of God to be revealed. Each Soul refracts the Light of God accordingly, and you are that unique Soul that was able to catch the illuminating Light of God's Divine Plan. It's that simple, O."

"That's the only thing that makes sense to me" I replied, recalling how Soul revealed this to me when Carl Jung and I talked in my dream. He had also read my book *The Way of Soul* on the inner, and I was pulled into his gravitational field because he wanted to ask me some questions about the alpha and omega of the self. "But I can tell you J, having worked out the Divine Plan of God I no longer look at life in the same way. Man's fear of death is a joke that Kal plays upon mankind to keep Soul trembling. I realize that life is a school for Soul, but must the lessons we learn be so damn hard? Cannot these lessons be learned with less suffering? You yourself were a puppet on Kal's string. Your crucifixion, metaphor or not, goes a long way to firming up the way of blind suffering. The world has even made a cliché of your crucifixion with sayings like 'That's the cross I have to bear.' Can Christians help but keep this kind of stupid suffering foremost in their mind?"

"Enough," said Jesus, holding up his hand. "I know what I've done. I had no choice but to see the spiritual logic of my life to its conclusion. Do you think I wanted to become crazy with God? Do you think I wanted to impress my way of self-sacrifice upon the psyche of the world with my crucifixion? I had no choice, O. I had to do what I did just as you had to do what you did to initiate yourself into the Holy Current of God. I was no less caught up in the currents of my own way than you or any other Soul that connects with the inner currents of his spiritual life. When a Soul is caught in the currents of its own destiny, it has no choice but to see itself to the end; and that's all there is to it!"

I was shocked by Christ's abruptness, but I had to ask: "So I was right, then?"

"About what?" he asked, as though taken aback by my question.

"Self-sacrifice," I said. "I won't ask you now J, or ever; but if you ever feel free to tell me I would appreciate it very much. It would make my life complete."

"What would make your life complete?" Jesus asked, feigning ignorance.

"If you staged your own death on the cross to fix upon the psyche of the world the central premise of the Way of Christ," I said, with a nervous smile.

"You're right, I won't tell you. That's for you to figure out," he replied, and broke into a hearty laugh to relieve the emotional tension of my unasked question.

Feeling thwarted by his response, I reacted: "Well, J; when it comes to matters of the Way my intuition has never let me down. I found my own way home to God, and I feel that you choreographed your crucifixion for messianic reasons — and I trust my intuition!"

Jesus just stared at me, with the biggest grin on his face.

8. *Keep Your Eye on the Ball*

Suddenly I was filled with doubt. An enormous, overwhelming, and terrifying sense of doubt. I felt the absurdity of the whole experience. Sitting on a park bench in the center of the beautiful little city of Southlake, Ontario talking with Jesus Christ, one of the most powerful spiritual forces ever to affect the world, I felt the horrifying responsibility of helping him to reveal the truth of his gospel and wake Christianity up from its spiritual stupor, and a feeling of nausea overcame me. I wanted to throw up.

Jesus reached over and grabbed my hand. Energy flowed from him to me, and all fear left me. I looked at him, and said, "Thank you, J."

"You're welcome," he said softly. "Yes, it is an enormous responsibility to introduce the Divine Plan of God to the world; but if not you O, who?"

I thought for a moment, and then replied, "The world is what it is, and according to the Living Soul Master everything is where it's supposed to be; so what does it really matter if we decode your sayings or not?"

"Do you remember the story of the starfish that the Living Soul Master told at one of the Worldwide Seminar talks?" Jesus asked.

"'What does it matter to this starfish?'" I said, recalling the story of the young boy on the beach with thousands of starfish that had been washed up on shore. One by one, the boy threw the starfish back into the sea. An old man was walking the beach and asked the boy what he was doing. He told him he was saving the starfish. The man looked about and saw all those starfish, and seeing the absurdity of trying to save them all said to the boy, "What does it matter?" The boy, who was holding a starfish in his hand ready to throw back into the sea, said to the cynical old man, "It matters to this starfish."

"Yes. It matters to that one starfish, does it not?" said Jesus.

"You're saying that if one person out of a million or ten million is awakened by our dialogue, then it won't be for naught?" I asked, feeling a little foolish.

"Exactly," said Jesus. "One awakened Soul affects hundreds, if not thousands of sleeping Souls in its lifetime. That's how the Spiritual Law of Service works."

"Our dialogue is for that one Soul, then?" I asked, for clarity.

"In effect, yes. Look at your own life. How often have people thanked you for your spiritual wisdom? Look at Kevin Archer. He's exploring his spiritual life through his art now with a vital new passion, and he thanks you for showing him the way. Now he's teaching young students how to connect with their inner self through art. You are that little boy and Kevin was the starfish you helped connect with the Holy Current of God. You have become a Keeper of the Flame, O; and you have touched many Souls with the Holy Flame of God. Do you see the point now?"

Kevin Archer was a real life artist in my waking dream novel who was responsible for inspiring my book *The Way of Soul*. "Yes, of course," I said. "I'm just in awe of this whole thing, that's all. I felt overwhelmed there for a moment."

"And well you should be," said Jesus. "The Law of Service washes pure the mind of man. As long as we occupy a physical body we will always be subject to these great moments of spiritual doubt. It is to the nature of mortal human consciousness. Just keep your eye on the ball, as the expression goes."

"That's good. That way doubt won't have a place to enter, will it?"

"Exactly," said Jesus, with a generous smile.

"Tell me, J," I said, feeling emboldened; "what have you learned from your remarkable life as the sole savior of the world?"

Jesus snickered. "That's the Gospel conspiracy! To set the record straight, O; I was never the savior of the world, because the world did not need to be saved. The world is what it is, and Soul takes it for what it is. That's the Law of God. My life as a teacher of the Way taught me many things. It taught me that love is the purpose of life, which I was asked by the Nine Silent Ones in charge of these lower planes to bring to the world. We are born to learn how to give and receive love. In the giving and receiving of love man fulfills his destiny in life, which is to expand the Consciousness of God. God grows through the giving and receiving of love, and if my sacrifice on the cross pried open the heart of one Soul it was worth it. It does not matter what path one takes in life, in the end all paths lead home to God; if not in this lifetime the next, because it is written in Soul's DNA."

"True enough," I said, smiling at the thought of how I had come to the same realization as I worked out the Divine Plan of God; but not until I had worked it out though did I remove all doubt about spiritual paths. "Some paths however," I was nudged to add to Christ's surprising confession, "are more circuitous than others; and it will take many more lifetimes than I think necessary to find the way out of the cycle of life and death."

"But find it they will because it is destined," Jesus stressed.

"So you admit that the Way of Christ is a difficult path, then?"

"Of course it's a difficult path," replied Jesus, smiling at my little dig. "It was never meant to be easy. That's what the times called for, O. I did what I was driven by Holy Spirit to do. Like I said, I had very little choice in the matter."

"But the Elders at the community begged you to stay and calm the raging fire of Holy Spirit; why did you not listen to them?" I asked, genuinely perplexed by Christ's passion to sacrifice his life on the cross to get his message out to the world.

"And do you think I could hear them through the roar of the Holy Fire of God?"

"Probably not," I said, with a nervous laugh.

"The world is blissfully ignorant of the circumstances that led to my crucifixion," Jesus continued, with a touch of sadness in his voice. "That's why we have to dispel the Gospel conspiracy that keeps me hanging on the cross. I would have thought by now that someone would have broken the code of my sayings, but the world is still muddling the puddle. I understand now that I did not even exist as a person. I'm just a myth like Osiris. When will they smell the coffee, O?" Jesus asked, with a straight face.

I laughed at the irony. I had just read *The Pagan Christ* by a Christian writer who argued that Jesus did not exist as a historical person, but there sat Jesus beside me, on a park bench in Southlake. I reached over and grabbed his hand and started shaking it. "Hello Jesus." I said, still laughing. "What a thrill it is to shake the hand of a myth!"

Jesus laughed as he shook my hand. "The pleasure is all mine, O," he said, and grabbed my hand with his other hand and squeezed mine in both of his small, but powerful hands and vigorously inspired a new round of laugher.

When we settled down Jesus smiled at me. His eyes were so full of love for me that I could hardly look into them. "You are a special Soul, O," he said. "You have dared to go where few Souls have the courage to go. Your lifetime as the lost Soul of Paris was one of the most courageous lifetimes that any Soul can live in this world. With that lifetime to work with, you forged your way to the Divine Plan of God in this lifetime."

Taken by surprise, I said, "And how did I do that, pray tell?"

"You dared to let ego devour you whole and died trapped by your own nothingness that had to be resolved by very difficult future lives," Jesus replied, his eyes looking askance at me as he read my Soul records. "It was a pivotal lifetime. Few Souls have the courage to go by way of non-being. You are right to believe that there are two paths in life: one by way of being, and the other by way of non-being. You have captured the essential nature of each path in your writing because you have lived both paths, and the world needs to know that the Way of Christ was a teaching that short-circuited the way of non-being. This is the mystery of my teaching that the scholars cannot fathom."

"Because they can't fathom the reality of the non-self!" I burst out.

"Exactly. It is impossible to see the self that is not a self," Jesus explained, with a big grin. "They go back and forth like a pendulum, and not until life gives them the experiences they need to see the false self of their own ego will they ever catch a glimpse of the mystery of my teaching and find the correct interpretation that will set them free."

"But your sayings tell us how to solve the mystery of your teaching!" I instinctively responded, and broke into an ironic chuckle.

41

"Of course they do," Jesus calmly replied. "But few people have taken my sayings all the way to the Soul Plane and experienced their immortal Soul self as you have. Since the Church instituted the sacrament of confession people cannot cultivate a will for the Way of Christ. Do you understand now why Christians want their cake and eat it, too?"

"Of course I do," I said, and laughed at the absurdity of Christianity's logic. "Let's look at this from the three levels of human consciousness; the exoteric, mesoteric, and esoteric circles of life. The less spiritually evolved Souls in the outer circle of life don't have sufficient spiritual maturity to live the Way consciously. These Souls need a crutch to lean on, and Christianity has become that crutch—"

"But how long must they walk through life with a crutch?"Jesus cut in. "This is why we're having this dialogue to help them let go of their crutch. You cannot imagine how many Souls there are out there that have outgrown their crutch but cannot let it go. Some even deny me my very life in their vain efforts to hold onto their crutch. They say that my life is a parable created by those clever Gnostics to teach the world about the Way. They want the Christ but not Jesus, and if that doesn't take the cake nothing does!"

I burst into a fit of laughter at Jesus' sense of the absurd. He stared at me, smiling as I laughed. "You do see to what lengths Christians will go to have their cake and eat it too?" he said, and snickered at the absurdity of his non-existence.

I broke out again. Jesus caught the infectious spirit and we laughed with abandon at man's outrageous capacity for self-deception.

9. *Dig for Dig*

"Alright," I said, sitting up on the bench, "let's look at this whole thing from the perspective of the seeker."

"No," Jesus cut in. "It's not the seeker that I wish to address. It's the whole psyche of Christianity. The seeker will find his own path to the Way eventually. It's the mind of Christianity that I hope to wake up with a clear understanding of the Way of Christ."

"Then you're dreaming, J. You couldn't wake Christianity up with an atomic bomb of spiritual consciousness. Besides, isn't this dialogue for that one starfish?"

"Of course it is; but the overall purpose is to plant the seeds of this atomic bomb of spiritual consciousness so we can blast the Gospel conspiracy into oblivion," replied Jesus, with that delightful twinkle in his playful, God-realized eyes.

I snickered at the image of all those tiny bombs of spiritual consciousness exploding in the mind of my readers as they read *Jesus Wears Dockers*. "I follow you," I said, still laughing. "Do you have an overall game plan?"

"I do," said Jesus, amused by my laughter.

"And can you share it with me?"

"This is it, O. Don't you think this dialogue will intrigue the Christian reader?"

"Dialectical fiction or not," I added, just to be smart.

"It's ironic, but it doesn't really matter for our purpose whether I'm real or a myth like the Egyptian Horus-Osiris myth; Spirit is Spirit, regardless which medium it uses to reconcile Soul with God. It was this creative genius that inspired the Gospel writers, and to a great extent Paul's letter; that's why I singled you out to help me dispel the Gospel conspiracy. You are no less courageous in your own expression of the Way. Soul has to wake up to its own destiny, and this cannot be done until it takes karmic responsibility for its own life. This is the spiritual bomb that will wake Soul up from its Christian stupor."

"But how do you propose to set this bomb off when the very foundations of Christianity support the illusion of instant salvation through your death upon the cross? Do you see the dilemma?" I asked, pushing the envelope as far as I could.

Jesus had his answer ready. "I'm hoping that by demystifying my sayings we can shatter this illusion of instant salvation with my death on the cross. Once your reader sees that the premise of my sayings has to do with the transformation of consciousness, he will wake up to the illusion of instant salvation because my sayings negate the very idea of instant salvation. My sayings are all about giving birth to one's spiritual self, which is the true salvation of my gospel. This is the messiah secret that the scholars cannot penetrate. But once the reader wakes up to his own karmic responsibility he will see through the false premises of Christianity that prop up this illusion of instant salvation—"

"You mean false premises like baptism, forgiveness of sins, perfect acts of contrition, final judgment day, rapture, eternal punishment in hell, and all that nonsense?" I said, just to make sure that I understood Jesus correctly.

"Yes," he confirmed.

"Well, good luck to you!" I exclaimed. "It's been my experience that no matter how ready Christians may be to throw away their crutches, they refuse to do so. People are what they believe even if they have outgrown their belief. Letting go of their crutches would be letting go of who they are, and how many people do you know who will die to their life to save their life, to borrow your famous line?"

"I confess, not many," Jesus said, with a look of seriousness on his face. "But you miss my point, O. I'm planting seeds. I don't expect this crop to be ready for many years to come yet. All I'm doing is planting seeds. That's all any Master can do."

I watched the people in the park as I thought about the long slow process of spiritual awakening. I thought of my own life, how long it had taken me to find my way to the Living Soul Master. I thought of all the books that I had read in my efforts to follow the scent of the Way, and all the spiritual paths that I had studied. I thought of all the trials, tests, and tribulations of my own life, and I broke into a wry chuckle.

"What's so funny?" Jesus asked.

"Me. I can't help but feel like a big fool now. God, what I wouldn't have done to have a mentor in my life! What nonsense I had to work my way through to get to where I am today! I could have been spared so much agony had I a mentor!"

"But you had a mentor, O," Jesus replied. "You had the Inner Master—"

"Oh for Christ's sake, J! You know what I mean!"

Jesus burst into laughter. "Of course I do. I couldn't help myself. Dig for dig, O," he added, and broke into another gentle bout of precious laughter.

"Yeah. That's what karma's all about, isn't it?" I sighed.

"Precisely!" exclaimed Jesus, and stood up to stretch his legs. He walked around the bench and stood in front of me and looked into my eyes.

His love just poured into me, and I smiled as his love healed me; then I giggled mirthfully to myself. I could not believe my good fortune!

10. *The Insidious Worm of Christian Conceit*

Jesus paced slowly back and forth in deep thought as I sat watching him. "J," I said, interrupting his pacing, "if I had one wish for this dialogue, guess what it would be?"

"You tell me," he said.

"Come on, humor me," I pleaded.

"Alright. I would say that your wish for our dialogue would be to snap one Soul out of the hypnotic hold that Christianity has over it—"

"Not one Soul! Millions!" I exclaimed. "That's what I would wish!"

"Why?" Jesus asked, and sat back down on the bench.

"Because the whole fabric of society would change, that's why!"

"But did not the Living Soul Master say that the world is as it is supposed to be?" Jesus came right back at me, and smiled his playful smile.

"Yes, he did," I said, smiling at his comeback. "But creative imagination is God's gift to Soul," I said, standing my ground. "With imagination we can expand the consciousness of life and let in the Light and Sound of God!"

"Excellent! I should have known you would get yourself out of that corner! But then, that's your spiritual gift; isn't it?" Jesus said, his eyes twinkling.

"Those born of the Spirit are unpredictable," I said, and laughed.

"For the sake of the reader, would you please explain that?"

Jesus was way ahead of me. As much as I wanted to believe that I had some control in our dialogue, I was beginning to see that I really didn't. I was just a servant of Holy Spirit, and Spirit was writing the script for both of us.

"Alright," I said, with a sigh of relief. "All I'm saying is that any point in life can be an exit point out of life. That's God's gift to Soul."

"That's the gift of Holy Spirit. It's the creative genius of Holy Spirit that liberates Soul from life. You're quite right, the creative imagination is God's gift to Soul; but how can Soul be creative when it is boxed in by a dogma that denies man his destiny of spiritual self-realization and God-consciousness?"

"You mean belief systems like Christianity, Judaism, Buddhism, Hinduism, Islam, atheism, and such fixed beliefs?"

"Exactly," said Jesus.

"That's the purpose of our dialogue, is it not; to expand the paradigms of spiritual thought?" I replied.

"Very well put," said Jesus, and stood up again.

"Yes," I said, with a sigh of relief. "I like how the creative genius of Holy Spirit flows out of me, J; but more often than not it falls on deaf ears."

Jesus looked down at me. "Holy Spirit speaks to Soul, not to the little human self. Don't fret about whether people hear you or not. I used to fret too until I realized that my Father in heaven spoke to Soul and not to the little self. Soul will act upon its human self from within. Should the little self be ready to hear our Father in heaven—"

"Stop!" I shouted, holding up my hand. "The Voice of Soul would be more appropriate for our dialogue than our Father in heaven. Father in heaven is too patriarchal for our times. Believe me, J; that won't cut it in today's emancipated world."

"I agree. Given that the self is ready to hear the Voice of Soul, it would be a bonus then; otherwise the Word will work from within upon the little self."

"How long did it take you to realize this?" I had to ask.

"I realized this in the first year of my mission. At first I felt great disappointment, because few people heard the Word of God. Then I began to speak to Soul directly, and that made all the difference. I bypassed the mind and addressed Soul's spiritual need, which I was doing in any event; and it dawned on me that many Souls were ready to be harvested but had to be made aware that they were ready. This is the problem with Christianity today. There are many Christians ready to be harvested, but they have to be made aware that they are ready; hence, our dialogue."

"How ironic! Christians ready to be harvested!" I exclaimed, and burst into another fit of irrepressible laughter.

"Isn't it?" Jesus said, and chuckled with me.

"But I doubt they will appreciate our sense of humor," I said to Jesus.

"Some will and some won't. Those who appreciate our humor will be ready to be harvested, and those who don't will have to have more experience," Jesus replied, in that no-nonsense voice I heard at the worship service earlier at the Southlake Public Library when he addressed Stanley Hansen's talk on love.

Stanley Hansen was a smug High Initiate, and Jesus' appearance confirmed my feelings that Stanley's High Initiate status stood between him and all the chelas that were not High Initiates. Holy Spirit gave me the experience with Jesus to let me see the spiritual conceit that had wormed its way into the spiritual community of the Way of the Eternal, and especially into what I referred to as "the cult of the High Initiate," and now Jesus sat on the park bench with me for a much greater purpose, which was to cast out the worm of Christian conceit that he called the Gospel conspiracy. "I have to ask you something, J," I said, my voice faltering a little.

"Go ahead," he said, his voice of authority reassuring me.

"Did you appear at the worship service this morning to confirm my suspicion of the spiritual conceit that I see worming its way into our spiritual community?"

"Yes," Jesus replied, without hesitation. "And to prepare the way for our dialogue that I hope will dispel the Gospel conspiracy and build a bridge to the new religion of the Light and Sound of God. Building bridges, O; that's all we're doing."

"I knew it!" I exclaimed, and jumped to my feet. "Tell me," I said, after a moment's quick reflection, "am I wrong to speak my mind about the Way as I do? It bothers some High Initiates, especially High Initiates from Toronto. *Am I wrong, J?"*

"Not at all," Jesus replied. "The Way of the Eternal is the most direct path to God. I realize that, and so does any Master worth his salt. But Soul needs all kinds of life experiences to learn its karmic lessons. You know that, O. Christianity is just another experience. As is Buddhism, Hinduism, Judaism, Islam, Theosophy, Anthroposophy, Sufism, metaphysics, spiritualism, or atheism for that matter. Soul has to experience many paths before it finds its way home to God. The truth is that I come from a different line of Masters than the Living Soul Master. I fulfilled my destiny in the line of my Jewish tradition, and other Masters have fulfilled their destiny in the line of their own ethnic tradition; but all spiritual lines converge in the Living Soul Master, because he is the Light-giver of the world; so you do not have to apologize for your perspective on the spiritual life. You found the Way of Life, and this grants you the privilege to speak of the Way in all traditions, including the Way of the Eternal; so if your spiritual perspective bothers some High Initiates in your community, that's their problem. Does that put your mind at ease?"

"It does. But tell me this, please. Why would Stanley — and not only Stanley Hansen; I had an experience with an H.I. who pulled the same stunt on me with my ID card that Stanley pulled on you this morning because he couldn't believe I wasn't a High Initiate. I only had my Fourth Initiation then. So tell me, J; what's the story here?"

"You're a member of the exclusive club of mystic lovers, and they're not!" Jesus burst out, with the biggest smirk on his adorable face.

I had to laugh at the irony. "It's as simple as that, then?"

"Not quite. But it will do for now." Jesus replied. "Now can we get on with our dialogue and leave this issue of vanity for them to resolve on their own?"

"You mean let these H. I.'s find their own way to the garden of mystic lovers?" I said, and burst into another fit of delicious laughter.

"You're shameless, O!" Jesus said, staring wide-eyed at me.

Unable to repress the irony of my fellow chelas who believed that they were superior spiritual beings because they were High Initiates of the most direct path to God — *just as Christians believe that only through Jesus Christ can we be saved!* — Jesus couldn't help himself and broke into laughter also at the insidious worm of spiritual conceit that we had both come to know so well!

49

11. *The Divine Imminence*

"Before we get to the meat of the last supper," I said, standing up to stretch my own legs because I felt them cramping, "I think for the sake of the reader we should explain the fundamental message of your sayings—"

"Not my sayings necessarily," Jesus cut in. "I garnered my wisdom from life, O; because only by living the wisdom sayings can they rightly be called yours. I have to stress that this gnostic wisdom exists in the experience of life itself, like veins of gold running through stone; and the seeker has to learn the secret of mining the spiritual gold of the Way. This is what drove me to slaughter sheep and master weaving, pottery, and brick making. I gave my all to life, and in my efforts to master life I mined the spiritual gold of the Way of Life. That's what Master Zadok wanted me to realize."

"I know what you mean. As I 'worked' on myself with Gurdjieff's teaching I also mined the spiritual gold of life; but shouldn't we explain what we mean by spiritual gold?"

"I called it *virtue,*" Jesus freely offered, and unexpectedly I felt Spirit pulling us deeper into the Holy Stream of Life. "The *virtue* of life is realized by mastering life," Jesus added. "The more one masters a life experience, the more *virtue* he will realize from that experience. That's what the Way of Life is all about."

"That's the point I wanted to make to Kevin Archer," I said, feeling the tide of Holy Spirit surging within me. "He had to connect with his art in a way that would allow him to mine the spiritual gold of his own life experience, and I did all I could to help him connect with his inner self in that special way. I tried to make it clear to him that by connecting with his inner self he would tap into the Creative Life Stream — the vein of spiritual gold that runs through all of life. To do that, he had to master the art process."

"Certainly," said Jesus, nodding his head in agreement. "Master life and you master the Way. Ironically, many people who become masters of their own discipline are not aware of the spiritual gold they are mining. Rather, they are aware of it; but they do not know how to use their wealth for their own spiritual good. That's the premise for my saying, *'Lay up for yourselves treasures in heaven, where neither moth nor rust doth corrupt, and where thieves do not break through nor steal.'* I quote that from St. Mathew's Gospel, Chapter 6, verse 20; but we can talk about this when we get into my sayings. You're absolutely right, O. We have to make it clear what this spiritual gold is so your reader will know what to expect from a correct interpretation of my sayings."

"Would you like me to give it a shot?" I asked, feeling very bold.

"Go ahead. Holy Spirit refracts the Light of God accordingly, and the prism of your individuality refracts a unique wisdom," Jesus said, with that twinkle in his eyes.

"Alright," I said, amused by the compliment. Silently, I called upon the Inner Master for the right words. "The spiritual gold of life is the energy of spiritual freedom," I began, feeling absolutely confident as I felt the Inner Master's presence. "At the risk of sounding too esoteric, I've come to see that the more pure the energy of life is the more spiritual freedom it has. The spiritual gold of life is the pure freedom of Holy Spirit. This pure spiritual freedom exists at the very heart of life. It is the vein of gold that runs through all life. But that's not an appropriate metaphor, because this energy of pure spiritual freedom is not a vein of spiritual gold, as such; it's more of a spiritual imminence."

"Well put!" Jesus exclaimed, startling me. "That's an excellent way of expressing the presence of Holy Spirit in life — *an imminence!* By living my sayings, one releases this spiritual imminence!"

"Hold on, J. We're getting ahead of ourselves," I said.

"Sorry. I was excited by your explanation, that's all!"

"I've struck the right chord, then. Okay, where was I?"

"You were talking about spiritual freedom," Jesus said.

"Right. This Divine Imminence, if we can call it that now, is the energy of pure spiritual freedom, and the secret teachings of the Way have to do with releasing this Divine Imminence to nourish Soul's need for total self-identity; meaning, spiritual self-realization and God consciousness. That's the gist of it, wouldn't you say?"

"It certainly is," said Jesus, with a satisfied smile. "All we have to do now is explain the secret knowledge of how to release the Divine Imminence of life."

"It's being released all the time," I replied, as the creative genius of Holy Spirit rushed the thought to my mind. "Life itself is made up of this Divine Imminence, and every experience we have releases spiritual freedom. The whole point of your teaching was to capture this spiritual freedom and contain it for the specific purpose of spiritual growth. Your saying about storing one's treasures in heaven speaks to this mystery. It may sound abstruse now, but we have to factor in the dense little human self here, don't we? After all, it's by way of the human self that the spiritual self grows, is it not?"

"Of course it is," said Jesus, almost sounding annoyed at the simplicity of the Way. "Now I think we should set down the fundamental premise for spiritual growth."

"Which is?" I asked, hoping he would continue with the logic of our discourse.

Jesus did. With that sense of divine authority in his voice, he pursued the irrefutable logic of the Way of Life: "The spiritual self of man needs the human self to grow. By cultivating the human self to live the spiritual life, man will learn to capture the Divine Imminence. The more Divine Imminence one captures, the more the spiritual and human self become one individuated Soul self. That's what I tried to get across in my gospel of spiritual rebirth. Unfortunately this concept got so distorted by the Gospel writers that it has made a mockery of my teaching of salvation."

I laughed at Jesus' blunt candor. "Don't feel bad, J. After all, it's to the nature of the little human self to do everything in its power to resist being spiritualized. This brings us to the three levels of human consciousness again — the exoteric, mesoteric, and esoteric circles of life; or, more precisely, the three stages of Soul's evolution through life."

"Of course," Jesus quickly agreed. "The seeds of the Way cannot take root until Soul has evolved to the middle circle of life. Only then will my sayings make sense, because Soul will be mature enough to resonate with the wisdom of the spiritual life force—"

"You mean the Way," I interjected. "The reader has to see that the spiritual life force is the Word; that the Word is the Way; and that the Way is this spiritual freedom, or Divine Imminence that exists in all of life!"

"I could not have expressed it better," said Jesus, with a contented smile.

"Alright, then; the point we have to make absolutely clear for the reader, if he is to get the wisdom of your sayings, is that the human self and spiritual self are in constant conflict in the exoteric circle of life; but I'll let you explain that, if you would?"

"I would be honored," said Jesus. "The human self is the primordial self of man that has taken millions of years of natural evolution to reach the point of self-awareness, and as the primordial self evolves in self-awareness from lifetime to lifetime—"

"*Stop!* The reader should know here that you, Jesus Christ, son of Mary and Joseph and sole savior of the world, are talking about reincarnation; right?"

"Yes; absolutely. In the context of our dialogue, this should be obvious by now, don't you think?" Jesus replied, affecting his serious savior's voice.

I loved how Jesus played with me. We had caught the spirit of humor in our talk, and he did not want me to kill it with all the deadly serious talk about the Way.

"Sorry, J," I said, smiling to let him know I understood. "Please continue."

"Soul has only one eternal life; but the self evolves from one life to the next like different chapters of the same story," Jesus continued, in his casual voice that sounded like a young college professor giving a tutorial. "The more the self grows in its own identity through karma and reincarnation, the more it grows in spiritual consciousness and works its way through the outer circle of life to the second stage of evolution. That's when I entered the scene with my teaching. I came to liberate the spiritual self of man trapped by its human self; but unfortunately my teaching got so distorted by the Gospel writers, with John leading the pack, that only a handful of people understand the real message of my gospel."

"And now we're going to demystify your sayings for the world," I said, and laughed at the audacity of our presumption. "If you would then, J; choose the first saying that you want us to demystify. *A saying that will stand the world on its head!"*

Without thought, Jesus quoted the first saying that he wanted us to decode, from St. Mathew's Gospel, Chapter 5, verse 37. ***"'But let your communication be, Yae yae; Nae nae; for whatsoever is more than these cometh of evil,'"*** he said, and gave me a look that challenged every fiber of my Soul.

"Wow!" I exclaimed. *"That's a real doozie!"*

"I knew that would get you, O," he said, and broke into laughter.

"It did get to me," I said, still reeling from one of the most powerful and perplexing sayings in all the Gospels of Christ. "So, who's going to take this on; me or you?" I asked, hoping that it would be Jesus.

"Let's flip on it," Jesus said, to my surprise. He reached into his pocket and took out a toonie. "Heads you reveal the gnostic wisdom of this saying, tails I do."

"Okay, flip it!" I said, loving the excitement.

Jesus flipped the toonie, caught it, and slapped it onto his other wrist. Lifting his hand, he looked at the coin and said, "Heads."

"My honors. *Thanks a lot, J!"*

"You're welcome," he said, and thus began our unbelievable dialogue on the messianic meaning of the enigmatic sayings of Jesus Christ!

12. *The Dual Consciousness of Man*

"You could not have selected a more revealing saying to penetrate the mystery of Christ's Way," I said, and sat back down on the bench.

I crossed my legs, closed my eyes, and did a short HU. I called upon the Inner Master. *"Thy will, not mine,"* I said, silently. I opened my eyes, turned to Jesus, and said, "I have to paint a picture now for the reader to see the profound meaning of your first saying for our dialogue. I beg your indulgence, J."

"Of course. If I may, O; I chose this saying because I wanted to cut to the very quick of my teaching and get to the heart of the matter."

"I'll say! I don't think any other saying can get to the heart of your teaching more quickly than this one!" I said, feeling like I had just been thrown into the lion's den.

"And what do you perceive to be the heart of my teaching?" Jesus asked, with that mystifying twinkle in his loving eyes.

I didn't think about what to say. I just opened my mouth and let Soul speak: **"The heart of the Way of Christ is the gnostic knowledge of the dual nature of human consciousness,"** I replied, with absolute confidence in my understanding of Christ's teaching. "Once one realizes this, all the sayings of Jesus fall into place."

Jesus reflected a moment, and said, "I agree. Little does man realize that he is not a human self that possesses a Soul; he is a Soul self that is split in two, one higher and one lower. And my gospel to the world had to do with reconciling the lower self of man with his higher self. This is what you mean by the dual nature of human consciousness, is it not?"

"Yes. You can continue. I won't mind," I said, and laughed.

"Sorry. You won the toss, O. You explain the saying," Jesus said, with a straight face.

"Alright," I said, jumping right in. "Perhaps it's best we begin *Jesus Wears Dockers* with my explanation of your first saying, because I can express the wisdom of this mind-boggling saying in contemporary language. I can employ the idiom, ideas, spiritual insights, and concepts of today's world to make sense of your metaphorical genius—"

"Perfect!" Jesus exclaimed, cutting me off. "That's precisely what I hoped you would do, O! *Thank God you won the toss!"*

"Don't thank yourself, J," I replied, with a straight face. "That would be terribly immodest, don't you think?"

Jesus broke into laughter. I stared, smiling at the spectacle of the world's most famous savior bent over with laughter at the absurdity of being worshiped as God.

As Jesus laughed, I got the feeling he was overdoing it; but before it took hold of me he explained himself. "It's good to get this out of my system, O. You cannot imagine how long I have waited to find the right context to reveal how I feel about my life as the crucified savior of the world!"

Again, with a straight face, I said, "I've been called a lot of things in my life, but never a context. That's all I am to you, a context?"

Jesus' eyes lit up with such warm love that he made me feel like the most special person in the world. "Yes, O; you are the perfect context to reveal the hidden meaning of my sayings. Scholars have been trying for centuries to penetrate the mystery of my gospel teaching, but only the chosen few have dared to take my sayings as far as you have. This is the context that you provide for our talk."

"You mean my life experience?" I asked, to be certain I understood correctly.

"Precisely! Mine is not a teaching for the mind of man. It is a teaching for the Soul of man. It will do no one any good unless my teaching is lived. This is the context that you provide. Many people have lived my sayings, but few have connected the dots as you have. This is what I hope to do with our dialogue. By unraveling the mystery of my sayings I hope to let your reader catch a glimpse of the divine mystery of the Way."

"If I may, you mean the natural way of spiritual self-realization consciousness," I said, putting Christ's gospel teaching into a modern context.

"Yes. Man has to get over this concept of instant salvation. If we can accomplish this with our dialogue I will be happy indeed!"

"Then why don't we talk about this for a moment before I let Soul speak on your first saying?" I said, hoping for a little respite.

"Why not?" Jesus said, surprising me. "What do you want to say about this foolish notion of instant salvation at the heart of the Gospel conspiracy?"

"Again, Gospel conspiracy? I think I'm beginning to see what you mean," I said, not quite yet grasping the full significance of what he meant by Gospel conspiracy.

"Good. That should make it easier for Soul to speak. You were saying?"

I had to pause. "Okay," I said, smiling at Jesus' playfulness. He wasn't going to spell it out for me, so I put on my brave face and continued. "The first thing I would say about instant salvation is that the idiocy of this concept lies in the idea that one man's death can atone for the sins of the whole world. How the Gospel writers fixed upon this idea is the real mystery, because it goes against the fundamental integrity of the natural Way of Life, which they must have known. Life has its own rules, and for man to believe that he can sneak his way out of the cycle of karma and reincarnation with instant salvation is about as foolish as man can possibly be. This concept of instant salvation through your death upon the cross has turned your teaching on its head; and Kal is laughing in your face, J."

"Don't I know it?" Jesus exclaimed, his eyes popping as wide as saucers. "Let me set the record straight. **I did not die on the cross to atone for the sins of the world. My crucifixion was a calculated ruse to fix upon the psyche of man the central premise of my gospel teaching—**"

"Self-sacrifice?" I instinctively interjected, to be absolutely certain.

"PRECISELY! Self-sacrifice is the engine that drives the Way of Christ, not my death upon the cross. It is the death of the lower self—"

"Stop!" I shouted, holding up my hand. "That's too far into the mystery for the reader. We have to work up to this before it makes any real sense to him. I kid you not, J; Christians are fixated on this idea of instant salvation, and if we accomplish anything with this dialogue I would hope it to be shattering this mindset all to hell. And

the only way we can do that is to lead the reader into the mysteries of your teaching with the spiritual logic of the Way. We have to connect the dots of your sayings. Once the reader sees the connection of your sayings, he will be forced by the spiritual logic of the Way to realize the mystery of your true teaching, and the real reason for your crucifixion."

"Yes," Jesus said, with a heavy sigh. "I took too much for granted when I revealed the Way to the world, didn't I?"

"Perhaps," I said, feeling the sadness in Christ's voice. "The exoteric world cannot grasp the mysteries of the Way. Nicodemus was too spiritually immature to hear what you were saying. You had no choice. You had to speak in metaphor. Well, the problem we have today is that your metaphors have never really been properly explained."

"BINGO!" Jesus exploded. *"We have to explain the metaphors to release my sayings from the prison of the insidious Gospel conspiracy!"*

"This is fun," I said, smiling at Christ's unbridled excitement. Then for some odd reason I cast my gaze out at all the people in the park, like I was being directed from within; at the two men and three women waiting to have their fortune read; at the man and woman at the hot dog vendor's cart; at a young couple walking hand in hand; at the two children frolicking with innocent abandon with their parents looking on; at a well-groomed man in checkered dress shorts walking his well-groomed black poodle on a tight leash; and the very idea of Jesus and I having a dialogue that would dispel what Jesus called the insidious Gospel conspiracy seemed so absurdly relevant to the panorama of life that I burst into a fit of giddy laughter, and I just sat there shaking my head in wondrous disbelief!

58

13. *Life Is a Waking Dream*

As I took in the people in the park it suddenly hit me. I looked up at Jesus, who was wondering what I was laughing at, and exclaimed, *"Life is a waking dream!"*

"Of course it is," Jesus replied, with the casual manner of a man whose sayings have made clichés of some of the most profound philosophies of life, "What did you think it was?" he added, just to tease me.

"Don't get smart, J! You came to me, remember?" I quickly responded, still giddy with the joy of my new revelation.

Jesus couldn't help himself and burst into laughter also. The spirit of levity had possessed us once more, and I began to feel light-headed again.

"It's no wonder the Way chose you to bring out the Divine Plan of God," he said, when he stopped laughing. "You could level the gods with your sense of humor!"

Instantly I saw the opening that Spirit had just provided, and I responded, "But isn't that the whole problem, J? The enormous gravity that people, including many Masters I might add, have placed upon the spiritual life? In the Divine Plan of God there is no time set for the liberation of Soul from these lower worlds. In the Divine Plan of God no experience is more relevant than any other to Soul's journey home to God; so tell me, why all this gravity about the Way? Even in my spiritual community, the most spiritually enlightened group of people in the world today, this gravity dampens the spirit of laughter. Why all of this seriousness about spiritual liberation, J? Can you tell me? No. Don't bother. Your crucifixion went a long way to making the Way a cross to bear. When I realized that in the Divine Plan of God your crucifixion was no more relevant to Soul's liberation from life and death than a farmer hoeing his potatoes, or a housewife washing her dishes, or an architect designing a new building to replace the twin towers in New York City, or Robert Bly working on his daily poem I felt the death throes of this spirit of gravity and you cannot imagine my relief. *It felt like the world had been lifted off my shoulders!"*

I expected Jesus to respond to my outburst, but he said nothing. He just sat there with a bemused smile on his face. Finally, he said, "You're right, O; the world is much too serious about salvation. After all, the world has never needed to be saved because this is how God realizes Itself. Through life, God grows. Life is a process that does not need improving upon, because whether it is improved upon or not the fundamental purpose of life would remain the same. So you're absolutely right; there is no need for all this gravity about spiritual liberation. Perhaps this is the spin that we should put on our talk?"

"What other spin can I put on it given my realization of the Divine Plan of God? That's why I say that the world can find its own way," I said, with a wry snicker.

"Yes, of course," Jesus said. Then after a moment's thought, he added, "Perhaps it's my attitude that needs to be adjusted."

"Perhaps," I said, with an ironic smile. "From what I've experienced of you so far, I would be inclined to say that you feel the same way about life as I do," I added, playing along with Jesus.

"I wasn't aware of it until you brought it to my attention," Jesus replied, with a revealing twinkle in his eye. "For centuries the world has treated me with uncompromising seriousness, never once with the lightness and humor that I am experiencing with you. You cannot imagine how refreshing you are to me, O!"

"Good. Now can I get back to the point I started to make?"

Jesus laughed at my feigned seriousness. "By all means," he said.

"Alright," I said, slipping from feigned to real seriousness. "I was telling you that all of life is a waking dream. Well, Spirit just lifted the veil and let me see the whole drama of Soul's journey through life in the ordinary events of people's lives out there. Take a look, J. See those people waiting to have their fortune read?"

"Yes. What about them?"

"Holy Spirit opened up my spiritual eyes and let me see that those people symbolize man's innate desire to know himself."

"Excellent! What else did you see?"

"I saw that young couple over there walking hand in hand. Two young lovers are connecting with the Creative Life Stream with their love for each other — a waking dream pointing to the most natural way back home to God!"

"Absolutely!" said Jesus.

"Love. That's what they revealed to me. Love is what all of life strives to realize, and that young couple in love speak the Way better than all the literature on the Way!"

"Wonderful! What else did your waking dream reveal to you?"

"A man and woman buying a hot dog or Italian sausage or what have you, which speaks to man's natural desire for life."

"Good! What else?"

"Children playing. They revealed the innocence of the self, which is the secret of spiritual self-realization consciousness. To use one of your most famous sayings, *`Lest ye be as little children, thou shall not enter into the kingdom of heaven!'"*

"Bravo!" Jesus exclaimed. "What else?"

"A man walking his dog on a leash," I replied, and chuckled.

"Why the chuckle?" Jesus asked.

"Because he revealed the dilemma of Soul's journey back home to God," I answered, and laughed some more.

"How so?" Jesus asked, his eyes just brimming with love.

"The dog was in front, walking the man as it were; and his 'dog of desire,' to use a Sufi expression for man's ravenous appetites, is what keeps man from becoming as a little child," I answered, and instantly burst into a fresh fit of laughter.

So did Jesus. He couldn't help himself. *"What a wonderful waking dream!"* he exclaimed, unable to contain the irony. "First you saw man's need to know himself, which symbolizes Soul's desire for total self-realization consciousness; then you saw that Soul must connect with the Holy Current of God's Love to realize its divine essence, which the young lovers symbolize; then you saw a man and woman satisfying their natural desire for food to sustain their life; then you saw children playing, which reveals the key to the kingdom of heaven in the purity of their innocence; and then you saw Soul's dilemma in the waking dream of the dog walking the man, which symbolizes Soul's constant struggle with the desires of its lower self. *What a wonderful waking dream, O!* Is there more?"

"Yes," I said, so elevated by the joy of spiritual awareness that I felt extremely light-headed again. "And you and I sitting here talking about the Way. We symbolize that part of the spiritual journey where all these people are going to be one day — *but even we in the garden of mystic lovers are no closer to the mystery of God than they are!*"

Jesus could not contain the irony of our dilemma and burst into such a fit of laughter that he had to hold his stomach with both hands!

14. *For the Sake of the Reader*

I could not believe how perfectly the Golden-tongued Wisdom of Divine Spirit spoke to me. My waking dream revealed the whole story of Soul's journey through life. I sat back with a big smirk on my face basking in the afterglow of God's love.

"It is gratifying, is it not?" Jesus said, with a satisfied smile.

I turned to Jesus. "It certainly is," I said.

His eyes danced with light. "It is food for Soul, is it not?" he said.

"Holy Spirit is forever nourishing Soul. We just don't realize it, that's all. Take my waking dream. In one glance Spirit let me see Soul's whole journey through life, and I can't help but feel a profound sense of spiritual satisfaction in this awareness."

"How so?" Jesus asked. Not because he didn't know, which I'm certain he did, but just to carry the conversation along for the reader's sake.

I had by this time begun to see that for all of his human qualities Jesus was much more of a Master than he let on to me, and he knew just what to say to keep our talk fresh and exciting. His playful smile told me he suspected I had found him out, but he didn't let on. He continued to play the role he had assigned himself, human and intimately familiar, but still the Master who knew what was both on my mind and in my heart.

"Well, J," I said, playing the part that Spirit had assigned to me; "it satisfied my need to know that I'm still in agreement with life. Spirit gave me the waking dream to reaffirm my knowledge of Soul's fundamental purpose in life, and that was very gratifying."

"For the sake of the reader, when you write your story please explain what you mean by this sense of spiritual nourishment that your waking dream gave you," Jesus said, and put his arm on the bench to relax and enjoy our intensely revealing dialogue.

"Alright," I said, smiling playfully back at Jesus. I loved how he always kept the reader in mind. I didn't realize until just then how often he referred to the reader. It was as though Jesus was editing the book as it was being written on another level, and whenever he felt something had to be cleared up he caught it and pointed it out to me. "Soul needs food to grow as well as the body," I continued, silently beseeching my Muse for the right words, "but the problem people have is that they don't realize the literal truth of this spiritual need. People have the mistaken idea that Soul is a complete entity unto itself, and that it's simply a matter of doing this or doing that in order to be liberated from the karmic cycle of life and death. The truth is that Soul needs spiritual food, because Soul has to satisfy its encoded need for total self-identity. Every Soul self has to grow into itself. This is why we have come into these lower worlds. We did not come into the evolutionary process of life as complete spiritual entities. We came as — are you ready for this, J?"

"Yes, of course. I was wondering when you were going to reveal the DPG."

"DPG?" I said, puzzled.

With a big smile, Jesus said, " Divine Plan of God."

I couldn't quite read his smile this time. It seemed to be a magical blend of love and mischievousness. More loving than mischievous, I thought.

"Alright," I said. "We came from the Ocean of Love and Mercy. The Body of God, if you will —*for the sake of the reader!"*

"Please, continue," Jesus said, disregarding my sarcasm.

"The Body of God is made up of individual atoms, which are Souls that have Soul consciousness but no self-consciousness," I continued, letting Soul speak; "just as those Canada geese over there that have group consciousness but no self-consciousness. Well, the whole purpose of life is to give each atom of God the opportunity to evolve an individual identity. Each atom of God is a Soul seed encoded to become totally self-realized. Just as the acorn seed is encoded to become an oak tree, so is each atom of God encoded to become a spiritually self-realized, God-conscious Soul. This, then, for the sake of the reader, is how God expands its consciousness in the lower worlds and becomes more God. Through the growth of individual Souls God realizes itself. That's the GDP in a nutshell."

"And what does all of this information, precious though it may be, have to do with nourishing the higher self?" Jesus asked.

"It satisfies man's need to know," I replied.

"Please, explain that," Jesus said.

"For the sake of the reader, right?"

"Yes, of course."

"See those people getting their fortune read," I said, looking at the little crowd waiting to have their ten minute fortune read.

"I see them," Jesus said.

"Well," I said, very gently letting Soul speak, "they have a need to know about their life. This need to know drives us through life. But we have a need that is even more fundamental than our need to know. It is even more fundamental than our need for air, food, water, sex, and emotional succor even. We have an *a priori* need for total self-identity."

"Spiritual self-identity," Jesus amplified.

"Yes; we are driven to become spiritually self-realized and God conscious. This is our fundamental need in life. Each atom of God is an un-self-realized Soul seed, and the whole purpose of life is to nourish the atom of God's need for total self-identity. And my waking dream gave me the satisfaction of seeing the whole drama of Soul's purpose in life. Spirit lifted the veil and let me see the divine purpose behind the drama of life in those few people; and that, for the sake of the reader, is what constitutes a waking dream!"

"Excellent!" said Jesus, with a satisfied smile.

"If I may now, at the risk of being redundant — but then, repetition is the teacher's best tool, is it not?" I said, and laughed.

Jesus loved my laughter. "Yes, it is. Please, continue."

"Well," I said, summing up my insight, "in the people seeking to have their fortune read, I saw man's *a priori* need to know himself; in the young lovers, I saw that love is the path home to God — or, if you will, the natural way to nourish one's need for total self-identity; in the man and woman getting something to eat, I saw man's need to satisfy his natural bodily desires; in the children playing, I saw the path of purifying our human consciousness with the virtue that leads to innocence, because only the pure of heart can enter the kingdom of heaven; and in the man walking his poodle I saw the whole drama of the conflict between the lower self, which is driven by human desires, and the higher self, which is driven to become spiritually self-realized and God-conscious. And seeing all of this, Holy Spirit filled me with

65

a sense of certainty that satisfied my need to *know* my purpose here today, which is to serve God by helping you explain the secret of your gospel to the world. That's what I mean by spiritual nourishment. This waking dream is like spiritual candy, and in all honesty it's very, very satisfying!"

"Thank you," Jesus said, on behalf of the reader I'm sure; and then he laughed because he knew that I was finally onto his game with me.

"That should satisfy the reader's need to know, don't you think?" I said, just to confirm that I knew and didn't mind being used that way.

"For now. We still have a long way to go before we dispel the Gospel conspiracy," he said, and instantly his eyes changed from playful to serious and I knew that from that moment on our dialogue was going straight to the heart of his secret teaching!

15. *The I of God*

"Do you think I'll remember all of this when I get to write *Jesus Wears Dockers?*" I asked Jesus, with a self-conscious smile.

"What you don't remember you can fill in. You have an exceptional imagination for spiritual truth, O. That's why the Way chose you to help me dispel the Gospel conspiracy and set the record straight."

"It will never be settled, will it?"

"What, the story of my life?"

"That too," I said, thinking more of his teaching.

"Of course not. As you have correctly reasoned, there are three levels of human consciousness, and countless levels within each of these three levels. Each level satisfies its own need in its own way. There are those that will believe what they want to believe because it satisfies their level of consciousness, and there are those that will not believe because it does not satisfy their level of consciousness. Nichodemus could not believe me when I told him that man must be born again to enter into the kingdom of heaven, because his level of consciousness could not digest the rich spiritual food of my sayings—"

"Stop!" I interjected. "That's the point I was getting to — the spiritual food that nourishes Soul!"

"Yes, I know. If you would, then," Jesus said, and motioned for me to explain.

"Consciousness is the spiritual food of life," I began, with a pressing urgency to reveal this impenetrable mystery. "The spiritual nature of consciousness was one of my most liberating insights. Without it, I could not have connected the dots in the Divine Plan of God. For whatever merciful reason, Spirit revealed to me that consciousness is the energy that the atom of God needs to grow, and it was only a matter of time before I came to the realization that the consciousness of life is the un-self-realized 'I' of God!"

"Wow!" Jesus shouted, excited by this disclosure. "Do you think it wise to reveal this divine truth to the reader now?"

"How can I not? What would be the point of revealing Soul's *a priori* need to become God-realized and not disclose what energy it needs to grow in spiritual self-realization and God consciousness?"

"You're logic is sound. I fear for the readers, though," Jesus responded, with a concerned look. "This is much too deep. They will not fathom the mystery of the 'I' of God until they begin to live the Way consciously. Not until Soul begins to nourish itself on Holy Spirit by living the Way consciously will man see what this spiritual energy really is; but I will leave that for you to disclose or not. It is your book after all."

"It wouldn't be much of a book without you, would it?" I said, and sniggered.

Jesus laughed. "So, do you plan to reveal the deepest mystery of the self of man?"

"I have no choice, do I? Spirit has set the stage for us, and we have to play our part, don't we?" I said, feeling very much like I had just crossed the point of no return.

"I agree completely," said Jesus, and patted my knee.

"What was that for?" I asked.

"There's no turning back now, O," he said, confirming my feelings.

Then Jesus smiled and the love poured out of his eyes and filled me with such confidence that all of my fear vanished. Taking a deep breath, I jumped into the heart of the divine mystery of the self of man. "The deepest mystery of the self is this: **consciousness is the un-self-realized 'I' of God**. By living life, man nourishes himself with the 'I' of God. As man nourishes himself with the 'I' of God, he individuates the 'I' of God into a spiritually self-realized and God-conscious Soul. This is the purpose of the Divine Plan of God — *to individuate the 'I' of God and give birth to God with each new Soul self!*"

"WOW!" Jesus exclaimed. *"It's finally out!"*

"Yes. And it's a big mouthful to swallow, isn't it?"

"Some people are going to choke on it," Jesus said, and laughed.

I laughed too. The relief felt good "What can I say, J? I'm sure there are people out there that have an appetite for this truth."

"No doubt. But what do you think it will do to those whose entire belief system will be thrown into disarray?" Jesus asked, looking concerned.

"That's not my problem, is it? Life is life, and people can do as they please with this sacred knowledge. As I said, J; the world can find its own way—"

Jesus laughed. Then, thoughtfully, with what sounded very much like regret in his voice, he said, "I wish I would have adopted this attitude two thousand years ago. It would have made all the difference in the world."

I couldn't believe my ears. *"Are you serious, J?"*

"Yes. I took the Way much too seriously for my own good. You have no idea the karma that I precipitated in my fever to establish the kingdom of heaven on earth. I will have to answer to the Lords of Karma until the end of time for whatever people do in my name. The good that they do in my name honors me, but I am responsible for all the evil that people do in my name. Believe me, O; it's no fun being Jesus Christ!"

Nonplussed by Christ's candor, I had to sit back and reflect for a moment. I had never thought of Jesus creating karma for himself, so this came as a shock to me. After all, how could I see Jesus and karma in the same boat together? But there they were. I became very emotional. Suddenly I felt for Jesus in a way that I would never have imagined.

"If I may," I said, my voice full of emotion, "can I ask how you go about resolving all the evil in the world that is done in your name?"

"It's not quite as simple as all of that," Jesus replied, with a twinkle in his eyes and what seemed to be a shadow of a smirk on his face. "Karma is, after all, a personal responsibility. I'm called by the Lords of Karma to explain myself. Each Soul that does evil in my name has to be made aware that they have misunderstood my teaching. I am not literally responsible for the evil done in my name; I am nominally responsible. There's a difference. Even so, I am getting tired of being hauled up by the Lords of Karma to keep explaining myself. I do hope our dialogue will set the record straight, O. It just might make my life a little simpler."

With that, Jesus burst into a fit of laughter at my expense. I couldn't share in his laughter, but I sure felt a big sigh of relief for Jesus!

16. *The Way of Love*

The two young lovers were sitting on the grassy bank of the murky river that flowed through the heart of Southlake. He put his arm around her. She turned to him, and they kissed tenderly on the lips. It was very touching.

Jesus saw me smiling at the lovers. "Did you like what I said about love at the worship service this morning?" he asked.

"Very much," I replied.

"I had to speak up, O. For the sake of your spiritual community, Stanley had to hear that it takes consciousness to keep love alive."

"I agree," I said, smiling at the irony of Christ's response to Stanley's message on love. Stanley Hansen, for all of his spiritual maturity as a High Initiate, saw love as the magic elixir for all of life's problems, and I was growing impatient with Stanley's one song repertoire. Jesus pointed out to Stanley and everyone at the service that love is a powerful force that has to be invested wisely or it will go sour. "I'm glad you appeared," I added. "I was beginning to feel all alone out there."

You're not alone by any means, O. Your love is true. That's why you don't make a fuss about the Way of Love."

"There's a chapter I could write!"

"What?"

"The Way of Love!"

"Perhaps you should. Why don't we talk about that now to set the stage, as it were?"

I was happy to take the plunge. "Where should we start?"

"Take that young couple over there," said Jesus, nodding in the direction of the lovers who embraced each other now as if they were the only two people in the world. "They don't know it, but their love for each other has introduced the God-force into their life."

Jesus stopped, expecting me to say something. I didn't. He beckoned me with his eyes to respond. "This is not news to me, J," I said, unable to resist. "What is God if not love? And love is love, regardless how it is expressed."

"Yes, of course" Jesus confirmed. "But falling in love and keeping one's love alive are two entirely different things. Falling in love like those lovers is a gift from God, be it the result of their own karma or not. The real question is this: can they keep their love alive?"

"This is like your parable of the talents, isn't it?"

"Precisely like my parable of the talents!" Jesus exclaimed, excited that I had made the connection. "The precious gift of love has to be invested wisely for it to grow!"

"That's why you said that the spiritual life is not unlike the economic life at the worship service this morning, isn't it?" I asked, to draw Jesus out.

"Exactly," Jesus replied. "These young lovers have to take the gift of love that God has bestowed upon them and invest it wisely in their relationship. If they don't, they will exhaust their precious gift and do one of two things."

"Which are?" I asked, very eager to know.

"They can go their separate ways and hope to find a new love, or they can stay together and be unrequited for the rest of their lives," Jesus replied, without compromise.

"Probably the latter," I said, and laughed.

"Why?" Jesus asked.

"As you said this morning, it takes consciousness to invest one's love wisely; and most people just don't have that level of awareness."

"And why do you think that is?" Jesus asked, in that solicitous voice which told me that he was asking on behalf of the reader.

I slouched back on the bench, stretched out my legs, and thought long and hard. Jesus waited patiently for my answer. "Values," I finally said, and fell silent.

My one word answer wasn't enough. "For the sake of the reader, O," Jesus beckoned.

"Of course, the reader," I said, and snickered.

"What about values?" Jesus insisted.

"Alright," I said, and sat up. I crossed my legs, rested my arm on the back of the bench and looked at Jesus directly in the eye when

I spoke. "The values that one lives by determine one's level of spiritual consciousness. The more self-serving one's values are, the less spiritually conscious one will be. The more life-serving one's values are, the more spiritually conscious one will be. The more spiritually conscious one is, the more one's love will grow, because love grows or dies in direct proportion to the consciousness of one's personal values. Love and consciousness, J. They co-exist!"

"Good. Would you break that down, please?"

"For the sake of the reader, right?"

"We have to keep him in mind," said Jesus, with a hint of irritation in his voice. "After all, this dialogue is for him, isn't it?"

"Alright," I said, smiling at the memory that flashed across my mind. "As I used to say in my past lifetime as Daniel, Earl of Wellington Manor, 'if I'm in for a penny, I'm in for a pound.' But I need help on this one, J. So give me a moment please."

"Certainly," Jesus said.

I closed my eyes and called upon inner guidance. I wanted the right words to explain the Way of Love. I used my secret word because it opened me up to the Soul Consciousness of my higher self, which in essence was the Inner Master.

Silently, I repeated my spiritual power word a dozen times or so. I began to feel the Inner Master's presence. Then I heard his soft, gentle voice: *The secret of love is the secret of life. Speak from the heart, O. Just don't be too casual about love. The world takes love much more seriously than you do.*

I chuckled out loud. Jesus smiled, but said nothing. I was ready to explain the Way of Love; and I just stepped back and let Soul speak: "The secret to keeping love alive in a relationship, as you said in your parable of the talents, is wise investment," I began, with absolute confidence in myself. "But how does one invest one's love wisely? Is it wise to keep one's love locked up in one's heart where the flourishing Light of God cannot get to it? No; I don't think so. Love is the energy of life, and from what I have experienced in my many lifetimes in this world I can tell you that life is the natural way back home to God. Life is the Way, and if love is the God-force that nourishes life it follows that one has to be true to the principles of the

Way of Life if he wants to keep love alive in his life. The logic is impeccable."

"Yes, it is. And what are these principles?" Jesus asked.

"The Spiritual Laws of Life," I replied, feeling Spirit surging within me. "One of these laws is the Law of Reciprocal Return. You get love by giving love. So the more one learns how to give love—"

"Wisely!" Jesus cut in. "One has to learn how to give love wisely."

"Yes, of course. May I continue, please?"

"Yes," Jesus said, smiling at my seriousness.

"Thank you. The more one learns how to give love, the more love one will receive, because the Spiritual Laws of Life are exact. On the other hand, the less love one gives the less love one will have in his life. Those young lovers have just embarked upon the greatest adventure of their entire life — *a journey into the divine mystery of God!"*

"I agree," said Jesus, smiling. "But to be honest with you, O; I'm not completely satisfied with your explanation. If you don't mind, I'd like to add my two cents."

"I won't take anything less than a pound," I said, and laughed.

Jesus chuckled. "That was Daniel speaking, wasn't it?"

"I suppose it was," I said, as the memories of my lifetime as the quick-witted *bête noire* of London's aristocracy rushed to the surface. I had a sharp tongue in that life.

"Pound it is, then," said Jesus, and grinned. His grin faded, and in the same gentle but firm voice that he used at the worship service with Stanley, he continued. "True love is pure love. It is not tarnished by life. When two people fall in love and feel the Current of God flowing through them, they know that they have been blessed. Their love has connected them with the Holy Current of God, which raises them up to the lover's heaven of divine bliss; but as they come down from their heaven of bliss life begins to dampen the ardor of their love, and it is here that the true story of their love is told."

"How so?" I asked, smiling at Christ's description.

"Priorities," Jesus replied, and fell silent.

"And by that, you mean?" I asked.

"To stay in love one has to make love a top priority in their life," Jesus answered. "And making love a top priority takes time, patience, wisdom, kindness, and a never-ending supply of sensitivity—"

"CONSCIOUSNESS!" I erupted.

"Exactly," Jesus said, smiling at my outburst. "This is precisely the point that I was trying to impress upon Stanley Hansen this morning."

"I don't think he got it," I said, and laughed.

"Oh, he got it," Jesus said. "He doesn't know it yet, but he got it!"

"So tell me, J," I mused; "what's the most important thing that we can say about love for the chapter I'm going to write on the Way of Love?"

"Love is true to you when you are true to love," Jesus replied. With that we both fell silent, as if Spirit had cut us off for the moment, and we just sat quietly enjoying the young lovers as they hugged and kissed and whispered sweet promises to each other as all lovers do when they first fall in love.

17. *A Grease Monkey for God*

I felt my stomach rumbling. "I could use another hot dog. How about you, J?" I asked, standing up.

"Yes, please," Jesus said. "I'll come with you."

We walked over to the vendor's cart. "I think I'll have an Italian sausage on a bun. How about you?"

"That'll be fine," Jesus said.

"Cold drink?" I asked.

"Sure. I'll get this," he said, and reached into his pocket.

"No way! It's not every day that one gets to treat Jesus Christ!"

Jesus laughed. The vendor gave us a strange look. I laughed, and said, "I'd like you to meet Jesus Christ. And I'm St. Peter. Jesus here saves them, and I reject them if I don't approve. Not a bad team, eh?"

The vendor smiled, and then laughed. "It's a pleasure to serve Jesus and St. Peter," he said, when he handed us our hot sausages on a bun. Then he got our sodas.

I paid the vendor, gave him a generous tip, and we walked back to our bench. There was a stout, elderly gentleman with a punched-up boxer's face sitting in the middle of our bench with an arm resting on either side of the backrest. He had on plaid green trousers, a plain rumpled white dress shirt open at the chest with the sleeves rolled up once, and sandals on his bare feet. I bid him a nice day.

"Yeah, but it's calling for rain tonight," he gruffly replied.

"We can use the rain," I said, and smiled at the man.

"Yeah, but not too much I hope. Wouldn't that be something, if we could control the weather? Sure would make life a lot simpler!"

Both Jesus and I laughed. Then, from out of nowhere Jesus made the comment, "Nature patterns itself after man, not man after nature."

"I beg your pardon," the man said.

"Oh, nothing," said Jesus. "I was just musing."

"Well, it's a good muse," the man said, with a twinkle in his eyes. "Take that storm down below in the U. S. of A. Hurricane Katrina blew through New Orleans and cleaned up a whole lot of stuff down there. That's what you mean, isn't it?"

Jesus smiled. "Yes. That's precisely what I mean."

"But we can't say that too loudly, can we? After all, karma is not a subject people warm up to easily," the man said, and stood up. "Well, I'll leave you two to it. Have a nice day," he said, with a wave of his hand and a smile on his boxer's face.

Jesus and I sat down. I watched the man saunter away. Something about him intrigued me. I took a sip of soda. "That was a Soul Master, wasn't it?" I said to Jesus.

"I believe it was," Jesus casually replied.

"And he wants us to talk about karma, doesn't he?"

"I'm sure of it," said Jesus, as though it was all so normal.

Nonplussed, I didn't know what to say. We ate our sausage and sipped our cold drink in silence. I couldn't help but wonder who that man was, and Jesus was not volunteering the information, so I had to ask. "Well? Are you going to tell me or not?"

"You wouldn't believe me if I told you." Jesus said.

"Who?"

"Socrates."

"No way!"

"Yes."

"Christ! Why didn't you tell me? Socrates is my favorite philosopher!"

"I know," Jesus said, and laughed.

"Then why didn't you introduce us?"

"It wasn't my place. If Socrates wanted you to know who he was, he would have introduced himself."

"Christ!" I exclaimed again.

"Stop shouting my name, will you?" Jesus said. "You have no idea how it annoys me when people use my name every time they have a need to vent. Please stop it, O."

"I'm sorry," I said, with a self-conscious chuckle. I took a drink of soda, and just as I was about to open up the subject of karma, Jesus said, "The more balanced society is, the more balanced the weather will be. Storms are nature's way of keeping man on his spiritual toes, as it were."

"From this perspective it would follow that man and nature — *of course they are!*" I interrupted myself, concluding my own thought.

"Man and nature are what?" Jesus asked, on behalf of the reader.

"Man and nature are intimately related," I replied.

"They are one," said Jesus. "Man is nature's most precious creation; but because of free will man has fooled himself into believing that he is separate from nature. That's the great tragedy of the scientific age."

"Mind over matter," I said, with a snigger.

"Something like that. Just because we can think our way through life doesn't remove us from the life process, as quantum physics has finally proven. Life is who we are. Life is a divine matrix of matter, mind, and spirit; and until the scientific community realizes this man will never control the weather."

"You're serious, aren't you?" I said, intrigued by this information.

"Of course. Let's get back to karma," Jesus said.

"But karma is related to the weather. That's what Socrates just said."

"Of course it is. Socrates said that just to open up the subject of karma. Karma affects the weather, but what is karma? That's what Socrates wants us to explore for your book."

"So this book's becoming a community project now, is it?"

"You didn't think I was in this alone, did you?" Jesus said, and broke into a mirthful chuckle. *"Come on, O. I need all the help I can get!"*

I didn't know what to say. I felt myself being pulled in deeper and deeper into what was becoming an unbelievable experience, but I couldn't help myself. I had my wits about me, but I was no match for the Masters. I had to let Jesus know exactly how I felt.

"So why me, J?" I said, my voice faltering a little. "Is it because I've worked out the Divine Plan of God? Is that it?"

"Essentially, yes. You see, O; we finally have a paradigm large enough for all the big questions of life. You have managed to connect all the spiritual dots with the missing pieces, and this makes your perspective precious to the Masters."

"What missing pieces?" I asked.

"Don't play coy with me. The time for coy is long past. It's time now for the meat of the last supper," Jesus said with a straight face.

I broke into laughter. Jesus could not contain himself and burst into laughter also. "So this whole thing is a set-up, then?"

"Yes."

"For what purpose?"

"Many purposes. You've always been a multi-tasker. Well, your book will serve many functions also," Jesus said.

"Name two," I challenged.

"Sure. One; it will do wonders for my new image. I kid you not, O. I'm tired of being the crucified Christ. That's why I wish you had pursued the publication of *Dear Jesus*. It would have gone a long way to taking me down off my cross. People cannot let go of this image. The crucifix has served its purpose, but it has too much power now. Sometimes I wish I had taken Master Zadok's advice; but I was too crazy with God to hear him. Now I have to live with it. That's what karma is all about, O — CONSEQUENCES!"

Jesus shouted the word. He even stroked his finger in the air to underscore it. And he had a tortured messianic look on his face.

I chuckled nervously. "Choices and consequences," I summed up.

"Exactly! Why can't the world connect these dots?" Jesus asked, as if truly perplexed by man's recalcitrant ignorance. *"Why can't the world see this connection?"*

"Because we make choices in the present and the consequences are in the future, and we don't want to look into the future for fear of not seeing the right consequences," I replied, to my own astonishment.

"There's a lot of truth to that," Jesus said, softening the stern, almost vengeful look on his Old Testament messianic face. "People only want to see the good of their choices, not the bad. That's the whole problem with—"

"Stop!" I exclaimed, holding up my hand.

"What?" Jesus asked, surprised by my outburst.

"You've just made a point that has to be addressed."

"What point?"

"ACCOUNTABILITY!" I shouted for the whole park to hear, underscoring the word with my right index finger just as Jesus had done.

"Please, explain that," Jesus said, with a big smirk on his face.

I wanted to say, "For the sake of the reader, right?" But I chose not to irritate Christ's Old Testament messianic personality. It gave me the willies.

"We fear looking into the future to see the consequences of some of the choices we make because we will be forced to see that we are responsible for consequences we don't want to own up to," I explained, and chuckled to release the tension. "That's why fortune tellers like that chap over there seldom reveal the bad stuff about a person's future."

"Yes, I know," Jesus said, now smiling at me. "So it's the fear of responsibility of one's bad choices that keeps man from becoming aware of the consequences of his choices; is that what you're trying to say?"

"Yes. Fear of personal accountability is what keeps the world blind to karma."

"Of course. And what do you propose we do about it?"

"Not a damn thing!" I instinctively responded. "As I told you, J; as far as I'm concerned the world can find its own way!"

"You're serious, aren't you?"

"Of course I am."

"What about your responsibility to the Way?"

"I beg your pardon?"

"You are an initiate of the Way, are you not?"

"Yes."

"Don't you have a responsibility to the Way?"

"I don't understand what you mean."

"You have a responsibility to get the Way out there for people to explore the conscious spiritual life, don't you?"

"What does it matter to me if the world explores the conscious spiritual life of the Way? I'm not responsible for the choices people make. That's the whole point about karma, isn't it? LIFE IS A

PERSONAL CHOICE!" I shouted again for the whole park to hear, and then I burst into a fit of gut-splitting giddy laughter.

Jesus just smiled at me, his eyes glistening with love. "Yes it is, O," he said, when I settled down. "But the awakened Soul has a responsibility to keep the wheels of the Divine Plan of God greased, if I may be allowed to express it this way.

"So now I'm just a grease monkey for God?" I quickly replied.

Jesus burst into laughter. "What an incredible sense of humor you have, O! You take all the gravity out of the spiritual life! I LOVE IT!" Then in a reflective, almost tormented voice Jesus said, *"Oh, how I long to be taken down off my cross…"*

18. *Out, O Damned Spot!*

Seeing how Jesus felt about coming down off his cross, I thought it appropriate to share something he might enjoy. "If you don't mind, J; I'd like to share an image I had of you a few years ago."

"By all means," he said, with no trace of remorse in his voice.

"Well, I saw you hanging on your cross," I said, not knowing how Jesus was going to respond to the irony, "but instead of what you said up there I put a few words from Shakespeare into your mouth."

"Probably, 'Out, o damned spot!'" Jesus said, to my surprise.

"That's good. That's really good. No. I never thought of that line. What I had you say instead was, 'the times are out of joint, o cursed spite, that ever I was born to set them right!'"

Jesus broke out, and he laughed long enough to let me know that he was back to his playful self again; and then he said, "That's very good, O. But to be honest with you, I prefer my quotation to yours. It's more to the point."

"The point being?"

"To remove that stain from the Soul of man."

"What, original sin?"

"Yes."

"Wow! That's really good! No wonder you prefer your quotation. I prefer it too!"

"Why don't we talk about this stain on the psyche of man, then?"

"The psyche? Not the Soul of man?"

"That's the point, is it not? To point out to the reader that this stain of original sin is an imaginary stain? Ergo, it's in the psyche of man, not the Soul of man," Jesus replied, with a playful smile on his loveable, jowled face.

"How stupid of me! And to remove this imaginary stain from the psyche of man, what do you propose we talk about — the evisceration of Christianity?"

Jesus couldn't help himself. He burst into laughter again. "That's exactly what it would do to Christianity, wouldn't it?"

"Eviscerate it? Yes, of course. What would Christianity be without original sin?" I replied, smiling to myself at the mounting irony of our dialogue.

"So how do you propose we eviscerate Christianity?" he asked.

I looked at Jesus and thought to myself; if only the world could see Jesus as I saw him sitting there people wouldn't be so damn serious about salvation. *"That's it!"*

"What?" Jesus asked, surprised by my outburst.

"If we eviscerate Christianity we can remove all this seriousness about salvation!" I exclaimed. "We should talk about salvation and work our way backwards!"

Jesus thought for a moment. "I see where you're going. Good. I like the methodology. By taking the fear out of salvation we can remove the spot of original sin. *Excellent, O!"*

"And I know just the place to start," I said, as Divine Spirit flashed the thought across my mind. Silently, I thanked the Inner Master.

"Where?" Jesus asked.

"With my regressions. I had seven past-life regressions last year, and my fourth regression gave me one of the vital missing pieces that I needed to work out the Divine Plan of God," I said, just bursting to tell my incredible story.

"That's wonderful," said Jesus, his eyes shining with love. "It was your regression to the Ocean of Love and Mercy, wasn't it?"

Surprised, I looked at Jesus. "Of course," I said, when it hit me. "You've read my book on my past lives on the inner, haven't you?"

"Yes. Go on with your evisceration. I'm curious to see how you're going to remove the stain of original sin from the psyche of Christianity."

"Now it's the psyche of Christianity?" I said.

"Yes. It's all part of the Gospel conspiracy, O," Jesus said, in his serious voice.

"Alright," I said, following suite. "Let me get right to the point, then. In my fourth regression the Inner Master took me to the Ocean of Love and Mercy where I experienced myself as an un-self-realized atom of God. The Ocean of Love and Mercy is the Body of God and ground zero of the Divine Plan of God—"

"Ground zero?" Jesus interrupted, for the sake of the reader.

Smiling, I continued. "In the same regression the Inner Master took me to my first human life where I experienced the birth of my own reflective self-consciousness. I called myself Grunt for this lifetime because I grunted all the time. It was a power grunt to keep my clan in check. As an atom of God, I had climbed up the evolutionary ladder through millions of incarnations all the way up to the primordial life of man. Because I had this experience I know that the Divine Plan of God is a living reality. I was there. I experienced myself as an atom of God in the Body of God, and then in the world as a primordial human being, and along with my other regressions I pieced together the Divine Plan of God!"

"Could you give us a synopsis of the DPG?" Jesus asked.

"Us?" I said.

"Myself and the millions who are going to read your book."

"Millions? Will I get to see this in my lifetime?"

"Yes."

"Promise?"

"No. I don't make promises anymore."

I smiled. "Okay, where was I?"

"The DPG. A quick synopsis, if you would?"

"Okay. For the sake of the reader. We are all atoms of God. What the poet Keats called, 'atoms of perception.' We come from the Body of God into these lower worlds to create a self-identity, which incidentally Keats also discerned in the letter to his brother called 'The Vale of Soul Making.' So we come from God into the evolutionary process of life to create a Soul self. As atoms of God, we have Soul consciousness but no self-consciousness. We go through the evolutionary chain of life to create a Soul self. We are Soul to begin with, but Soul without self-identity. After millions of years of evolution we come to the point that I did in my first primordial human life where I had the dawning of my own reflective self-consciousness. From that lifetime on with every incarnation I built upon my own identity until I began to get a sense of my immortal self; and the rest, as they say, is history. That's the DGP in a nut shell!"

"Good. Now, how did you build upon your identity?"

"Through experience. From lifetime to lifetime. By creating karma and resolving karma. Life experience collects the God-force that nourishes the spiritual self."

"By God-force, you mean the 'I' of God?"

"Yes. The God-force is the consciousness of life, and the consciousness of life is the un-self-realized 'I' of God. By experiencing life we take in the consciousness of life and individuate the 'I' of God. That's how we create our Soul self."

"And that's how God grows also," Jesus added.

"It follows. The important thing here is this: at no point in this entire process did I experience original sin. So it's from personal experience that I can say that this whole concept of original sin is a figment of Christianity's imagination, and you would have been a different Jesus Christ today had you uttered the bard's words upon the cross!"

"Shakespeare wasn't even thought of then," Jesus said.

"Real cute, J!" I said, and laughed.

"Please continue with your evisceration of Christianity, O. I'm enjoying this very much," Jesus said, with a satisfied grin on his face.

"What do you mean *my* evisceration? Do you think I want this on my shoulders? *No way!* You created Christianity, and you can share in the responsibility of eviscerating it!"

"Christianity wasn't founded upon my gospel, O. This is why we're having this dialogue. But you're right. We have to see this through together even if the reader will never know if this dialogue took place or not," Jesus said.

"It doesn't really matter, does it? Real or imagined, it's all woven out of the same miraculous fabric of God," I said, and laughed.

"We know that; but there are people out there who are particular about these things. But then, it's all part of God's Plan, isn't it?" Jesus said.

"Exactly! So, where were we?"

"Original sin. You didn't experience it in your regressions."

85

"Yes. I didn't have original sin in the Ocean of Love and Mercy. As an atom of God, I was the seed of my own Soul self, and as I evolved through life all the way up to my first human life where I had the dawning of self-consciousness I did not evolve with the stain of original sin; so for whatever reason Christianity created this myth of original sin, it's not true. And once we inform the reader that original sin does not exist, your death upon the cross becomes redundant."

"Redundant!" Jesus exclaimed. "My sweet God," he added, for dramatic effect, "Jesus Christ, the only Begotten Son of God, savior of the world — *REDUNDANT!"*

"How's that for the evisceration of Christianity?" I said, giving Jesus new cause to keel over in laughter, and I joined him.

19. *My Sense of Life*

I felt comfortable talking with Jesus now. It was still quite surreal, but that was only because part of me failed to acknowledge the eternal nature of Jesus and kept him locked up in history. But the more we talked the less hold the historical Jesus had upon me.

"Would you like to talk about my saying now?" Jesus asked, snapping me out of my thought. "We don't want to digress too far, do we?"

"Your yae yae, nae nae saying?"

"Yes. Are you ready to let Soul speak on what we can call the first saying of my true gospel teaching?" Jesus asked, with a generous smile.

I thought for a moment. "To be honest with you, I don't think I'm ready just yet. I'm still too much in my own way. I have to be free of the little me to let Soul speak on this powerful saying. Why don't we just continue talking freely to open up my creative channel? After all, this is no ordinary book you've asked me to write. It's going to take all I have to give, because I know damn well how the creative process works."

"May I?"

"Yes."

"Would you not use cuss words, please? It's acceptable in the culture of your workaday trade, but you are talking with Jesus Christ now. There are readers out there who will not understand your sense of life."

"My sense of life?" I asked, intrigued. "What do you mean by that?"

"This is your Gurdjieffian background," Jesus explained. "Gurdjieff was an extraordinary man who lived life fully. His influence upon you runs much deeper than you realize. You even went further than Gurdjieff, because you saw through the tragic flaw of his incredible teaching of self-transformation. You saw that Soul pre-exists life, and this gives you a perspective which allows you to treat life equally in all of its expressions. For you, Soul equals Soul;

but you have a tendency to be much too literal about this, and the reader won't understand. He will not be able to see that one aspect of life is as relevant to the DPG as any other aspect of life, because for the reader life is a progressive line of natural growth and dissolution. For you, life is just life, as it is for everyone that has been initiated into the divine mysteries of the life process; so if you would, please keep in mind that there is a time and place for the language you choose."

"Wow!" I exclaimed.

"Why the wow?" Jesus asked.

"I've just been lectured to by Jesus Christ!" I said, and laughed.

"I know. It's not something we like to do. But in your case, I had to."

"Why?"

"BECAUSE I'M IN YOUR BOOK!" Jesus shouted.

Jesus took me by surprise. He had on his tortured messianic face, but I knew that he was playing with me now. "So I have to censor my thoughts because I'm talking with the only Begotten Son of God, is that it?"

Jesus couldn't keep a straight face, and laughed. "It would be nice to keep our dialogue free of cuss words. Cuss words—"

"Expletives," I interjected. "I have a lot of emotion, J. I need all the expletives I can use to keep my energies in balance. You read my last novel, didn't you? Look at what my energies did to our glass coffee table?"

"That was something, wasn't it?" Jesus said.

"I also blew out a transformer one day while I was on a taping job. I was still writing my waking dream novel at the time, so my energies were running very high. I plugged in my drill to mix my mud and the power went out. I checked the rest of the house, and it was out all over. I went outside and asked a neighbor, and their power was out also. It was out on the whole block. It may sound far-fetched, but it was too much of a coincidence for the power to go out the instant I plugged in my drill. I know I blew out a transformer; so I'm sorry J, I'm not going to censor my thoughts."

"Why, because your energy level is so high?" Jesus asked.

"Yes. It has to do with who I am. I'm all of me, not just part of me. I'm both my lower and higher self. I'm both my being and non-being. Actually, I'm both but neither; I am Soul. The point is that I trust all of me, both my lower and higher self. I'm a good person, J. And being a good person, whatever I think and say is an expression of who I am; so if I use an expletive to relieve some emotional pressure, it's simply an expression of who I am, that's all. I don't use expletives for dramatic effect like so many people do."

Jesus burst into laughter. *"What a wonderful rationalization!"*

"You think so?" I said, with a nervous smile.

"Yes," Jesus said, giving me a stern look. "You have to refine your language if we're going to discourse on the subject of God."

"What about the subject of man?" I asked, just to see if I could push Christ's buttons, if he had any buttons to push. "We can't talk about God without talking about man, can we?"

Jesus cracked a smile. "No; of course not. After all, God needs man to grow as much as man needs God to grow. It is a symbiotic relationship."

"I know; and I speak for man," I retorted, feeling very confident in myself now. "My language expresses my experiences as a whole man. I'm a tradesman by vocation, and tradesmen are by nature very down-to-earth. Our language is the no-nonsense language of life. I'm also a creative writer. This gives me the advantage of letting my Muse speak freely, and I do just that. The creative Spirit is neutral. It speaks for both the lower and higher self of man. It does not censor thoughts. It just flows!"

"Very convincing, but still a rationalization," Jesus said.

"You won't give me an inch, will you?" I said.

"Nope," Jesus bluntly replied.

"Why not?" I asked.

"Because you should know better, that's why."

"Alright, here's a question for you. Why are you telling me this? I was under the impression that Soul Masters never point out a student's faults. They always address them obliquely. Why this frontal blow with me?"

"Because you can take it, O. Most people can't."

"I see. Well tough luck, J! I told Stanley that I wasn't going to censor my thoughts for him at our functions, and I'm not going to censor my thoughts for Jesus Christ either! When I speak, I let all of me speak, and that's that. So either you trust me or you don't!"

Jesus burst into laughter. *"You're something else, you know that!"*

"I know," I said, once again feeling very foolish.

"Alright; have it your way," Jesus said. "It is your book after all, so why not let the reader hear your voice *in toto?*"

"Good," I said, grateful for Christ's generosity. "Now if you don't mind," I added, to firm up my wounded confidence, "let's go over something that came up just now."

"I know," Jesus said, with a grin on his face. "And yes, I think we should talk about man's symbiotic relationship with God."

I burst into laughter. Jesus just stared at me. "It's fun talking with you, J," I said, as I scrambled for solid ground to stand on. "I've never experienced this kind of creative exchange in my life before. *It's so damn liberating!"*

I expected Jesus to respond to my cuss word, but he didn't. He just stared at me with that generous smile on his loveable face. "What, no comment?" I asked.

"You were going to tell me something," Jesus said.

"Oh, right," I said, once again feeling foolish. "Alright. The reason I want to talk about man's symbiotic relationship with God is to inform the reader — or, rather, to demystify for the reader the issue of man being made in the image of God. We're told in scripture that our body is a temple for God, but this concept can be given a much better explanation now that we have penetrated the mystery of the DPG."

"Excellent. You have the floor, O."

I felt myself centering, thanks to Christ's generous spirit. "Well, all I want to say is that the lower human self and the higher spiritual self are one Soul self. This one Soul self is made up of the individuated consciousness of the God-force, which is the un-self-realized 'I' of God. So, the self of man is made up of the consciousness of God. This is why man is made in the image of God. We're both made of the same divine substance!"

"Bravo! A thousand times bravo!" Jesus exclaimed, with so much joy in his voice that it brought instant tears to my eyes.

After a minute or two of silence, I said, "Thank you, J."

"For what?"

"For letting me be me."

With the sweetest smile, Jesus said, "You're welcome."

20. *The Meat of the Last Supper*

I glanced at my watch. I couldn't believe the time. "I have to call Cathy, J; but my cell phone is in the car," I said, and stood up. "Do you mind if we walk back to the library? I'd like to get my notebook as well. I'll never remember everything we're talking about."

"Sure," Jesus said, and stood up.

We walked back to the library. While Jesus waited on the bench in front of the library I walked to my car and called Cathy. I told her I would be late and would explain later. I got my notebook and jotted down key words, phrases, and images. I was still jotting notes as I walked over to Jesus. He saw me coming and stood up.

"Did you tell Cathy you were having a conversation with Jesus?" he asked, with a big smile.

I laughed. "I'll tell her later."

"Do you think she will believe you?"

"After what we went through with my regressions, she'll believe anything!"

"It was difficult, wasn't it?" Jesus said, very sympathetically.

We started walking back to the park. I kept my notebook open to catch all the key words in our dialogue. As we walked, I thought about my regressions. I opened up to Jesus.

"People have no idea how much our past lives affect our present lifetime," I said, very thoughtfully. "It took centuries for Cathy and I to come together in this life to work out our karma from our lifetime in Genoa, Italy. It was not a pleasant experience dealing with our karma. It almost broke up our relationship. Believe me, neither Cathy nor I thought that was possible. That's how close we thought we were."

With compassion in his voice, Jesus said, "The Holy Fire of God burns deeply, O. There is no other way to cleanse the heart of crystallized karma. You chose this lifetime to resolve your karma because you both had the Inner Master's love and protection; otherwise you would never have taken on that responsibility. This is why man needs the Way-shower to connect him with the Holy Current of God."

I stopped and turned to Jesus. "Do you realize how strange it is to hear you talking about karma and the Way-shower? After all, you're the man responsible for Christianity. *'I am the way, the truth, and the life'"*—

Jesus smiled, shaking his head at my sense of humor. "Yes, it is strange, isn't it? But all spiritual paths lead to the Living Soul Master eventually, so why not get this out of the way before we get to the meat of the last supper?"

"You like that phrase, don't you?"

"Very much."

"We're of the same mind on this phrase, aren't we?"

"If you mean by your phrase the secret of my sayings, yes; we are of the same mind. Is that what you mean by it?"

"That's precisely what I mean. Let me tell you something, J. I've read a whole library of books on your life and teaching, but no one has ever taken on the meaning of your sayings. It's more important for scholars to figure out if you authored the sayings attributed to you than it is to delve into the mystery of your mind-boggling sayings. Would you like to know how I finally managed to crack the code of your sayings?"

"Yes, please," Jesus said.

"It was Gurdjieff's teaching that began to awaken my spiritual senses. The more I lived G's teaching, the more I began to hear the Word. I didn't know what the Word was, except that it was a special way of living my life. This way of living my life affected a change in my consciousness that transformed my life. I need not go into detail here, because I've done this in my writing. For the sake of the reader though, I have to say that the only reason I cracked the code of your sayings was because I had begun to live the Way consciously with G's teaching of 'work on oneself.' But I have to explain this—"

"For the reader," Jesus cut in, with a chuckle.

"Of course," I said, laughing at Christ's sense of play.

"I'm sorry for interrupting, O. Please continue."

I smiled. I must have sounded too serious, and Jesus was just trying to diffuse the deep emotional content of my feelings that my

Gurdjieffian experience had awakened. "As I was about to say," I said, once again very much appreciating Christ's love for me, "Gurdjieff had some techniques for transforming one's consciousness which were very difficult, if not impossible to practice. But if one persisted he created that special energy that one needed to create his own Soul. According to Gurdjieff, not everyone is born with an immortal Soul; so we have to create our own Soul if we aren't born with one. He was both right and wrong on this point; but I need not explain this now. Suffice to say that the more I practiced his techniques, the more—"

"If I may," Jesus interrupted. "Please explain what these techniques are. I think our reader would want to know this information."

"Our reader?" I said.

"Of course," Jesus replied, with that playful smile.

"Alright," I said, and stopped to think for a moment; and then I wrote out the four fundamental techniques in my notebook. "Gurdjieff's system for creating the special energy we needed to create our own Soul comes down to these four powerful techniques. First, NON-IDENTIFICATION. This is the most difficult technique to practice, but the most effective. I'm not going to explain it here. If the reader wants to know what this technique is all about, he can read my books. The second is VOLUNTARY EFFORT. The third is CONSCIOUS SUFFERING. And the fourth is SELF-REMEMBERING. With these four techniques one can transform his life and literally change his personality. This is why the Living Soul Master said to me one night in a dream, 'Your name and you don't fit.' That's how effectively I had lived G's teaching. By working on myself I had transformed myself so much that I no longer reflected my family consciousness!"

Jesus laughed. "That's exactly the same effect that my sayings will have on a person if he lives them!"

"I know. That's why I was attracted to them. I saw the transformative power of your sayings. That's why I took your gospel to heart and your sayings with me everywhere I went. I lived your sayings, J. I lived them daily as I lived G's techniques until I penetrated the mystery of the Way of Christ!"

"Bravo! So the meat of the last supper can be defined, how?"

"How? I would say that the secret to the Way of Christ is the power that the Word of God has to transform one's consciousness and liberate Soul from the endless cycle of karma and reincarnation, and by Word of God I'm talking about your sayings."

"I agree completely. But how does this transformative power take place? That's what the reader would like to know."

Just as I was about to answer I got a very strong nudge from the Inner Master to wait, so I said, "Let's not get into this now. I think we can talk about this when we unpack the secret meaning of your sayings."

"You're right. There's no point getting ahead of ourselves."

"I do want to ask you one thing," I said, and stopped again to look at Jesus. "When did you first realize the power of the Word?"

"To be honest with you, O; I did not have one specific epiphany. I grew up with the secret sayings that my father gave me to practice daily. Joseph was an Essene Elder, so the Way of Life was my catechism growing up. I did not come into this world with the glorious God-realization consciousness that the world would like to believe I was born with. I grew into my divine nature, as all Souls must if they live the spiritual life of the Way. I suppose you could say that I lived the Way of Life consciously from the time of my youth."

"And as you lived the Way of Life the Way revealed itself to you, did it not?" I asked, to continue our dialogue on the Way.

"Exactly. The more you live the Way, whatever expression of the Way you choose to live, the more the Way will reveal itself to you. It's axiomatic," Jesus replied.

"So we can say that the meat of the last supper is the Word of God; and the Word of God is the Way of Life; and the Way of Life is the Creative Life Force; and the Creative Life Force is the consciousness of life; and the consciousness of life is the un-self-realized 'I' of God. So as we live the Way of Life we individuate the 'I' of God—"

"*Stop!*" Jesus interrupted. "The Word is Holy Spirit. Holy Spirit is the God-force. And the God-force is the Law of God that reconciles Soul with God. That's how I would define the meat of the last supper."

95

"I see the distinction," I said, and chuckled. "It's very subtle, but I see it. Of course, the God-force has to be the Law of God, which is Holy Spirit. The Word of God then is the reconciling power of Holy Spirit. But we're in a bit of a quandary here."

"How so?" Jesus asked.

"I experienced the genesis of life on Planet Earth. I was there, J. The Inner Master took me to that moment in time when gases from the planet collided with gases from the sky and created the first building blocks of life in the amino acids that these gases created. I experienced myself entering into the amino acids and life began, so I know from personal experience that the consciousness of the life-force is the consciousness of Soul!"

"Yes; but Soul not yet realized," Jesus added.

"Certainly. But I prefer the Jungian terminology. The consciousness of Soul that is not yet *individuated*. Yes, the consciousness of Soul is the unrealized self; or, if you will, the un-self-realized 'I' of God. So Spirit is dual in nature."

"Excellent!" Jesus exclaimed.

"What?" I asked, wondering what had excited Jesus.

"We have just revealed one of the deepest secrets of God!"

"What, the dual consciousness of God?"

"Yes!" he exclaimed again.

"Well, if we have a symbiotic relationship with God it would follow, wouldn't it?" I said, and burst into a bout of relieving laughter.

So did Jesus. "We've just opened the door to one of the deepest of mysteries," Jesus said, with that mystical twinkle in his eyes.

"What, the mystery of Holy Spirit?"

"Yes," Jesus said. "Holy Spirit is both the reconciling power of the Word of God as well as the un-self-realized 'I' of God!"

"That's the conclusion I was forced to see as I worked out the DPG," I said, smiling at Christ's excitement. "In a word then, the Word is simply the 'I' of God both realized and un-self-realized!"

"Yes! This is one of the most impenetrable of the divine mysteries!"

"But what does it mean, J? What can the reader make of it?"

Jesus smiled. "Why don't you let Soul speak on it, O?"

"Sure, why not," I said, feeling very confident now. I stopped for a moment to silently connect with the Creative Life Stream with my secret word that the Inner Master gave me to use for the rest of my life when I received my Third Initiation, and then I just let Soul speak freely: "In the Way of the Eternal we know that the God-force splits into the positive and negative currents of life when it hits the worlds below the Soul Plane, so the positive current of Holy Spirit would be the reconciling power of the Word, or the redemptive consciousness of God if you will, and the negative current of Holy Spirit would be the un-self-realized consciousness of God; and the whole point of the evolutionary process of life is to make conscious the unconscious nature of God — just as Doctor Jung concluded with the mystical marriage of the *individuation process* of the unconscious."

"Yes, the un-self-realized atoms of God becoming the self-realized atoms of God," Jesus very happily summed up. "Soul becoming self-realized!" he concluded.

"By living the Way," I added, for the reader's edification.

"And that's the meat of the last supper!" Jesus exclaimed.

I laughed at the thought that popped into my mind. "The body of Christ is the Holy Word of God," I said, with a smirk on my face. "We have to stress this spiritual truth or the reader will never understand what we're talking about, will he?"

"Exactly! The body of Christ is the Holy Word of God, and the Word of God is revealed in my sayings!"

"But only if one lives your sayings," I added, and laughed.

"Precisely! As one lives my sayings one eats the body of Christ and is born again in Holy Spirit," Jesus concluded.

"AND THAT'S THE MEAT OF THE LAST SUPPER!" I shouted unselfconsciously for the whole world to hear, and I put my arm around Jesus' shoulders and we walked across the street to the park like the best of long-lost friends.

21. *In the Shoes of Christ's Sayings*

A young mother was sitting on our bench. Her baby stroller was in front of her. She was rocking it gently, lovingly. Jesus greeted her, and softly asked, "Boy or girl?"

"Girl," she replied in a loud whisper, her face beaming with pride.

"May I?" Jesus said, and bent over the stroller.

The young mother bent over also to check her infant daughter. She was wide awake. She picked her up and held her in her arms. Jesus leaned to look, and when their eyes met the baby's eyes lit up and her face beamed like a miniature sun.

Jesus tickled the infant's cheeks. The child giggled with laughter. Jesus smiled. Love poured out of his eyes like a milky fountain of pure joy. "Sweet child, may your life be full of longing," he said, touching her little forehead with his hand.

The mother looked at Jesus with wonder in her eyes.

"Longing for what?" I asked, with a puzzled smile. "Perfect love?"

"If only," the young mother said. "But is there such a thing as perfect love?"

Jesus had his cue. "Of course there is. Unconditional love is perfect love. It is the purest and highest form of love. But we can love unconditionally only when we have exhausted all other forms of love. What I meant was a longing for life, because only the longing for life will bring Soul to unconditional love."

The young mother was amazed. She stared at Jesus in awe. I had to keep the spell alive, so I said, "By longing, you mean the desire to live life fully as opposed to just existing, or putting in time as it were?"

"Something like that," Jesus replied, his face just glowing. "This beautiful little Soul is destined to live her own life. I can see it in her mother's eyes."

The young mother's face lit up. "Thank you," she said. "I want my daughter to be all she can be. I want her to have every opportunity to realize her dreams in life. I promised her when she was born. And she will. I know she will."

"Of course she will," Jesus said. "Continue to love her with all your heart, for love nurtures a child's dreams. Have a beautiful day," he added with the most loving smile I had seen on Christ's face all day, and then he turned to leave.

"You too," the young mother said, her eyes beaming with pride.

We found another bench under the shade of a large oak tree and sat down. Shaking my head in wonder, I said to Jesus, "That was incredible!"

"Why?" Jesus asked.

"That young mother and child have just been blessed by a Soul Master, and Jesus Christ to boot!"

Jesus laughed. "A Master's blessing goes a long way to helping Soul find its way out of the life cycle. That infant was destined to be blessed by a Soul Master."

"How so?"

"I know that Soul. She was with me in Palestine during my silent years."

"No kidding?" I said, excited by the information.

"Of course not. She studied the secret teaching with me as we made mud bricks. She was a man then, and my apprentice. When I left Palestine I promised him that we would meet again one day, and that day was today."

"And you knew that this Soul was ready to find the Way again in this lifetime?"

"Yes," Jesus said, with a big smile.

"Wow! I like hanging out with you, J!"

Jesus laughed. "Life is never dull when you hang out with a Master. But then, life is never dull for a chela of the Way, is it?"

"If it is, something's wrong," I said, and broke into a hearty chuckle.

Jesus understood what I meant and laughed with me. "Tell me, O," he said, with that playful smile, "What do you mean by that exactly?"

"For the sake of the reader, right?"

"Of course," Jesus said, still smiling.

"I mean that the spiritual life is never dull. If one's life is boring it simply means that the creative life force has stopped flowing in their life. It's the creative energy of the life force that keeps one's life exciting. Is that satisfactory enough?"

"Not quite," Jesus said, wanting a full explanation. "Just how does one keep the creative life force flowing freely in one's life?"

"On our spiritual path, we do the spiritual exercises daily. Like the HU chant. We call the HU chant a Love Song to God. But I don't want this discourse to turn into a sermon on the Way of the Eternal. As I told you already, J; I honestly don't care if the world finds its own way or not. I've paid my dues, and I've earned the right to be indifferent about the Way. I've outgrown the seductive power of the Way to save the world, because I know that the world does not need to be saved. The world is what it is, and that's that!"

Jesus sniggered. "That was my problem, O. So seduced was I by the redemptive power of Holy Spirit that I could not help myself; I had to save the world. Now I'm paying for the pleasure of my spiritual arrogance."

"What, Jesus Christ, arrogant? You, the most humble servant of God, arrogant? You, who sacrificed your life on the cross to atone for the sins of the world, arrogant?" I said, and burst into laughter.

Jesus waited for me to have my fun, and then said, "The world knows very little about the real Jesus Christ, O. You have come closest to what I really am, and that's only because you dared to walk in the shoes of Christ's sayings."

"You're making a point here, aren't you?"

"Yes," Jesus replied.

"Give it to me in a word or two," I said, pen in hand.

"A man becomes what he believes," Jesus replied.

"What he lives by, you mean?" I asked.

"If you will. Live by my sayings long enough, and you will take on the consciousness of the Christ. That's all I meant."

"Well, to be honest with you J; once I cracked the code of your sayings I began to feel an affinity with you that I never felt before. And I'll tell you something else that may surprise you and all of my readers. *This affinity that I felt for you was responsible for my leaving Christianity!*"

Jesus broke into such a spontaneous fit of laugher that it took me off guard. Instantly I experienced the same intense joy of irony and joined him in laughter. The blessed Spirit had possessed us once again, and we laughed to our heart's content!

22. *The Seductive Power of the Way*

After a few minutes of refreshing silence, Jesus turned to me and very casually said, "O, do you think it's worth exploring?"

"What?" I asked.

"As you so poetically expressed it, the seductive power of Holy Spirit," Jesus said, with that loveable twinkle in his eyes.

"Listen, J," I said, feeling playful myself. "If you're going to quote the O, quote me accurately, please."

"Oh? And what exactly did you say?"

"I said, 'the seductive power of the Way.'"

"La meme chose," Jesus said.

"It may be. But isn't this what all the fuss has been about in your teaching — the accuracy of your words?"

"Yes, I know; and it's preposterous. Take your expression and my version of it. You used the word Way and I used Holy Spirit. You and I both know that the Way is Holy Spirit, so there's no truth lost, is there?"

"None whatsoever," I replied.

"Why the fuss, then? Jesus said, alluding to the scholars.

"I suppose it's because they can't see that the truth the vessels contain is the same truth," I replied. "They can't make out the wood for the trees, if you will."

"Exactly! So, do you want to explore the seductive power of Holy Spirit, then?"

"For the sake of the reader, right?" I asked, being smart.

"Of course. It's for the reader that we're doing this. You and I don't need this information, do we?"

Still smiling, I said, "And you think the reader does?"

Jesus picked up on my provocative tone. "On the whole, the reader is ignorant of the spiritual life," he responded, in what sounded like his messianic voice. "Man enjoys the search for truth because it excites him. His blood pumps hot. And the closer he gets, the more excited he is. But seldom does he take truth into his heart when he finds it, because with truth comes the responsibility to live it. This responsibility is too much for most people, because it takes courage to live the truth. More courage than most people have."

"Why?" I asked, to keep Jesus talking.

"When one finds the truth it is often at the expense of what one believed to be the truth. This means letting go of the old and embracing the new, and few people have the courage to let go of the old. This is why religions like Christianity are so slow to reform. They cannot keep up with the unfolding spiritual consciousness of life because they have too much invested in their old truths."

"We've moved from the reader to the religions of the world? How deft of you, J!"

"Let's get back to the reader," Jesus said, without missing a beat. "He needs to know how the Way works so he does not have to face the fear of letting go of his old beliefs, which will definitely be threatened with what we're going to reveal to him. We have to build up his confidence slowly with our discourse on God, and—"

"By God, you mean the Way?" I interjected.

"La meme chose," Jesus repeated, in mellifluous French.

I smiled. I loved Jesus talking this way. It was so spontaneous and natural that it gave him a whole new dimension, which I thoroughly enjoyed because the Jesus of scripture was so dry and humorless. "I love it when you talk like this," I repeated out loud.

"I hope the reader will too. So, to continue. We cannot treat the reader like a child, which is what the religions of the world persist in doing."

"And by that, you mean?"

"They refuse to let their followers think for themselves."

"BINGO!" I exclaimed, and bounded to my feet. Looking down at Jesus, I said, "I have two experiences that attest to this very fact!"

"Good," said Jesus, with a big smile on his face. "Can you share them?"

"Of course I can," I said, full of excitement at the memory of my discovery. "I was only fourteen when I discovered Darwin's theory of evolution. I brought my book to my parish priest to see what he had to say about it. Instead of giving me an explanation, Father 'Bud' patted me on the head and told me not to worry about it. 'Keep

103

your faith in the Church,' he said to me. When I was fifteen I discovered reincarnation in Plato's dialogues, and Father 'Bud' patted me on the head again and told me to keep the faith. Well it was inevitable that a conflict would brew in the depths of my Soul, because my heart began to disagree with my mind — *and here I am today!"*

"Well said," Jesus said, with a big smile. "Well said indeed!"

"You're absolutely right, J!" I exclaimed, my blood still running hot from the memory of my discovery. "We have to give the reader the benefit of the doubt!"

"We certainly do," Jesus confirmed.

"Ironically, I've always treated my reader with respect; too much respect in fact, given the response that I got to my books in my hometown!"

"True. But when the dust settled the people of St. Jude had time to reflect. I assure you, O; in the privacy of their mind they respect you for what you wrote. They will never admit to it in public, but that shouldn't matter to you. The reader's journey through life is the same as the seeker's, and it's a solitary journey; so don't fret over how the people of St. Jude treated you and Cathy. You did what the Way called upon you to do. And now the Way has called upon you again to help me dispel the Gospel conspiracy."

"If I may, what can I expect from the readers of this book?"

"A new and exciting dialogue on Christianity," Jesus replied.

"A dialogue? What good will that do? Dialogues are like Royal Commissions. They cause a lot of fuss for a short time and then they end up on the dusty shelves of history!"

"Not this time, O. Your perspective on the spiritual life will inspire change. No reader of our dialogue will ever be the same again, because it is to the nature of your writing to pry open the mind and introduce the Light and Sound of God to Soul. Your readers will not be able to avoid the spiritual wake-up call that your writing affects. It does not matter how far they take your thoughts, because they will never again trust what they are told about the spiritual life. Such is the power of your spiritual perspective!"

"I just got an image of slashing my way through life with the spiritual scythe of my personal truth!" I said, and broke into a mirthful chuckle.

Jesus smiled at my image. "So for the sake of the reader we have to inform him about the seductive power of Holy Spirit," he continued, with that same messianic seriousness in his voice that made me feel slightly uneasy. "If we don't inform him, the reader will continue to buy into the illusions that the God of these lower worlds keeps spinning."

I burst into laughter again.

"What's so funny now?" Jesus asked.

"I don't want to go there."

"Why not?"

"Because it might shock the reader."

"Shock the reader? How?"

"Do you really want to know?"

"We all do," said Jesus.

"Alright, I'll tell you," I said, relieved to see Jesus back to his normal non-messianic, playful self. "There are many new spiritual paths out there today, and disaffected people are taking them very seriously. But as I read this new crop of gurus from the perspective of the DPG, I see the same tired old truths re-spun into exciting new webs of mesmerizing illusion. It makes me laugh, J. It's unbelievable how seductive the reconciling power of Holy Spirit can be! *It can seduce even the most stalwart Soul!"*

Jesus laughed. He knew what I was talking about, but he could not bring himself to say it. I had to say it for him, because it had to come from someone that had been seduced by the spiritually reconciling power of the Way but who had also broken the hypnotic spell of the spiritual seduction. Jesus hadn't, and he was crucified for the Way.

"I agree," said Jesus, reading my thoughts. "This is why we have to reveal the secret of my sayings. It's the only way I can dispel the Gospel conspiracy that keeps me hostage to the illusion of instant salvation through my crucifixion."

"And how will this change anything?" I asked.

"It will reveal the true meaning of life's purpose. Spiritual truth is the only thing that will cut through the illusions of life, and I have all the confidence that the spiritual truth of my sayings will

105

encourage the reader to take this new crop of gurus with a grain of salt."

"I hope so. But if I may, let me clear up a possible misunderstanding—"

"I'll do that," Jesus cut in, reading my mind again. "Every Soul is an individual Ray of God's Light, if I may borrow your phrase. Each Ray refracts one aspect of the Way. The illusion arises when one Ray of God's Light is taken to be the whole Light of God, as the Gospel conspirators Mathew, Mark, Luke, and John especially have done with my life. This is the seductive power of Holy Spirit. Hopefully, by revealing the truth of my sayings we can dispel this illusion and let the reader in on the mystery of the DPG—"

"*I like that!*" I exclaimed, excited by Christ's candid explanation. "If I may add my pound's worth, I would emphasize that the Way is always one truth, but every expression of the Way does not always refract the oneness of the Way. That's where the seductive power of Holy Spirit spins its magnificent illusions in these half-baked gurus!"

"*Excellent!* If I may express it another way," Jesus added, his face glowing radiantly. "The Whole exists in all of its parts, but the parts of the Whole don't necessarily refract the Whole. Each part of the Whole is as relevant to the Whole as any other part, but it would be an illusion to take one part for the Whole as the Gospel of John and to a lesser extent the Gospels of Mathew, Mark, and Luke have done with my life and teaching!"

"I think you've just muddled the puddle, J!"

"Maybe," Jesus said. "But I assure you, O; by the end of our dialogue the puddle will be crystal clear. *And that's a promise your reader can take to the bank!*"

23. *A Tricky Question for Jesus*

I had never talked with anyone who was such an open channel for the Way as Jesus was, but I had to clear up something I knew would hinder the flow of our dialogue. I mustered my courage. "I have to ask you something personal, J?"

"What now?" he asked, in a tone that anticipated me.

"It's a tricky question. I don't quite know how to ask it."

"Just ask it, O. I can take it," he said, softening his tone.

"I'm sure you can. But will I be able to take the answer?"

"In that case ask the Inner Master for guidance."

"Good idea," I said, and closed my eyes. I did a silent HU first, and then I switched to my secret word as I often do whenever I want a really good connection. Slowly I began to sense the Inner Master's presence. *"Should I ask Jesus?"* I asked silently.

"Yes," he replied, in the quiet of my mind. *"It will clear up a lot of confusion about Jesus that exists out there today, especially in our spiritual community."*

"Okay," I said out loud, and turned to Jesus. "Why did you appear as a chela of the Way of the Eternal at the worship service this morning?"

"Why do you ask?"

"Because I know from the Living Soul Master's writing that you belong to a different line of Masters," I replied, feeling a little guilty for prying into his private life.

"Didn't Pat Montamuri write about St. Paul in his book, *Talks with Soul Masters*?" Jesus asked, with a twinkle in his eyes.

"Yes."

"And wasn't St. Paul introduced as a Soul Master?"

"Yes, I believe he was."

"Well?"

"Well, what?"

"Why can he be a Soul Master and not me?" Jesus said, teasing me.

"Because you're only a Second Initiate!" I retorted, and laughed.

"Touché!" Jesus exclaimed, and burst into laughter also.

"Well?" I asked, pushing Jesus.

"That is a tricky question, O," he replied. "How can I put this?"

"Any way you can," I said.

"Well, the short answer is that all Soul Masters are Ascended Masters and one with Divine Spirit. This eliminates all distinctions between different lines of Masters. In my case, I'm responsible for bringing the Way of Christ into the world, which St. Paul helped mushroom into the world religion of Christianity. I have to bear responsibility for the Way of Christ. But that's not the answer you're looking for, is it?"

Jesus read my thoughts accurately. "Not quite."

"I appeared as a chela at your worship service this morning because I am a chela of the Way of the Eternal at heart, as are all Masters. I came as a Second Initiate because this is what I was at the time of my mission on Earth. As you know, Master Fubbi Quantz gave me my Second Initiation at the Katsupari Monastery in northern Tibet; but even a Second Initiate can realize God-consciousness. That's what you want to hear, isn't it?"

"I knew it!" I exclaimed. "I just needed confirmation, that's all!"

"Why? Don't you trust your own intuition?" Jesus asked.

"Touché," I responded, feeling foolish for prying.

"Never doubt what you feel in your heart, O," Jesus offered, with a warm and generous smile. "Your heart knows best. I have to stay in the line of Masters that I was born into, because that's just the way it is. I came to your worship service for two reasons. First, to reveal the worm of spiritual conceit that has found its way into your spiritual community, especially among High Initiates, just as it found its way into Christianity; and second, to bridge the gap between Christianity and this new religion of the Light and Sound of God, because essentially all religions come from Holy Spirit. *Capisce?*"

I burst into laughter, despite how foolish I felt. "So you came to the worship service this morning to set the stage for our dialogue on your gospel teaching?"

"That was my main reason for coming," Jesus said.

"You want to bridge the gap between Christianity and the Way of the Eternal with our dialogue?" I asked, just to be certain of Christ's purpose.

"I can't promise anything. Look at what happened the first time I tried to bridge the gap between the outer and middle circles of life. It could backfire on me this time also. Nonetheless we should explore how we can bridge this gap."

"Now?" I asked, astounded by Christ's frankness.

"If you like," Jesus said.

"But there are huge differences between Christianity and the Way of the Eternal," I said, genuinely perplexed. "How on earth can these two paths ever be bridged?"

"Let's be frank, O. When I introduced the Way to the world two thousand years ago I had no idea that it would mutate into the bizarre creature that it is today. But it does introduce man to the reconciling power of Holy Spirit, and we can be thankful for that."

"Regardless of the preposterous premises that Christianity is founded upon?" I asked, as I felt the Holy Current pulling me deeper into our discourse on the Way.

"Yes. When Soul is ready to move on it will find another path that will nourish its need to grow. You did."

"At what price, J? That's the question, isn't it?"

I expected Jesus to come to the defense of Christianity, but he surprised me. "You're right, O. The price is much too steep for many Souls to pay. This is why I want to reveal the truth of my sayings. Hopefully we can dispel this illusion of instant salvation through my death on the cross and get on with the show, as the expression goes."

I chuckled at the image that flashed across my mind. Jesus stared at me, waiting patiently for me to explain myself. "Bishop John Shelby Spong and his like-minded followers are on a crusade to change Christianity," I explained, and snickered again. "But the sad truth is that they're still fishing in a lake with no fish!"

"Please explain yourself," Jesus said, with that satisfied smile.

The irony was too much and I broke into laughter again. "That's the tragedy of trying to reform Christianity from within," I said, shaking my head in disbelief. "As long as Christians hold onto the one life theory and forgiveness of sin nothing will change. Until Christians come to the realization that we live more than one lifetime and that we are karmically responsible for our own liberation from the cycle of life and death they will remain asleep to their spiritual purpose in life. This is why I contend that the price is too steep for most Christians to pay. You know damn well that I speak from experience, J. I'm sorry for the cuss word, but that's my Christian past coming out. I couldn't breathe. I was suffocating in my Christian faith. I had outgrown it, but I couldn't get out. No! That's not true! I tried every which way to get out, but it wouldn't let me go! That's why I have this thing with Christianity. *It would not let me go, and it made my life hell!*"

Jesus reached over and grabbed my forearm and squeezed it gently. I felt his love flowing into me. Within seconds, I calmed down.

"Thank you," I said, feeling very foolish again.

"You have every right to be emotional," Jesus said, smiling at me. "You paid a dear price to free yourself from the hold that Christianity had upon your psyche. Not many Souls are willing to pay this price in one lifetime. What you did in one lifetime would normally take Soul half a dozen lives to work through, so don't be too hard on yourself. But that's neither here nor there now. The point is that we have to build a bridge for those Souls that are ready to move on. It's not our place to judge the role that Christianity plays in life, because it's all part of the DPG. Our place is to help the Living Soul Master with his mission to help Soul find its way back home to God. Fair enough?"

Again, I felt very foolish. I couldn't respond.

"Fair enough?" Jesus insisted.

"Fair enough," I said, and fell silent; and then I just sat back and waited to see what Divine Spirit wanted us to talk about next…

24. *A Curious Pair of Bridge Builders*

Spirit nudged me to explore the thought further. "What's going on, then?" I asked Jesus. "You're a chela of the Way of the Eternal at heart, but you have to continue in your role as the founder of Christianity; and I'm a chela who found the Way in your sayings before I found the Way of the Eternal. This makes me no less of a puzzle to my spiritual community than the real Jesus would to the Christian community. What's going on here, J?"

"We do make a curious pair of bridge builders, don't we?" Jesus said, and crossed his slender legs to face me while we talked. "It's precisely because of our unique relationship with the Way that we have been brought together to build a bridge from Christianity to the new religion of the Light and Sound of God."

Suddenly it hit me! My relationship with Christ's sayings was exactly the same as his relationship with the Way of the Eternal — *we both saw the Way in each other's path, and this gave us the freedom to speak of the Way as one!* I laughed. Then I said to Jesus, "The Living Soul Master says, 'Truth is one, but there are many paths leading to it!'"

"If we substitute the word Truth with the word Way everything will fall into place," Jesus replied. "Truth is one, and the Way is one; but there are many paths that lead to the Way. But then," he added, with that playful glint in his eye and subtle smile on his lips, "what would the scholars of my life and teaching say?"

I laughed at Christ's sense of irony. But he was right. Truth, the Way, Spirit, Logos, God-force, Sound Current, Light and Sound of God, Audible Life Stream, the Word, Baraka, Chi, creative life force, élan vital, gnosis, Tao, Holy Ghost, and "juice," as my literary mentor Ernest Hemingway called the creative energy of his writing — they all spoke the same divine reality. This realization was the only way that Jesus and I could hope to build a bridge from the purest teachings of the Light and Sound of God to Christianity and all other religions in the world — not by diminishing their expression of the

Way, but by allowing each religion to play its part in the Divine Plan of God!

"It all comes back down to the three levels of human consciousness," I said to Jesus, to make it absolutely clear what I believed the purpose of our discourse on his gospel teaching would be about. "We have to take the esotericism out of your sayings for the outer circle of life to understand them, don't we?"

"*Exactly!*" exclaimed Jesus, and slapped me on the knee.

"But only those Souls that are ready for the mesoteric circle of life will understand us," I further explained. "For example; last night I was watching the Larry King show on TV. He had his holiness the Dalai Lama on as well as a Christian minister from New Orleans. He was asking them for their perspective on the damage that hurricane Katrina had wrought in the Gulf Coast, especially in the devastated city of New Orleans. The Dalai Lama spoke of the law of causality, and he even went further to say that the damage wrought by Katrina was a karmic cleansing, that people are responsible for what befalls them. The minister said that Katrina was a natural disaster brought on by God, that it was not his place to question the works of God, and all he could do was put his faith in God's wisdom. He was totally blind to the Spiritual Law of Karma. He represents the Soul stuck in the outer circle of life where life is a mystery and it is not one's place to question the works of God. The Dalai Lama on the other hand represents the middle circle of life where Soul has become aware of the Spiritual Laws of Karma and Reincarnation. Our purpose with this discourse would be to reach all those Souls in the outer circle that are ready for the middle circle of life where they can begin to live the spiritual life of the Way more consciously and not blindly like that Christian minister on the Larry King show last night."

"*Precisely!*" Jesus exclaimed again, with that big grin of satisfaction on his face that I began to notice every time we made a point he wanted made. "You could not have found a better example to illustrate what I hope to accomplish with our dialogue. Are you ready then to let Soul speak on my first saying?"

"Let's not rush it, J. There are still a few things we have to get out of the way before we get down to the meat of the last supper."

Jesus broke into a mirthful chuckle. "This is priceless, O. I have never had occasion to be so human. That's the problem with

Christianity. It has taken all the humanity out of my life. All I am for the Christian world is a free pass to heaven. I can respect that, because they don't know any better; but I hope we can shift the responsibility of salvation from my shoulders to where it belongs on their shoulders — and to Holy Spirit, of course!"

"Of course," I said, smiling at Christ's uncompromising candor. "But you do realize that we will only reach those Souls mature enough to be pulled into the gravitational field to our dialogue. People like that Christian minister on the Larry King show have a lot of life yet to experience before they wake up enough to take the full karmic weight of their own personal choices. We can't hope for the moon, can we?"

"If anything, I'm very much a realist now," Jesus snickered.

"I know. That's the problem with Christianity. It's taken the realism out of your teaching and fabricated this Gospel conspiracy nonsense. But let's not go there now. Let's just let that delusion evaporate on its own as we disclose the truth of your sayings."

"You're ready, then!" Jesus said, slapping my knee again.

"Hey! Why are you being so pushy?"

"You're just putting off the inevitable, that's why!"

"Not so. To be perfectly honest with you, J; I was hoping to dig my Bible out of the boxes of books I have piled in the basement of our new house. I want to read the Gospels a few times before I let Soul speak on your sayings. I'd like to reacquaint myself with the full flavor of your sayings again so when we discourse on them I'll have them fresh in my mind. That way I'll be able to give your sayings all the contextual relevance they deserve so we can reveal their mind-boggling secrets to the world!"

"Ahhhhhhh, so that's why you're putting it off! Okay, what do you say we chat for a while longer to see if Soul has anything more to say? Then we can meet again after you have reacquainted yourself with my sayings. Fair enough?"

"I was hoping you would understand. Besides, it would reassure me that this is not some kind of dream vision — *if we meet again, that is!"*

With that playful twinkle in his eyes, Jesus said, "Tell me, O; what would be the difference between a dream vision and an actual experience with me?"

"I have no idea. But you know what I mean."

"I do," said Jesus, with that all knowing smile.

"Then explain it to me, please," I said.

"Truth is one, O; but there are many paths that lead to it," Jesus said, and broke into a gleeful chuckle. *"All ways lead to the Way!"*

"I can appreciate that, J; but will the reader?"

"We can only hope, O. *We can only hope..."*

25. *The Scales of Divine Justice*

We sat in silence for the next few minutes, watching the squirrels scampering about, people walking to and fro, birds flitting from tree to tree, cars driving by, and listening to the murky river falling over the cement falls. My mind wandered back to my youth, to that spring morning when I confessed to my parish priest my venial sins and that one grievous mortal sin that I feared would condemn me forever to the burning fires of hell.

As I walked down the cement church steps and up Newton Street free of the guilt and fear of going to hell, I had a sudden spiritual insight that changed my life forever. I had to share this with Jesus. Without looking at him, I said, "I know what we should talk about before we get to your cryptic sayings. The Inner Master just told me."

"What?" Jesus asked.

"Guilt," I said.

"Now, there's a subject worthy of a book!" Jesus exclaimed. "Yes, O; I think we should let Soul speak on guilt!"

"We do see eye to eye, then?"

"We do," said Jesus.

"And we can pull out all stops?"

"I would prefer it," said Jesus, to my surprise.

"You realize that if we do that we will shatter the illusion of Christian faith?" I said, just to make sure that we understood each other completely.

"I know," Jesus replied, with that playful smile that lit up his whole face.

"After all, what's Christianity without guilt?" I added, to his further amusement. The irony was delicious, and we both laughed. Then I shared the epiphany I had that memorable Saturday morning in St. Jude, my hometown that was appropriately named after the patron saint of hopeless causes. "When I came out of the confessional that spring morning, I was free of the guilt and fear of going to hell forever when suddenly like a miracle sent by God it dawned on me that there was something terribly wrong with the logic of sin."

"How so?" Jesus asked, his eyes devouring me.

"For some reason I saw the terrible injustice of it all. I held my hands up in front of me, like this," I said, and positioned my hands palms up in front of my chest like two weigh scales. "In one hand I placed my mortal sin, and in the other hand I placed eternal damnation in hell. It just didn't feel right, J. My hands had become the scales of Divine Justice, and it shocked my psyche to realize that one mortal sin committed in a moment of time could equal an eternity of suffering in hell-fire!"

Jesus smiled, but said nothing. I continued.

"In a flash I realized that this was not right. I realized that God would not punish Soul for eternity in hell-fire for one mortal sin committed in a moment of time. It was inconceivably unjust. I just *knew* this in the depths of my Soul. A flash of light had pierced the darkness of my blind Christian faith, and my life changed forever!"

"In what way did it change?" Jesus calmly asked.

"I was twelve or thirteen years old when this happened. This experience let me catch a glimpse of the spiritual light that existed outside my Christian faith. As I told you, I discovered Darwin's theory of natural evolution at fourteen and reincarnation the following year, but it still took me years to break free of the hold that Christianity had upon me. My repressed guilt was the hold that Christianity still had on my psyche. It went so deep that it puzzled me all my life until I had my past-life regressions last year. That's when I learned of my lifetime as the infamous *Scoundrel of Paris*."

Jesus chuckled, but again said nothing.

"My depraved lifetime in Paris was primarily responsible for all the Christian guilt that I suffered growing up in my current life," I continued, smiling to myself for having made the connection. "I could not believe how guilty I felt every time I committed a mortal sin. Even after my confessions I still felt the shadow of guilt lurking in the back of my mind like an ominous specter. I had a terribly anguished youth, J. I could not enjoy my innocence because of this menacing shadow of guilt. As the infamous *Scoundrel of Paris* I blasphemed your name and all that you represented. You cannot believe what I did to you, J!"

I stopped. The emotions of my spiritually depraved lifetime surfaced, and I had to collect myself. Thankfully, Jesus remained silent.

"Even now," I continued, with a self-conscious smile, "I still feel guilty for what I did to those women to get back at you and the Church. The world has no idea how insidious Christian guilt can be. It will haunt you throughout the ages. And only when Soul can no longer bear the anguish of guilt will it seek a way out of the darkness of spiritual ignorance. That's what happened to me. Now I have to ask you something. What good does guilt serve in the DPG? Tell me, what possible good does Christian guilt serve Soul?"

Jesus sniggered. I turned to look at him. His eyes glistened. They sparkled like two brilliant jewels. I was forced to smile at the radiance that shone from his face.

"The joy I feel at this moment cannot be expressed," Jesus said, his words flowing out of his mouth like golden honey. "You have opened a door to the Light of God that will bring so much comfort to your readers that it makes me want to dance with the angels!"

"Why? What did I say that makes you feel this way?"

"Your past-life experiences have garnered enough spiritual wisdom to shatter the illusion of Christian guilt," Jesus replied. "It's not what one believes that gives Soul the incentive to complete its journey home to God, but what one experiences. You dared to live a life of such depravity that it haunted your future lives until you could bear the anguish no longer in your current lifetime. This was your lifetime as the lost Soul of Paris. This is why I have such love for you, O. Your courage to do what you did for the sake of your honor in that life set the stage for your spiritual liberation in this life. Yes, Christian guilt is responsible for keeping Soul trapped in the cycle of life and death. Christian guilt represses Soul to the point of unbearable anguish. But Christian guilt will eventually free Soul from the hold that life has upon it."

"You're really putting a positive spin on Christian guilt, aren't you?"

"Of course. After all, I am the savior of Christianity!"

Jesus forced a laugh out of me, but I had a lot more to say. "If I may continue," I said, silently calling upon the Inner Master to guide me, "I'm not quite satisfied with this whole Christian guilt thing. I realize that Soul is here to learn from life, which is the standard answer that all you Masters seem to give us, but I have a different take on Soul's journey through life ever since I worked out the DPG; and I'd like to run this by you, if I may?"

"By all means," Jesus said.

"Alright," I said, casting my mind as far and wide as I possibly could to make the point I felt had to be made. "As we've already said, Soul needs experience to satisfy its divine need for total self-identity. Well, I've had the experience of three incredible events that give me the freedom to speak of Soul's journey through life from the lofty perspective of the DPG, and by lofty I mean as objective as one can possibly get."

"I understand. What were these three events?" Jesus asked.

"My experience of the inception of life in the material worlds; my regression to my first primordial human life where I experienced the dawning of my own self-consciousness; and my experience in the Ocean of Love and Mercy as an un-self-realized atom of God. With these three experiences I confirmed the fundamental purpose of life."

"Which is?" Jesus asked, on behalf of the reader.

"Soul's encoded need for self-identity and God-realization consciousness," I replied. "Let's fast-forward this to the role that Christian guilt plays in Soul's journey to total self-identity. True, as you say, guilt creates anguish; anguish leads to despair; and despair gives Soul the incentive to seek a way out of its mental prison. But is all of this anguish and suffering necessary? This is my concern, J. I can't help but feel — and you did tell me to trust my heart over my mind, didn't you?"

Jesus smiled "Yes, I did."

"Alright, then. I can't help but feel that the time for Christian guilt is over. It has served its purpose in the DPG. It's time to dispel the horror of this unconscious karmic process of liberating Soul from the cycle of life and death and introduce the world to the conscious spiritual path of the Way of the Eternal. I just feel this, J. I can't help myself!"

"Why do you feel this?" Jesus calmly asked, again for the reader's sake.

"You may not believe this, but I honestly feel that all of this Christian guilt contributes to many of the social horrors in the world today."

"Such as?"

"For one thing, wanton sex and violence. This is Soul's blind way of liberating itself from the unbearable anguish of unresolved karma, and not until the spiritual consciousness of the world has been raised will this change. Soul has to release the pressure of karmic guilt, and sex and violence are natural emotional outlets. However, this only creates more karma that will have to be resolved eventually. This is the dilemma of Soul's journey through life, and the only way out of this dilemma is to raise the spiritual consciousness of life. But we can't do that without revealing the truth about Christian guilt, can we?"

Jesus couldn't help himself, and laughed. "I never thought that you would get to the root cause of society's primal horrors. *I'm impressed!*"

"Primal horrors?" I repeated, hoping that Jesus would elaborate.

"I agree with you completely. Guilt is unresolved karma. It is the unresolved energy of the 'I' of God trapped in the unconscious self of one's spiritual personality, and not until this unresolved 'I' of God has been spiritually processed will Soul free itself of the hold that life has upon it. That's good, O. *That's incredibly perceptive!*"

"It may be perceptive, J," I said, grateful for his confirmation, "but we have to make this absolutely clear for the reader."

"Be my guest," Jesus said, gesturing with his hand.

"Alright. The guilt that I packed with me from lifetime to lifetime because of what I did as the *Scoundrel of Paris* had to be resolved. The question that I have to ask for the reader now is this: exactly how did I realize such profound guilt?"

"Yes; please tell us," Jesus said.

"I violated the sanctity of spiritual freedom, that's how. Guilt, whether it comes from breaking the Ten Commandments, our own moral code, ethical principles or what have you, is essentially born of one's violation of the Spiritual Laws of Life. Guilt is nothing more than the individuated 'I' of God trapped in the consciousness of one's spiritually unresolved personality, or what Doctor Jung called the shadow; and not until this tortured I-consciousness of God is resolved will one be free of the hold guilt has upon Soul!"

"And just how is guilt resolved?" Jesus asked.

"Certainly not by going to confession or praying for your forgiveness," I quickly responded. "That's my beef with Christianity. Karma can't be resolved by going to confession once a week as I used to do. Karma has to be resolved by the natural process of spiritual growth. Soul has to live up to the responsibility of its actions. If I violated the sanctity of spiritual freedom by seducing those women to denounce you and the Church for denying me the love of my life, I had to pay for my violation of the spiritual law. That's why I had a future lifetime as a black slave in southern Georgia. I had to resolve the karma that I created as the *Scoundrel of Paris* by forfeiting my own freedom. The guilt that I packed from that lifetime for violating the sanctity of spiritual freedom with every woman that I seduced into forfeiting their precious virtue to me took many lives to resolve, and even today I can still feel the horror of my arrogant violation of the law of spiritual freedom for what I did to those women to avenge myself with God for betraying my love!"

"So we've come from Christian guilt to the unresolved karma that Soul creates from breaking the spiritual laws of life?" Jesus said, smiling. *"How clever of you, O!"*

Again, Jesus forced me to laugh. "I guess we have. But the point I want to make is that forgiveness of one's sins by you or one's parish priest does not resolve one's karma. Karma is repressed to the unconscious. That's the source of this haunting guilt that we carry from one life to the next. This is why growing up in my current life I always felt the shadow of my guilt lurking in the background. It did not matter how many times I went to confession and received Holy Communion, I could not get rid of this guilt that haunted me. This is my point. I just cannot get over the feeling that Christianity's role in the salvation of Soul has to be reconstituted for the modern world. This whole concept of guilt and forgiveness of sin has to be put into its proper perspective in the DPG!"

"I couldn't agree more," Jesus said. "Soul does not sin. Soul has life experiences. As the noble bard expressed it, 'There is nothing either good or bad but thinking makes it so.' If an experience creates karma that has to be resolved, then Soul must resolve it. Confession will not resolve one's karma. The most confession can do is remind one not to do it again. Your experience with guilt proves this. This is why I'm delighted that you brought up this subject of Christian guilt. Readers can relate to experience much more easily than to theory, or blind faith; so thank you, O."

I couldn't help myself, and burst into laughter.

"What's so funny?"

"Nothing."

"What?"

"It's this whole thing. I can't get over how the creative dialectic of our discourse can take a thought and run with it. We started with Christian guilt and ended up with the Spiritual Law of Karma. It's amazing how Spirit works!"

Jesus laughed. "It does have its own agenda, doesn't it?"

"It certainly does. But this opens the door to the question of free will versus the will of God, doesn't it?" I asked, as the thought flashed across my mind.

"Not now, O," Jesus said, with that beaming smile that told me how happy he was with our discourse. "I think we should give the reader a break, don't you?"

"Okay," I said, and got up to stretch my legs. "Let me jot down a few notes so I don't forget this part of our talk."

"Guilt," Jesus said. "That's the only word you need to jot down. It will all come back to you when you start writing your book."

"Perhaps. And if not, I'll just let my Muse fill in the blanks. That's what the Gospel writers did, didn't they?" I said, with an ironic chuckle.

"If only," said Jesus, very soberly. "The problem with the Gospel writers is that they took it upon themselves to be their own Muse, with John being the most audacious. That's how they fostered their conspiracy. But we won't get into this now. Suffice to say for now that when truth is filtered through the mind it has a tendency to serve Kal's purpose, not Holy Spirit's."

"That's the writer's dilemma," I said.

"What is?" Jesus asked, with a puzzled look

"Ego," I replied. "That's the artist's biggest obstacle. I know you don't want to talk about it now, but can I ask you one question about the Gospel conspiracy?"

"I'd prefer you didn't just yet," Jesus said.

"*'Ask and thou shall receive,'*" I pleaded, and smiled.

Jesus relented. "Ask your question."

"Was the Gospel conspiracy deliberate?"

"That's a loaded question, O."

"I know. But, I have to know."

"Why?"

"Ego or Divine Spirit, J? I have to know."

"Why don't we just wait and see how our dialogue unfolds?" Jesus replied, and stood up to stretch his legs also. "That way we will know one way or the other what Soul wants to reveal about the Gospel conspiracy story."

"Fair enough," I said, and dropped the subject.

26. *The Three Stages of the Self*

"Why don't I leave it to you to let Soul speak," I said to Jesus, after I sat back down and stretched my legs out and put my hands behind my head. "I'd be very curious to see what Divine Spirit has to say from Christ's perspective on the subject of free will."

"Are you sure you want to take this on right now?" Jesus asked.

"What's the difference? The reader will probably be so engaged by this stage of the game that he might just want to jump right in."

"Free will is God's gift to Soul, but only when Soul has a sense of self," Jesus answered, jumping right into the discourse on free will.

"That makes sense," I said, catching Christ's point immediately. "Speaking from my past life experience as Grunt when I experienced the dawning of self-consciousness, I cannot fathom the concept of free choice before that. Group consciousness functions as a collective will with an instinctive capacity to choose for the survival of its species. With the dawning of self-consciousness this instinctive will for group survival is now directed to the survival of the newborn self. Would you agree with that, J?"

"Yes. But where does this sense of free choice come from?"

I thought for a moment and then closed my eyes. As I did a silent HU I rode the Holy Current of God back into time, going all the way back to my lifetime as Grunt. I don't know how long I sat in silence, but I sensed myself in my first primordial human life exercising authority over my ten or twelve clan members with brute force and incessant grunting. The louder my grunts, the more power I threatened. This kept my clan in check. I sensed myself being separate from my clan. I sensed the strange sensation of this separateness. It was both exciting and frightening. I could not put words to this sense, but I was distinctly aware of it. I sensed this sensation every time I grunted. It was like my grunt told me that I was separate from my clan even though a big part of me was still present in my group consciousness. I chuckled. "Of course," I said, out loud. "I've only got a dim sense of self. The rest of me is still merged with the group consciousness of my species!"

I felt myself being pulled deeper into my first primordial human life. I felt the pull of my group consciousness and the pull of my dim sense of self, and I felt conflicted. *"Wow!"* I exclaimed, to Christ's astonishment.

"What?" Jesus asked.

"I think I've just experienced the root source of our most fundamental conflict as human beings!" I exclaimed.

"This should be interesting," Jesus said, smiling at my epiphany.

"It is! I've just gone back to my first human lifetime and experienced the most peculiar sensation of primal conflict!"

"Primal conflict?" Jesus asked.

"I don't know what else to call it. I sensed my sense of self, and I know that it was only a partial sense of self. The rest of me was still a part of my group consciousness. I sensed the primal conflict that existed between my group consciousness and my dim sense of self. I wanted to be more myself and my group would not let me go, so I grunted all the time. My grunt was my way of threatening the group to let me get my way, to let me be my newly realized sense of self. Does this make sense to you?"

"It makes perfect sense," Jesus confirmed. "Your emerging self-consciousness must fight to remain a distinct self. This, as you say, is the primal source of the conflict that exists between the individual and society."

"Wow!" I exclaimed. "So it doesn't matter at what point in the history of mankind, there will always be this primal conflict between the individual and social consciousness?"

Jesus laughed. "I wouldn't have put it so bluntly, but yes; essentially society will always try to keep Soul from realizing its individuality. This is why it's so difficult to break away from the status quo and be yourself in society."

"I can't believe this!" I exclaimed, jumping to my feet. "Do you realize what just happened here, J?"

"Of course. You've just opened the door to the divine mystery of free will," Jesus replied, with a big smile on his exceptional face. I still could not get over how different Jesus looked from any painting I had seen of him.

"I have?" I replied. "Are you saying that — *of course!"* I blurted out. *"Free will is the 'I' of God, isn't it?"*

Jesus laughed. "In essence, yes."

"Then it follows that the more the 'I' of God is individuated the more free will Soul will have — *right?"*

"It follows," Jesus calmly replied.

"So this is why they say that total freedom and responsibility are the goals of the spiritual life — because the more spiritually self-realized we are, the freer we will be! And with spiritual freedom comes the responsibility of — what? You tell me, J. Where does responsibility come into the picture here?"

"The responsibility to sustain the freedom to be yourself," Jesus replied, with the sweetest smile. "This may sound strange at first, but responsible freedom is what defines the God-force. It may be a crude analogy, but it's the best that I can do for now. Responsible freedom is to the God-force what wet is to water. Do you see where I'm going with this?"

"Strangely enough, yes," I replied.

"Good. So the more spiritually self-realized one becomes, the more freedom he will have. With this freedom comes the consciousness of one's God nature. Here we have a similar situation to your experience when you had the dawning of self-consciousness."

"Don't say it! I think I see where you're going with this!"

"Please," Jesus said, and gestured for me to continue.

"If I understand you correctly, the newly realized spiritual self would be akin to the dawning of my primordial human self; right?"

"So far," Jesus said, with a big smile.

"And as the group consciousness of my primordial life tried to hold me back, so does social consciousness try to keep me from realizing my spiritual self?"

"In essence, yes," Jesus replied.

"Okay. To be more myself as Grunt I had to assert myself, which I did. This speaks to the struggle that Soul has to make in daily life to hold onto its self-identity; right?"

Jesus smiled. "Continue."

125

"Soul does this by exercising its own choices. The more power it has to exercise choice, the more it grows in self-identity; right?"

"Yes. But at this stage Soul's self-identity is all too human," Jesus replied.

"*Of course!* This is the egoic human stage of Soul's journey through life, isn't it?" I said, bursting with excitement. "This is the exoteric evolution of the self, if you will."

Jesus smiled his happy smile. "Go on, O. You're almost there."

"Alright. When Soul has realized enough self-identity through exoteric evolution to want total self-identity, it will seek the Way. When Soul finds the Way and lives the Way consciously it becomes more spiritually self-realized. Soul does this by choosing to live the mesoteric spiritual life over the exoteric material life; right?"

"Good so far. Keep going. You're almost there."

"Then when Soul has finally realized its spiritual self it is driven to realize God-realization consciousness; right?"

"Yes."

"As Soul had to exercise its freedom to live the spiritual life over the material life to realize its spiritual self-identity, so must it now exercise its freedom to live the new kind of life that it must live in order to realize God-consciousness; right?"

"You've almost got it," Jesus replied, his face beaming.

"*I think I have it!*" I said excitedly. "*In fact, I know I have it!* I worked this out in the DPG. But I hesitate to reveal this, J. It might be too much for the reader!"

"We can't stop now. It wouldn't be fair to the reader."

"If you say so," I said, chomping at the bit. "I just don't want to take all the responsibility for revealing this insight into the divine mystery of the self."

"I'll share it with you," Jesus said, and laughed.

"Alright," I said, and anxiously paced back and forth in front of Jesus. "To realize our own sense of self we have to assert our self-will. This is the only way we can grow in our own individuality. This is the exoteric stage of the individuation process. This leads to the second stage where we realize that to become more self-realized we have to play by a different set of rules. We can no longer be primal, aggressive, and blindly selfish because the consciousness of our human self has to be processed by a different set of values for the self to realize its spiritual identity, which is driven by its divine conatus to do so; so the new values have to be inherently self-transcending values. This means that in the second stage of the individuation process the self must choose to live the spiritual life if it wants to grow more into its spiritual self!"

"Why?" Jesus asked, on behalf of the reader. "Why cannot the human self continue to grow, and grow, and grow?"

"The human self can only grow so much in the consciousness of the lower worlds," I heard myself saying. "This is what I experienced in my lifetime as the *Scoundrel of Paris*. Ego can only grow so big before it collapses in on itself. But I don't want to explain this here. We can talk about ego when we get to your sayings. Right now I have to complete this thought about free will and the will of God before I lose it."

"Then please do," Jesus said.

"Alright," I said, silently appealing to the Inner Master to let me carry the insight all the way to its conclusion. "It seems to me then that at the primal stages of self-individuation we are aggressively selfish in our choices. This is our primal animal nature choosing. We can say that we are purely self-motivated here. But as we grow in self-identity from lifetime to lifetime we have to get along with life, and our choices become less self-motivated and more socially accommodating. In effect we're learning to become less selfish in our choices. The more we grow in self-identity, the more we realize that to grow in our spiritual self we have to be less selfish and more social in our choices. We have to learn how to live by spiritual values that will transform the consciousness of our human self. But even so, we're still self-motivated in our choices even though our values are less self-serving. In effect, as I experienced my own spiritual growth through the second stage of the self-individuation process I realized that the more you give of yourself the more of yourself you will have to give. This sums up the ethic of the spiritual life of the second stage of human evolution. But as I said, it is still self-motivated even though one is giving of oneself unselfishly. Then, when the unselfish self grows enough in spiritual consciousness to seek God-realization, which is the third and final stage of Soul's individuation, it must once again play by a different set of rules. This is the path of unconditional love."

"Aha!" Jesus exclaimed. *"You got it, O! You finally got it!"*

"Please, let me get this out before I lose it," I said, too excited to be excited by Christ's unexpected outburst.

"Be my guest," Jesus said, his face beaming with so much love that I wanted to rush over and hug him. I continued.

"So, the spiritually self-realized Soul must now surrender its will to God in order to realize the third and final stage of its journey home to God; right?"

"BINGO!" Jesus shouted.

I sat down to catch my breath. I shut my eyes, took in a few long breaths, and thanked the Inner Master. *"Thank you, Z,"* I said, and let out a long sigh.

"You're welcome, O," I heard him say, in the quiet of my mind. I opened my eyes. Jesus was staring at me, his face smiling like a radiant, full jowled sun.

27. *The Sacred Mantra*

Jesus was enchanted. We had taken the atom of God from the primal stage of its growth in the world through to the mature human stage, the spiritual stage, and right to the doorstep of God-realization consciousness, the third and final stage of Soul's journey through life; but Jesus felt that there was more to say on the subject of free will. "I'd like to clear up this question of free will before we move on. Do you mind, O?"

"Not at all," I said.

"Good. For the reader's sake, I'd like to clear up this issue of divine guidance in daily life. I'm thinking of television evangelists in particular when I say this."

I picked up on Christ's thoughts instantly. "Let me give you the most brazen example of divine guidance that I have ever witnessed," I said, smiling at the memory. "I'm going to quote one of these Christian evangelists to make my point. This is one of the best examples of brazen *chutzpa* that I have ever seen. After building up his audience to make their monetary donation to his ministry, this shameless evangelist then said, 'God has instructed me to tell you to give until it hurts — *and then to double it!'*"

"Exactly," said Jesus, without cracking a smile. "How on earth do those poor people distinguish the Voice of God from the voice of the preacher's self-serving ego?"

"That's the question, isn't it? One could also ask, which God is talking to them?"

"One could, but we won't go there now. It would only confuse the reader to learn that a separate deity rules the lower planes of consciousness. Let's concentrate on the Voice of God and the voice of ego. How do you tell the difference, O?"

"Me? I wish there was an easy answer. It's probably the most difficult thing for people to do. I find it very difficult. The only answer I can give you has to do with what I call self-coincidence. This is a difficult concept to get across, and I don't know if I can. I've tried a few times at our spiritual functions, but it seems to fly right over their heads."

"Try for the reader's sake," Jesus said. "I think I know where you're going with this. If you need help, I'll let Soul speak."

"Would you?"

"Of course. This is the whole point of our discourse."

"To let Soul speak?"

"Yes."

"Why? So the reader can see Creative Spirit in action?"

"If you like. The answer I would give is to let the reader come to his own conclusion about the true gospel of Jesus Christ. That's how we're going to dispel the illusions of the Gospel conspiracy story."

"That's the agenda, isn't it?"

"You were saying?"

"I was about to say that I was getting very tired of the chela's sacred mantra, but I don't know if I should go there."

"What sacred mantra?" Jesus asked.

I hesitated. "I'm not sure about this, J."

"I'll be the judge," Jesus said.

"If you wish. *'Just give it to the Master.'* That's the sacred mantra of my spiritual community. That's what they all say when they want God's help."

Jesus laughed. *"I hear you, O!"*

"J, you have no idea how frustrating it has been to get the simple point across that we have to do our best to make our own decisions in life. I could not make myself understood. One chela in particular, and a High Initiate at that, was forever casting his load off to Divine Spirit. He would always begin with, 'I just gave it the Master.' One week he was going to build his new house because the Inner Master gave him signs to go ahead, and the following week he was not going to build his new house because the Golden tongued Wisdom of Holy Spirit gave him signs to not go ahead. This seesawing went on for three months. The same thing with his new business venture. One week Spirit told him to pull out, and the next week he got signs from Spirit to stay in. Finally one day I said to him, 'At what point do Soul and Spirit meet in happy agreement?' He missed my point entirely. I quoted the Living Soul Master. *'The true man of God does not ask God for help, he works out his own problems.'* He missed that point also. Don't get me wrong, J. I've asked God for help many times in my life, and probably will do so many more times before I die, as well you should know because I prayed for your help when I had to deal with my father's unclean spirit—"

"That was the Holy Ghost that came to you, O," Jesus interjected.

"I know now it was. But the Holy Ghost came in your image because you were the one I prayed to at the time, and I'll be forever grateful for your help. I could not have dealt with the Evil One on my own; so, thank you, J."

"You're welcome," Jesus said, with the warmest smile.

"Alright. The point I wanted to make is that this H. I. began to fatigue me. I could no longer stand to hear the sacred mantra every time I attended one of his *satsang* classes."

"Satsang?" Jesus asked, for the reader's benefit.

"Sorry. *Satsang* means a spiritual gathering."

"Good. What was it about this sacred mantra that bothered you?"

"My sense of self-reliance was offended. I believe in the principle of letting go and letting God, but it annoyed me whenever I heard my fellow chelas mouth the sacred mantra at every turn. It seemed that they abandoned their responsibility to the Inner Master, which is counter-intuitive to the goal of the Way of the Eternal of becoming a Master in our own right. How can one become a Master in his own right if he abandons his responsibility to Divine Spirit at every turn? Am I wrong, J; or do I have a point here?"

"Both," Jesus replied, to my surprise. "If you don't mind, let me clarify this for you, O. This sacred mantra that your fellow chelas live by is the crutch they need to build up their spiritual legs. There is legitimacy to the use of this aid, which the Living Soul Master grants his chelas; but as the chelas grow in spiritual strength they have to rely more on their own intuitive resources which, ironically, is still Divine Spirit."

"My point exactly! That's what I meant by self-coincidence!"

Jesus laughed. "Yes. To make your point, then. When you prayed for my help, you prayed to Divine Spirit, did you not?"

"Absolutely. You and Spirit are one. That's precisely what I mean by self-coincidence. The lower self has to coincide with the higher self in order for one to become a Master in his own right. The more we work out own problems, the more Spirit is going to help us because we are closer to Divine Spirit. Is that so difficult to understand?"

"For most people, yes. From what you have said then, I would say that there is still a small but powerful part of you that refuses to let go and let God. In good time this part will give way to Soul. Your logic is impeccable, O. This pleases me, because few Souls can make this distinction with as much clarity. And humor, I might add!"

With that, Jesus laughed, and I joined him.

"Alright," Jesus said. "We've had our fun. Now let's resolve this issue with these holy rollers that have taken my gospel to such heights of absurdity that it has fatigued even my own high level of godly tolerance!"

I burst into laughter. *"Be my guest, J!"*

"I know there's no getting through to them, but for the sake of the reader we have to explain the absurdity of blind reliance upon God," Jesus began, and then paused.

"In itself, it's not absurd to let go and let God," I said, to clarify Christ's point. "It's the context from which this blind reliance on God springs, is it not?"

"I see where you're going with this. If the context is false, then one's abandonment to God would be equally false. Is that what you're trying to say?" Jesus asked.

"Yes. The context is instant salvation, be it salvation in whatever form. It could be a healing salvation, financial salvation, romantic salvation, career salvation, or whatever; and not until one realizes that salvation is a personal responsibility will he understand the legitimacy of letting go and letting God. As the Living Soul Master said in one of his talks, we have to do everything we can to solve our own problems; only then should we ask God for help. Does that make sense to you, J?"

"Absolutely. How else can we exercise our spiritual muscles?"

"Exactly. We become spiritual cripples if we continue to rely on the sacred mantra for everything we want out of life, won't we?"

"You do have a way of seeing the humor in everything, don't you?"

"I'd go nuts otherwise!" I said, and laughed. Then I sat back and took notes on our discourse on free will and God's will.

I jotted down everything I could remember. Then, to my delight, my Muse gave me one line that summed up our whole talk on free will: **The more true we are to ourselves, the closer we are to God; and the closer we are to God, the more our will and God's will become one. That's the mystery of free will.**

I turned to Jesus, and said, "That's that topic. Just give me a few minutes, please. I feel Spirit coming through with something else…"

28. *The Confession of Jesus Christ*

Not unlike the modern day founder of the ancient spiritual teachings of the Way of the Eternal who was given his chapter titles for every book he wrote by Divine Spirit, so was I privileged. While Jesus waited patiently, I jotted down the title for twenty-eight chapters of my Jesus book, with a note or two for each chapter.

That was all I needed for my book thus far. The titles opened up the door to whatever Spirit wanted from our dialogue on each specific theme, and the twenty-eighth chapter was called "The Confession of Jesus Christ."

I stopped writing and turned to Jesus. He knew that the creative consciousness of Divine Spirit, which I simply referred to as my Muse, had nudged me to ask him something, and he opened the door for me. "What does Spirit want us to talk about now?" he asked.

I read the twenty-eighth chapter title: "The Confession of Jesus Christ."

"Yes. It's about time the world heard the real story," Jesus said, with a reluctant nod.

Some thoughts flashed through my mind, and I knew my Muse wanted me to address them. "Do you mind if I ask you some pointed questions?"

"Not at all," Jesus said with his voice, but his eyes weren't as willing.

"Are all Soul Masters aware of the Divine Plan of God?" I asked.

"As you have experienced the DPG; no. You have been privileged to connect the spiritual dots in a way that lends invaluable clarity to Soul's purpose in life. Every Soul Master is God-realized, but every Master refracts the Light of God according to the prism of their unique individuality. Despite the fact that we are all aware of the DPG, some Masters give it more clarity than others; but it is always implied in our teaching. Indeed, how could it not be? We all speak the same divine truth. Does this clear up the issue for you?"

"And hopefully for the reader," I said.

"Of course," said Jesus, with another nod of his head.

"Given the DPG then, every Master must be aware that Soul's encoded purpose in life is spiritual self-realization and God-consciousness. Is this not the case?"

"It is," Jesus said, and fell silent.

Suddenly I got a vision of a courtroom with Jesus sitting stone silent in the witness box, and I was the prosecutor questioning my own witness. I felt nervous and laughed.

"What's so funny?" Jesus asked.

"I feel like a prosecutor," I said, with another nervous chuckle.

"You speak for the reader. Just ask the questions that you feel the reader would want answered," Jesus said, but sounding very much like a reluctant witness.

"I feel a tough one coming on right now," I said, and took a deep breath for courage. "Did you die for the sins of the world?"

"My sacrifice upon the cross symbolizes the resolution of sin by the Way of Christ. Self-sacrifice is the Way of Christ, and my sacrifice upon the cross was supposed to symbolize the death of the lower self. By resolving the consciousness of one's lower self through self-sacrifice, one resolves one's sins. That's the message of my crucifixion."

With that, Jesus fell silent. *In fact, the whole park fell silent. Dead silent. I couldn't believe it. I stared out into the park, but heard nothing. Absolutely nothing. Not a sound. I looked at the street and saw cars driving by, but they were silent. It was like I had gone stone deaf. I stared in awe and began to feel very uneasy.* Suddenly the sound returned, and I turned to Jesus and saw a faint smile on his face. "Did you do that?" I asked.

"My Father in heaven," said Jesus, with a telling snigger.

I laughed. I couldn't help myself. I was nervous and had to release the tension. "Is this how Soul Masters communicate?" I asked, trying to make sense of the silence.

"Sometimes. It's not all ball and chains, you know," Jesus said.

I didn't know what to say; but I knew Jesus was telling me something. "I feel privileged to experience this with you," I said, very puzzled by the whole experience but strangely excited. "I have another reader-question, if I may?"

"You may," said Jesus, not volunteering an explanation for the eerie silence.

"Okay," I said, still reeling from the experience. "If you survived your crucifixion, did you and Mary get married and have children?" I asked, for my reader's sake.

"There's a loaded question. I'm not quite sure we're ready to answer this one yet," Jesus said, and fell stone silent again.

I felt the silence creeping in again and quickly responded to ward it off: "As witness for the prosecution, I feel you must answer this question. My reader wants to know." And no sooner did I say this and I *knew* that the eerie silence was Christ's way of telling me that I had gone where I had no right to go; but I felt compelled to continue.

"Yes, I survived my crucifixion; thanks to my Essene brethren who were in on my crucifixion plot," Jesus replied, to my astonishment. "And as to Mary Magdalene, let me just say that I shared my dream with her of making my sacrifice upon the cross the symbol of my gospel teaching to the world. Mary understood me better than all of my disciples, and we shared our life after my crucifixion. That is all you need to know."

"This leads me to ask the following question—"

"Never mind," Jesus abruptly interrupted. "We can dispel this notion of a bloodline, if that's what you're after. A bloodline does exist, but not in the context that the world has been led to believe. Salvation is a personal responsibility, not a bequeathed legacy."

"Holy bloodline," I said, delighted by Christ's response because it answered the burning question raised by the best-selling novel *The DaVinci Code* that had just been made into a Hollywood movie that was condemned by the Vatican. "The following question is mine. Are all Soul Masters aware of the three levels of human evolution?"

"The exoteric, mesoteric, and esoteric circles of life? Yes and no. You have defined these three levels because it helps to articulate the DPG as you have experienced it, but every Master is aware of the many levels of consciousness. Indeed, how can they not be?"

I laughed at the absurdity of my question. "When a Master talks about harvesting Souls, he's referring to all those Souls that have evolved enough to take evolution into their own hands and live the Way consciously, is he not?"

"In effect, yes," Jesus replied, and fell silent again.

"Are you the Son of God?" I felt compelled to ask.

"Every Soul that realizes God consciousness becomes a Child of God. I need not expand upon this for fear of obfuscating the clarity of this simple truth."

"Obfuscating?" I repeated, and laughed. "I wonder what the scholars of your life and teaching will have to say about that."

"It is they that should worry about obfuscation," Jesus curtly replied.

"Touché!" I exclaimed.

"Any more questions?" Jesus asked, with a hint of impatience.

"Yes. This one is from my readers again. Did Judas betray you?"

"Yes."

"Why?"

"Judas was called but not chosen. The Spirit of Christ was too much for him. Judas could not help himself. This happens to everyone that is called to the spiritual life but is not willing to be resolved by the reconciling power of Holy Spirit. Judas could not let go of ego. In the end his lower self won over his higher self and he turned on the apostles first, on the Holy Word of God which he could not hear, and on me personally. That is why he betrayed me; which, I might add for the sake of history, helped to bring my mission to fruition."

"Are you going to come back as the Second Coming of Jesus Christ?"

"No. Once was enough, thank you. I have been assigned to the Fourth Plane of Consciousness for an indefinite period," Jesus replied, with a definite edge to his voice.

"Probably until Christianity has run its course," I said, with a nervous smile.

Jesus said nothing, but his face told me I was right.

"I have a personal question that has bothered me for a long time, and I just have to ask you. May I?" I asked, pressing my luck.

"You may," he said, again as though he was directed to respond.

"Did you become crazy with God, or was that just an expression used by the Elders at the community of Qumran to explain the strange phenomenon of being possessed by the reconciling power of Holy Spirit?"

"Both," Jesus replied, and fell silent. A moment or two later, he added, "Yes, I did become so overwhelmed by Holy Spirit that I lost my spiritual balance. My crucifixion was the result of this imbalance, however cleverly plotted it may have been. My death was calculated for the sake of my gospel, because I was driven to establish the kingdom of God on earth. Those were harsh times. Society needed the Holy Word of God to shed new light upon the Way, which was in grave danger of being lost to the strict letter of God's Law. In my arrogance, I made myself a sacrificial lamb to reveal man's self-redemptive nature through my life and teaching; but my message got turned on its head by the Gospel writers when they made me the Son of God and savior of the world. Again, for the sake of history; I am the messenger, not the message. That's all I'm going to confess at this time. If you will excuse me, I need a cold drink. May I get you one?"

"Yes, please," I said, and stood up to walk with Jesus; but he held up his hand for me to stay. I understood. I had crossed a line I had no right to cross.

29. *Many Are Called but Few Are Chosen*

As I watched Jesus walking to the vendor's cart, tears came to my eyes. He had bared himself to the world, and I was responsible. When Jesus returned, I said, "I'm sorry, J. I had no right to probe you as I did."

"But you did," he replied, to my surprise.

For whatever reason, whenever I felt that Jesus would respond one way, he replied another. This intrigued me. He handed me my orange soda and sat down. He took a long, refreshing drink of his coke, and then looked at me. The love that shone from his eyes was so overwhelming that I heard myself say, "Let's talk about the Master's love."

"Which Master? The Living Soul Master, or Masters in general?"

"Both. But isn't it the same thing? The love of the God-realized Soul is the love of God, is it not?"

"Of course," said Jesus. "What do you wish to know about love? Was not what I said about love at the worship service this morning enough?"

"It was enough to prick Stanley's balloon, but that's not what I'm after. When I wrote my book on my past lives Spirit let me catch a glimpse of the God-realized Soul. What I saw explained the phenomenon that people experience whenever they are blessed by the presence of a Soul Master. The love that a Master emanates is so great that it leaves an indelible impression. If you don't mind telling me, can you explain why this is so?"

"Not at all. Love is the Holy Current of God that runs through life. The Holy Current of God has to be stepped down to adjust to the consciousness of life. The lower the consciousness of life is, the less the Holy Current of God flows through it. The higher the consciousness of life is, the more the Holy Current flows through it. A Soul Master is a clear channel for the Current of God, so the flow of love from God through a Master is unimpeded by the individual self, because the self of a Master is pure Spirit. The Hand of God touches a

Soul blessed by a Master's love, as it were. Does this make sense to you?"

"It does to me; but I'm sure the reader will have to reflect on it."

"Then why don't we explain what it means to become one with Holy Spirit?"

I thought for a moment. "Isn't this what the Way of Christ is all about, transforming the consciousness of the lower self of man to become one with Holy Spirit?"

Jesus smiled. "Yes, of course. I'm glad you brought this home. I thought for a moment we were getting off topic."

"All roads lead to Rome, J," I said, with a self-conscious laugh.

"Indeed. What is it you would like the reader to know about a Master's love?"

"I want to tell the reader that a Master's love is to him what wet is to water, if I may use your analogy," I replied.

"It's appropriate. But you do realize that you're going to take all the mystery out of a Master's love, don't you?" Jesus said, with that playful twinkle in his eyes.

"I know. But I want to take advantage of your company, J. How often does a person get to probe the mind of a Soul Master, let alone Jesus Christ?"

"More often than you realize," Jesus responded, once again surprising me with his answer. "You don't think that all the great advances in the world were made by mere mortal minds, do you? Plato, Shakespeare, Rumi, DaVinci, Keats, Wordsworth, Washington, Lincoln, Whitman, Mozart, Einstein, Gandhi — they all had a Master by their side guiding them, just as you have the Inner Master—"

I couldn't help myself and burst into a fit of laughter. Jesus smiled at me as I laughed. "What a joy you are. You have a way of opening one's heart with your laughter. Would you like to know how you came by your gift?"

"What, my sense of humor?"

"Yes."

"Please, I'd love to know."

"You dared to suffer the insufferable, that's how."

I thought for a moment, but I couldn't make the connection. "Pardon me?"

"You risked eternal damnation to honor your love for Claudine," Jesus said.

"Oh!" I exclaimed, as memories of my past lifetime as Riel Laforchette rushed to the surface. "I follow you. You're saying that because I dared to risk eternal damnation I've seen through the veil of illusion, and this frees me from the hold of life?"

"BINGO!" Jesus exclaimed.

"Well, we'd better explain this for the reader because he'll never know what the hell we're talking about!"

"You do have a way with words, don't you?"

I smiled self-consciously. "I thought it appropriate."

"So it was. But hell is not a word people take lightly. It has deep emotional resonance for a lot of people. But you know that, of course. Why don't you explain how it is that you saw through the veil of illusion, and why this should bless you with the gift of humor?"

"Certainly. From the perspective of the DPG, there is no such thing as damnation, temporal or eternal. There is only experience. Soul has the experiences it needs to complete its journey through life to total self-realization consciousness. But I didn't see this until just recently, shortly after I had my past-life regressions. I had my sense of humor long before this, and if you want I'll tell you when it came to the fore in my life."

"Let me guess," Jesus said.

"You have to guess?"

"Sometimes," Jesus said, with a big grin. "After you experienced your own immortality in your mother's kitchen; right?"

"Yes. Once I squared the circle I never again feared the siren call of my own nothingness!"

"That, you will have to explain!" Jesus said, with a snicker.

I laughed also, because I did not expect to say that. "Squaring the circle is the metaphor I used in my novel to explain my journey to the Soul Plane of Consciousness. This is the plane of one's true self. One's own nothingness is the consciousness of one's lower self. The siren call of one's own nothingness is the seductive power of the lower self that keeps one's higher self from squaring the circle, if I may express it this way."

"You may not. Keep it simple, O," Jesus said.

"Alright. All I'm saying is that one's lower self is made up of the unresolved consciousness of one's spiritual self, and resolving the consciousness of one's lower self is how one gets to experience his own immortal nature. This is what I mean by squaring the circle — *because it's damn near impossible to do!* And this, incidentally, is why you and I are having this dialogue, is it not?"

"Essentially. And we're going to explain to the reader the spiritual power that my sayings have to resolve one's lower self—"

"To the point where one is born again!" I excitedly jumped in.

"Exactly," Jesus calmly replied, with a big smile on his face. "Spiritual rebirth is what my gospel is all about, not the instant salvation of the Gospel conspiracy. And the most effective way to resolve one's lower self is by the Way of Love. There, how do you like the way I brought our talk back to point?"

"That's good. But let me finish, if I may. I'm blessed with my sense of humor because I know that we're all free to do whatever we want, because there is no such thing as eternal damnation. This realization came to me because of my lifetime as the *Scoundrel of Paris*. I died in that life expecting to go to hell for eternity for what I did to you and the Church with my whores, but I didn't go to hell. I took my guilt with me into my next life, as well as the emptiness of my insatiable egoism that I had to karmically process in future lives, starting with my next life as a black slave in Georgia. And here I am today, a spiritually self-realized Soul. So, what does this tell you about the fear of hell?"

"The reader will appreciate your experience," Jesus said. "You risked damnation to honor your love for Claudine, and you died an empty shell of a man; but you did not go to hell. You were reborn into a life of slavery to redress the karma that you created as the lost Soul of Paris, and this information will be invaluable for the reader's edification."

"Good. If I may then, my humor springs from the knowledge that Soul is free to do whatever it wishes, because the journey to the Higher Worlds of God is open-ended. It does not matter if it takes one lifetime or a million lifetimes, Soul will complete its journey. This is just the way it is in the DPG. It's all a matter of choice. There is no deadline for total self-realization consciousness. This knowledge gives me license to speak my mind; and this, I believe, is why I have an uninhibited sense of humor."

"Yes," Jesus said; and then with a little snicker added, "And also why you chafe people. It's the absence of the fear of consequences that lets you speak your mind so freely. Not that you are unaware of karmic consequences; but because you are aware of the open-endedness of Soul's journey home to God you are free to risk whatever consequences may come for what you say. Does that make sense to you?"

"Perfectly," I said. "Is this why we're having this discourse, because I can inject humor into this dreary subject of Christian salvation?"

"This and more. The sad truth is that the world has taken me so seriously it has lost all perspective on the life well-lived."

"The life well-lived? Is that something like the complete life that Pythagoras taught?"

"Not quite. Pythagoras sought to impress upon his students the spiritual advantages of the responsible family life. What I mean by the life well-lived is a life in which one is not afraid to take risks to satisfy his inherent longing to be whole."

"I like that!" I exclaimed. "And it's so true, isn't it? Let me recite a poem I wrote that makes this very point," I enthusiastically added. "I wrote this poem a few years ago, but believe me it's as relevant to your point as any poem can possibly be!"

Jesus smiled at my show of emotion. "Please," he said. "I'd love to hear how you distill the gnosis of your life experiences into poetry."

"I love poetry, J!" I exclaimed, revealing my appreciation for all the inspiration that poetry had given me over the years. "Poetry pierces the veil of life and reveals the essential truth of *what is,* to borrow a phrase from Adrienne Rich. Poetry is to literature what wisdom sayings are to the Way of Life. As a matter of fact, I gave a talk to a group of artists last year on the spiritual nature of the artist's way. I used poetry to make my point just as I'm going to do now. I

want to give my reader an insight into the heart of our discourse, because poetry has the power to speak the Word more clearly than any other art form!"

"That's debatable," Jesus said, still smiling at my display of emotion. "Music is my favorite art form. But please, continue."

"Fair enough," I said, and calmed myself to recall my poem. "Okay. My poem was inspired by an experience I had with a man whom you would have described as shallow soil for the seeds of God's kingdom. Spirit brought him into my life because he was going through his dark night of Soul. I introduced him to the Way of the Eternal, but he was afraid to take the risk of what propriety might say if he stepped outside the safe little box of the status quo. My poem opens a window onto the life of this pusillanimous Soul."

"Pusillanimous Soul?" Jesus frowned. "That's a bit harsh, don't you think?"

"Not at all. This is how he revealed himself; and if poetry is anything, it dares to rend the veil of life," I replied, with unabashed conviction in my poetic insight.

"Pusillanimous Soul it is then," said Jesus.

"Okay. I hope I don't offend you, because my poem does feature you as the object of this man's cowardice. He was afraid to risk leaving you to embrace the Way of the Eternal. The title of my poem, which I borrowed from one of your sayings, reflects the soul of St. Jude in this one conflicted Soul. It's called, *Many are Called but Few are Chosen:*

> From deep within the holy seed sprouted,
> the desire to be more; but the path he walked
> had grown empty, and he prayed to God
> for guidance. In a dream one night he saw a sign
> when his fishing hook snagged a power line;
> but afraid of what people might say,
> he refused to walk the Way. True to his nature
> he played it safe, because it takes courage to
> believe; the fear of ridicule mocked his spirit,
> and stopped his seed from growing. Desperate,
> he returned to Jesus Christ, savior of the
> status quo; but the emptiness within could not

be filled, and he refused to see why.
He looked for answers in all the wrong places,
because it kept him far away from home; but alone
at night he saw his life's lie, and he could do nothing
but cry. Again he prayed to God for guidance,
and in a dream he saw the sign of an ass; but
his obdurate mind objected, and now he lives his
lonely life waiting in fear to die.

"Savior of the status quo?" Jesus said, and snickered. "How fitting. Well, I hope to change all of that with our dialogue, O. Thank you for your insight into the troubled soul of the paralyzed Christian. I'm sure your reader will find it very informative."

"You're welcome," I said; but I still felt very uncomfortable for probing Jesus the way I did. I forced myself to look into his eyes, and just as I was about to apologize for my impertinence he gave me the sweetest smile and put his finger to his lips; so I said nothing, and we just sat in silence and waited for Spirit's guidance...

30. *Savior of the Status Quo*

I could feel our dialogue coming to an end for the time being, but I wanted to make sure I had all I needed from Jesus before I dug up my Bible.

I had already gone through half of my boxes of five thousand books looking for my Bible. I needed it to reference Christ's sayings for the novel I wrote on my regressions, but I couldn't find it. It had to be there somewhere, though.

As I thought about my Bible it occurred to me to ask Jesus what he thought about preparing the reader for what I knew would be the world's most profound discourse on the enigmatic sayings of Jesus, and he said, "What kind of preparation?"

"We can't just jump in and explain the metaphysics of spiritual transformation, can we?" I replied. "The reader's psyche would be affronted. If what I suspect is going to happen with this book, it'll be read by Christians that have outgrown their faith like the man in my poem but who don't want to take up another path for fear of propriety—"

"Stop!" Jesus said, holding up his hand. "Why don't we talk about this fear of propriety? You're right, O. I think we should make every effort possible to dispel this fear for the reader."

I chuckled. Jesus looked at me. "Did I say something funny?"

"I can't help but laugh at the thought that you are responsible for this fear that so many Christians suffer from."

"Me? In what way?" he asked, playing dumb for the reader's sake.

"As I said in my poem, Jesus Christ has become the savior of the status quo. I can't tell you the number of times that I've seen criminals on the news go to court with a Bible under their arm because they found Jesus, nor how many times I've seen people use you to cover up for their deceit. Why you, J? Because you are the savior of the status quo, that's why. You are the paragon of moral rightness. The moment someone says he has found Jesus Christ he's welcomed back into the fold. As ironic as it may be, you have become the gateway to spiritual salvation as well as spiritual enslavement; that's why I was chuckling."

"Don't I know it," Jesus said, with a heavy sigh. "You have no idea what it's like to live with this on my mind. Of course I know that people use me to cover up for their deceit, but there's not much I can do about it. Do you think I would not like to see these mercenary television evangelists struck with a bolt of Light like St. Paul was? Of course I would. But I can't do anything about it because I serve Holy Spirit. I do what I can within the boundaries of the spiritual laws. That's all I can do, O."

Surprised by Christ's revelation, I had to ask, "Were you responsible for St. Paul's experience on the road to Damascus?"

"Yes and no. As I said, I do Spirit's bidding. Holy Spirit woke Saul of Tarsus up from his spiritual stupor to prepare him for the Way of Christ. So powerfully did Holy Spirit smite Saul that it transformed the molecular structure of his body. That's why he had such a profound transformation. It was necessary for Saul to have this transformation, because Holy Spirit needed him to disseminate my gospel. But don't ask me why, because I'm as ignorant of Holy Spirit's design as the next Master. We just serve God, O. We don't question God."

"Wow!" I said, delighted to hear Jesus speak so frankly. "So, you do feel responsible then for all the nonsense done in your name?"

"Nominally responsible, not karmically responsible. Every Soul is responsible for its own life. That's the spiritual law. But it's all this nonsense done in my name that often leaves me to wonder if I served God as well as I could have," Jesus confessed, with an obvious hint of regret in his voice.

I felt for Jesus. "There's no use crying over spilt milk," I said, smiling at the thought of being a shoulder for Jesus to cry on. But I had to dispel that thought, which only served my vanity. "As I've come to realize since I worked out the DPG, every experience is an entry point to spiritual freedom. It doesn't matter where one starts the spiritual journey; the door exists everywhere because, as you said, the kingdom of heaven is everywhere. Spilt milk or not, Soul is never denied the opportunity for salvation. What does it matter to the grand scheme of things if you had done it differently? The door to the kingdom of heaven would still be everywhere to be found, would it not?"

"I agree. But I may be allowed a moment of self-pity, may I not?" Jesus replied, in a surprisingly maudlin voice.

"If you wish. But what kind of image are you creating for the reader?"

"A real one, I hope. I'd like the reader to see Jesus Christ the man first, then the savior. Can you appreciate that?" Jesus asked, sounding all too human.

"I can, because I know how the DPG works," I replied. "Soul does not come ready-made into the world. Soul has to unfold through the evolutionary process of life to realize its spiritual identity. I know that all Masters have earned their stripes. What the world needs to understand is that Jesus was very human, with all the faults that man is heir to, and that you had to earn your stripes as well. That's what your sayings are all about, aren't they?"

"Exactly. My sayings are all about taking one's spiritual destiny into one's own hands; and not until the world realizes this will Christianity ever change."

I laughed. "It'll never change, J. All we can hope for is to reach those Christians that have outgrown their faith but who need all the help they can get to liberate themselves from their fear of propriety."

"From the savior of the status quo, you mean," Jesus said, and snickered.

"Yeah, I guess they're one and the same, aren't they?" I said, and laughed.

"I would say so," Jesus said. "But how do you propose we help Christians liberate themselves from the savior of the status quo?"

I burst into laughter again. Jesus joined me in the humor of the irony. "This is priceless," I said, still laughing. "You, Jesus Christ, are asking me to help liberate Christians from Jesus Christ!"

"The savior of the status quo!" Jesus shouted, throwing his hands into the air in mock exasperation.

After we had our fun we got serious again, and I shared with Jesus an experience I had with a United Church minister on one of my painting jobs in St. Jude. "Just to make the point about self-deception, let me tell you about this Christian agnostic—"

"Christian agnostic?" Jesus interjected. "What kind of creature is that?"

"That's what I tried to figure out. This United Church minister had outgrown his faith, but out of fear of losing his meal ticket he rationalized his spiritual doubts by calling himself a Christian agnostic. He doubted that you were the Son of God, having come to believe that one can never know God, but he just did not have the courage to go out into the world and look for the Way. He stayed in his safe little ministry because he was getting a free meal ticket on the backs of his parishioners. He wanted his cake and eat it too. He was a self-deceiver, J; and all because he did not have the courage of his convictions."

"Many Christians fall prey to the spirit of self-deception," Jesus replied. "That's a sad fact of life. But that's their journey, O. That's what they have to experience to strengthen their spiritual resolve. Did you not also fall for a Christian solar cult teaching?"

"Yes, I did," I said, and my face instantly flushed red with humiliation. "And you cannot imagine — of course you can," I corrected myself. "I went through horror with that teaching. I'm still paying for it with my damaged eyesight. But let's not go there. Let's get back to the issue of the disaffected Christian's fear of propriety."

"Fair enough," Jesus said, generously giving me my space.

"To what would you attribute this fear?" I asked.

"Being alone," Jesus replied. "It's a frightening world when you're all alone out there, O. Christians ready to embrace a higher expression of the Way are afraid they may not find it and be left stranded. This happened to me several times during my silent years. After I left Qumran with the sayings that Master Zadok had given me—"

"May I?" I interrupted.

"Certainly," Jesus said, knowing that I was excited because of my past lifetime as Samuel the Essene.

"Jacob the Elder told us that Master Zadok gave you some of the most powerful sayings from the Great Book of Life. I have to know this. Did those sayings make it into the Gospels of Christ?"

"What do you think?" Jesus asked, with a big smile on his face.

149

"I think they did. In fact, I'm certain they did; especially in the Gnostic *Gospel of Thomas.* And as I lived your sayings I transformed my consciousness enough to be able to say, as you did, 'Get thee behind me Satan!' If that's not proof, nothing is!"

Jesus laughed. "As I was saying, in my own journey I felt stranded and alone a number of times. I had outgrown one aspect of the Way and had not yet initiated myself into a higher expression of the Way, so I can appreciate what Christians who have outgrown their faith are up against."

"Let's back up for a moment, if we may. If you had the sayings from the Great Book of Life, what do you mean that you had outgrown one expression of the Way and were left stranded? The Way is the Way. The sayings from the Great Book of Life were a direct link-up with the Way of the Eternal, so how could you feel stranded and alone?"

"Good question. But why don't you answer it with your own experience with the Way of Christ? You lived my sayings. You must know that they will take you through the many valleys of despair—"

"*Many valleys is right!*" I exclaimed. "We never have one dark night of the Soul on this journey, do we? We have many dark nights of the Soul!"

"There you go, then," Jesus said with a big smile.

"So it's the fear of being all alone out there that keeps the nascent Christian seeker from leaving the security of his faith, despite the fact that he has outgrown it?"

"I would say so," Jesus confirmed.

"*I find that hard to believe, J!*"

"Why? Do you doubt my wisdom?"

I broke out. Jesus joined me in laughter. "It's not that I doubt your wisdom," I said. "It's more like I trust my own wisdom more. In this case, anyway."

"Why?" Jesus asked.

"This is the digital world, J. People have access to the world's largest library. All one has to do is ask and Google provides. To excuse the nascent Christian seeker because he may feel all alone out there if he steps outside the suffocating little box of his spiritual faith is to rationalize his lack of courage for breaking out. That's my theory anyway."

"And a valid one it is. To what do you ascribe their fear, then?"

"We're back to propriety. My poem describes the fear of propriety that one Christian seeker was afflicted with. He was a retired RCMP officer very conscious of his image in St. Jude; and he feared being ridiculed by the community if he embraced this new religion of the Light and Sound of God, despite the fact that he was given all the signs to embrace it. He had those dreams that I mentioned in my poem. The power line that he snagged with his fishing line told me that he was fishing for a new spiritual path, and he snagged the Holy Current of God by accident. His own good karma snagged the Way of the Eternal, to be precise; and his dream of the ass told me that his stubborn nature kept him from taking up the Way of the Eternal. This man's fear of propriety speaks to my primordial experience as Grunt, my first human life. I felt the pull of my group consciousness and the pull of my need for greater self-identity, and I had to be very aggressive to get my own way. This is how I grew in self-realization consciousness. I contend that this primal conflict exists in every person; and it's responsible for the fear that the nascent Christian seeker has when he feels the pull for more self-realization consciousness but is held back by the pull of social consciousness. This is why I feel it has to do more with courage than anything else. If the Christian seeker's need for more self-identity is not strong enough to resist the pull of the status quo, then I'm afraid he will be destined like the man in my poem to live his life in quiet desperation and go to his grave with the song still in him, just as Henry David Thoreau said. He will die with his courage stuck in his throat, and that does not make for a nice death. I know, because I had a past-life death just like that."

"Oh? Which lifetime?" Jesus asked, drawing me out for the reader.

"My lifetime in Genoa, Italy. I dishonored my wife, family, and friends for the love of my mistress. I was a wealthy textile baron. My name was Don Giovanni, and I was a man of the world; but behind my back they called me *'Don Ciuco'* for the ass that I had made of myself with my mistress on the dance floor of Genoa's most prominent social event. I died choking on my lack of courage in that

151

life. But I don't want to talk about this now. That life was responsible for the devastating karma that I had to come to terms with in my current life with Cathy, who was my wife la Donna Francesca in Genoa, and my regressionist who turned out to be my mistress in that life. The point I want to make is simple, J. I just want to say that the nascent Christian seeker — and by this I mean the Christian who has outgrown his faith but is afraid to step outside his box to seek a spiritual path that will satisfy his need for wholeness — this Christian has to muster his courage and step outside his faith, because his faith now impedes his spiritual growth."

"And live the life well-lived!" Jesus exclaimed.

"Exactly. So I don't buy into this notion that they would be all alone out there. They will and they won't. That's the reality of the spiritual quest. It's always been an individual journey, but we are never alone; and I have no desire whatsoever to coddle the pusillanimous Soul. That's not my function in this life. These disaffected Christians can find their own way when life makes them ready for the next step. All I can do is be there for them, like I was for the man in my poem; and what they do with what Divine Spirit gives them is entirely up to them. Fair enough?"

"Fair enough," Jesus said, thus ending part one of our dialogue.

PART TWO

<u>THE SAYINGS OF JESUS REVEALED</u>

31. *My Jesus Book*

Cathy believed me. I told her the whole story, and that I would be starting my book in the morning. "I don't think Jesus will show up again until I've written our story this far," I added, to Cathy's disappointment.

"Do you think I'll get to meet him?" she asked.

"I don't know. Maybe. Do you want to?"

"Yes, I think so. I was a Christian for a while. I think it would be nice to meet Jesus," she said, with that innocence that charmed me from the first day we met.

"Why did you leave Christianity?" I asked. It just occurred to me that I had never asked her before, and I smiled to myself in amazement.

"It didn't give me the peace of mind I needed," she replied.

"And you just left?" I asked.

"Yes," she said.

"You must have had a reason," I said, pressing for an explanation.

"I suppose," she said; and then she went into characteristic thought mode. I waited patiently. "I didn't grow up practicing my religion," she explained. "My parents didn't take us to church, so I didn't owe Christianity anything. I got married in the church because I had to. Reverend Iverson gave us lessons, and then we got married; but I never went to church. After my brother died of cancer I begin to look for answers, but the minister didn't have any answers. He meant well, but he couldn't help me. I asked him simple questions and he gave me passages from the Bible to read. I wanted to know if I would meet my brother when I died, but he didn't know. He told me to pray to Jesus. That's when I started looking someplace else for answers. I read a few books, and then you came into my life."

"That's how life works," I said, smiling at how we met in her corner store shortly after her brother died. "When the student is ready, the teacher appears."

That night I took Cathy to meet Jesus on the Mental Plane of Consciousness, which St. Paul called the third heaven in his Second Letter to the Corinthians. He was dressed in his casual tan Dockers and light cream polo shirt. They shook hands, and with a radiant smile Jesus said, "Finally, we get to meet in person."

Cathy's face lit up. "I wanted to meet you when I was a little girl," she said, her eyes as wide as saucers. "Can I ask you my question now before I forget?"

"Please," Jesus said, with the most beatific smile.

"Is my brother in heaven?" she asked, very anxious to know about her favorite brother whose unexpected death by cancer at thirty-five devastated her.

Jesus smiled, his eyes shining with love. "You know better, Cathy."

"I know; but I had to ask you," she said, and laughed.

"Yes, he's in the first heaven. The Astral Plane, actually; and he's doing very well. He's planning to return to earth in a few years," Jesus freely offered.

"Thank you. May I ask you one more question?"

"By all means," Jesus said.

"Is my sister going to be okay?" she asked; her voice fraught with emotion. Her young sister had just been diagnosed with breast cancer.

"That's in the hands of Holy Spirit," Jesus replied.

"I know. I thought I would ask anyway," Cathy said.

Jesus looked long and deep into Cathy's eyes, his eyes shining with warm, healing love. "I can see why you two get along so well. You share the same spirit."

We laughed. That's all I remember of my dream. Cathy didn't remember our experience on the inner planes. "I guess the Dream

Master doesn't want me to remember," she said when I shared it with her. "Why do you think that is?"

"I think because you met Jesus on the inner you won't have nagging doubts about my project with him out here," I conjectured. "That's why the Inner Master let us have the experience with Jesus last night. He was just reassuring you, that's all."

"I'd be much more reassured if I could remember," Cathy replied, with a look of disappointment. "How long will it take to get the first part of your Jesus book written?"

"I don't know; maybe a month," I said.

"Then you think he'll show up again?" she asked.

"I have no idea. I may continue to meet him on the inner, but it's more exciting out here. You've read Pat Montamuri's book *Talks with Soul Masters,* haven't you?"

"Yes. I enjoyed it too," Cathy said.

"So did I; but he must have a great memory to remember all those talks with the Masters that appeared to him. I hope Jesus and I talk out here so I can record our talks before they slip into the great void of my mind."

"You remember everything, O. You just think you don't, but I know you do."

"In one form or another," I said, smiling at how well Cathy knew me. "I don't have a very good memory for details, but I have a great memory for impressions. I pick up on a person's energy. I can sense their frequency. That's why I can identify people just by the sound of their voice. When I write about people I tap into their consciousness through the impressions they made on me. When I write my book it'll be the impression Jesus made on me that I'll be drawing on, because there's no way I'll be able to remember the actual words we spoke. But that's alright. The dialogue may not be verbatim, but the spirit of our dialogue will be true. I just hope I can do our dialogue justice, that's all."

"You will," Cathy assured me. "I like the way you blend real life with what you imagine. It makes your stories more real."

"That's what good literature is supposed to do," I said, and laughed.

155

"Yes; but you're problem is that you make it too damn real," Cathy said, with implied reference to the shocking effect that my first two books had on the people of St. Jude. "That's why people react the way they do to your writing. It's too much for them."

"Bob Niemond still hasn't made any comments about my books," I said, to confirm Cathy's point. "It's been three months since I gave them to him."

"I know. Except for the comment he made at our *satsang* class last month."

"What comment?"

"'*There's a thought that'll fry your brain,*'" Cathy said, quoting Bob's response to something I said at the class. "That's the effect I think your books had on him."

"What; fried his brain?" I said, with a chuckle.

"Yes. That's why he can't bring himself to talk about your books. He's a High Initiate, and he's supposed to be on a higher level than you; but you blow him away at our *satsangs*. I think that's why he wanted to see our ID cards. He wanted to see what level of Initiation you were. I'm sure of that. He's intimidated by you, O."

"Yeah, just like Stanley Hansen. Bob's never brought up the subject of writing again, either," I said, smiling at his literary pretensions. He had written a thin spiritual book that read like a dry business report, and he was working on a novel based on his experience of how Spirit brought him to the Way of the Eternal after his wife left him.

"I don't think he realized the talent you have and he's not big enough to admit it," Cathy said. "Just like our family and friends. He's no different."

That's what my dream that Carl Jung analyzed for me in my dream with him was all about; the world wanted to fit me into a pair of pants much too small for me. How do you think our spiritual community will respond to my Jesus book when it comes out?"

"Who cares? You're not writing it for them. You're writing it for the public. It's the public that needs to understand Jesus Christ's teaching, isn't it?"

"That's why Jesus wants my help to decode his sayings."

"Then do it. Don't worry about what our community will think about it. Most of them are just as resentful of you as Bob Niemond is anyway."

"I just hope they'll be able to see past their nose, that's all."

"I don't think they will. They're no different than anybody else. They just think they're different, that's all," Cathy said, revealing her true feelings.

"To be fair, sweetheart; they are different. But I know what you mean."

"I don't think they're any different than anybody else," she insisted. "If anything, I think they're more like everybody else than they think they are!"

I knew what she meant, because living the spiritual life forced our shadow to the surface for the whole world to see and tested our relationships; but I still had to be fair to our fellow chelas. "Cathy, don't take it away from them," I said. "They've earned the privilege of the most direct path to God. They just have to come to terms with their ego, that's all; and that comes in its own good time for all of us, including you."

"I can't help how I feel. They think they're better than everybody else because their on this special path, and I don't care for their attitude," she said, almost in anger.

Cathy also saw the worm of spiritual conceit that had found its way into our spiritual community, and it bothered her more than it bothered me; that's why she hated going to our spiritual functions. She only attended once in a while for my sake. "The Inner Master did tell you on your walk one night that your powers of intuition would be magnificently amplified," I said, to calm her down. *"Well I think they've kicked in!"*

We shared a good laugh; and then we had a late dinner of maple chicken that Cathy had prepared, and the next morning I began working on my Jesus book.

32. *Why Me, Jesus?*

It always takes a few chapters of a new book before it speaks to me. After I wrote chapter seven ("Disemboweling Christianity"), I heard the voice of my Jesus book. It spoke loud and clear that it was time to give the world an entirely new perspective on the Way of Christ — a new paradigm of spiritual thought, as Jesus said in the park.

That should have been obvious from my dialogue with Jesus, but it didn't hit home until I caught it on paper, as faithfully as my creative memory allowed me to do so. More importantly, I wanted to capture Jesus' unbelievable sense of irony.

Perhaps it was because Jesus and I enjoyed so much laughter that we connected in that special way. Perhaps this was the Jesus he wanted the world to see. It didn't really matter to me. All I knew as I wrote my chapters was that I laughed all over again. I saw more of the real Jesus than I experienced in our dialogue, and this fascinated me.

Such is the magic of creative writing. Spirit always reveals more during the creative process, and I decided to go with it. The voice of *Jesus Wears Dockers* had spoken, and I had to go with the emerging soul of my book. But still, I had to ask myself: *why me, Jesus?*

I had a whole library of books on Jesus and Christianity, world religions, and spirituality; but there was always something missing. I was given incredible explanations for the packaging, but little understanding of the contents; and only because I was so caught up in my own quest did I begin to see beyond the packaging and into the contents.

It was more than seeing. I *experienced* the contents of Christ's teaching. I *tasted* the truth of Christ's Way. In fact I gorged myself on the sayings of Jesus because I could not get enough of the Way of Christ. That's why I also devoured St. Paul's Epistles.

St. Paul spoke the same language of the Way that Jesus spoke. If one were to substitute *Holy Spirit* for the name *Jesus Christ* in St.

Paul's letters it would offer a much clearer picture of the Way of Life; which is what Jesus hoped to do with our dialogue.

The Way of Life is the natural way of transforming our consciousness and realizing our spiritual self, but this concept is much too deep for the exoteric Christian mind because Christianity has lost its foothold in the mesoteric circle of life. It has become firmly ensconced in the outer circle where the spiritual consciousness of man is not mature enough to appreciate the hidden meaning of Christ's sayings.

Christianity is so introverted now that all its power is focused on keeping Soul trapped in the paradigm of instant salvation through Jesus Christ. Rather than give Soul the peace of mind it needs to heal from life's painful journey, it fosters more spiritual anguish by not giving Soul the freedom to realize its divine nature.

This is why I felt suffocated by my Roman Catholic faith. As one of my elderly painting customers who had also outgrown her faith expressed her feelings, "Christianity doesn't nourish my Soul anymore." But just like the lost Soul in my poem and disaffected Christians everywhere, she was afraid to leave her religion for fear of what the community would think of the woman who had started the first bridge club in St. Jude; hence the inspiration for writing my Jesus book. *But still, why me, Jesus?*

Is it because I broke the code of Christ's sayings? Is it as simple as that? Of course, that isn't simple at all. If it were that simple Christianity wouldn't be what it is today, for such is the transformative power of the sayings of Jesus!

So profound is Christ's secret that the sayings of Jesus, if lived as Jesus intended, can take one all the way to God-realization consciousness as Jesus himself revealed when he said, *"I and my Father are one."*

Jesus was initiated into the Creative Life Stream that flows from God and back to God, and he received his Second Initiation in the Way of the Eternal by the guardian of the Golden Wisdom Temple in the remote regions of northern Tibet during the last three of his "lost years," but it was his commitment to the natural Way of Life that elevated him to the heights and made him the savior of the world that inspired the Gospel conspiracy.

The Way of Life *is* the reconciling energy of God. It is the natural wisdom of the Way that life reveals as Soul evolves from one experience to the next. As an Essene during the time of Jesus, it was my duty to scribe this special gnostic wisdom into the Great Book of Life that my fellow Essenes brought back from their sojourns in the world. I failed to penetrate the secret of the sayings in my lifetime as Samuel, and it was not until I lived many more lives that I began to drink in the gnostic wisdom from the "cups of God," which is what we called the wisdom sayings.

I have Gurdjieff to thank for this. The sayings of Jesus gave up their secret as I "worked" on myself with Gurdjieff's teaching, and if I were to guess why Jesus chose me to help him dispel the Gospel conspiracy it would be because I connected the dots all the way back to the Ocean of Love and Mercy where Soul comes from. From the inception of life on Earth all the way up the ladder of natural evolution and back home to God, I connected the dots of Soul's journey from God and back to God, and I believe Jesus chose me to reveal the role that his sayings played in helping me work out the Divine Plan of God.

In the Divine Plan of God no one religion is more relevant than another for Soul's evolution through life. This was my experience, and he wanted me to share it. One may study the sayings of Jesus until the cows come home, but not until he *lives* them will they give up their secret, and I lived them to the point where I was blessed to look into the Face of God. That's why Jesus chose me to help him dispel the Gospel conspiracy that makes him the exclusive gateway into the kingdom of heaven; or so I think, anyway.

33. *So, What Is the Way Then?*

I like the Jesus in the park. I love his sense of irony. I'm not sure I like the Jesus of the New Testament Gospels. He's much too dry, remote, and mystifying. The Jesus I saw at the worship service at the Southlake Public Library and in the park was no less mystifying, but at least he was accessible, and so down-to-earth that he made me feel like a fellow traveler on the road of life. And we are fellow travelers, really.

If what Spirit revealed to me in the Divine Plan of God is true, and I trust Divine Spirit implicitly, Soul equals Soul. No person is greater than any other person. We are all at various stages of our journey to the higher worlds of God. Jesus would be a fellow companion then, because there is no end to God-realization consciousness.

Perhaps this realization allowed us to meet. But for whatever reason Jesus chose me to help him decode his sayings, I felt so privileged that I dared not think about it too long for fear of waking up like I did at the worship service.

Jesus was there and then not there. He was an obvious member of our community, and everyone saw and heard him but only I remembered; and it put me on the spot during fellowship after the service when I asked my fellow chelas what they thought of his amazing talk on love. They gave me strange looks, like I had lost it. That's why I called it a dream vision. I don't know how this happened, nor do I know that my experience in the park with Jesus wasn't a similar experience; but he was real to me.

We ate hot dogs together. We talked to people. I touched him and he touched me. But then, the experience with Jesus at the service was no less real but only I remembered. My fellow chelas had no memory of Jesus being there; so I have no way of knowing for certain whether my experience with Jesus happened in this world or another.

That's why I asked Jesus if it mattered whether he had authored all the sayings in the Gospels. I know that the Way just *is*. I penetrated this mystery. The packaging of the Way no longer fascinated me as it once did, and by packaging I mean the medium by which the Way expresses itself in the world — be it Christianity, Judaism, Buddhism, Hinduism, Sufisim, Gnosticism, Taoism, Alchemy, Gurdjieff's Work, Jung's *individuation process*, art, poetry, running *("In running I found my salvation,"* said Dr. George Sheehan), or whatever path one finds in life. The Way is the Way is the Way, regardless how it's packaged; but the Way will only reveal itself as one *lives* the Way. This is the mystery of Christ's teaching, and the heart of the book that Jesus wanted me to write.

Descriptions of the Way are endless, because the Way is life itself. As long as there is life there will always be the Way. But this is much too esoteric for the world to see, and it will do nothing to help the reader understand what the Way is. The best way to help the reader see what the Way is would be to describe the essential purpose of life.

The spiritual journey is one of experience, and in my fourth past-life regression I experienced myself as an un-self-realized atom in the Body of God. This revealed to me that we begin our existence as atoms in the Body of God; and an atom of God is the seed of a new Soul self, like an acorn is the seed of an oak tree.

We are all un-self-realized Souls before we begin our journey through life. We have consciousness but no self-consciousness, and our purpose in life is to realize our human self-consciousness first, then our spiritual self-consciousness, and then God-realization consciousness; and we realize our encoded purpose in life through evolution.

The more experiences we have, the more we grow in our own identity; and the more self-identity we have, the more spiritually self-realized we will be. And the more spiritually self-realized we are the more conscious we become of the Spiritual Laws of Life. And as we become conscious of the Spiritual Laws of Life we begin to understand why Soul Masters come into the world to help us break the recurring cycle of life and death.

Karma and reincarnation govern our journey through life. From lifetime to lifetime, we experience life and grow in our spiritual identity. When we have realized enough identity to want to return to the higher worlds of God, we seek out the Way. We do not do this consciously, which is why one person may say "I don't know what it is about this teaching, but it feels right for me," and another person will shun the same teaching for equally unknown reasons. Every Soul is attracted to the teaching it needs for its journey back to God, and no one teaching is better than another. All teachings serve the same purpose in the Divine Plan of God, which is to help us realize our divine nature.

The sayings of Jesus are powerful precipitators; but they are mystifying because they cut through all the red tape of life. As one *lives* these sayings he speeds up his spiritual journey, and Jesus never explained how this miracle happened. He sealed the mystery of spiritual rebirth in metaphor, and this has puzzled the world.

This is why Jesus wanted to unlock the mystery of his sayings and tell the world that salvation is a personal responsibility. There is no eleventh hour salvation in his teaching. There is only spiritual growth and understanding. Having experienced this spiritual growth with his sayings to the point of experiencing my own immortality, I welcomed Christ's challenge to help him dispel the Gospel conspiracy. *So, what is the Way then?*

Besides being the experience of life itself, the Way is the conscious knowledge of spiritual growth. As an apprentice must learn the skills of his trade with effort and commitment, so must a student of the Way learn the skills of the Way to realize his divine nature; but to appreciate what the Way is one must understand man's essential purpose in life, which was revealed to me as I worked out the Divine Plan of God.

The atom of God is a soul seed that comes into life from the Body of God and evolves over eons to the stage of the primordial life of man where it has the dawning of its own self-consciousness, which I experienced during my fourth past-life regression. From this lifetime on, this dim sense of self-consciousness evolves through karma and reincarnation to the point where it begins to sense its own spiritual essence.

This is the first stage of Soul's evolution through life. It began at the inception of life, when the gases of the material world created the first building blocks of life in the amino acids. Soul entered the emerging life process of the amino acids and evolved through millions of life forms all the way up to the dawning of self-consciousness in the primordial life of man, and Soul continued to evolve through the creation and resolution of personal karma to the point where it experienced the dawning of spiritual self-consciousness.

The natural individuation process of the self in the exoteric circle of life takes place over millions of years, guided by karma and reincarnation. But nature can only evolve Soul so far in the first stage of evolution; and here, at the limits of the exoteric circle of life, a Master appears to help us realize our destiny by introducing us to the conscious knowledge of the Way, as Jesus did with his gospel of salvation.

With a conscious knowledge of the Way, man begins his journey through the mesoteric circle of life where he takes evolution out of the hands of nature (karma and reincarnation) and accepts responsibility for his own spiritual growth. It is here that the sayings of Jesus play their role in the Divine Plan of God.

Christianity can only take Soul to the mesoteric circle of life. Because Christianity believes in salvation through Jesus Christ's death upon the cross it hopes to bypass the entire mesoteric stage of evolution, which cannot be done. It is an illusion to believe that this stage of evolution through life can be short-circuited. This is why the founding fathers of Christianity condemned the Gnostics as heretics, and why Jesus wanted to reveal the hidden wisdom of his sayings to dispel the wicked Gospel conspiracy.

Christ's sayings contain the conscious knowledge of the Way, but this knowledge will only reveal itself as one *lives* the sayings; so the mesoteric circle of life can be described as that stage where Soul learns how to *live* the Way consciously. Soul takes evolution into its own hands, which is what St. Paul meant when he wrote in his Epistle to the Philippians, *"work out your own salvation with fear and trembling."*

The secret of the Way is simple: the more one *lives* the Way, the more the Way will reveal itself; and learning how to *live* the Way is what the mesoteric circle of life is all about. This means that the sayings of Jesus can best be understood in the context of taking our spiritual destiny into our own hands. In short, Jesus did not come into the world to save us, but to give us the means to save ourselves.

Salvation is Christ's metaphor for spiritual rebirth, which means spiritual self-realization consciousness. This can only take place on the Soul Plane, the first plane of the spiritual worlds of God. The lower worlds are the Physical, Astral, Causal, Mental, and Etheric (subconscious) Planes, which constitute the exoteric circle of life.

The mesoteric circle of life introduces the spiritual consciousness of the Soul Plane into the evolutionary cycle of life, and this is done by living the Way consciously (as one does by *living* the sayings of Jesus); and the more conscious one becomes of the Way, the more spiritually conscious he becomes of the Soul Plane of Consciousness.

Hence the more spiritually self-realized one becomes, the more he dwells on the Soul Plane. When one has created enough spiritual consciousness by living the Way consciously he will shift his spiritual center of gravity from the exoteric circle of life (the lower planes) to the Soul Plane where he will experience his own immortal self, as I did that memorable day in my mother's kitchen while she was kneading bread dough on the kitchen table.

Spiritual self-realization consciousness can only be experienced on the Soul Plane. This is what the sayings of Jesus are all about. He gave us his sayings to help us take our destiny into our own hands so we can evolve to the Soul Plane where we will experience our own immortal self, which Jesus called being born again. We are all Soul, then; but we are not awakened Souls. We are in the process of becoming conscious of our spiritual nature, and we awaken to our spiritual nature by living the Way consciously.

There is no instant salvation in the Divine Plan of God. There is only experience, growth, and understanding; and one day we will be spiritually mature enough to find the Way-shower who will initiate us into the Creative Life Stream which will take us all the way back home to the higher worlds of God where we came from. The Way-shower is the Way incarnate, and all ways lead to the Way-shower. It is *ipso facto*.

Strangely enough, I initiated myself into the Creative Life Stream with Gurdjieff's teaching, the sayings of Jesus, and the gnostic wisdom that I garnered from life; and because I found the Way before

I found the Way-shower I awakened to the Way of Life before I was initiated into the Way of the Eternal, which gave me what Jesus needed to help him dispel the Gospel conspiracy; and I couldn't wait for our next talk...

34. *Levi Virtue*

I had not dug out my Bible yet, so it came as a pleasant surprise to see Jesus in the food court of the Bay Mall in Carlton nursing a cup of coffee. It was as though he was waiting for me. "I'm glad you could make it," he said, with that playful smile on his distinctly memorable face. "Let me get you a coffee. Just cream?"

"Yes," I replied, bemused by Christ's appearance.

I had drafted my book as far as I could, but I didn't think he would appear until I was ready to delve into the mystery of his sayings. Maybe he felt I was ready. I had to ask when he returned with the coffee, "Why now? I haven't dug out my Bible yet."

"What's taking you so long?" he asked.

"I have a way of putting things off, I guess. But I did write our story so far."

"And?"

"And what?"

"What do you think of it so far?" Jesus asked.

"It's found its own voice," I replied, with a proud smile.

"Good," said Jesus. "That means your book speaks for the collective consciousness of our individual perspectives. When we get to my sayings it will broaden its voice to include the magnificent voice of the Way."

"I think it's done that already," I said.

"I'm not surprised," Jesus said, and took a sip of coffee. He was wearing Dockers again, a light olive green color this time, with another yellow polo shirt with a golfer's logo, and a pair of designer sunglasses hanging from the neck of his shirt. He had on a pair of New Balance runners and a gold watch on his left wrist.

"You look good in casual wear," I said, and smiled.

"Thank you. This is the new Jesus for the times. I'm not as relevant as I used to be, you know," Jesus said, with a big smirk on his face.

I couldn't help myself and broke into laughter. "And I like the message you're sending with your shoes," I instinctively said, with an ironic chuckle.

"New Balance? I thought it appropriate. After all, the spiritual life is all about finding the right balance. Don't you think so, O?"Jesus said, with a slightly provocative tone that magically dislodged the memory of my first pair of New Balance runners that I bought at PHEIDIPPIDES in Winnipeg while visiting my sister long ago, and all those wonderful memories of running along the lake in my hometown of St. Jude washed over me — including the memory of my dream that connected the holistic benefits of running with the "work" I was doing on myself with Gurdjieff's teaching and Christ's sayings!

"Is there such a thing as wrong balance?" I said, taking up the challenge.

"Of course. A person can be stuck in the outer circle of life—"

"The exoteric circle?" I pointedly interjected.

"Yes. And not until he is ready for the middle circle—"

Again I jabbed, "The mesoteric circle?"

"Yes," Jesus said, smiling at me. "Not until he is ready to find the Way will he be ready for the right balance between the material and spiritual life."

As if on cue, a young couple walked by our table. In their late teens, they both wore Levi jeans all frayed and full of tears and holes. I couldn't help but snicker to myself as they walked by. Jesus picked up on my thoughts and gave me a big smile.

"False virtue," I said, replying to Christ's all-knowing smile.

"Yes. That's what I mean by right balance," he said. "That young couple is caught up in the currents of daily fashion, which speaks to the outer circle of life—"

"The shallow end of life, you mean!" I interjected.

"Yes, it is shallow. But at least they have a sense of the virtue that they wish to affect with their clothes," Jesus said.

"What? The virtue of honest labor?"

"Of course," he said.

The irony forced me to laugh. "If only those kids knew what I had to do to get my jeans to look like theirs. *Talk about work!"*

"Why don't you tell me, just to see where the Way will take us today?"

"I'd love to," I said, and just as I said that my Muse flashed the title for my next chapter across my mind and I burst into laughter.

"What?" Jesus asked.

"Levi Virtue," I replied, repressing the irony.

"Levi virtue?" Jesus said, puzzled.

"That's the title of my next chapter. My Muse just flashed that across my mind to reveal the ironic nature of the affectatious life."

"Affectatious? Is there such a word?" Jesus asked, with a subtle smile.

"If there isn't, there is now," I replied, returning the smile. "Affectation. Noun for pretense, display, or assumed manner of behavior. Affectatious. Adjective. Those kids would say they're making a fashion statement with their clothes, but in truth they want to affect the virtue of honest labor with their stressed jeans; ergo, affectatious."

"The affectatious life? That makes my point," Jesus said. "By affecting the virtue of life it shows they are at least conscious of the real virtue of life. You were telling me about your own jeans. No; don't bother. You were going to tell me how hard you worked to wear your jeans out to look like the stressed jeans that young couple is wearing."

"I wore out three pairs of jeans by the time I finished building my triplex up north, so I know the difference between the virtue of honest labor and Levi virtue!"

"I love it. You've made your point so it never fades. You've even created your own words — *affectatious* and *Levi virtue*. That's your creative genius, O!"

Something about Christ's voice made me feel more foolish than proud, like he was poking fun at my disarming wit. "Let's not get carried away, J," I replied, centering myself. "I connect the dots more quickly than most people; that's all."

"Same thing," Jesus said, with that playful twinkle in his eyes. "For the sake of the reader, explain the difference between false and real virtue?"

"Yes, of course, the reader. We mustn't forget him, must we? Well there's not much more I can say, is there? Either one works for one's virtue or one doesn't. You can't slap on virtue like after-shave lotion. It doesn't work like that. In fact, even if one is living the spiritual life he can still get caught up in Levi virtue!"

"Pardon me?" Jesus said, with a puzzled look. "I don't follow that. How can one living the spiritual life fall prey to false virtue?"

"*'Get thee behind me Satan!'*" I quoted, with a wry chuckle "Didn't you say that to one of your own disciples?"

Jesus sat upright and stared at me long and hard. "As a matter of fact, I said that to Peter. Of course, I see where you're going with this. Please, continue."

"Alright," I said, smiling at the insight Spirit had just given me to make my point about virtue. "You see that young couple with their stressed Levis?"

Jesus turned to look. "Yes. What about them?"

"Let me show you the other end of this spectrum," I said, as Bob Niemond popped into my mind. "I know a High Initiate in my spiritual community who refuses to wear jeans altogether. He feels he's above wearing blue jeans. They're too pedestrian for him."

"There's no end to the ironies of life, is there?" said Jesus.

"Not only does he refuse to wear jeans," I added, with that guilt that gets stuck in my throat whenever I feel that I'm gossiping, "his personality is fraught with all kinds of amusing idiosyncrasies that prop up the elitist image he wants to project to the world."

"Name one," Jesus said, with hint of mischief in his voice.

"I can't. He'd only spot himself when I write this chapter," I said.

"Do you think he won't see himself as it is? Don't count on it, O. The male ego is much more sensitive than the female ego will ever be. The moment he reads that he is above wearing blue jeans it will set off a cataclysm of reactive emotions. Be that as it may, you do make your point about false and real virtue. This is what we want to do for this book. My sayings are all about seeing the distinction between the two selves of man."

"*And learning how to create real virtue!*" I added excitedly.

"Of course. It's the virtue of real life that nourishes Soul."

"That's the conclusion I came to as I lived your sayings, J," I said, smiling at how Spirit had made its point. "This is why I made goodness my ideal virtue. If I may, let me quote my favorite lines in all of literature. 'He labors good on good to fix, and owes/ To virtue every triumph that he knows.' They're from *'Character of the Happy Warrior,'* by William Wordsworth. They make my point about the spiritual life better than anything I've ever read — including your sayings, J. Let me take this theme one step further, if I may."

"By all means take it all the way to its conclusion. That's what a good Socratic dialogue should do."

"Speaking of Socrates, do you think I can get to see him again?" I asked.

"We'll see. Continue with your thought, if you would," Jesus said.

"My thought has to do with the consciousness of authenticity," I continued, and suddenly stopped in mid thought. I was nudged to connect more deeply with the Creative Life Current. I shut my eyes to call upon the Inner Master. I did a silent HU, and then I used my secret word for a better connection. I opened my eyes. Jesus was smiling, waiting patiently. I continued: "There's a difference between the authentic life and spiritual life. I didn't realize this until I worked out the Divine Plan of God. I had always thought that the more authentic one became, the more spiritually realized he would be; but I learned that the spiritual life presupposes the authentic life. One can be as authentic as one can be and still not realize his spiritual self. As I learned from my spiritual community, one can be a High Initiate and still be false in many ways. It takes a long time to resolve the consciousness of one's falseness, as I pointed out with the H. I. who's above wearing jeans—"

I burst into laughter. From the lofty perspective of the DPG, the absurdity of clinging to such petty pretensions reminded me of the scales of justice of my youth when I measured the absurd imbalance of one mortal sin against eternal damnation. The irony was too much, and I keeled over with laughter. Jesus waited for me to have my fun. The look on his face told me that I had gone far enough, and I composed myself.

171

"What are you saying, then?" Jesus asked. "That there is a difference between the consciousness of authenticity and spirituality?"

"In effect, yes. The authentic life is by no means the spiritual life. Take the image of *Cool Hand Luke,* for example. Paul Newman's portrayal of a natural man; or a *blasé* Parisian intellectual smoking his *Gauloises* with the casual intensity of a man whose every pleasure speaks his whole life. Sartre, Camus, Hemingway. Their novels reek of authenticity. But this authenticity speaks to the existential self, not the spiritual self. That's what I'm trying to say. Even the consciousness of authenticity has to be transformed for one to realize his true spiritual self. To be honest with you, J; I'm not so sure the consciousness of authenticity is any less difficult to transform than one's falseness — *if not more so!"*

With that, Jesus smiled and stood up. "This coffee is going right through me," he said. "Look, O; find your Bible and refresh your memory, please. Given what you've just said, I think we're ready to reveal the secrets of my sayings."

"I think so, too," I was forced to agree.

"Have a nice day, O," Jesus said, with a wave of his hand.

"Thank you," I said, and watched Jesus softly walk away.

I wanted to see if he would come out of the washroom, but he didn't. I wanted to go and check, but I couldn't. I got another cup of coffee and made some notes in my pocket notebook that I always carry with me whenever I'm working on a new book, and I couldn't wait to share my surprise Jesus experience with Cathy.

35. *Would You Take Out the Garbage for Me, Please?*

I reflected for days on my last conversation with Jesus, which I shared with Cathy the moment she came home from work. Her response brought to mind what the Living Soul Master's wife said to him while he went on about some lofty spiritual subject. "That's nice, dear," she said. "Would you take out the garbage for me, please?"

He laughed when he told this story in one of his public talks, because he saw the wisdom of right balance. He was bringing out the ancient teachings of the Light and Sound of God, and he was forever thinking about how to best present the teachings to the modern world, so his mind was always preoccupied; but his wife kept him balanced.

"That would make a great title for my next chapter," I thought, as my Muse flashed the thought across my mind. Taking out the garbage was a wonderful metaphor for the process of self-transformation, which Christ's sayings were all about; but I didn't have Jesus to share my thought with. That's when the idea struck me.

I went to my bonus room above the garage of our new home a few minutes' walk from Georgian Bay, which I used for my writing den, and sat at my desk with my eyes closed. I did a long HU chant, visualizing the HU flowing in spiritual waves all the way to Jesus in the inner worlds, and then I visualized him riding the HU waves back to my den and sitting in my reading chair beside my desk. This was the same technique that the Living Soul Master used to call his own teacher before he became the Living Soul Master.

"What do you think of my metaphor?" I asked, out loud.

"I think it's wonderful," I heard Jesus reply. I opened my eyes. *Jesus was sitting in my reading chair!* "You haven't dug up your Bible yet," he added, with that same playful smile on his clean-shaven, striking face.

"I meant to," I said, nonplussed. "I got caught up writing my last chapter."

"I can accept that. What is it you want to talk about this morning? The metaphor of spiritual cleansing?" Jesus asked, with a casual indifference that made me smile.

"It's not really a metaphor, is it?" I said, and laughed. I couldn't help myself.

"Of course not," Jesus said, in the same tone of indifference. "It's as much a cleansing process as taking out the garbage. But there is no other way around this, is there? Didn't Socrates say something to that effect? *'And what is purification but the separation of the Soul from the body, the habit of Soul gathering and collecting herself into herself?'"* Jesus said, quoting from Plato's *Phaedo*.

I thought for a moment. "What we're saying then is that in order to have the right balance in life we have to remove the garbage from our life? That's the gist of this concept, isn't it?" I asked, amazed at how quickly Divine Spirit had set the course of our talk.

"Exactly," said Jesus, his eyes now alight with love. "But we have to talk about what this garbage is so the reader will know what to take out."

"What about the passions of the mind? That's a good place to start."

"Good. I never thought of the five destructive passions of the mind. I was thinking more in terms of the seven deadly sins."

"No way!" I exclaimed. "Let's get out of this whole sin thing! We want the reader to step outside the box of blind Christian faith, not deeper into the box!"

Jesus laughed. "If he's ready."

"Of course. I wouldn't expect every Christian to understand what we're talking about. No doubt there will be those that will denounce my book as the Devil's work!"

"That's par for the course. But let's not go there, O. I have no heart for that topic today," Jesus said as he crossed his legs for comfort.

"But we'll have to deal with it one day, won't we?" I said.

"Of course. How can we talk about my sayings and not reveal the truth about the Devil's work?" Jesus said, so matter-of-factly it made me feel foolish for asking.

"If only Christians knew the truth about the Devil's work!" I quickly responded.

"If only," Jesus said, with a heavy sigh. "But we're not there yet, O; so let's talk about taking out the garbage."

"The reader won't have a clue what we're talking about unless we establish the principle that your whole teaching is based on," I said, to Christ's surprise.

"I give you the floor," he said, with an approving smile.

"You don't mind?" I said.

"Why should I? If you can reveal the principle upon which my whole teaching is based, I'll be in your debt forever!"

"Sure you will. Let's get one thing clear, J. There is no one way to capture the teaching of the Way, because the Way cannot be revealed by one way only—"

"But it can," Jesus interrupted. "Each perspective of the Way reveals the whole Way. What you're trying to say is that each perspective of the Way is unique in its revelation of the Way. The Way is always the Way, regardless how it is revealed."

I reflected on Christ's words. "I'm not sure I meant it like that. I agree with you, but I think I was going for something else. What I hope to get across to the reader is that the principle of your teaching opens the door to the Way. Once one captures the principle of your teaching, he will have the key to unlocking the secret of all your sayings."

"Wow! Please, let's hear what this principle is," Jesus said.

"I don't know what it is yet," I replied, with a self-conscious smile. "I feel it approaching, but it's not here yet. I'll have to do a short contemplation to see if I can capture it before its time."

"Before its time?" Jesus queried.

"If it was meant to be revealed now, it would be here. I'll see if I can entice it with the HU," I said, and silently called upon the Inner Master's help.

"By all means," Jesus said, and sat back in his chair.

I did a short audible HU. Jesus joined me. With each chant of HU, the thought approached me. Finally, I saw it clearly. "The principle upon which your teaching is based is the principle of metaphorical death. Once the reader sees that your whole teaching has to do with this metaphorical death, he will understand your sayings. In one way or another, your sayings all come back to the death of the lower self. So, taking out the garbage is just another metaphor for this death of the lower self. Didn't Socrates also say in the *Phaedo*: *'The true disciple of philosophy* (by philosophy he meant the Way) *is likely to be misunderstood by other men because they do not perceive that he is ever pursuing death and dying?'* This Socratic death is the same in your sayings. But the reader will never grasp this concept of dying metaphorically unless he can see the logic behind it."

"Then explain the logic," said Jesus, with a big smile on his face.

"Nope. I give the floor to you. This is your teaching; and you can take the mystery out of it for the reader," I replied, and laughed.

"The ball's in my court, is it? Okay, I'll take the mystery out of my teaching; but I have to speak in the idiom of the day."

"Of course," I said, smiling with anticipation.

"What I could not get across in my time was the complex nature of the self," Jesus said, very thoughtfully. "St. Paul's phrase 'selfsame thing' comes closest to the true nature of the self, but even this expression has its limits. To be honest with you, O; I like the way you captured the self in your waking dream novel. In your talk with Doctor Jung you made it very clear what the self is. I'd like to borrow some of your concepts, if I may."

I laughed at the thought of Jesus quoting from my book that wasn't even published yet. Jesus picked up on my thoughts, and laughed too. "We are in this together, aren't we?"

"You're right. What difference does it make if you quote me, as long as we get the point across? Please, be my guest."

"Okay," Jesus said. "I want to get across the simple point that the atom of God is both the human and spiritual self. You make this clear in your book *The Way of Soul* that Doctor Jung liked so much. Each Soul is an atom of God, and this atom of God evolves in life. As it evolves it creates a human self. Out of this human self is born the spiritual self. For the atom of God to become fully self-realized, it has to transform the consciousness of its human self. This transformation of the human self is what my teaching is all about. You are absolutely correct to hold that the principle upon which my teaching is based is the metaphorical death of the human self. There, does that meet with your approval?"

"My approval? What the hell is the reader going to think about me when he reads that Jesus Christ needs my approval?"

"That you're an awakened Soul helping me to explain the mystery of my teaching. And please cut out the swear words, will you?"

"Sorry. I just don't want the reader to get the wrong impression. I'm a writer with a gift for letting Soul speak, so there's no need to foster a false image. Fair enough?"

"Fair enough. Can we get to the point now?"

"Which is?"

"Taking out the garbage."

"I thought we had captured that in the principle of your teaching?"

"You give the reader too much credit. Don't make the same mistake I made two thousand years ago. That's why I'm here to explain my teaching."

"I'm stuck between a rock and a hard place, aren't I?"

"Yes. You're damned if you do and damned if you don't. Finding the right balance is not easy; but you'll find it. I have all the confidence in you, O," Jesus said.

"Amazing!" I exclaimed. "But does such a balance exist?" I asked. "Where is that happy medium where the spiritually blind can see enough to understand the Way and the sighted are not offended by the simplicity of the Way? Does such a medium exist, J?"

"That is a challenge, isn't?" Jesus said, with a big smirk.

"If only the reader could appreciate our sense of humor!" I burst out.

"That's the whole point, isn't it? He has to see enough to capture what we imply in our talks but not be offended by what he captures. So, O; your challenge is to make clear the unclear," Jesus calmly said.

"That's the challenge of your whole teaching! If you had made your gospel clear in the first place Christianity wouldn't have muddled the bloody puddle, and you wouldn't be here trying to undo centuries of misunderstanding; would you?"

"I know," Jesus sighed. *"Ain't hindsight grand?"*

36. *Breaking the Law of Silence*

It felt strange knowing that Jesus could appear at any moment. It was like being transported to another world within the same world where everything was exactly the same but entirely different. I couldn't quite wrap my head around the concept of parallel worlds, but that's what the spiritual life was all about.

My spiritual community knew this. The spiritual experiences that chelas have on a regular basis would shock most people. That's why Soul Masters stress the Law of Silence for initiates of the Way. Yet I was writing a book that would tax even the most devout believers of the spiritual life; but I felt compelled to reveal the Way.

Indeed, the whole point of our dialogue was to decode the secret of his sayings so Jesus could dispel the Gospel conspiracy. I had stepped into the esoteric circle of spiritual evolution and looked into the Face of God, and I had no choice but to help Jesus.

"God-realized people know that they must pass along all the knowledge they have. You cannot keep the knowledge to yourself unless you would lose it for yourself," said the Living Soul Master in *The Heart's Wisdom*. *"Besides, didn't Jesus also say that we should not hide our light under a bushel?"* I said to myself, and snickered.

"That's precisely what I said!" Jesus exclaimed, in my mind.

I bolted in my chair. After a moment or two, I said, "So now it's telepathy, is it?"

"Are you receiving me?" Jesus asked, in a playful voice.

"Loud and clear," I replied, out loud.

"Good. I just want you to experience this form of communication to broaden your spiritual horizons. I can manifest if you want."

"No, please don't," I said, telepathically. *"Let's do it this way for a while. I want to experience this private mode of communication with another Soul Master. I've read about it, and I experience it with the Living Soul Master in small doses; but I'd like to carry on a conversation telepathically just for the sake of the experience, if you don't mind."*

"Of course not. Have you dug up your Bible yet?"

I laughed out loud. *"No,"* I said.

"Do you really need to?" Jesus asked.

I had an urge to speak out, but I caught myself. *"Yes,"* I replied.

"Why?" Jesus asked.

"I want the reader to see the context of your sayings. I think it's important that we let the reader come to the realization that it's what you say that's important to their spiritual growth, not you per se."

"That's good. Do you want to talk about the Law of Silence?"

"Yes. What can you tell me about it?"

"Nothing you don't already know," Jesus said, and laughed.

Something about Christ's laughter made me sit up and take notice. *"Are you trying to tell me something?"* I asked.

"Yes."

"What?"

"How do you know the voice you hear is the voice of Jesus Christ and not some astral entity, or an archetypal matrix of energy conjured up by your own mind?"

"Stop messing with my mind, J!" I exclaimed vocally.

Again, Jesus laughed. This time it was out loud. He was sitting in my reading chair with a big grin on his face! "Why did you do that?" I asked.

"To give the reader a taste of the broad range of the spiritual life. That's the problem with the modern world, O; it has little imagination for the spiritual life. Science has stifled man's spiritual imagination. It's time we took the straightjacket off, don't you think?"

"Yes, I do," I agreed. "This is why I'm happy to see programs on television like *The Other Side, Beyond Reality, Mysterious Ways,* and *Crossing Over with John Edwards.* They speak to the full potential of man. But they also offer the skeptic's perspective, like the magician James Randi; or that neuroscientist Michael Persinger from Laurentian University in Sudbury who reduces the spiritual life of man to brain chemistry!"

Jesus smiled. "There will always be skeptics, O. But that's not our concern here. As you're so fond of saying, 'there is only self-initiation into the mysteries of life.' This brings us back to the point. The Law of Silence is there for a reason. Initiates of the Way must obey the Spiritual Law of Silence until they are strong enough to withstand the cynical blows of life. But the world cannot harm you any more, O. You do remember the early days of your quest before you took your vow of silence, don't you?"

"I certainly do," I said, with some embarrassment. "I got the strangest looks from people until I woke up to the effect I was having on them. That's when Gurdjieff made me promise in a dream one night to not speak about the Work. This gave me an incredible sense of freedom. I became invisible. What a sweet feeling it was, knowing that the world couldn't see the real me. I created a mystique about myself, and I loved it. I still do, despite how vociferous I can be about the Way without talking about the Way. I just love the irony of being in the spiritual know, J; especially since I've been initiated into the holy mysteries of the Divine Plan of God. But that goes with the territory, doesn't it?"

"Yes, it does. Even so, you still have to protect yourself from the world. You can't be too mysterious, O. Society can't deal with anything that threatens its image, and this image does not include the spiritual dimension of life as you experience it."

"And my spiritual community," I quickly added.

"Yes. Your community threatens society also with its comprehensive understanding of the Way. But that's changing. The more your spiritual community grows, the less threatened society will be by the new religion of the Light and Sound of God."

"Isn't that amazing, J?" I said, bemused by the whole thing.

"What?" Jesus asked, with a puzzled look.

"The world will accept you with open arms if you show an interest in the spiritual life, and even commend you for it; but woe to you should you actually begin to experience the mysteries of the spiritual life, like I'm doing with you for example. *God forbid!*"

"That's so true," said Jesus, and laughed at the irony.

"We're not breaking any spiritual laws with *Jesus Wears Dockers*, then?" I asked.

"Not that I'm aware of. It's a free country, isn't it? Freedom of expression is the cornerstone of our democracy, is it not? Not to mention God's gift to Soul. Don't worry about it, O. Keep writing, and one of these fine days we'll get to my sayings—"

I burst into laughter. I just loved Christ's non-judgmental cheeky sense of humor. But when I stopped laughing Jesus was gone. He had made the point he had come to make, so I sheepishly went down to the basement to dig up my Bible!

37. *The Greater Wisdom in My Box of Books*

It took most of the afternoon, but I finally found my Bible. It was in a box full of reference books, which I found rather amusing in that Golden-tongue Wisdom kind of way that Spirit sometimes humors me with, because I had not packed my books; Cathy did, and she had no way of knowing the message that Spirit was sending me.

My Bible was at the bottom of the box. My five volume set of *The Dictionary of the History of Ideas*, my *Psychiatric Dictionary*, my *Reader's Digest Great Encyclopedic Dictionary*, and the *Cambridge Biographical Dictionary*, all speaking to man's perennial quest to expand his mind, were piled on top of my Bible; but when I took my Bible out, I said, "How fitting that it should be at the very bottom!"

The sayings of Jesus were in the Bible. They were the most valuable information in my box of books, despite the impressive stature of the other books; and I found it ironic that the gnostic sayings of Jesus Christ should be so burdened by all of man's mental knowledge, because this was Divine Spirit's way of telling me that one has to dig deep into the box of life to find the wisdom of the Way!

As I leafed through my Bible just to recapture the feeling of the thousands of times that I had it in my hands ferreting out the hidden meaning of Christ's sayings, I said to myself, *"Okay, J; now we can begin the book proper and dispel this Gospel conspiracy that you're so fixed on!"* And the next morning I opened my Bible to Mathew and read the first Gospel, and all the memories came flooding back. The first thing I noticed was with what greater clarity I discerned the Way in the red letters of Christ's words!

I hadn't picked up my Bible in years; but I had grown considerably in spiritual consciousness with each new initiation that I received in the Way of the Eternal, not to mention the wisdom I received from my experience of taking in the Golden Light of God on the Ninth Plane of Consciousness during my last past-life regression. I looked forward to reading the Gospels of Christ again, just to see how they would read from my new spiritual perspective that now included my initiation into the Divine Plan of God!

After I read Mathew's Gospel I knew that I would have to make it clear to Jesus that we would have to explain the central metaphor of his teaching that he used to introduce the Way to the world; so I made a note to begin my next chapter with the title that my Muse had provided for me — "The Greater Wisdom In My Box of Books."

This greater wisdom was the wisdom of the Way, which all of life's quests lead to. This is what Jesus meant with his saying, *"Seek ye first the kingdom of God and all else will be given unto you,"* because this is what life prepares Soul for. I didn't really have to read the other Gospels to begin the discourse proper on the sayings of Jesus, and I couldn't wait for Jesus to show up again.

I sat at my desk after I read Mathew's Gospel and tried the same technique to connect with Jesus, but Jesus neither spoke to me nor did he appear in my reading chair. "So, what's the problem?" I said, out loud. I waited for an answer, but none came. I decided to begin my new chapter anyway after I saw Cathy off to work. As I wrote the first few pages I felt someone watching me. I turned to look, and I saw Jesus standing behind me.

"I waited for Cathy to leave for work," he explained.

"Oh," I said, relieved to hear his explanation. "Okay, before I forget let me say something at the outset of our discourse—"

"Hold your horses," Jesus said, holding up his hand. "Just relax, O. Let the waters of living truth flow gently. We have plenty of time to let Soul speak. Just relax. We should do a short HU to set the right atmosphere."

I chuckled. "Yes, we should. I'm just excited, that's all."

We sang the Love Song to God for a minute or so; and then, in unison, we said, "May the blessings be." We opened our eyes, looked at each other, and smiled.

"You wanted to say something?" Jesus said, breaking the sweet silence.

"I wanted to begin with your first metaphor for the Way in the Gospels, but during the HU I got the strongest nudge to begin with the narrative of your life."

"Why do you think that is?" Jesus asked, with that all knowing smile in his eyes.

"It's the narrative of your life that has the greater impact on the reader's psyche," I said, suddenly catching on to why he wanted us to do a HU first, so he could plant the seed of our talk. "Your life can be overwhelming when it's laced with all those mystifying parables and metaphors, and I think we have to address this technique that the Gospel writers used for creating images in the reader's mind. Don't you think so, J?"

"I'm not following you," Jesus said, again teasing me with his smile.

"I doubt that very much. You're just saying that for the reader's sake, aren't you?"

"Of course," he said, with a playful wink.

I laughed. "Alright, let me tell you then. The more I got into Mathew's Gospel, the more convinced I became of the Living Soul Master's comment about the Bible."

"Which is?" Jesus asked.

"That it's mostly a work of dialectical fiction," I said.

"You're saying that as you read the Gospel of St. Mathew you felt more and more like it was a work of the imagination?" Jesus asked, setting the stage.

"It's not quite as simple as that. You see, J; I'm good at blending the real with the imagined. I have two novel memoirs that attest to this narrative technique, as well as several boxes of manuscripts. This skill can be very effective. In fact, the narrative can be so convincing when the author blends the real with the imagined in that special way that magnifies truth that it can affect a reader's life. Like *The Glass Bead Game* by Hesse; *The Old Man and the Sea* by Hemingway; and especially *The Razor's Edge* by Somerset Maugham that combusted my quest for my true self when I was in high school; and at the risk of offending our readers, my gut tells me that Mathew's Gospel falls into this category of great writing!"

"Great creative writing, you mean?" Jesus said, his eyes sparkling with excitement.

"Yes. Exactly," I said, trying to read the expression on his face.

"I agree. Mathew took what he knew of my life, blended it with his knowledge of the Way, and created this great narrative about my life — *and the rest, as I keep telling you, is the Gospel conspiracy!"* Jesus burst into laughter. He couldn't help himself.

I joined him. When we stopped laughing, I said, "But it's not the narrative of your life that we're going to focus on here, is it?"

"Nope," Jesus blurted out.

"Then you'd better explain to the reader why not."

"I want to focus on the secret knowledge of my sayings. The Gospel conspiracy will keep the scholars busy until the end of the Christian cycle, so why bother? It's my sayings that I want to talk about, because that's the real narrative of my life."

I chuckled, and then I broke into a full laugh.

"What?" Jesus asked.

"I was just thinking of one of the writers that I studied in my own quest."

"Who?" Jesus asked, drawing me out for the reader.

"Carlos Castaneda. I was fascinated by the main character of his books, a man called Don Juan, because I spotted some of Gurdjieff's principles in this 'man of knowledge.' But by the time I got to Castaneda's third book I began to smell something fishy."

"Meaning?" Jesus asked.

"My writer's instinct flashed a red flag. I dug a little deeper and found other skeptics who felt as I did, like the novelist Joyce Carol Oates who spotted the creative writer's technique in his so called non-fiction books. I studied *The Don Juan Papers* by Richard de Mille, and then I read a few more of Castaneda's books just to convince myself, and I dropped his teaching altogether. Castaneda proved to be a clever writer who could weave a great tale of fact and fiction. He got stuck in the psychic worlds and brought his readers along with him in the fantasies that he spun. He seduced a lot of people with the mystique of his occult teaching; but not as many people as the Gospel writers have fooled!"

I broke into laughter. Jesus just stared at me. "What can I say, O? I did what I had to do. What the Gospel writers did with my life is their responsibility, not mine."

185

"You can't pass the buck like that," I shot back. *"The Gospels are responsible for the greatest monumental edifice of illusion that the world has ever known!"*

"You mean Christianity?" Jesus calmly replied, with a subtle smirk.

"YES!" I blurted out, full of explosive emotion.

"That's the Gospel conspiracy, O. But Soul has to start its journey back to God somewhere, doesn't it?" Jesus quietly responded, his eyes glowing with glee.

"I know that. But Soul doesn't have to be stuck in one place for centuries, does it?" I said, not understanding Christ's calm composure.

"You're right. And what do you propose we do about it?"

"Tell the truth about your teaching!" I exploded, and burst into laughter.

"But I did tell the truth," Jesus very calmly replied, smiling at my show of emotion.

"I know you told the truth. I can see that. And so can anyone who has eyes to see. What we have to do now is make this truth accessible to the partially sighted—"

"The partially sighted? Now who's talking in riddles?" Jesus said, and laughed.

"Never mind," I said. "I'll explain this as I write my story. What we have to do now is let the reader know that it's not the narrative of your life that's important — your birth, mission, crucifixion, and resurrection, if you will — but the hidden truth of your sayings."

"Fair enough. So, we're going to start with Mathew, Chapter 5, verse 37."

"Which is?" I asked.

"Look it up," Jesus said.

I did. It read: ***"But let your communication be, Yea yea; Nay, nay; for whatsoever is more than this cometh of evil."***

Instantly Gurdjieff came to mind, and I quoted the explanatory saying that was inscribed on a special script of Gurdjieff's aphorisms on the wall of the study hall of the Priory in Fontainebleau, France where Gurdjieff had established his Institute for the Harmonious Development of Man: *"Blessed is he who has a soul, blessed is he who has none; but woe and grief to him who has it in embryo."*

Jesus gave me the sweetest smile, his eyes lighting up with all the love they could reflect, and I felt the atmosphere of the room change as it filled up with the overwhelming love of Holy Spirit, and for the first time I smelled the sweet scent of the Holy.

"You're off to a good start," Jesus said, his words filling me with all the confidence I would need to let Soul speak on the mysterious sayings of Jesus Christ.

Smiling at Jesus, I said, "Thank you. I think I know why you chose this saying to begin our discourse; but if you don't mind, I'd like to take a break. I feel a powerful tide surging, but I need my best energies to let Soul speak freely. What do you say we continue this tomorrow morning? I need time to consolidate my perspective."

Jesus nodded. "I understand completely," he said. "Until tomorrow morning then," he added, and disappeared before my eyes.

38. *A Journey through the Consciousness of Jesus Christ*

After Cathy left for work the next morning I did a twenty minute Love Song to God. As I was HU-ing I heard another voice. I knew it was Jesus, but I did not open my eyes. We brought the HU to a gentle close, and then I said, "May the blessings be."

"Good morning, J," I said, with a contented smile.

"And a good morning to you, O," Jesus replied. "Would you like to sit in silence for a few minutes?"

"We could," I said.

"Good," said Jesus, and closed his eyes.

The silence was necessary to listen to the Holy Sound of God that we had set free with the Love Song to God. As I listened, I heard the Voice of Silence; and it inspired me to read the entire text of the saying that Jesus wanted me to explain.

I opened my eyes, opened the Bible, and read Chapter 5 of Mathew's Gospel. As I read, I felt the surging tide of Spirit again, and I knew I was ready to take on what I felt to be the second most challenging creative effort of my entire life after working out the Divine Pan of God — *a journey through the consciousness of Jesus Christ!*

I turned to look at Jesus, who waited patiently for me to begin the discourse on his sayings. "We can begin," I said, with excitement and fear in my voice. "But before we do, I would like to ask for your blessing. I know my Muse is going to explore the consciousness of Jesus Christ, and it would be fitting to have your blessing before I set out on this incredible adventure into the mystery of your sayings."

Jesus stood up, took a few steps to my chair, put one hand on each of my shoulders, and said: "In the name of Jesus Christ, son of Joseph and Mary, I grant you permission to enter the mind and Soul of the savior of the world. You may reveal the secret of my sayings." With that, he bent over and kissed the top of my head and sat down.

Surprised by the drama, I said, "Thank you."

"You're welcome," Jesus replied, with that playful smile.

"Savior of the world?" I queried, playing along.

"Yes. I have to be true to form, don't I? After all, I did hear the voice of Holy Spirit speaking to me when John baptized me. Did not Mathew write, 'He saw the Spirit of God descend like a dove, and lighting upon him. And lo a voice from heaven saying, This is my beloved Son in whom I am well pleased?' Chapter 3, verses 16 and 17."

"So, because the voice called you 'my beloved Son' you took that to mean that you were the savior of the world?" I asked Jesus.

I could tell by the twinkle in his eyes that he was leading me somewhere, but I had no idea where. I asked him my question to get an answer to his comment about being the savior of the world, because I had to clear up this concept before I took my first step into his private life.

"I did and I didn't," Jesus replied, his eyes now sparkling. "Why don't you flip to Mathew 13, verses 37 and 38, and then tell me what I meant."

"Tell you, or the reader?" I said and smiled because I got a very strong feeling where he was taking me.

"The reader, of course," said Jesus.

I flipped to Mathew 13, and read: *"'He that soweth the good seed is the Son of man. The field is the world, the good seed are the children of the kingdom; but the tares are the children of the wicked one.'"*

I was right. Jesus wanted me to see that he was the savior of the world only insomuch that he brought the Way into the world for Soul to liberate itself from the cycle of life and death. I continued to read, because I saw an opportunity to have Jesus explain the mystery of the end of the world: *"'The enemy that sowed them* (the tares) *is the devil, the harvest is the end of the world; and the reapers are the angels.'"*

I stopped, but Jesus said, "Complete the chapter, and we will reveal the truth about damnation once and for all."

I turned to my Bible and read the rest of Chapter 13, verses 40-43: *"'And therefore the tares are gathered and burned in the fire; so shall it be in the end of this world. The Son of man shall send forth his angels, and they shall gather out of his kingdom all things that offend, and them which do iniquity. And shall cast them*

189

into a furnace of fire: there shall be wailing and gnashing of teeth. Then shall the righteous shine forth as the sun in the kingdom of their Father. <u>Who hath ears to hear, let him hear.</u>'"

I deliberately underscored with my voice the last line **"Who hath ears to hear, let him hear,"** and then I broke into laughter because I caught on to what Jesus had done.

Jesus smiled. "I knew you would see the humor," he said. "But the reader will have absolutely no idea what you are laughing at."

"I know. But your tactic—"

"My tactic?" Jesus said, feigning surprise.

"Don't pretend with me, J. I see through your ploy. I just got a flashback of this same tactic that I was trained to use when I was a salesman the year before I went to university to study philosophy."

"Oh? Then maybe you should explain this tactic?" Jesus said, with a big grin.

"Of course," I said, laughing at the brilliance of Christ's tactic. "It's the hit-them-between-the-eyes tactic. In other words, give the customer the full price of the product that you're trying to sell them first, and shock the hell out of them — if you will pardon the pun," I added, and laughed some more. "After they have been hit between the eyes with the full cost of the product, you explain all the benefits of the product; how it works, what it can do for you, and why it's worth every cent of the price they are asked to pay. This, if I may say so, is a stroke of pure genius on your part to start our discourse on your sayings by telling the reader the price it will cost him for the product you tried to sell the world two thousand year ago!"

Jesus burst into laughter. "You're amazing!" he said. *"You heard, and now you speak!* What a joy it is to watch how your mind works! Please explain for the reader what we have just done here."

"Where to start?" I said, still laughing at the brilliance of Christ's tactic. "Okay, I know where," I said, as Spirit flashed the thought across my mind. "You tried to sell a product two thousand years ago. This product was the Way. You dressed the Way up in parables and metaphors, but the price tag you put on the product puzzled people, because they could not see the meaning of your parables and metaphors. In fact, I would say that the world has taken

190

the packaging for the content. This is where all the problems with Christianity arise. The world has taken your sayings much too literally, because only those who are evolved enough spiritually can see through the packaging into the content of the Way. I can see the Way in your teaching, so I have to explain to the reader what you were trying to do."

"Please do," Jesus said, with an eager wave of his hand.

"Another thought just crossed my mind. Remind me to explain the product that I sold, because it is coincidental to my explanation of the Way of Christ," I said, and laughed again at how Spirit was directing the drama of our first discourse on Christ's sayings.

"Tell me now," Jesus said.

"Okay. I sold a product called University Scholarships of Canada. It was a trust fund. Parents put money aside each month for their child's university education. This speaks to your metaphor of storing our treasures in heaven. The point being that wise investment is necessary to get to the kingdom of heaven."

"Brilliant!" said Jesus. "Alright, let's hit the reader between the eyes with the cost of my product, as you put it!"

"In the simplest terms possible," I said, knowing exactly what to say, "the product that you're selling is the Way, and the cost of your product is the sacrifice of the lower self. Pay the price, and you enter into the kingdom of God. Don't pay the price, and you will remain in the endless cycle of life and death until you are mature enough to be harvested by another savior. But it's your product that has to be explained. What is the Way? What can it do for you? And how do you use the Way? That's what the reader wants to know."

"Yes, certainly. Please continue," said Jesus.

"Now that we have hit the reader between the eyes with the cost of your product, which is the death of the lower self, we have to ensure him that the cost is well worth the product; and the only way we can do that is to ensure the reader that there is no such retributive payment as eternal damnation, because in the DPG there is only opportunity for Soul to grow and liberate itself from the cycle of life and death. So there is no eternal damnation in hell if one can't pay for the product; right?"

"Absolutely!" Jesus exclaimed. "Please, continue."

191

"Let's go back to Mathew. We have to explain the hidden meaning of your seed parable for the reader to make sense of your product."

"Exactly. So explain for the reader what I meant by sowing the good seed. What do I mean by good seed here?"

"The good seed is the Word of God. But that won't mean much to the reader, will it?"

"No. It won't. Break it down, then," Jesus said.

"Okay. Your product is the Way. The Way is the reconciling power of Holy Spirit. The reconciling power of Holy Spirit resolves the consciousness of the lower self and reconciles the lower self with Soul. The more resolved the lower self is by the reconciling power of Holy Spirit, the more Soul passes through that straight gate which you refer to elsewhere. But I better not confuse the reader here. Suffice to say that the good seed is the methodology of the Way of Christ. This is why you admonish the world to *do* your sayings — because it is only by *living* your sayings that the good seed, which is the reconciling power of Holy Spirit, is released in man to do its work of resolving the consciousness of his lower self. But you know what, J? We can't go any further until we explain the purpose of the DPG. The reader has to see the blueprint of the Way in the Divine Plan of God to appreciate the methodology that you gave the world to free Soul from its bondage to life."

"I agree," said Jesus. "Shall I, or would you like to continue?"

"Why don't you? It might mean more to the reader if you describe the blueprint of the Divine Plan of God."

"Fair enough. The blueprint is simple. Each Soul comes from the Body of God. Soul comes into the world to create a spiritual identity. Soul goes through the many stages of life before it evolves into a human being. Karma and reincarnation govern Soul's growth. When Soul has evolved enough through the natural process of evolution, the Son of man appears to sow the good seed. The Son of man is any God-realized Soul, and the good seeds are the teachings of the Way. When Soul hears the Word of God in the teachings of the Way, it has a choice to live by the Word of God or not live by the Word of God. If Soul lives by the Word of God, it will set free what you have so aptly described as the reconciling power of Holy Spirit. This divine love resolves the lower self of man, and by resolve we mean that it spiritualizes the lower self. This is the difficult part of my teaching, because it takes courage, effort, and commitment to reconcile the lower self with the higher self. This is why Christianity has opted for the illusion of instant salvation with my death upon the cross. *It is here, at precisely this point, that the Gospel conspiracy was born!"*

Jesus paused. He wasn't looking at me when he talked. He was staring into space, as though scanning the Soul records of life. "It costs to be saved. Not all Souls are willing to pay the price for my product. Soul must create its own identity to return back to God, and the Way is the means by which Soul can complete its destiny in these lower worlds. Do you have anything more you would like to add?"

Jesus turned to look at me. I thought for a moment, and said, "I would add that the Way of Christ is not the only way to reconcile the lower self with the higher self. There are many spiritual paths in life that will take Soul back home to God, and yours is only one path. It's a very effective path; but, in all honesty, I have to tell you that the price you ask for your product is too much too soon. You ask for payment in one full shot with the death of the lower self, and that scares the bejeezes out of people!"

Jesus smiled. "I like that! Yes, I did put the fear of God into a lot of Souls, didn't I?"

"You sure did," I said, smiling at Christ's light-hearted response to the deathblow that had just shattered the Gospel conspiracy. "So much in fact that this paralyzing fear completely distorted your message to the world and gave birth to the Gospel conspiracy," I added, just to nail the point home. "Well, J; now's your chance to set the record straight."

"I hope so, O! I really hope so!" Jesus burst out, with a look of relief.

With that we ended our first discourse on the secret meaning of Christ's sayings, because I had to get dressed for work. I excused myself, and Jesus remained sitting in my reading chair with the most satisfied smile on his adorable face.

39. *Who's Going to Pay My Bills, Jesus Christ?*

I had already stained the oak stairs of the house I was working on in Allenwood for a Croatian family who had built it as an investment home, so after I left Jesus for work I began applying the first coat of varnish. I was working on the third spindle when it hit me, and I burst into laughter. "I can't believe I did that," I said to myself, out loud.

I was alone. I had the radio on to CBC. There was a lockout at the CBC network, so they were repeating old programs. I had already heard the interview that Shelagh Rogers was doing with a journalist and one of her old high school teachers who was afflicted with Parkinson's disease, so I wasn't paying close attention.

My mind was on my talk with Jesus. "What on earth will the reader think when I tell him that I left Jesus sitting in my reading chair because I had to go to work? *Jesus Christ, for Christ's sake!*" I added, and broke into a new fit of laughter.

Who in their right mind would just get up and walk out on Jesus Christ? That's the question I had to answer for my reader. "But how?" I asked myself.

I tried to put myself in my reader's shoes. I let my mind relax, and I heard myself saying, "Was your work so important that you left Jesus Christ just sitting there? You are self-employed, are you not?"

"Yes," I replied to my imaginary reader.

"Then it doesn't matter if you're late or not, does it?"

"Not at all. I don't have many perks in my work, but that's one of them. I can pretty much come and go as I please," I replied, totally honest in my answer.

"So why in God's name would you just leave Jesus Christ sitting there to go and varnish a set of oak stairs?" my dumbfounded reader asked.

"Because someone has to take care of the stairs to heaven!" I exclaimed, and broke into a fit of laughter at my spontaneous response.

It was humorous. Jesus Christ versus a new set of oak stairs. "This is a waking dream?" I said to myself, as the thought connected. A waking dream is an experience that happens in real life that speaks to a spiritual truth, and the spiritual truth of my waking dream was that I was putting the finishing touches on a new set of stairs that would lead to an enlightened understanding of Christ's secret teaching. *"Besides; who's going to pay my bills, Jesus Christ?"* I asked myself, and broke into another fit of laughter.

I knew that it would be inconceivable for the reader to appreciate where I was coming from, so I had to make it absolutely clear why I left Jesus sitting in my den. I continued varnishing for two or three minutes when I was strongly nudged to listen to the teacher talking about her old students, whom her former student who was now a journalist had contacted so they could pay their gratitude to their old teacher who was suffering from advanced Parkinson's disease. One student called in from Switzerland. I stopped working to listen to his story. He thanked his teacher for her encouragement to pursue his dream, which he was living; and another student told her story of how desperate and suicidal she was, but whose life got turned around by her old teacher's genuine concern for her. It brought tears to my eyes to hear of the teacher's love for her work; and then like a bolt out of the blue it hit me, and I exclaimed, *"That's what I have to explain to my reader!"*

It was my work that released the God-force in my life! It was my work that brought me out into the world to ride the currents of the Creative Life Stream to the higher worlds of God! It was my work that honed and tempered my spirit! It was my work that forced me to confront the many hidden layers of my vanity and self-deceptions! It was my work that gave me all the random opportunities that I needed to test the sayings of Jesus in the affairs of daily life! It was my work that gave me vast treasures of *virtue* to store in heaven! And it was my work that paid my way through life!

I had made self-reliance the bedrock of my life. Despite the fact that I was so possessed by the spirit of the Way that I had become pathological in my quest for my true self, I still had to work to pay my way through life; so my trade became my spiritual path! That's why I took to Gurdjieff's teaching. It was a perfect fit for my life, because

G's teaching of "work on oneself" was transportable. I took it with me everywhere. So were the sayings of Jesus. As I worked my trade I *lived* G's teaching and Christ's sayings, and this *doing* realized all the *virtue* that I would need to transform my lower self and grow in spiritual consciousness; and so much did I grow in spiritual consciousness that I experienced my own immortal self one day in my mother's kitchen!

I heard the love in the teacher's voice. She loved her work, and her love touched the lives of her old students. And this love was obvious in her students' voices as they told their stories. That brought tears to my eyes, because I knew what this love was!

This love was the God-force. This love was the reconciling power of Holy Spirit. This love was what I called *virtue* in my own lexicon of the Way. *This love was the Way!* The more excellence I put into my work, the more *virtue* I realized to nourish my spiritual self. That's why it didn't bother me to leave Jesus sitting in my room while I went to work — *because my work had become my way to spiritual self-realization consciousness, not Jesus Christ!* But could I ever get the reader to see this?

Jesus never tired of saying that one had to *do* his sayings to realize the spiritual benefits of his sayings. I did. That's why my work was so important to me. My work was my way, and my way opened the door to the Way; so I knew what Christ's teaching was all about. I had penetrated the secret of his sayings. But I had already realized the spiritual benefits of my work. I had taken Christ's teaching to its conclusion. I had given birth to my spiritual self. So why couldn't I just sit with Jesus to round off our discourse?

As I varnished the stairs I let my mind wander. The interview was over, so I didn't pay much attention to what followed. Then the thought came to me about what I said at the last worship service that I had attended in Southlake. The cleric, who never tired of telling us that her goal in life was to become a Soul Master, asked all of us to reply to the question "What does the Way of the Eternal mean to you?"

One by one each chela revealed their feelings, and collectively they spoke to the question of just how important the Way of the Eternal was for them. They could not conceive of their life without the Living Soul Master, just as Christians cannot conceive of their life without Jesus Christ. Each chela had their story to tell, and some were quite moving; but when it came to my turn, which happened to be last in the circle, I said, "The Way of the Eternal means absolutely nothing to me."

At first there was stunned silence, then shock, and then horror. I broke into a mirthful chuckle. One or two chelas smiled, because they sensed my playful sense of humor; but even so I could see their dumbfoundment. I had to explain. "On the other hand," I said, with a mischievous smile, "The Way of the Eternal means absolutely everything to me. It means both nothing and everything. That's what spiritual freedom is all about. As Jesus would say if he were here today, *'But let your communication be Yae yae; Nay, nay; for whatsoever is more than these cometh of evil.'* That's what my life is all about — nothing and everything. Would you like me to explain that?"

"Please," the mystified cleric said, with a look of alarm in her eyes.

"Okay," I said, and took a deep breath. "The Inner Master let me catch a glimpse of the Divine Plan of God last year. I'm not going to explain this, because now is not the time. Suffice to say that from the perspective of the Divine Plan of God no experience in life is more important to Soul than any other experience. Everything is of equal importance. Our spiritual path then means nothing to me insomuch that it has the same relevance to my life as everything else; so it both is and isn't relevant to me. Just as everything else in life, our path just *is*. I'm an initiate of the Way of the Eternal, and I live my life in the conscious awareness that I am Soul and that life just *is*, and that's the most I can say on the subject."

Some chelas may have heard me, but by the look on their face most didn't; and that spoke to one of my favorite of Christ's sayings— *"he who hath ears to hear..."*

"I hope some of my readers have ears to hear me," I said to myself, with an ironic chuckle; and then I turned my attention back to my work and continued brushing the spindles of my waking dream stairs with the first coat of shiny varnish.

40. *Once Again, Jesus Surprised Me*

Jesus did not return until I brought my book up to date. On the morning that I wrote my last chapter, I realized we couldn't proceed until we had cleared up what I believed to be the central mystery of his teaching. I waited with excitement for his next appearance.

I went downstairs to get a fresh cup of coffee and bid Cathy a nice day as she left for work. When I returned to my bonus room, I found Jesus in my reading chair. "What, blue jeans?" I said, with some surprise.

"Why not? They're very comfortable."

"You're not above wearing jeans?" I asked, just to see where he was going.

"What, me? Get serious, O! I'm only the savior of the world. Now if I was a dashing upwardly mobile entrepreneur like your fellow H. I., I wouldn't want the world to get the wrong impression of me; would I?"

"What impression?" I asked, enjoying Christ's sense of play.

"The impression of mediocrity, of course," he replied.

"God forbid!" I said, and laughed. "Okay. Let's start our discourse here, then. I had another thought that I wanted to explore before we continued with your sayings, but I think we should get this out of the way first; don't you?"

"Why do you think I'm sporting jeans?" Jesus asked, his eyes twinkling.

I laughed. "Alright. Let's play this out. Self-coincidence. That's the phrase I would use to open up this discussion on man's egoic need to be more than what he is."

"And by that, you mean?" Jesus asked, now playing the provocateur.

"Until one has coincided with his inner self he will always have this egoic need to be more than what he is. It's nature's way. Nature has evolved the human self. The human self is the ego self. The ego self forever strives to be more than what it is. Because the human self is born of the consciousness of life, ego is driven by the material values of life. These values are essentially social approval, social success, and social acceptance—"

"Status!" Jesus cut in. "Ego forever seeks status, be it on whatever level of the social ladder!"

"I would say so," I replied, smiling at Christ's fervor.

"But the ego is never content with the level it's on," Jesus quickly added, with a wry smile. "So it strives for the next level, and the next level, and the next level until it gets to where you were in your past lifetime as the Earl of Wellington Manor, the pinnacle of social status — *to the aristocratic summum bonum of social life!"*

"You make your point well," I said, and smiled self-consciously as the humiliating memories of my hypocritical lifetime in high society London, England flooded me.

Jesus had nailed his point. But I could not resist one more jab at the insatiable ego, which I knew only too well, not only from my past lifetime in London's aristocracy but from my lifetime as the infamous *Scoundrel of Paris.* "Yes," I said. "And from these lofty heights of social status one can afford to look poor if he wants to!"

"And wear jeans even!" Jesus added, categorically nailing the point.

"Alright, J, we've had our fun," I said, eager to move on. "Can we get serious now?"

"Why? Don't you think the question of self-coincidence is serious enough?" Jesus persisted. "What do you think my sayings are about if not self-coincidence? Incidentally, O, I love this phrase *self-coincidence.* It addresses the metaphysics of spiritual rebirth in my sayings very nicely."

"I know. And I have the existentialists to thank for the concept."

"Anyone in particular?"

"Jean Paul Sartre."

"The atheist?"

"Yes."

"Ironic, isn't it?"

"Life is becoming one big irony for me, J," I said, and snickered.

"Good. That means you're still growing spiritually. That's what I feel we should talk about today."

"What, spiritual growth?"

"Yes."

"Why? Won't this be implied in our discourse on your sayings?"

"Of course it will. Why don't we address it explicitly so the reader can see where we're coming from?"

"I give you the floor, then."

"Thank you," Jesus said, and crossed his legs and made himself comfortable. "Spiritual growth is all about attitude—"

"Attitude?" I cut in, with some surprise.

"Yes, attitude," Jesus repeated.

"Doesn't attitude speak more to ego than it does to Soul?"

"Of course. But how can one address attitude if one is not aware of it? Do you think the High Initiate who is above wearing jeans is conscious of his superior attitude?"

"As a matter of fact, I got the distinct impression that he was defiant in his attitude about not wearing blue jeans. When a woman in our *satsang* class last month told him that she had spotted him that afternoon walking down the main street of Collingwood in blue jeans he reacted instinctively. *'It couldn't have been me,'* he said to her. *'I wouldn't be caught dead in a pair of jeans!'*"

"That's attitude," Jesus said. "This man has trapped a large part of himself in his own ego, and until he breaks down this elitist attitude he will never set himself free and coincide with his true self."

"But he's a High Initiate of the most direct path to God. Shouldn't he know better?"

"You tell me," said Jesus.

I felt challenged. "To be brutally honest, J — which, incidentally, is the attitude that I've adopted for my writing—"

"Not just your writing, O," Jesus interjected, and grinned.

"Alright. You've made your point. As I was saying, this attitude of feeling superior has spilled over into his spiritual life. Being an H.I., he feels he's made it, if I may use the phrase so common to man's egoic need to be more than what he really is; and it's this spiritual conceit that's spawning the cult of the High Initiate in my spiritual community. But let me ask you this, J. Is this H. I.'s attitude still ego; or is it a spiritual conceit now?"

"And what is ego if not the un-spiritualized self?" Jesus replied.

"Of course," I said. "They're one and the same, aren't they?"

"Precisely," said Jesus, and poof — *he was gone!*

41. *The Shocking Truth of Christ's Message Two Thousand Years Ago*

"Look, J; we can't continue our discourse until we clear up the central mystery of your teaching," I said to Jesus the following morning after I saw Cathy off to work.

"Which is?" Jesus asked, his eyes bright with anticipation.

"You know what I'm going to ask, don't you?" I said.

"Yes. And I've done all I can to prepare the reader for the shocking truth of my message two thousand years ago," Jesus said, in his serious voice.

"I knew it! I was right, wasn't I?"

Jesus said nothing. He just looked at me.

"I was right, wasn't I?" I insisted.

"You were," Jesus replied, with reluctance in his voice.

"Then I think you should tell the reader the shocking truth of your message two thousand years ago," I said, giving the floor to Jesus.

"Would you, O? I fear I may only confuse the reader. Would you do me this favor?"

"Gladly," I said, delighted for the opportunity to share my wisdom. "But tell me, J; why do you think I can do your shocking truth more justice than you?"

"You're an initiate of the DPG. You can put the central mystery of my teaching into the context it deserves to be properly understood today. I fear I won't be able to do that."

"Come on, J; you have to do better than that!" I exclaimed, pressing Jesus.

"Why? Do you think Masters resonate with every Soul? Not on your life. A Master resonates with one Soul and not another. Why this is so it does not matter at the moment. You have the gift of making yourself heard, to the point of chafing people I might add. It doesn't matter for our purpose if the people you chafe shoot back slings and arrows, which some will definitely do; what matters is that these people will be touched by your spiritual logic. That's why I would like you to explain my message."

Jesus had just revealed why people react to me the way they do, especially some High Initiates in my community. Whether it was true or not was immaterial. Jesus trusted me, and I felt honored; but that playful smile on his face gave him away, and I started to laugh.

"You know that it's going to be your baby if you reveal it," Jesus confessed.

"That's not fair," I said, shaking my finger at Jesus.

"Fair or not, the giver of the truth must bear responsibility for the truth," Jesus said, with affected seriousness in his voice.

"*Bear responsibility for the truth?*" I exclaimed. "If I tell a man that his wife has cuckolded him, does that make me responsible for how he reacts to this truth?"

Surprised by my analogy, Jesus just stared at me. For whatever reason, he waited. Finally, he said, "What if this man is so devastated by this truth that he murders his wife, or the man who cuckolded him, or both? Would you not feel responsible?"

"Not in the least. Life is life, J. Why should I take responsibility for a birch tree being a birch tree and not an oak? What people do with the truth of life is their responsibility, not mine; because if it falls upon the giver of the truth to be responsible for what people do with the truth they are given then free will would mean absolutely nothing. Free will defines the fundamental nature of Soul. This is the central mystery of the DPG. The Creator gave Soul the freedom to choose its own destiny in life, and how Soul evolves is a matter of free choice. We create the karma that defines our unique identity, and we create this karma entirely by choice — be it conscious or unconscious. If the cuckold chooses to murder his wife, her lover, or both, that's the choice he will have to live with. All I did was inform him about the truth of his marriage because he happened to be a good friend of mine—"

"*Pardon me?*" Jesus said, as though taken by surprise. "How did your friend respond to his wife's infidelity?" he asked, seeing the spiritual wisdom of my experience.

"He got lucky because Providence intervened," I replied. "He sat up with his hunting rifle in the basement apartment of his so-called best friend's house where he was staying for a few weeks to give his wife the space she had asked for to work things out in their marriage, and he waited for him to come home. His so-called friend didn't come home that night, though. He was an OPP officer, and he was out all night on a manhunt. The next day my friend thought about the consequences of what he could have done had his so-called best friend come home, and he went home and packed his bags and left his wife."

"He was spared murder by divine intervention?"

"I guess you could say that," I said.

"And you don't feel responsible for breaking up your friend's marriage?"

"Why should I? It was my friend's choice to leave his wife."

"Yes. But his marriage was no longer the same after you revealed the shocking truth about his best friend and wife sleeping together. Don't you feel that you should take some measure of responsibility?" Jesus asked.

"Once again, why? Or better still, let me ask you this: would it be better for the cuckold to live the lie of his marriage, or to be aware of the humiliating truth that he has been cuckolded by his best friend?"

"Is it better to live a lie and be relatively happy," Jesus pondered, "or to know the truth and live with the consequences? I don't know. That's a personal thing; don't you think? I'm sure there are those that would want to know if they have been cuckolded, and those that would prefer not to know. I would want to know whether my wife and best friend are making a fool of me. But that's me. What would you do, O?"

"I would pack my wife's bags, not mine," I replied, and broke into a hearty chuckle. "But then, if I were the cuckold I probably wouldn't have the balls to do that; would I?"

Jesus shook his head. "You're shameless in your honesty, aren't you? Tell me, O; how do you think the reader will respond to the shocking truth of my message two thousand years ago?"

I snickered. "If we can use the analogy of the cuckolded husband, I think some readers will pack their bags and leave their unholy union with Christianity, some will turn a blind eye to it, and some will stay and never be happy again in their relationship."

"On the other hand, some may try to patch things up and get on with their life," Jesus added, with a loving twinkle in his eyes.

"It's possible, but I don't see how. I'm sure one's faith would melt down with the realization of your true teaching. But Soul has been melted down before, hasn't it? After all, what's the meaning of the wailing and gnashing of teeth in your gospel if not this spiritual meltdown? This is nature's way — or, to be specific, karma's way — of melting down the consciousness of selfishness so that Soul can enter into the kingdom of God. But one can take destiny into his own hands and transform his lower self with your sayings. You may be right, J; it's possible to rebuild one's relationship with Christianity if one has the wisdom and fortitude, but I doubt that will happen. I've yet to see anyone do it. Bishop John Shelby Spong has tried, and as sincere as he may be he's still chasing his own tail, just like the author of *The Pagan Christ* who believes you weren't even a real person."

"But you have," Jesus replied, with the sweetest smile on his face. "If you hadn't, we wouldn't be having this dialogue, would we?"

"You've got me all figured out, haven't you?"

"Not quite; but enough to respect your wisdom. So what do you say we reveal the shocking truth of my teaching?" Jesus said, playing to my vanity.

"You mean your teaching two thousand years ago," I said, smiling at Christ's tactics. "That's not the same message today, is it?"

"Right," Jesus curtly replied. "Today I have to address the spiritual needs of our times. Two thousand years ago Soul was so trapped by the crushing weight of material oppression that it had to be shocked awake. That's why I gave my message the way I did with my death on the cross. Soul does not need to be shocked awake today. Society has a long history of the Way, and the consciousness of man has been expanded enough for him to reason his way out of the consciousness of materialism. This is why I hope our dialogue will ameliorate some of the devastating effects that the Gospel conspiracy has been responsible for over the centuries. Before we continue then, we have to start fresh. I give you the floor, O. Please reveal the shocking truth of my message two thousand years ago."

"Okay," I said. I took a deep breath, silently invoked the Inner Master for guidance with my secret word, and after several minutes of connecting with the Holy Current of God I relaxed my will and let Soul speak: "The shocking truth implicit to your teaching two thousand years ago has a long tradition. The Essenses taught it long before you brought it out into the world. It goes as far back as Atlantis and much further. This is the truth of the real nature of Soul. This is the truth of Soul giving birth to itself. Unless Soul gives birth to itself, it will never break the cycle of life and death and destine itself to roam the lower worlds forever. This shocking truth is that only by creating the right kind of self can Soul give birth to itself and break the cycle of life and death. If Soul creates the wrong kind of self it will have to be melted down in the furnace of life's karma and create a new self that is pure enough to enter the kingdom of heaven. You dared to reveal the true nature of Soul's destiny in life. Your sayings provide Soul the means to melt down the consciousness of one's selfish nature, which keeps Soul from giving birth to itself. The shocking truth of your message two thousand years ago is that unless one sacrifices his ego he will never enter the kingdom of heaven, because the lower self of man is not allowed into the higher worlds of God. This shocking truth is that the creation of the right kind of self that Soul needs to give birth to itself can only be created through one's own conscious efforts. Every Soul is destined to become a Child of God. This is scripted in the Divine Plan of God. But the only way to become a Child of God is to create a self so pure that Soul will give birth to a new I of God. The shocking truth of your message is that God gives birth to God through man. `***Be ye therefore perfect even as your Father which is in heaven is perfect,**' you told the world. The mystery of your teaching is the secret knowledge of how man can create this perfect self for Soul to give birth to itself and complete God's nature. That's it, J; that's the shocking truth of your message two thousand years ago. Have I done justice to your secret teaching?"

Jesus got up, put his hand on my shoulder, and said, "Thank you, O."

"You're welcome," I said, smiling at Christ's sense of drama. *"All we have to do now is wait and see who packs their bags!"*

206

Jesus burst into an irrepressible fit of laughter, and I joined him; and we laughed and laughed until we had tears in our eyes.

42. *Leading a Horse to Water*

It wasn't a coincidence that at our next worship service in Southlake the cleric would ask what we could do to help bring our spiritual teaching to the public. The group had plenty of ideas, but I could not help but feel that there had to be a more effective way to introduce the spiritual teachings of the Light and Sound of God.

I thought of the modern day founder of the Light and Sound of God, which he simply called the Way of the Eternal. *"There are two kinds of seekers,"* he said. *"Those that seek the Way, and those that the Way seeks out."* I thought I would share this with the group, but it didn't resonate; and then I said: "If you want to go fishing for Souls that are ready for the Way of the Eternal, if I may use a Christian metaphor, you have to know where the fish are. I think most seekers are Souls that the Way seeks out. The other seekers will find the Way eventually because they are spiritually programmed to find it. It's those Souls that are trapped by life that have to be reached, because they're crying to be set free."

"I don't understand," someone said. "What do you mean, trapped by life?"

She was a young chela. "Take marriage, for example, or any relationship for that matter," I replied. "I've known people who felt trapped by their relationship and sought help to extricate themselves. Soul is no different. It may be trapped by its religion, politics, career — whatever; Soul has outgrown its way, but it can't extricate itself. There may be many reasons why. This is the case with many Christians. They've outgrown their faith, but they can't leave it. I've known Christians like this, and I tried to help them free themselves. In fact, I'm working on a new book on this very subject. I think we have to understand where these Souls are in life if we want to go fishing for them."

"But how do we reach these Souls trapped by their faith?" asked Janet, with genuine concern in her voice. Her husband was a devout Baptist who was seriously threatened by her involvement in what he called "that dangerous New Age cult."

"Only people that have outgrown their faith are ready for another path," I replied, with genuine sympathy for Janet's situation.

"I understand. But how do we reach those people that can't break free?" she asked.

"Actually, Janet; I've given this a lot of thought," I said, and took a deep breath because I didn't want to go there. I asked the Inner Master for guidance. *"Use your best judgment,"* he replied, in my mind. "All spiritual paths prepare Soul for the Way," I explained; "but we know that all spiritual paths are born of Divine Spirit, so we have to appeal to Soul's familiarity with the Way in its own path. That's how we can span the chasm of unbelief to the Light and Sound of God. I think we have to respect the fact that all spiritual paths are expressions of the Way and let people know that they can access the source of their own path in the pure teachings of the Light and Sound of God."

"Is this what you're doing with the book you're writing?" Doreen, the owner of a used book store that specialized in New Age literature, candles, and sundries asked.

"Yes," I replied.

"You're building a bridge to other spiritual paths?"

"One in particular," I replied.

"Which one?" she asked.

"Christianity," I said.

"If I may ask, how are you building this bridge?"

"Doreen, you wouldn't believe me if I told you."

"With you O, I'd believe anything!" she said, and laughed.

Everyone laughed. Doreen asked another question. "Why do you think Christians who have outgrown their faith are afraid to leave their religion? This puzzles me. I was Roman Catholic. I outgrew my faith, and I just knew it was time to move on. But I know Christians who are afraid to move on. I've never understood why. Can you tell me?"

"I'd like to hear what everyone else has to say," I answered.

"Can you tell us what you think first? Then we can ask everyone else," she said.

"Okay," I said, smiling at Doreen's faith in me. "Social consciousness, or propriety if you will, holds many Christians back.

They're afraid of how they'll be perceived if they step outside their safe little box of Christian faith."

"That's ego," Stanley Hansen quickly offered, forcing me to smile. "That's all that is. Ego doesn't want to look bad. Ego wants control."

"True," I replied, with a wry chuckle because his own ego was so bloated that it made him believe he was even superior to Jesus Christ because of his High Initiate status. "But I think it runs a little deeper than that, Stanley. It takes courage to step out of one's safe little box of faith. It means going against one's family, friends, and even one's community. A closet gay, for example. It takes courage to step out of the closet. He or she is not what they pretend to be, but they know that once they step out of the closet their world will change forever. But they get tired of living the lie of their life, and out of sheer fatigue some will step out. In like manner, there are many Christians whose life is a lie but just cannot step out of their faith. I met a United Church minister who calls himself a Christian agnostic. That's a contradiction in terms and a form of self-deception to cover up for his loss of faith. That's the kind of power propriety can have over Soul. So it takes courage to leave one's path. One may no longer believe, but he still feels some measure of security in his faith. That's why people are afraid to try something new. The familiar drives society, not the new."

"In my case, it was my mother," Doreen said. "You have no idea what I had to go through to convince her that there's nothing evil about this teaching. Why do Christians think that all other paths are evil?"

"I'll ask Jesus the next time I see him," I said, with an ironic chuckle.

And I did. After the worship service Cathy decided to drive to New Lowell to visit her friend and I went to my bonus room to work on my book. As I was writing, I heard Jesus, "I understand you would like to ask me something?" he said, to my surprise.

I turned to find Jesus happily sitting in my reading chair. "Yes," I said, trying to act natural. "A fellow chela would like to know why Christianity has a tendency to call other spiritual paths evil. Why is that, J?"

"Let's be fair, O. Not all Christians are like that," Jesus replied.

"I know. But it's still a conceit that runs through the whole body of Christianity. There isn't one Christian denomination that is spared the conceit that you are the savior of the world and all other religions are false."

Jesus laughed. In his laughter, I felt his tears. "You're right, O. It's the conceit of the Gospel conspiracy. I can only hope that our discourse will help free those Souls that are ready for the pure teachings of the Way. Believe me when I tell you this, there are more Souls ready for the Light and Sound of God than you realize."

"How do you know, J? Do these Souls pray to you for liberation?"

"As a matter of fact, they do. In one form or another all Souls pray for liberation," Jesus replied, his face just glowing with divine radiance.

I chuckled to myself. "Now you can appreciate why I wrote my open-letter book asking you to come down off your cross. The symbol of your crucifixion has served its purpose, and it's time for the world to move on."

"*Amen to that!* You should have published *Dear Jesus.* It would have set a lot of Souls free," Jesus said, once more surprising me with his omniscience.

"That's what this is all about, isn't it?" I said.

"What?" Jesus asked.

"Liberating Soul," I replied.

"*It's time to harvest this new crop of Souls!*" Jesus exclaimed.

"You're right," I said, smiling at his emotional outburst.

"The world has never known such a bountiful crop," Jesus said; and then he burst out with, "*and you are destined to become one of life's most remarkable fishers of Souls!*"

"Let's not go there, J," I said, catching on to his little game. "You know very well that as far as I'm concerned the world can find its own way. If what I write helps to free Soul from the cycle of life and death, that would be a happy coincidence; not design."

"*Doing without doing! Brilliant, O!*" Jesus replied, still playing with me. "That's what I tried to get across to my disciples when I told them to be in the world but not of the world. But today they call this detachment, don't they?"

"I call it compassionate indifference," I responded, with a big smile.

"Better still!" exclaimed Jesus, still affecting emotion to convince me.

"I mean it when I said that the world can find its own way," I insisted. "I have no desire whatsoever to martyr my life for anyone. I want to be clear on that, J."

"You just keep saying that, O. Maybe you'll convince yourself yet," Jesus said, with a sarcastic smirk on his loveable face.

"I'm serious, J. You can lead a horse to water, but you can't make it drink."

"Leading a horse to water is not the same as letting the world find its own way. Your books lead the horse to water, O; don't they?"

I thought for a moment. Jesus was right. "I suppose they do. But the premise of my writing is the fundamental truth that the journey back home to God is an individual journey, and all I'm doing is telling the story of my own journey; that's all."

"In the process you are leading the horse to water," Jesus insisted.

"But whether the horse drinks or not is a matter of complete indifference to me."

"Of course," said Jesus. *"And you talk about attitude!"*

I burst into laughter. "I should include this in my book, shouldn't I?"

"It's your book, O. *Use your best judgment,"* Jesus replied, deliberately emphasizing his words with a bright twinkle in his all knowing eyes.

Startled by the familiarity of his advice, which was exactly what the Inner Master had just said to me when I asked for his guidance, I looked at Jesus and was just about to confront him on it when he said, "Until we meet again," and vanished.

43. *The Golden Thread of God*

"Alright, J," I said the following morning after I kissed Cathy goodbye for work, "we can get to your sayings today because my book is starting to grow out of control."

"Spirit is in charge of this project, O," Jesus replied, with a big smile. "Every word you write is WRITTEN LARGE in the Golden Light of the Way. Didn't Shakespeare say, 'by indirections find directions out'?"

"That's several times you've quoted Shakespeare," I said, smiling at Christ's literary tastes. "I also find his insights astonishing. As a matter of fact I quoted Shakespeare a few times at our spiritual functions, which contributed to Stanley Hansen's objection to my literary references. He took me out for coffee after an introductory talk on our spiritual path where I quoted half a dozen writers, and he told me that if what I had to say wasn't directly related to the teachings of the Way of the Eternal I shouldn't say anything."

"And what did you say to that?" Jesus asked.

"I told him that I wasn't going to censor my thoughts for him or anybody else. Just because he couldn't see the relevance of my quotations to the Way didn't mean it wasn't related to the Way. It's all Spirit, J. You and I know that. It's all a question of seeing the relevance, that's all. As much as it cost me to tell Stanley to butt out, I had to."

"Yes," Jesus sighed. "That's why he had to be told about love and consciousness at the worship service. Be that as it may, we should inform the reader that the Golden Thread of Spirit is woven through the divine matrix of life. As you say, it's all spiritually relevant; and it's only a matter of seeing this relevance, that's all."

"Relevant to what?" I asked, on behalf of the reader.

"Of course," said Jesus, picking up on my thoughts. "Relevant to the reconciling power of Holy Spirit. Holy Spirit is the Golden Thread of God that runs through the tapestry of life. If one can see this Golden Thread in a line from Shakespeare, Pascal, Plato, John Milton, or Rumi he sees the Way. When one sees the Way, it means that he has heard the Word of God calling Soul home. That's what you tried to tell Stanley, wasn't it?"

"Stanley suffers from *High-itis* — pun on High Initiate, of course," I said, and laughed. Jesus smiled. "This spiritual conceit blinds him to the finer Golden Threads of God in the tapestry of life and spawns the cult of the High Initiate. It's too bad this had to be brought to his attention; but hey, that's how Spirit works. By hook or by crook, vanity will be found out. So, J; what do you say we get to your yae yae, nay nay saying now?"

"Not yet, O," Jesus said, to my surprise. "I think for the reader's sake we should explore this concept of the Golden Thread of God. After all, the Golden Thread of God connects all of my sayings to the Way. In effect then we will have to get to my sayings eventually, but with a much greater spiritual clarity for the reader."

"True," I said, and smiled at the image that just popped into my mind. "It's like following Ariadne's string, isn't it? So, what more can we say about the Golden Thread of God that we haven't said already?"

"The reader should be made to see that the tapestry of life is woven out of this Golden Thread of God, and there is not one experience that Soul has that is not related to the Way. Is this not why you stress in your writing that life itself is the Way?"

"Precisely!" I exclaimed. *"*I found the Way in life, J. That's why I see the Way in all of life's experiences. But how can we get the reader to see that the tapestry of life is woven together by the Golden Thread of God? We know that there's only self-initiation into the mysteries of life, and seeing that the tapestry of life is woven out of the Golden Thread of God is one of the most profound spiritual mysteries — which, incidentally, quantum physics is beginning to realize with the unified field theory. But despite this scientific breakthrough, we can talk about the Way until we're blue in the face; because unless the reader is ready to be initiated into the mysteries of life what we say won't mean a damn thing, will it?"

"Not necessarily," Jesus said, giving me a disapproving frown. "How many times has the course of your life been affected by a book that you read?"

"Touché! You're right, J. It may not affect the reader right away, but it will leave an impression," I said, catching onto to what Jesus meant.

"As long as they hear the truth, Spirit will find its way into the reader's heart eventually. We should talk about resonance, then."

"Pardon me?" I said, not following Christ's logic.

"Resonance," Jesus said, stressing the word. "Truth resonates with one's personal level of consciousness. Truth is one. It is not two, three, or a thousand different truths all fragmented but related by a common denominator; truth is the same reality everywhere."

"As the Living Soul Master said in one of his talks, 'truth and existence are one and the same reality,'" I added for the reader's clarification.

"Excellent. But how one resonates with truth depends upon their level of consciousness," Jesus continued. "As one's level of consciousness expands, their perception of truth grows also. This is because they now resonate with truth on a higher level."

"And by resonate, you mean?" I asked, for amplification.

"To resonate with something is to be in sympathy with it," Jesus explained. "Ultimately it all comes down to vibrations. Life is all about vibrations. As one grows in consciousness, one's personal vibration changes. As one's vibration changes, they resonate with life on a new frequency. This is where you get expressions like 'misery loves company,' 'it takes money to make money,' 'nothing succeeds like success,' 'birds of a feather flock together,' 'it takes one to know one,' and so on; all of which attest to the Law of Attraction. Resonance defines a person's life. A Christian resonates with the truths of Christianity, but as he grows in spiritual consciousness he will lose sympathy with the truths of Christianity and will no longer resonate with the truths of Christianity—"

"May I?" I interjected.

"Please," Jesus said, gesturing permission with his hand.

"Shouldn't we make it clear that many of the truths that Christianity holds dear are founded upon false premise; ergo, they're not truths at all? Won't the reader be confused?"

"Yes," Jesus said, and smiled at me because he saw the opening I had given him to talk about the Gospel conspiracy; but he surprised me. "The tapestry that Christianity has woven out of the Golden Thread of God does not present a clear picture of truth," he explained, with that twinkle in his eyes, "but it is all woven out of the same fabric of God. Truth is truth. How the tapestry of truth is woven depends upon the weaver."

"You were a master weaver, weren't you?" I said, probing Jesus.

"I spent three years mastering the craft. I know of what I speak," Jesus said.

"If I may, then; I'd like to ask you a personal question."

"Please."

"Alright," I said, and took a breath. "Your sayings and parables seem to come from a profound level of personal experience, which is why they have such resonance with the world at large. Is this what you mean by the level of a person's consciousness resonating with truth on his or her own level of frequency?"

"Yes. One's level of vibration resonates with truths on that same frequency. But truth contains all frequencies. That's what makes the same truth seem different to different people. Go on; you were going to ask me something."

"I'd like to know if you worked in vineyards during your silent years. I get the feeling from your sayings and parables that you weren't just quoting from the Great Book of Life. You were drawing from your own experience, weren't you?"

Jesus laughed. "Of course I was. How foolish of the world to think that I came ready-made! No Master comes into the world ready-made. Every Soul evolves in spiritual consciousness. This is the Law of God. The only way for Soul to evolve is through life experience. Yes, I worked in vineyards. I also slaughtered sheep; I made mud bricks; I built homes and furniture; and I even frequented houses of pleasure to experience sex. Life is about experience, and Soul must experience life to grow in spiritual consciousness. I lived my life as completely as I could, and my sayings and parables are fraught with the consciousness of my experiences. Does that satisfy your need to know?"

"It confirms what I suspected," I said, making a mental note to inquire about his sex life later. "Are we done with the golden thread of God, then?"

"Just a few more thoughts. What I would like to make crystal clear is that the fundamental nature of the Way is experience. From the experience of life we extract the wisdom of life just as juice is extracted from the fruit of the vine. It is this gnostic wisdom of life that we can properly call the Way of Life. But why would we call it that, O? Can you clarify this for the reader?"

"I believe I can," I said, happy for the opportunity. "One person's experience can save another person a lot of hardship and pain. For example, a carpenter learns the hard way that it's better to measure a board twice before making his cut just to make sure that he doesn't make the wrong cut and spoil a perfectly good board. This is how the expression *measure twice cut once* came to be. In this expression you have the experience of the way of the carpenter distilled into a little pearl of gnostic wisdom. In like manner, all of life's wisdom pearls speak to the Way of Life. In essence, **the Way of Life speaks to the best, most efficient, and least troublesome way to negotiate one's way through life.** This is gnosis, and what I learned during my Essene lifetime. It was my duty to scribe all the new wisdom sayings that were brought back to our community by our brethren who had gathered them in their sojourns in the world, but it wasn't until my current lifetime that I actually experienced the gnostic purpose of the Way of Life. This is why I took Gurdjieff's teaching and your sayings to heart. I felt such resonance for G's Work and your sayings that it opened the door to the Way for me. Does this make sense to you, J?"

"*Absolutely!*" Jesus replied, and gave me a big smile that lit up his whole face with love. "Now we have to convince the reader that his own life is the way, because it is one's own experiences that reveal the Way. If we can get this point across I believe the reader will eventually come to see that all ways lead to the pure teachings of the Light and Sound of God and the Way-shower. Do you have anything more you would like to add?"

"Not really. But I'd like the reader to understand that although life is the Way, the Way is Divine Spirit; and the purest expression of Spirit can be found in the Way of the Eternal, the modern day religion of the Light and Sound of God. I don't want the reader to think I'm

217

promoting this teaching. I'm just leading the horse to water, that's all."

Jesus laughed. "Yes, I know; and if he drinks or not is a matter of complete indifference to you. I understand. Now I think we can get back to my sayings."

I smiled at Christ's sarcasm as I glanced up at the clock. "I have obligations, J."

"Yes, of course. Tomorrow morning, then?"

"I'm looking forward to it," I said, and bid Jesus farewell. Then I went into my bedroom to change into my work clothes.

44. *Jesus Lets the Big Cat Out of the Bag*

"We have a dilemma, J," I said.

"What dilemma?" he asked, making himself comfortable in my reading chair.

"You, Jesus Christ, are pointing Soul to the new religion of the Light and Sound of God. That's a dilemma, wouldn't you say?"

"Why? Because the world has made a religion out of my life and teaching? Does that mean that my life must come to a standstill?"

"Not at all," I said, catching the sarcasm in his voice. "It's your life, and you can do with it as you please. All I'm saying is that being the savior of Christianity it would appear problematic to point Soul to another religion. I'm sure you can see the dilemma."

"Of course I do!" Jesus exclaimed. "That's the point of this dialogue, isn't it — to point the reader to the pure teachings of the Light and Sound of God? Where do you think I got my teachings from, anyway?"

"Directly or indirectly, from Divine Spirit," I replied, smiling at Christ's playfully defensive mood. "But how much you got from Spirit directly, I don't know. From memories of my lifetime as Samuel the Essene, I know that you received the secret teachings from Master Zadok who was the Living Soul Master at the time. You also received the golden teachings from Master Fubbi Quantz at the Katsupari Monastery in Tibet; but that's all I know about you. You tell me where you got the rest of your teachings," I challenged.

"I found my way into other mystery schools in Egypt, Persia, and India," Jesus replied. "But essentially life was my teacher. I put to practice all the sayings that Master Zadok gave me when I left Qumran to fulfill my destiny, and as I lived these powerful redemptive sayings I extracted all the virtue that I needed to grow into the consciousness of Christ; so where's the dilemma, if I may ask?"

"In the premises of Christianity," I replied. "They don't coincide with the reality of your life and teaching. That's the dilemma."

"And what can I do about that?" Jesus said, with a shrug. "As I said, Christianity must complete its cycle before it fades into the light of common day, if I may borrow another phrase from Shakespeare."

I laughed. "And it doesn't bother you then that the reader will see that the man responsible for the religion of Christianity is pointing him to the pure teachings of the Way in the new religion of the Light and Sound of God?"

"Not at all. Holy Spirit is Holy Spirit wherever it is found. If Soul resonates with Holy Spirit in the religion of Christianity, then that's where Soul belongs. I'm not taking anything away from Christianity. All I'm doing is revealing the truth of the Way of Christ, which transcends the premise of the Gospel conspiracy. I see no dilemma in that."

"Not when you put it like that. But in all fairness to the reader, it sounds like a ploy to get the reader to see that the tapestry the Gospel conspiracy has woven is not a very clear picture of the Way of Christ, and at the risk of offending you I think you're just using me to state your case."

"Didn't I ask you at the outset to help me set the record straight?"

"Yes, you did."

"Well?"

"Well, I just get the feeling now that you're throwing the Christians to the lions," I replied, and broke into a hearty chuckle.

"I guess I am, aren't I? My God, how ironic! Imagine that, Jesus Christ throwing Christians to the lions? *But of truth!*" he quickly added, with that dazzling twinkle in his playful eyes. *"I'm throwing Christians to the lions of truth!"*

I lapped up Christ's delicious irony. "You know what, J? That's not a bad metaphor. Truth can devour one whole if it's powerful enough, and our dialogue has the power to do just that; doesn't it?"

"Yes. What do you say we introduce the reader to the leader of the pack, then?"

"No kidding? You mean we're ready to explain the transformative power of your communication saying?"

"Yes," said Jesus, with a big Cheshire cat-like grin. "But only in the context of its revelation," he added, to my total confusion.

"Meaning?" I asked.

"We have to let the reader see why I summed up my teaching of self-transformation the way I did with my yae yae nay nay saying. Context, O; it's all about context."

"Okay. I follow you. So, to explain your communication saying I have to address the metaphysics of self-transformation?" I asked, just to be sure I was following.

"Exactly. Please take the reader to the last verse of Mathew, Chapter 5 and reveal the ultimate purpose of all my sayings, which my communication saying points to. Can you do that for me, please?"

"Of course," I said, and went straight to the verse. As I read it, I smiled because it summed up the entire body of Christ's secret teaching of spiritual transformation and rebirth: ***"Be ye therefore perfect even as your Father which is in heaven is perfect."***

As I looked at Jesus I felt the tide rising, and I was free to let Soul speak: "It's impossible to explain the secret teaching in metaphor as you did. The consciousness of man has evolved considerably since you gave your teaching to the world, and I don't believe we can disclose the metaphysics of self-transformation without a conceptual understanding of the dynamics of the self of man. I can do this, J. This has been my spiritual quest. I understand now why I was attracted to all the teachings that I studied in my search. I had to work my way through all the stages of this dynamic. This is why you have come to me. Don't say anything just yet. I have to get out what Spirit wants me to say, and the tide is surging fast. If I may, let me continue."

Jesus motioned with his hand for me to continue. I took a breath, paused to reflect, and continued: "In my conversation with Doctor Jung in my dream we talked about the individuation of the self. Jung was amazed that I had managed to see the alpha and the omega of the self, and I revealed to him the secret of the self that he had spent his whole life looking for. This secret exists in your teaching. All of your sayings and parables speak to this secret. But to disclose this secret in the context of your teaching I have to translate your metaphors into modern language. This is what I mean by a conceptual understanding of the dynamics of the self; and the first concept that I have to reveal refers to the dual consciousness of the evolving self of man, the concept of the lower and higher self. Unless the reader gets a clear picture of this dynamic he will never penetrate the secret of your teaching. You understood this dynamic of the self, as all Masters do; but each Master reveals it in his own way and in cultural context. You had a genius for metaphor, J. This is why your teaching touched so many lives. Metaphor touches all levels of consciousness. But metaphor is still metaphor; and for the sake of spiritual clarity we have to unpack the wisdom of your metaphors and disclose the fundamental nature of this dynamic.

"I have the freedom to draw upon every stage of my own dynamic process because I gave birth to my spiritual self with your teaching. I can conceptualize the secrets of your metaphors, and the first thing I feel compelled to reveal is that the self of man must transform itself with the disciplines of the Way in order to realize its inherent purpose in life, which is to become an 'I' of God. This is why you said that we must be as perfect as our Father in heaven. The whole dynamic of self-transformation in your teaching has to do with spiritualizing the consciousness of our lower self until it is subsumed by our higher self, which results in the birth of a new 'I' of God.

"You called this being born again in Spirit. The world has very little idea of just what goes into this spiritual birth. As I said, Christianity has completely bypassed the mesoteric stage of this dynamic and granted the self instant spiritual self-realization; or salvation status if you will. This is an illusion that every Christian will have to dissolve one day with the karmic reality of life. The irony of Christianity lies in the fact that your very teaching dissolves this illusion by the sheer transformative power of your sayings; but only if one *lives* them. I did, so I know that this power is real. But to make sense of the spiritual power of your sayings one has to grasp what the dynamic of the self of man is all about. If I may, let me explain just what I mean by this dynamic"

"By all means," Jesus said.

I paused for a moment, and continued. "The self is an atom of God. An atom of God is the seed of an 'I' of God. Just as an acorn seed is a potential oak tree, so is the atom of God a potential new 'I' of God. The atom of God is planted in the soil of material consciousness, and through natural evolution it creates a sense of self. I realized the dawning of self-consciousness in my primordial lifetime as Grunt, which I experienced during my fourth past-life regression. From the dawning of self-consciousness comes the next stage of evolution. As the newly realized reflective self evolves from lifetime to lifetime, it begins to realize a sense of its own immortal essence; and after thousands of incarnations man realizes that he is more than human, and he seeks to realize his spiritual nature. Here religions are born. But let's not explore this now. Suffice to say that you came into the world to help man realize his potential as an 'I' of God; and your gospel has to do with how man can facilitate his own spiritual birth.

"It seems like I'm talking in circles here; but what I have to make crystal clear is that realizing one's spiritual consciousness takes time, effort, and commitment. It cannot be done by embracing Jesus Christ as one's savior and forswearing all of one's karmic debt to life. Just as there are various stages in the birth of a child in life, so are there stages for the birth of the spiritual self. Christianity has bypassed all of the stages from the conception of the 'I' of God to the birth of the 'I' of God by conferring instant salvation status upon the Soul that embraces you as its savior. This is an illusion. No mother gives birth to a child the day after its conception. There is a gestation period in the mother's, womb. The embryo grows until the fetus is ready to be born. It is this stage of the dynamic of the self that Gurdjieff refers to when he said, `Blessed is he who has a soul, blessed is he who has none, but woe and grief to him who has it in embryo.'

"Well, I was one of those who had it in embryo. I know exactly what Gurdjieff meant. But I'll explain this later. For now, I want to make it clear to the reader that the teaching you brought to the world facilitates the birthing of one's spiritual self. And the birthing of one's spiritual self requires the conscious effort of transforming the consciousness of one's lower self. Now I have to take a break because a wave of fatigue has just hit me. If you don't mind, J; I need a cup of coffee. Would you like one?"

"Just milk, please," Jesus said.

I went downstairs and poured two cups. I put a teaspoon of honey into mine and milk into Christ's and brought them upstairs. We both took several sips, and then I said, "What do you say we do a short HU? I want to capture this because the tide is still surging, but I need to energize myself."

"You should explain why you need to energize yourself, for the reader."

"Alright," I said, and took another sip of coffee. "Spirit is the creative life force, and when I say I feel a tide surging I mean that Spirit has something it wants to reveal. But Spirit can only do this through the medium of one's consciousness — or self, if you will; but one can get exhausted letting Soul speak. A creative thought will use up one's life force to express itself, and after it is spent one has to rest because one is literally exhausted. Artists describe this as being creatively spent. I felt spent after my explanation; so if you don't mind, I'd like to do a short HU to energize myself."

"Of course," Jesus said, and closed his eyes and began chanting HU.

After several minutes of singing HU, I felt myself re-energized and opened my eyes and Jesus said, "May the blessings be."

"To continue, then," I began, "I'd like to explain that the heart of your teaching is the concept of self-sacrifice, which you immortalized with your crucifixion. This self-sacrifice speaks to the transformation of the lower self of man. This lower self is made up of the individuated consciousness of the Physical, Astral, Causal, Mental, and subconscious Planes of Consciousness. This lower self is our human self-consciousness. It is our mental self, or ego if you will; and what we have to make clear is that this lower self is our spiritual self *in potentia,* if I can express it this way."

"May I?" Jesus interrupted.

"Please," I said.

"Just to clarify, because I can feel the reader's confusion here. The lower self of man is Soul trapped in the consciousness of these lower levels of consciousness—"

I burst into laughter. "You're not helping any. I think that only confuses the reader more. Let me give it another shot."

"By all means," Jesus said, and reached for his coffee.

"The self of man is one self, but it is split in two. One part of the self is aware of its divine essence, and the other part is not. The part that is not aware of its divine essence is our human, or ego self; and your teaching makes this part aware of its divine essence by transforming its consciousness. In the simplest terms possible, the human self is too impure in consciousness to be aware of its own divine essence, and your teaching is all about purifying the consciousness of our human self. This is what your saying about being perfect as our Father in heaven is all about. Our Father in heaven is our higher self, and we have to perfect our lower self to give birth to our higher self. Does that explain it?"

"Perfectly!" said Jesus, and smiled contentedly.

"Should I continue, then?" I asked.

"Only if you feel up to it," Jesus said, giving me the option.

"I think I'm up to it. Do you have something you would like to add before I get to the nitty-gritty of your saying?"

"By nitty-gritty, you mean?" he asked.

"I mean the metaphysics of spiritual growth," I said.

"If only I had today's concepts to explain my teaching back then," Jesus said, with a sigh. "Society wasn't evolved enough to discern this play of energies. People had primal awareness, and the strong exploited the weak. All I did was make people aware of how to store their energies in heaven where they would nourish their higher self; but you can explain the metaphysics of this play of energies, O. You have created a conceptual framework that speaks to my teaching very nicely."

"Thank you. If I may digress for a moment, may I ask you something — and I would like you to be brutally truthful, J. Don't coddle me, okay?"

Jesus laughed. He knew that I knew Soul Masters seldom if ever answered a chela's question directly. "Alright, ask and you shall receive," he replied.

"I want to know if anybody will ever get to read these talks. This is an unbelievable dialogue, J; so my question is this: is there any point continuing our talks on your sayings?"

"Why not? If not for the reader's edification, what about yours? You're exercising your spiritual muscles in a way that few Souls ever get the opportunity to experience. If you could gauge your own spiritual growth because of our dialogue you wouldn't dare ask me to suspend our talks. And if you can grow from the spiritual energy that is released in our talks, think of the spiritually famished readers. You have absolutely no idea how much your reader will benefit from our dialogue, O. *No idea whatsoever!"*

"That's why I asked." I said, relieved to know that as exciting as it was for me it was not going to end up on my pile of unpublished manuscripts. "We can continue, then?"

"By all means," Jesus insisted.

"Then I want the reader to know that the lower self of man has an appetite for the lower energies of life, and the higher self of man has an appetite for the higher energies of life; and the desire to feed both selves plays itself out in the drama of our personal life. And until one realizes that we cannot feed the lower self at the expense of the higher self or the higher self at the expense of the lower self, the lower and higher self will always be in conflict. And this conflict will never be resolved until the two selves come to an agreement to grow together in a harmonious relationship defined by their mutual need for total self-identity. Spiritual balance, J; that's what it's all about. Man has to be made conscious of the fact that the human self is created by natural evolution to serve the atom of God's divinely encoded purpose to become spiritually self-realized and God-conscious. Or, to put it in the simplest terms possible, the human self is the womb that gives birth to the spiritual self; and giving birth to the spiritual self is what your teaching is all about."

"Absolutely! And if I may be so bold and add my two cents, I would further say that the human self is the key to spiritual self-realization and God-consciousness; because the spiritual self is born out of the human self, and if the human self is flawed the spiritual self will only have to return to repeat the process until the human self is perfected enough to allow the new 'I' of God to be born!"

"Wow!" I exclaimed. *"Talk about hard ball spirituality!"*

Jesus laughed. "I really have no choice, O. The context of our discourse has allowed for the brutal truth to be revealed. I, too, am a servant of my Muse!"

I burst into laughter. That was one of my favorite expressions. I had to ask Jesus if the reader wouldn't be swallowed whole by the truth we had just revealed.

"In all honesty, O," he replied, with that Cheshire grin, "I think it's time to let the big cat out of the bag, if I may take liberties with an old saying. Why not tell your reader about the logic of karma and reincarnation? For what other reason does Soul keep coming back into the world if not to create a self perfect enough to give birth to a new 'I' of God?"

I burst into laughter again. Jesus stared. "What?" he asked.

"That's exactly what the modern day founder of The Way of the Eternal used to say. *'You just keep coming back until you get it right!'*" I quoted, and burst into another fit of irrepressible laughter. Jesus joined me.

45. *The Historical Duplicity of Christ's Life and Teaching*

I had known for years, of course; but for some reason it hit very close to home as I read the remaining three New Testament Gospels. Perhaps it was because of my talks with Jesus that brought it to the surface, or perhaps it was a keener insight into the dialectic of the four Gospels; whatever it was, I could not shake the pervasive feeling of the historical duplicity of Christ's life and teaching.

By the time I finished reading the amazing Gospel of John the feeling had taken hold of me, and for the next few days I could not shake the disturbing Gospel deception of bypassing the entire stage of Soul's critical growth in life. "What would the world have been like had Christ's teaching been understood?" I asked myself.

The thought of a world conscious of the mesoteric stage of evolution that John's Gospel completely bypassed boggled my mind, because that would mean an entirely different kind of society. The mesoteric stage gives rise to a consciousness of spiritual accountability. This is the stage where man becomes aware of the spiritual laws of life. Man takes evolution out of the hands of nature and becomes responsible for his own spiritual growth. In St. Paul's words, the mesoteric stage is where man puts away childish things; and the thought of the historical duplicity of Christ's life and teaching would not go away.

I felt the incredible wrongness of the direction humanity had taken with this false perception of Christ's life and teaching. I no longer believed in my mind what Jesus meant by the Gospel conspiracy, I *knew* in my gut what he meant; and it didn't matter if the conspiracy was perpetrated by the Gospel writers Mathew, Mark, Luke, and John or by the bishops assembled by the Roman Emperor Constantine at the First Council of Nicaea to come to a mutual agreement on Christ's life and teaching, or directed by Constantine to doctor the Gospels to give credence to the concept of Jesus being the only Begotten Son of God and sole savior of the world for the purpose of bringing all the divisive Christian factions under one roof, I just felt that it was wrong; and I had to ask Jesus.

"So?" I bluntly said to him, when we met again in my bonus room after I saw Cathy off to work. It was one week since we last talked. I had down time from my jobs, so I read the remaining Gospels and brought *Jesus Wears Dockers* up to date. I had to get what I felt off my chest, because I could not continue our discourses until I did.

"What?" Jesus asked.

I stared at him. He was dressed in casuals again, tan Dockers, light cream polo shirt, matching socks, and sandals, and he had the faint shadow of a beard which gave him a new look, but I made no comment. For some strange reason, I felt an oppressive weight in knowing that the world had been deceived by the Gospel writers, and I had to get it out of my system. I sighed, took a sip of coffee, and said, *"Damn!"*

"Damn?" Jesus said.

"Damn damn damn!" I said, and shook my head in disgust.

"What's the matter, O?" Jesus asked.

"I don't know what's going on!"

"Tell me," Jesus said.

"It's Christianity! It's this whole damn thing! What the hell are we doing, J?"

"What do you mean?" Jesus asked, with seeming perplexity.

"We're just feeding the fire, that's all we're doing!"

"What fire?" Jesus asked.

"Of the bloody illusion!" I exclaimed.

Jesus fell silent. Then he perked up. "Oh, I see where you're coming from."

"Do you really?" I asked.

"I believe so," he said.

"Tell me then," I said, challenging Jesus Christ's omniscience.

"You're afraid our dialogue will have the opposite effect on social consciousness and just add more fuel to the fire that Christianity refuses to let die out," Jesus said.

"Exactly!" I burst out, and sat back in my chair and looked Jesus in the eyes. "What the hell should I do? I can't live with the thought that I would only be adding more fuel to the greatest conspiracy the world has ever known!"

Jesus chuckled. But it wasn't his normal chuckle. He felt what I felt, and he had to address my disturbing feelings. "Life is a school for Soul, O," he began, in his gentle, healing voice. "It doesn't matter which course the world takes, Soul will always experience life and learn the lessons it must learn to grow. From this perspective, you should not be bothered by the deceptions of Christianity. If not the Christian religion, it would be something else because Soul has to experience the false consciousness of life. This is how Soul grows. It transforms the false consciousness of life just as you had to. Yours was a journey through the complex consciousness of your own false nature, and now look at you. Is this not proof enough that everything is as it should be?"

I thought before responding. "Everything you say makes perfect sense, but I don't agree with you. I'm sorry, J; but I have a feeling in my gut that won't go away."

"What feeling?" Jesus asked.

"That you gave the world a bum steer, and there's not a damn thing anyone can do about it!" I replied, letting it all out. "I know that any point in life can be an entry point into the secret teachings of the Way and Soul's liberation from the cycle of life and death, but that's not good enough to get rid of this feeling. *It's just not good enough!*"

"Could you be a little more specific?" Jesus asked, with concern in his voice.

Images of Christian churches and graveyards flashed across my mind from all the driving holidays that Cathy and I had taken over the years, and of all the times that I said to her, "Jesus sure has a lot of real estate," and I could not help but be overwhelmed by the thought of just how tightly woven the lie of Christianity was in the complex tapestry of social consciousness, and I wanted to gasp for air.

"All ways lead to the Way-shower," I said, after taking two or three deep gulps of air. "I know that. But to bypass the entire mesoteric stage of life with this Gospel conspiracy nonsense is wrong. *It's just wrong!* That's the feeling in my gut. It's just wrong for the world to go on being deceived by the great lie of Christianity! You can no more spare a Soul from going through the mesoteric stage of its spiritual growth than I can turn the clock back and undo some of the most stupid things that I have done in my life, and I have done some doozies! Does the world have to go on living the lie that you came into this world to confer instant salvation status upon Soul with your death on the cross? I know we can't change the past, because that's just the way it is; but I can't help feeling the way I do about the wrongness of this deception. Please tell me I'm wrong to feel this way, because it horrifies me to know that your life and teaching are responsible for this monstrous illusion that Soul does not have to take responsibility for its own salvation!"

Jesus said nothing. His eyes were closed. Then he smiled. His face took on a different look. It seemed to metamorphose before my eyes into a different face, one that I recognized but could not put my finger on; but the image vanished the moment Jesus spoke. His voice had authority: **"Those that are ready for the Way will find the Way, and those that are not ready will experience more life until they are ready.** That's the sum of it. What you feel about the Gospel conspiracy is born of your own relationship with Christianity, and you have to live with that. In time you will be less bothered by the deceptions of Christianity. For now, decide whether you want to continue our talks. I will respect your choice."

As pivotal as Christ's ultimatum was, I didn't have to think about my response. "I really don't know what to do," I said. "I've always wanted to write a book on your sayings, because I have an insight into your teaching that few people have, and it's unbelievably joyous talking about the Way with you; but I'm in a quandary. I feel like I might be an accomplice to this great deception, and I can't have that on my conscience. *I can't!"*

Jesus surprised me. He burst into laughter. "How can you be an accomplice if what we are doing helps to undo this deception?"

"It's stupid, I know; but that's how I feel. I feel like I'm being used, and I'm uncomfortable with this feeling. *It feels like I'm whoring myself!"*

"And what does that make me?" Jesus asked, with a twinkle in his eyes.

I burst into laughter. "Let's not go there! That would be too much for my psyche!"

"And mine. Alright, then. Are you uncomfortable with our talks?"

231

"Not at all. I like how they address the secret teachings of the Way. I guess what bothers me is this oppressive feeling of sadness — *that's it!*" I exclaimed. *"I'm feeling an overwhelming sense of sadness for all those Souls trapped by the lie of Christianity!* That's what I'm feeling! I feel sadness for all those Souls that cannot extricate themselves from a faith that keeps them hostage to their self-deception! I feel for them, J; I honestly do! And no; I will not discontinue our talks! If we can inspire one Soul to pack its bags and get on with its journey through life this project will have been worth it! *Just one Soul, J!"*

Jesus' face lit up like the sun. In his face I saw the image that I couldn't put my finger on. It was the same image that the Inner Master let me see when I asked him in a dream one night, *"What do I call you?"* He smiled and put his arm around my shoulder, turned me around gently, and I found myself staring into the Face of God! I could not contain my emotions as I stared into Jesus Christ's face, and I broke down and wept with joy.

Jesus waited for me to compose myself. Then, very softly, with a smile that wrapped my heart in his hands, he said, "Your heart center has expanded since we began our talks. Your empathy has overwhelmed you. As we progress in our talks you will get used to your greater love for Soul. Love is a powerful force, O; and only the most selfless Soul can receive the pure love of God."

"Another thought just came to me," I said, as an incredible feeling of hope washed away all of my sadness, "a thought that our talks will in some miraculous way help to shift the center of life's consciousness from the exoteric to the mesoteric circle of life."

"Indeed they will," Jesus very calmly said. "The more conscious people become of the Way, the more the mesoteric circle of life will expand; and the more it expands, the less hold the material values of life will have upon Soul."

"That's it exactly!" I shouted, so full of excitement that I could not contain myself and jumped out of my chair and looked at Jesus. "We can lessen the grip that the Gospel conspiracy has upon Soul just by explaining the true meaning of your sayings!"

"We will indeed," replied Jesus, with the sweetest smile.

"You know what, J? I feel better! Suddenly I feel like a player in the game of life! I really do! But I don't mean this in an egotistical way—"

Jesus broke into a gentle laugh. "More of a player than you realize, O. What you take so much for granted about yourself, the world will one day hold in awe and wonder."

"Why?" I asked, and sat down. I had to know to satisfy the insecure writer in me.

Again, Jesus laughed. "It is truly marvelous how you can be so far outside the box, even for High Initiates of the Light and Sound of God. But you also inspire a sense of dread, my fine friend. You have a way of waking people up to their inherent destiny, which can be too much for most people to bear; hence the spiritual dread that you inspire."

"Is this the dread of taking complete responsibility for your own spiritual life?" I asked, just to be certain that I understood Jesus correctly.

"Yes," he replied.

"And this is what inspires all those nasty little slings and arrows that I have to keep suffering from Old Whore Life; right?" I added, with a wry chuckle.

Jesus could not help himself and broke into laughter; and with this wonderful moment of irony we brought our discourse to closure for the day.

46. *Letting Soul Speak*

"Before we begin our discourse today, may I ask you a question?" I said to Jesus the next morning the moment Cathy left for work. "I'd like to clear up something."

"By all means," Jesus said.

"As I read what I've written so far of our dialogue, I got the feeling the reader might see me being somewhat cavalier with you. Am I?"

"The reader will get over this feeling the more he gets into your story," Jesus skillfully replied. "It's not that you're cavalier with me, O. It's more that you're not constrained by your own mind. You are free spiritually, and when you let Soul speak all bets are off. This can come across as being cavalier, but it's not."

"Then maybe we should let the reader in on the mystery of letting Soul speak?"

"Do you think they will better understand me now than when I said, '*Whosoever drinketh of the water that I shall give him shall never thirst?*'"

"That's only because they confused you with Holy Spirit," I replied, and smiled.

"True. But I did go on to say, '*but the water that I shall give him shall be in him a well of water springing up to everlasting life.*' John 4, 14. I did explain myself, O. Still, they missed the connection. The River of God flows through life, and every Soul can tap into this great river of everlasting life simply by living the disciplines of the Way, which I explained by telling the world to *do* my sayings. But the world misunderstood me; and we have to set the record straight once and for all."

"Then let's start by saying that this water that you gave to the world was drawn from the well of your own spiritual being—"

"No. Let's not say that," Jesus interrupted me. "If we say that the world will continue to confuse the message with the messenger. I was the messenger of Holy Spirit. I was, and still am the messenger of

Holy Spirit. Holy Spirit is the water of everlasting life, not me. I'm just the messenger. *Can I ever get this point across without tainting it?"*

I had to laugh at Jesus' passion. But I understood. "You're deliberately being very human in our talks, aren't you?"

"Of course. I want the reader to see that the Soul of man rises out of the human consciousness. I was a man long before I became the savior of the world, and my passion for life was no mean passion. How do you think I could be so fanatical about my mission if I was not so passionate about life? If the world only knew of my passion for life I would have been taken down off my cross long ago. The world refuses to see me as one of its own. In truth, I am very much one of the world's own because Soul is born of life. Soul may have its origin in the Ocean of Love and Mercy, but the spiritual self of man is born of life; and the more passionate the life lived, the more fierce the quickened Soul. Mine was a short life with a long history, but it could not have been more passionate. **I lived to live, not to die. My death was the death of death, not the death of life**; and I hope that we can make it clear with our talks that the death of the lower self does not deprive one of his passion for life. On the contrary, the most passionate Soul is the selfless Soul!"

I felt the intense joy of Christ's spiritual freedom, and I wanted to give him a hug. In fact I did just that. Jesus understood why I had to do it and thanked me.

"You're welcome. So, shall we let the reader in on the secret of letting Soul speak?"

"I've had my say for now, O. You can have the floor," Jesus said.

"Alright. Then I would say that letting Soul speak is being an open channel for the Creative Life Current, which is Holy Spirit. You call it the water of everlasting life. All great artists have learned to let Soul speak. Take Mozart. He was a great Soul open to the Sound Current of God. The Sound of God is the Voice of God, and the Voice of God spoke the Word through Mozart's music. Take Van Gogh. He was a great Soul open to the Light of God, which revealed to the world the wonder and splendor of God's creation. Or Shakespeare, another great Soul whose gift was tapping into the consciousness of life. The wisdom and passion of life flowed from his pen like sparkling water. The Word spoke through Shakespeare more than any other writer, except perhaps Rumi. Artists have always been channels for the Light and Sound of God, which together make up the Creative Life Current; and letting Soul speak is the equivalent of Mozart playing his music, Van Gogh painting his art, and Shakespeare writing his plays. It is the Voice of Soul speaking the Way of Life. That's all it means to let Soul speak. As you said two thousand years ago, the Word is the water of everlasting life, and when Soul speaks it speaks the Word; which can lead to everlasting life if one chooses to live by the Word. Otherwise one will continue to learn his lessons the natural way through the hard karmic knocks of life."

"Well said. If I may just add a word. One acquires the talent for letting Soul speak. The more one surrenders ego to their higher self, the more they will be open to the Voice of Soul. Letting Soul speak is being your true self, which is Soul."

"Wow! I wish I had said that!"

"You did, but in your own words."

"I love your words better. They speak to some of my favorite lines in literature!"

"Which are?" Jesus asked.

"'This above all, to thy own self be true, and it must follow as the night the day—'"

"'Thou canst not then be false to any man!'" Jesus interjected, completing my quote from *Hamlet*, and we ended our talk on that unbelievably high note.

47. *Frolicking With God*

I could feel the tenor of our talks changing. It was very subtle. After each talk I spent several hours capturing our talk on paper, after my day's work or very early the following morning; but for all the levity still, the tenor was changing. I wasn't too happy about this, because I didn't want *Jesus Wears Dockers* to become another one of those serious books on Christianity.

Of course, the secret of Christ's teaching would be so serious that it would change the reader's perspective on the life and teachings of Jesus; but I wanted to create an atmosphere of playful joy for the reader, like the playful joy that a long distance runner experiences when he hits his stride and feels so good that he wants to frolic with God. Jesus and I had connected in this special way, like two runners who had hit their stride and released so much goodness that we frolicked with God; that's why we laughed so much.

We could not contain God's love and had to let out the goodness with laughter. That was the playful, joyful atmosphere that I wanted to continue throughout the whole book; but I had to wonder: why did Jesus and I connect in this special way?

I knew from experience that whenever I have a conversation with a person within minutes I'm laughing at something or other, which instantly inspires laughter in the person I'm speaking with. Like the Dalai Lama who breaks into spontaneous laughter whenever he's talking with someone but no one but him knows why he's laughing. What is it about me that inspires this playful joy? Because whatever it is, Jesus possessed it in spades.

I thought about this for days before our next talk. When we met again in my bonus room I brought up the subject of playful joy which I felt defined our talks.

"Why do you suppose we laugh so much in our talks?" I asked Jesus, giving him no time to set the agenda. "Why such playful joy, J?"

Jesus gave me a big smile. "Have you ever seen children playing?"

"Of course," I said.

"And did you not notice the spontaneity of their play?"

"Yes."

"Soul is a happy entity, O; and innocence allows for this play of Soul. That's the insight you're looking for. You have realized this innocence that I tried to impress upon the world. `*Verily I say unto you, except ye be converted and become as little children, ye shall not enter into the kingdom of heaven,'* I said in Mathew 18, 3. And I went on to add, `*Whosoever therefore shall humble himself as this little child, the same is the greatest in the kingdom of heaven.'* In effect, the innocence of a child opens the door for Soul to experience the pure joy of life. In adults this innocence can only be recaptured with humility. But humility is not ego's strongest suite; so it is to the nature of ego that speaks to Soul's play in life. The more centered Soul is in its ego self, the less playful joy one will experience. Ego is much too full of itself to let Soul out to experience the pure joy of life. This is why self-centered people are so humorless."

An image flashed across my mind of a man I knew who had moved to St. Jude from an adjacent community. This man lived in a small paper mill town where he knew everyone and everyone knew him. When I saw him walking in St. Jude early one morning I could feel his newfound sense of freedom. He was happy because he was free of all the psychic constraints that his old hometown had on him; and I felt the same freedom when Cathy and I left St. Jude and moved to Georgian Bay.

"Soul is constrained by ego," I reiterated, to confirm what Jesus was pointing to. "That's why you stressed the virtue of humility. Humility checks the ego, and the checked ego gives Soul the freedom to come out and experience the joy of life. Is that it?"

"Very much so," Jesus said.

"If I may, J," I added, feeling a strong nudge to expand on this thought. "I used to be a long distance runner. I experienced the playful joy that distance runners experience when they hit their stride. But I also experienced something else that I think speaks to innocence. At some point during a long distance run one feels the self relax, to the point where one just experiences the simple joy of being. In fact some marathon runners have actually experienced a temporary loss of identity. They experienced the pure joy of being, and this pure joy of being is what I think the innocence of a child speaks to. However, because Soul needs a self to realize its teleological purpose of spiritual self-realization and God consciousness, this pure joy of being has to be understood; so becoming as an innocent child takes on a much more profound connotation than you imply with your saying. Am I correct in this understanding?"

Jesus reflected for a moment, and then said, "The consciousness of a child is free of all the baggage of life; that's why it is so innocent. What I tried to get across to my disciples was for them to be in the world but not of the world, just as the child. Children are in the world but they are not yet of the world, and I stressed the virtue of humility to keep the self from completely suffocating one's spiritual nature. My whole teaching addresses this point. Soul cannot realize itself in a human self that is so full of its own desires that it has no room for Soul to come out and be. This is what I meant when I said, *'It is easier for a camel to go through the eye of a needle than for a rich man to enter into the kingdom of heaven.'* Mathew 19, 24. By riches I meant the consciousness of one's ego, of course. Soul just *is,* O. The experience of pure being is a Soul experience. When a long distance runner experiences this sense of pure being, all he has done is shifted his I-consciousness from his outer to inner self; from his human personality to Soul. That's when this sense of playful joy kicks in, because one has been liberated from the constraints of the lower self. But why are we talking about this, anyway?"

"Because I felt that our talks were beginning to take on that dead-weight seriousness that all books on Christianity have, and I don't want our book to be like that."

Jesus laughed. *"I doubt that will ever happen!"*

"Why not?" I asked, smiling at Christ's playfulness.

"Because we can't help but be who we are, and who we are speaks to the pure spontaneous joy of life. As I said in our last talk, I did not die to life; I died to death. You also experienced this same death by living my sayings. That's how you experienced your own immortality. Did you not die to your life to find your life?"

"How else do you think I broke the code of your sayings?"

"Well then, stop worrying about how these talks will unfold. They will be what they will be because we are what we are. Now can we get on with the business at hand?"

"Which is?"

"Self-transformation."

"According to the sayings of Jesus?"

"Not necessarily. My sayings open the door to the mystery of self-transformation; but, yes, that's the business at hand."

"Not just yet, J. I want to explore this emotion of playful joy. I'd like the reader to understand exactly why you and I are having so much fun. I don't know if our humor will translate on paper—"

"But it will," Jesus interrupted. "The reader will catch the spirit of our humor and go with it. In fact, he will look forward to more of the same."

"Do you think so?"

"I know so."

"Why, because you're God?"

"I rest my case," Jesus said, and laughed.

"Alright," I said, with a mirthful chuckle, "I'd like to run a thought by you, which I believe speaks to this sense of playful joy."

"Please," Jesus said.

"First, let me ask you why you think all books written about you are so damn serious?" I asked, just to clear the air.

"Damn?" Jesus queried.

"Sorry, J; it just slipped out."

"No harm done. No doubt, these books are serious because they are written from the perspective of one's very mortal human consciousness—"

"DAMN!" I exploded. *"That's it exactly!"*

"Don't get excited, O," Jesus said, smiling at how quickly I had made the connection. "Now explain this for the reader please, because I'm sure it will need explanation."

"I'm sure it will too," I said, as I tried to calm myself. "The human self is very conscious of its own mortality, so it would follow that it would be deadly serious about the subject of immortality; and your teaching is all about the immortal nature of man; right?"

"Absolutely," said Jesus.

"But it's not quite as simple as all of that," I quickly added, as my Muse flashed the image across my mind. "The human self is conscious of its own mortality and therefore exists in a constant state of dread. This dread is repressed for the most part, but it's always there; and logic would dictate that the more centered one is in his lower self, the more intense the dread of his mortality will be. This is why the egoist is hell-bent on leaving monuments to his name when he dies, like Ozymandias in Shelly's poem. This is ego's way of dealing with the dread of its own mortality. Ironically ego is no more mortal than Soul is, because ego is simply Soul-not-yet-realized; and the whole purpose of your teaching is to transform the consciousness of one's lower self until one's lower and higher self become one self. That's when one's dread of mortality will disappear forever. I can attest to this with my own experience. And if I may say so now, this is why you and I have this irrepressible sense of playful joy in our talks; we're not constrained by the dread of our human mortality. Does that make sense to you, J?"

"Perfectly," said Jesus. "And I think it will make perfect sense to the reader also. Now can we get to the business at hand?"

"THIS IS THE BUSINESS AT HAND!" I exploded, and burst into laughter.

Jesus smiled, trying very hard to keep a straight face; but he could not contain the joy of the irony and burst into laughter too.

48. *The Parable of the Sower Revealed*

Jesus set the agenda this morning. He had a stern look on his clean-shaven face. He was wearing a short sleeve sky blue shirt, navy blue dress slacks, and dress shoes. Blue meant business. Blue is the Way-shower's color, so I wasn't surprised when Jesus said, "We're going to reveal the truth about my parable of the kingdom of heaven. It's time we took the mystery out of my teaching and dispel the Gospel conspiracy. Would you turn to Mathew 13 and read it out loud for me, please?"

I did. Jesus listened attentively, and then in the same no-nonsense business voice said, "Turn to John, Chapter 8, verse 51, please."

I flipped the pages to John, found Chapter 8, and read the verse Jesus wanted me to read: *"Verily, verily, I say unto you. If a man keep my saying he shall never see death."*

"Life and death," Jesus said. "That's what my teaching is all about. It is about the life of the spirit and the death of evil, and by evil here I mean everything that stands in the way of the spiritual birth that I promised the world with my gospel. Did I not say in John 3, verse 3, *'Except a man be born again he cannot see the kingdom of God?'* But we have to explain to the reader what we mean by the kingdom of God, don't we?

"The world has taken this phrase much too literally and completely distorted my teaching. The irony is that there is a literal truth to my phrase kingdom of God; but it is the metaphorical truth of this phrase that leads to the literal truth. By metaphorical truth I simply mean that the phrase kingdom of God stands for the Way. The Way is the key that opens the door to the literal kingdom of God, and by Way here we mean?"

Jesus looked at me, waiting for an answer. I wasn't sure what he was up to, so I replied, "The Way is the spiritual path of the Light and Sound of God."

"Yes, it certainly is that," Jesus replied. "But could you please explain what I meant by the Way in the context of my gospel of the kingdom of God? You have taken the Way into the modern world with your explanation, but I would like the reader to see what I meant by the Way in my teaching two thousand years ago. How would you define the kingdom of God for the reader as I use the metaphor in my teaching?"

I turned to the Gospel of Mathew and glanced at the first parable. It was the parable of the sower, which I had experienced many times in my own life; so I was intimately familiar with the truth of this parable because I had also sown the precious seed.

I looked at Jesus, pursed my lips in thought, and said, "By kingdom of God you mean the power of the reconciling Word of God. This reconciling Word of God is what has been called the Way throughout history. In your teaching, this reconciling power of Holy Spirit is released when one lives by your sayings. Your sayings are the key to your teaching, because they are like golden keys that open the lock to the mystery of spiritual rebirth. But I'm getting ahead of myself. What you mean by kingdom of God here is that body of secret knowledge that you shared with the world; that specific secret knowledge that will transform the consciousness of one's lower self. Your sayings release the reconciling power of Holy Spirit, which transforms the consciousness of the lower self. When the lower self is transformed enough, then one will experience his spiritual rebirth. Because I experienced this rebirth, I can explain it to the reader—"

"Please do," Jesus cut in, with a wave of his hand.

"What spiritual rebirth means here is that the power of Holy Spirit released by living the sayings of Jesus reconciles the I of ego with the I of one's higher self. Or, to put it simply, the I of ego is reconciled with one's unfolding spiritual self; and by reconcile we mean to make compatible, to harmonize, or bring into agreement with. So the reconciling power of Holy Spirit, which is released when one lives the Way — in this case, *doing* your sayings — harmonizes the ego self with one's spiritual self until there is a shift in one's center of gravity from the I-consciousness of one's human self to one's spiritual self. In other words, when one has released enough of the reconciling power of Holy Spirit by living your sayings and has resolved enough of the ego self to create a critical mass of spiritual consciousness he will shift his center of gravity from his human self to his spiritual self. This is what you refer to as being born again. This spiritual birth is simply a shift in self-consciousness from ego to Soul. Which means that one's I is no longer centered in one's lower, or human self; it is now centered in one's spiritual self. We call this spiritual self-realization consciousness. You called it spiritual rebirth. Can I take a break now?"

"Please," Jesus said, with a contented smile on his face.

"I could sure use a cup of coffee. Would you like one?" I asked.

"Yes, please," Jesus said. "That was an excellent explanation of my teaching, O. Thank you very much for that. I'm sure it will give the reader an entirely new look at my gospel to the world."

"I hope it takes the mystery out of your sayings," I said, getting up. "Just milk?"

"Yes, please," Jesus said.

I went downstairs, poured our coffee, and started up the stairs when the thought came to me to explain the parable of the sower as I had experienced it. I handed Jesus his cup, took a sip of my coffee, and said, "I want to share something with you, if I may."

"Is it related to our theme this morning?"

I smiled. "You're all business this morning, aren't you?"

"Yes."

"Why?"

"We have created enough of an atmosphere of credibility for the reader to be told the truth about my teaching," Jesus replied, like a calm executive at a board meeting.

"Everything we talk about reveals the truth of your teaching. This is the whole point of these talks, isn't it — to reveal the magic of spiritual self-realization consciousness?"

"Explain that, please," Jesus said, with a gesture of his hand.

"For you, or the reader?" I asked, trying to inject a little levity.

Jesus gave me a stern look. "The reader."

"You are all business today, aren't you?"

"Yes."

"Again, why?"

"We set out to reveal the truth of my teaching to dispel the Gospel conspiracy, but we always get sidetracked — *like now!*"

I laughed. "Okay. Let me explain what I meant. The spiritually self-realized person has the gift of speaking for Soul when the occasion calls for the Way to be introduced into a conversation."

"And by that, you mean?"

"I mean that when Holy Spirit sees an opportunity for the reconciling power of the Way to be revealed to a person, then Soul speaks," I replied, smiling at Christ's no-nonsense personality.

"And by Soul, you mean?"

"The Voice of Holy Spirit, of course."

"So, the spiritually self-realized Soul can speak for Holy Spirit?"

"Exactly. This is why I said that all of our dialogue speaks the Way, not just the part related to your teaching."

"Won't this lead the reader to make the same mistake with you that the world made with me — confuse the messenger with the message?"

I laughed. Jesus did not budge from his stern disposition, and just stared at me.

"I suppose it could," I replied, with a fresh chuckle. "But given my stance on the issue of messiahship, because I do adamantly believe in letting the world find its own way, I can't see how the reader could possibly ascribe to me what the world ascribed to you!"

With that, Jesus burst into laughter. "You win, O," he said. "I can't be serious with you. I wanted the reader to see you as you really are by playing the straight man, but I can't support that role. You were going to share something with me?"

"Yes," I said, happy to see the playful Jesus back. "I wanted to share my experience of sowing the seed like the sower in your parable."

"Excellent. This will put some real flesh into my parable. Please, I'm dying to hear," Jesus said, again with a motion of his hand.

"First, I should let the reader in on the simple fact that all spiritually self-realized Souls are sowers of the seed. It is *ipso facto,* because the spiritually self-realized Soul speaks the Way whenever the Way needs to be heard. In other words, life itself is the field which you refer to in your parable, and when a spiritually conscious Soul —

245

which in your teaching you call a Son of man, or a Child of God to be gender perfect — walks in the field of life, he or she is used by Holy Spirit to sow the seed in the soil-consciousness of all the people he or she meets. In other words, to take the metaphor out of your parable, each person that a spiritually self-realized Soul meets in life that is ready to receive the reconciling power of Holy Spirit will receive the seed, which is the Word, and take it to heart; but if a person is not ready he will dismiss it. In your parable you are more specific about this state of spiritual readiness in people. You refer to some people as being *not ready*, *partially ready*, and *ready*. This refers to different levels of spiritual maturity. If a person is spiritually ready to take his spiritual growth into his own hands, he will hear the Word — to use your metaphor. Which means that this person's higher self has enough authority over his lower self to put his hands to the plow — once again, to use your metaphor for taking up the spiritual life of the Way. In other words, soil in your parable refers to the spiritual consciousness of a person. If one is spiritually conscious enough to hear the voice of Holy Spirit, then he will receive the seed, which is the reconciling power of the Way; and if one is not spiritually conscious enough, he will reject the seed, or the reconciling power of Holy Spirit. And of course there are those who think they are ready but aren't spiritually mature enough yet to accept the responsibility of reconciling their lower self with their higher self, and these people I find very amusing—"

I burst into laughter, and Jesus broke into a mirthful chuckle. He knew exactly what I was laughing at, but for the reader's sake I asked Jesus to explain why we were laughing.

"The excitement! The joy! The jubilation! The commitment! The revenge! The love! The adulation! The fear! The dread! The despair! The anger! The guilt! The shame! And finally, the denial!" he exclaimed, playing out the whole litany of emotional responses to his teaching by those who thought they were ready for the Way but weren't.

Smiling at Jesus, I said, "That's the shallow soil speaking, isn't it?"

"Yes. And it pains me to reveal this to your reader because ninety percent of the people who read your book will fall into this category."

"Wow! That's hard ball spirituality, J!"

"I know. But I came not to liberate but to eviscerate!"

Surprised by Christ's comment, I said, "You're not serious, are you?"

"Of course not. I am allowed some measure of whimsy, aren't I?"

"With me you are. I wouldn't try this with anyone else, if I were you."

"There is truth to what I say, though. I do have to eviscerate Christianity of all that nonsense — *my God, O; I'm starting to sound just like you!"*

I broke into laughter. Jesus stared at me with a big smirk on his face. When I stopped laughing he calmly said, "Can we get back to the point now?"

"Right," I said, collecting myself. "I was going to share some of my experiences as a sower of the seed. My most memorable was with a Greek restaurant owner. John heard the Word, embraced the Way with passion for several months, and then abandoned it completely and could no longer look me in the eye for the shame he felt for not being strong enough to live the Way as I had shared it with him. He got cancer a few years after he abandoned the Way and went to Greece to seek out a miracle cure in a remote monastery on Mount Athos. He died, and when I met him on the other side in a dream one night I told him that he could try again in another life because that's just the way it was. I hadn't worked out the DPG at this time in my life, so I wasn't as compassionate in my understanding of the Way as I could have been with John. I was just as stern as you were when you gave your teaching to the world two thousand years ago — which, I might add, did not do your so-called image of the great giver of peace much good. In truth J, you were an extremely hard taskmaster."

Jesus smiled at my candor, and said, "I know; and I regret that. But that was then and this is now. Continue if you would, please."

"The next memorable experience I had of sowing the seed was with my nephew. He heard the Word, put it to practice, but then one day he said to me, 'I don't like what this teaching is doing to me. I don't feel right. I feel different.' And just as he said that I felt a sudden fierce rush of wind and I knew it was what you called 'the wicked one' come to take the Word away from my nephew. This was the Kal, the negative force of life, which protects ego from the reconciling power of Holy Spirit until the spiritual self is mature enough to embrace the Word of God. My nephew and I were never the same again; and, to make my point, my nephew abandoned the Way of Spirit for the way of the world and has been miserable ever since. His life is one big karmic mess today."

"Please explain that. The reader will never understand unless you do."

"Yes, I know. But how can I explain that there are two forces at play in life, and both of these forces are part of the Divine Plan of God?"

"Please try," Jesus said.

"Alright," I said, and silently called upon the Inner Master for guidance. "The two forces are the positive and negative forces. The positive is Holy Spirit, and the negative is the evil, or Kal force. Kal Niranjan is the Demiurge of the lower planes, just as the ancient Gnostics realized; and his mandate from the Supreme God of all planes of consciousness is to keep Soul trapped in the lower worlds by any means possible until Soul has all the experiences it needs to become spiritually self-realized. When I say that Kal will do anything, I mean anything! This is why we say things like, 'Who said that life is fair?' And, 'life is cruel,' 'it's a jungle out there,' 'it's a dog eat dog world,' and so on. However, Kal Niranjan is also responsible for the Law of Karma, so it has to operate within the boundaries of this spiritual law of just retribution; but even within these strict boundaries the Kal energy will do all it can to keep Soul trapped in the cycle of karma and reincarnation, because that's how Soul grows. The Kal will trick Soul into creating negative karma so that Soul will repeat life and learn its spiritual lessons the hard way. Kal loves to teach Soul its lessons the hard way. This is why Kal is called *Deus Deceptor*, or the Devil. In reality the Devil, or Satan, is just doing his job to temper Soul on its journey back home to God; and contrary to what the Gnostics believed Kal is not evil, as such. He's just perceived to be evil because not everyone can see the true spiritual purpose of this Demiurge.

"That's excellent," said Jesus, with a grateful smile. "But could you please amplify a little more? We should make it absolutely clear to the reader what we mean by evil."

"Alright. I'll give you the most modern definition of evil that I have worked out in my own efforts to put this whole issue into a context that does justice to how evil is perceived by the world and what it is in reality."

"This should be good," Jesus said. Then, with a playful smile, added, "If you can do that O, I'll kiss your feet!"

"Like hell you will! But that's how difficult you think it is, don't you?"

"It is difficult to define evil, I know; but creative Spirit knows no limits. Anything is possible," Jesus replied.

"I know, and I trust my Muse implicitly. But I'll only tell you on one condition."

"Which is?" Jesus asked.

"That we leave each other's feet alone!"

Jesus laughed. "I take it back, O. We don't want to create the wrong impression."

"No; we don't. Okay, evil. Well, it took years and countless hours of creative thinking to come to this definition, but I believe I found the perfect compromise for what the world takes evil to be and what it is in reality, and—"

"Drum roll!" Jesus exclaimed, and pretended to beat a drum on his lap.

Smiling at Jesus, I continued: "Evil is the unresolved karma of the world. Evil is the 'I' of God trapped in the unresolved collective I-consciousness of man's lower self. Evil exists only insomuch that it has not yet been resolved; so evil is both real and not real. It is real insomuch as unresolved karma is real, but not real insomuch that once it is resolved it ceases to be. As the unresolved karma of the individual ego, evil's name is legion. This is why evil is both one and many. Evil is the face, force, and spirit of all the negative karma in the world that has to be resolved in order for Soul to reconcile itself with God. In effect, all of this unresolved karma is personified in Kal Niranjan, or Satan, which Doctor Jung called the Archetypal Shadow in his psychology and which I have ironically identified as Old Whore Life that loves to screw us of our virtue; and it follows logically that the more one resolves their negative karma the less power Satan will have over them. This is the spiritual law of life. This is why Soul Masters seldom speak of evil as such, because in itself evil does not exist. It exists only insomuch that Soul creates evil by breaking the spiritual laws of life. In the strictest sense then, evil is man-made; not God-created. We are responsible for the evil in the world, not God. In effect, J; we are the Old Whore. And that, I'm afraid, is a truth that few readers will take lightly — especially Christians!"

Jesus stood up and very solemnly bent down, but I jumped to my feet knocking my chair over, and shouted, *"Like hell you do!"*

Jesus laughed and sat back down. "That was the best description of evil I have ever heard, O. *Excellent! Just excellent!"*

"Thank you. Now, if I may, I have other examples of sowing the seed, if you would like to hear them?" I said, picking up my chair.

"I certainly do," Jesus said.

"Okay. One in particular sticks out because I modeled a character in my last book on this man. He was an artist looking for his own way in art, and so thirsty was he for the Word that the waters of everlasting life just poured out of me. Honest to God, J; I could not believe how quickly the spigot opened whenever we got together. Every time the spigot opened the Way just poured out of me and he scrambled to take notes. Every word that came out of my mouth was like precious water to him. *It embarrassed me!"*

"I hear you," Jesus said, with a beaming smile.

"As I said, this man was a water color artist, and he had a desperate need to realize his own identity as an artist. This spoke to Soul's fundamental need for spiritual self-realization consciousness, and what came out of my mouth addressed this man's need for greater self-identity. It was one of the most incredible experiences of my life, watching how his insatiable need for greater self-identity pulled the Word out of me. The waters of everlasting life flowed in such abundance that I could not stop the flow. That's why I began dictating my Soul talk book *The Way of Soul* into my tape recorder on my way to and from work every day. I gave this artist the methodology he needed to satisfy his hunger for more self-identity, but the tide was so powerful that I had to let it out in my three Soul talk books, starting with the one that Doctor Jung read and wanted to discuss with me. That's when I became a Keeper of the Flame and Kevin Archer my first recipient of the Holy Flame of God; and I have to confess J, that I bear witness to the greatest Law of God in this phenomenal experience of letting Soul speak whenever I am called upon to serve life — **the more love one gives to a person, the more love he will receive from God!**"

Christ's face just glowed. He smiled, and said, "Would you please explain for the reader's sake what you mean by one's need for more self-identity? I fear he may not grasp this simple concept."

"Again?" I said.

"Yes, again," Jesus said, with authority in his voice.

"Okay," I said, acquiescing to Christ's request. "In the DPG we all come into the lower worlds to create our own spiritual identity, or Soul self if you will. As atoms of God, we all come into the world with Soul consciousness but no self-consciousness. As we evolve through the chain of natural evolution we nourish our spiritually encoded need for total self-identity with the consciousness of life. This consciousness of life is the I-consciousness of God, which we know as the creative life force. This life force is Holy Spirit. Life cannot exist without the energy of the creative life force. As we evolve through life, we take in more and more of this life force. As we take in the life force through our constant interactions with life, we individuate it through the process of natural growth. This can properly be called the individuation of the 'I' of God. When we have individuated enough of the life force to experience the dawning of self-consciousness, like I did in my primordial lifetime as Grunt, we will reincarnate with this rudimentary sense of self and continue to individuate our self-consciousness until we have a sense of our own spiritual essence; and we nourish our spiritual self-identity from one life to the next until we realize our Soul self in the experience of our own immortality, which I did with your teaching. This is what you referred to as being born again. Your whole teaching of sowing the seed is all about showing man how to take his spiritual growth into his own hands. In a word, J; your teaching is about becoming conscious of the Way so we can live the spiritual life consciously and realize our essential purpose in life."

"Which is?" Jesus asked, for absolute clarity.

"Which is to become a spiritually self-realized, God-conscious Soul. Or, as you put it, to become one with our Father in heaven."

"Excellent," said Jesus. "I think we're well on our way to taking the mystery out of my sayings and dispelling the Gospel conspiracy!"

"I think so," I said, smiling at Christ's enthusiasm. "Do you think we should explain your other parables of the kingdom of heaven?"

"Not necessary," Jesus said. "I think the reader should understand by now what I meant when I said in Mathew 13, 38, *'The field is the world; the good seed are the children of the kingdom; but the tares are the children of the wicked one.'*"

I quickly turned to Mathew 13 to look up the verse, and then I said, "I think we should further explain this, and the following verse."

"Read the following verse, please," Jesus said.

"*'The enemy that sowed them (the tares) is the devil; the harvest is the end of the world; and the reapers are the angels,'*" I read, and turned to Jesus for a comment.

"I think you should complete the whole thought to give it complete contextual meaning," Jesus said.

"I think so too," I said, and read Mathew 13: 40-43: *"'As therefore the tares are gathered and burned in the fire; so shall it be in the end of the world. The Son of man shall send forth his angels, and they shall gather out of his kingdom all things that offend, and them which do iniquity. And shall cast them into the furnace of fire; there shall be weeping and gnashing of teeth. Then shall the righteous shine forth as the sun in the kingdom of their Father. Who hath ears to hear, let him hear.'"*

Jesus nodded, but said nothing. I put my Bible back on my desk, and said, "This we have to explain for the reader, because you certainly led the world down the garden path with your metaphors for the transformation of the lower self. My God, J; what were you thinking?"

"Was it me, or the Gospel writers?" Jesus replied, with a big smirk. "No matter. It does need explanation. But I'll be very frank with you here, O. I have waited centuries to find the opportunity to undo the harm that the misunderstanding of this parable has done to the psyche of man, and now we can finally take the muddle out of the puddle!"

I laughed. I loved Christ's expression. But further still, I loved the fact that Jesus owned up to the effect that a literal interpretation of his parable had done harm to the psyche of man. "Would you like me to take the mystery out of your metaphors here?" I asked.

"If you would," Jesus replied.

"Okay," I said, and sat back in my chair. I closed my eyes and did a silent HU; and then I called upon the Inner Master to give me the right words, because as much as I understood Christ' parable I preferred that Spirit provide the explanation for the reader, and after a moment or so of silence I opened my eyes and let Soul speak: "This whole parable refers to the metaphysics of self-transformation. The dynamic of self-transformation is a very real experience, which takes place in the lower bodies of man — the physical, astral, causal, and mental bodies. As one puts to practice the sayings of Jesus, he sets into motion the dynamic of self-transformation. This happens as the reconciling power of Holy Spirit transforms the consciousness of the lower self. This transformation is not metaphorical. It is an actual alchemical experience that you refer to as the furnace of fire — or, more specifically, the wailing and gnashing of teeth. This wailing and gnashing of teeth is the spiritual anguish that one feels as the consciousness of his lower self is transformed by the reconciling power of Holy Spirit that one sets free as one *lives* your sayings. The end of the world that you refer to in this parable is the end of the world for the lower self, which is of this material world. As the consciousness of the lower self is transformed by the reconciling power of Holy Spirit, the individual becomes more purified in spiritual self-consciousness; and the more purified he becomes, the more he joins his Father in heaven. Which simply means that the lower and higher self are becoming one self. This one self is the individuated consciousness of the 'I' of God. This is why you can say that one becomes one with his Father in heaven. Just to make it absolutely clear for the reader, the end of the world in this parable refers to the end of the lower self's world. It refers to the death of the lower self and birth of the spiritual self, which I have called the birth of a new 'I' of God. This parable by no means refers to the end of the world, as such. It is a personal death, not a world death. The spiritually self-realized Soul then becomes what you call the righteous that shine forth. The angels in the parable are the Sons of man, or Soul-conscious people who help gather Souls ready for the kingdom of heaven — meaning, all those Souls that are ready to take spiritual growth into their own hands by living the Way consciously. The wicked one represents the negative forces of life, which will do anything to keep Soul trapped in the consciousness of its lower self. In effect, the two forces at play in the dynamic of your parable are the reconciling power of Holy Spirit and the negative material forces of life that you call the Devil; and all this talk about a literal damnation in hell is a misunderstanding of your parable, because what you meant by your parable is that the lower self has to be transformed in order for one to realize his spiritual self-identity."

I fell silent. Soul had spoken, and we both knew that we could do no more to explain Christ's Parable of the Sower; so we called it a day.

49. *A Man of Flesh and Spirit*

We turned a corner with our last talk. Jesus was in good spirits this morning. "What, shorts?" I said, with some surprise.

"Yes. It's going to be a hot one today."

I looked at Christ's legs, and smiled.

"I know, I know. I have skinny legs."

"I didn't say anything."

"You didn't have to. Your look said it all."

"Not only skinny, but hairy too," I said, and laughed.

"We are what we are," Jesus said, and crossed his legs. "Now can we continue?"

"Not just yet. Let's chit-chat. I'd like to know more about your personal life."

"Why?" Jesus asked, giving me a look.

"Why? Because you're Jesus Christ, that's why. You've been a part of my life — *my life!* Hell, you've been a part of so many of my lives that I feel you owe me an answer to every question that I ask you! Of course, you don't owe me anything. I'd just like to know more about you, that's all."

"Then ask," Jesus very calmly said.

Once again, Jesus surprised me. I think he liked doing that to me. I smiled, delighted for the opportunity to delve into the life of the most enigmatic person in history.

"If you don't want to answer this, I'll understand," I said, out of deep respect for Jesus' personal journey to God-realization consciousness, "but I'd sure love to hear what you have to say. I'm sure the world would too. You said in one of our talks that during your silent years you frequented houses of pleasure to experience sex. Did you do this for the reasons I think you did?"

"Tell me what you think and I'll tell you if you're correct," Jesus replied.

"The reader will never believe it if I'm right!" I exclaimed.

"Let's not keep the reader in suspense, then," Jesus said, with that playful smile.

"Okay," I said, taking up Christ's challenge. "I think you did what you did for the best of reasons. I can't believe that you just fell off the wagon, if I may express it this way."

"You had better explain that," Jesus said.

I chuckled nervously. "The reader knows what it means to fall off the wagon. An alcoholic who stops drinking is on the wagon. Falling off the wagon means that he has started drinking again. I believe you were so hell-bent on living the Way that you would never fall off the wagon of the Way; so, J, I suspect that what you did in those houses of pleasure had a spiritual motive. I think you gorged yourself sexually so you would have an enormous amount of sexual consciousness to process with the power sayings that you received from the Great Book of Life."

Without blinking an eye, Jesus said, "Which one in particular?"

"The Big Gun," I said, with a nervous smile.

"Please reveal the Big Gun of my sayings for the reader," Jesus calmly requested. "And then please explain why I did what I did so the reader can appreciate the full context of my Big Gun saying," he added, in a tone of voice that betrayed the detached state of consciousness that one realizes when he lives by the Big Gun of Christ's sayings.

"I'm not sure the reader is ready for this information — if I'm right about it, that is," I said, just to make certain Jesus and I were on the same page.

"You're right," Jesus said, without hesitation. "I was running out of steam and I had to satisfy my hunger for God. I put to practice one of the most dangerous techniques that a seeker of God can practice to satisfy his hunger for God. I gorged myself on the flesh of women until I could take no more, and then I went into the wilderness and transformed all of that sexual consciousness to satisfy my hunger for God; but unless we explain this, the reader will never understand the madness of this devastating spiritual technique."

I wanted to laugh, but couldn't; I had too much respect for Jesus and this unbelievable technique. "I suspected as much," I said. "I did the same thing. I also gorged myself on sex and then went into sanctuary to process my energy. Sanctuary is a state of absolute detachment that I created with Gurdjieff's technique of *non-*

identification. You called it going into the wilderness and I called it going to sanctuary; but I didn't gorge myself on sex for the same reasons you did. I had a past-life motive for doing it. I was a Sufi in ancient Persia. I belonged to the secret Order of the White Tiger, and I could not tame my tiger of desire. In my current life I had a driving subconscious need to make up for my past-life failure. My tiger of sexual lust got the best of me in my Sufi life, but in this lifetime I managed to get the best of my tiger of sexual desire. I know exactly why you did what you did, because by taming the tiger of my sexual lust — *that had been energized by the awakened kundalini, I might add!* — I fast-tracked my own experience of immortality!"

"Please explain this for the reader. I'm sure we lost him," Jesus said.

"Perhaps. Well, the best way to explain this spiritual madness is by way of metaphor. It's like converting unrefined natural gas. By refining the energy, the engine runs more smoothly. Sexual consciousness would be the unrefined energy that we take in by gorging ourselves on sex; then, as we practice the disciplines of the Way we refine this sexual consciousness and nourish our spiritual self. But the reader will have a hard time swallowing this remarkable spiritual technique unless he gets a fix on the dynamic of self-transformation."

"Absolutely! So reveal my Big Gun saying for the reader's sake, then."

"Okay," I said, and flipped through Mathew to find the saying that spoke to the issue at hand. I found it, and read, *"'For whosoever will save his life shall lose it, and whosoever will lose his life for my sake shall find it.'"* That's Mathew 16, 25. But we should explain here that when you said 'for my sake,' you meant for the sake of the Way, right?"

"Definitely. It's unfortunate that this phrase has caused so much confusion. It's not for me as such that one should lose his life, but for the sake of the reconciling power of Holy Spirit. One dies to one's lower self for the sake of Holy Spirit, because in dying to one's lower self one allows for the reconciling power of Holy Spirit to transform the consciousness of one's lower self, which in turn nourishes one's higher self. That's why I frequented those houses of pleasure. And I will tell you that I did so more often than I would care for the world to know."

"You pig!" I exclaimed. "You just couldn't get enough of God, could you?" I added, and burst into a fit of uproarious laughter.

Jesus laughed also. "What will the world think of me now?" he said, with the biggest grin on his loveable face. "My God, did we have to reveal this forbidden part of the secret teaching? Who would believe this but another initiate of the Way?"

"Any Sufi worth his salt," I said, with a snicker. "Rumi's father, for example; he knew the power of this spiritual technique. But I think the reader will be happy to know that Jesus Christ had to deal with sexual desire too. He may never understand the alchemy of transforming sexual pleasure into pure energy to nourish the spiritual self, but at heart he will know that there's more to sex than meets the eye. Don't you think so, J?"

"He may. But we should explain this transformation of energies. If we don't, the reader will only be more confused; and we don't want to muddle the puddle any more than it already is."

"I just had a thought," I said, excited by the insight. "My God, I wonder if this is why Christianity and sex don't get along. Rather than use sexual energy in a positive manner the way we did, Christianity is afraid that sex will only keep Soul trapped in that state of lower consciousness. Is that it, J? Is that Christianity's historical hang-up with sex?"

With the most radiant smile, Jesus said, "Christianity has lost the holy science of spiritual self-transformation. If Christianity understood the true meaning of my gospel it would not be so fixed in its aberrant doctrine on sex. Why don't we explain the secret of transforming the lower energies of life that nourish Soul's hunger for God?"

"You're right! Soul has a hunger for God that drives it from lifetime to lifetime, and it won't stop seeking God until it is completely satisfied in the experience of God-realization consciousness. Yes; we should explain how to transform the lower energies of life to nourish Soul's hunger for God! Should I, or would you like to?"

"Let me," said Jesus, to my delight because I would rather my reader heard it from Jesus himself. "Once the lower self has gorged itself on sexual pleasure," he explained, his eyes twinkling at the memory, "the seeker of God must then abstain completely from all thoughts and acts of sex. In his efforts to abstain from sex, he transforms the energy of his sexual consciousness. This is what I referred to as the furnace of fire—"

"Conscious suffering!" I interjected. "That's what Gurdjieff called it!"

"Yes," said Jesus. "In this case, it's conscious suffering. In the context of my gospel teaching, it refers to the natural process of karmic transformation. The wailing and gnashing of teeth is the pain that the lower self experiences as it is being transformed, either by the conscious discipline of the spiritual technique or the natural karmic process of dying to the desires of the lower self; but the real test of my discipline in the houses of pleasure was in the experience of being detached from the act of sex while performing the act of sex."

"And at this point we can reveal the meaning of your communication saying."

"Exactly!" Jesus exclaimed. "It's either yae yae or nay nay at this point, because if you get stuck between the two desires — the desire for God and the desire for the pleasures of the flesh — you will truly be in a state of evil. By evil I mean that state of consciousness where one is neither one nor the other, and the conflict is pure hell. That's why my experience in the houses of pleasure was so dangerous. Believe me, the pull of God and the pull of the flesh can drive one mad."

"As it did me in my Sufi lifetime!" I spit out, confirming Christ's explanation with my own experience of going out of my mind by the pull of my two stallions of desire. "It was a horrible life, J. I was torn apart by my desire for the flesh and my desire for God, and I died an utter fool of God. But let me say here that this secret aspect of the teaching can be bypassed altogether with the Love Song to God. I say this with all my heart, J. The HU can transform the consciousness of one's lower self with the gentleness of a mother's kiss; so there's no need for the reader to tease himself with the madness of this either/or technique. It's only for fools of God that will do anything to satisfy their lust for God."

"I agree," said Jesus, with a melancholy smile.

259

"I have to ask you something here, J," I said, as the thought popped into my mind. "Were you not familiar with the Holy Sound of God? You were familiar with the pure teachings of the Way. Were you not given the sacred HU?"

"Not until I went to the Katsupari Monastary," Jesus replied. "By that time I had done what I had to do to satisfy my hunger for God."

"I see. Well it's out now. But who will believe it?"

"Those that have eyes to see and ears to hear. To be honest, O; I'm glad it's out. At least now the world will see that I was as much a man of flesh as I was of Spirit."

"Well said, J!" I exploded, and laughed at Christ's shocking candor.

50. *A Foil for Christ*

The door into the private life of the savior of the world had been pushed wide open, and Jesus revealed himself to be very much a man of flesh and Spirit. I suspected as much, but it had to come from Jesus himself for the reader to believe, if he believed at all in the shocking truth of our dialogue. But it really didn't matter to me if the reader believed my experience with Jesus. What mattered was what was being revealed. What we revealed explained the Divine Plan of God from the perspective of an ancient culture that was desperate for a savior to open the door into the next stage of spiritual evolution.

I wanted Jesus to explain the meaning of *savior of the world*. I knew what it meant in light of the DPG, but the reader needed to understand the full context of the phrase responsible for the Gospel conspiracy; but something happened with our last conversation that I could not put my finger on, until I read my chapter to Cathy.

"You're hard on Jesus in this chapter," she said, after she got over the shock of Jesus doing what he did in the houses of pleasure for the sake of God.

"Am I?" I said, a little surprised by her comment.

"Yes," she firmly said.

"In what way?" I asked.

"You talk to Jesus like he's just another man. So he's got skinny legs. Did you have to tell the world that they're hairy too?"

"Why should that bother you?" I asked, in my defense.

"It just does. And when you said something about him pigging out on sex, did you have to say that? I don't think you're very respectful to Jesus."

"Is that how I came across?" I asked, surprised by Cathy's reaction.

"Yes. In this chapter, anyway. I like most of the chapters you read to me, but you're hard on Jesus here. I think you should apologize," she said, in her firm voice.

"Do I really come across disrespectfully?" I asked.

"Yes. Now smarten up and show Jesus a little more class," she said, and laughed to make me feel better; but I got her point.

"Okay," I acquiesced. "I'll tell Jesus how you feel. Fair enough?"

"Apologize to him first," Cathy insisted, and I did the next time we met.

"Apology accepted," Jesus said, with a warm smile. "In all fairness, O; I think it's good for the reader to catch a glimpse of the Christ in a body of flesh and blood. The world has lost sight of the fact that I was a man who became the Christ, not the Christ who became a man. Please tell Cathy that I'm not offended."

"Thank you. We can continue without anything standing between us, then?"

"Of course. What stands between us will be the reader's mind, not the dynamic of our relationship. You are a foil of Christ here, and you're playing your part well."

"A foil of Christ?" I said, suddenly feeling like a puppet on Christ's knee. "What do you mean by foil of Christ?"

Jesus laughed. "How does it feel to have the shoe on the other foot?"

"I don't know," I said, surprised. "I suppose it feels like — I don't know what it feels like! I think you've just thrown the reader a real curve here, that's what I think!"

"Curve?" Jesus said, playing dumb.

"Yes. I think the reader probably suspects by now that our roles in this relationship are the exact opposite of what you've just implied."

Jesus laughed. "You're right. After all, it is your book, O. Why would the reader believe that I'm directing this play?"

"There's a huge difference between you being the director of this play and me being a foil of Christ," I said, and laughed.

Jesus laughed too. "You're right. Bad choice of metaphor. Of course, you're not my foil. After all, you have free will. No Master interferes in the free will of a Soul. Free will is sacrosanct, and all spiritual laws of life stem from this one Great Law of God."

"Great Law of God?" I said, excited by the revelation. "Please tell me how this Great Law of God is expressed. I know what you're saying because I've caught a glimpse of this Great Law, but

262

how is it expressed in the language of the Way?"

"Any violation of Soul's freedom is a violation of the Great Law of God. All karma stems from a violation of the one Great Law of God; and the sooner man realizes this, the sooner the affairs of the world will be brought to order."

"You must be kidding?" I said.

"Why?" Jesus asked, looking surprised.

"Do you honestly believe this is possible? You, who introduced the world to the most concentrated teaching for the transformation of the self of man? How can you expect the world to respect the Great Law of God if the whole dynamic of life rests upon the principle of natural evolution? It's to the primal instincts of natural evolution for the strong to exploit the weak, so how can you hope the world to respect the sanctity of free will?"

"You're right, of course," Jesus replied, with an omniscient smile; "but I'm looking at the big picture, not just the first stage of Soul's evolution. Soul has to evolve through the exoteric stage before it is ready for the mesoteric stage of spiritual growth. It is here that saviors appear to show the Way. Despite the fact that the vast majority of mankind exists in the exoteric circle of life, the more spiritually conscious dimension of the mesoteric circle governs Soul's journey through life. This is what I meant when I referred to the world becoming more aware of the sanctity of individual freedom. Why do you suppose so much is being made of freedom of choice these days? Freedom of expression, freedom of behavior, and respect for individual rights? Why do you suppose this is such a focal point if not that the consciousness of the world has evolved enough to catch a glimpse of the mesoteric stage of spiritual evolution? Mankind is ready for the Great Law of God, as witnessed by the cry for individual freedom in many totalitarian countries today. This is why I'm here with you, O. This is the play that we are scripting."

"And I'm sure this is why there's such a proliferation of new spiritual interests in the marketplace today, like society's fascination with angels, spirit channeling, alternative spiritual paths and what have you" I added, appreciative of Christ's explanation. "People crave more spiritual freedom; and religions that tell people how to live their life run counter to Soul's growing need for individual expression—"

"Precisely. Soul's need for individual freedom is responsible for this proliferation of spiritual interests in the world today. Tear away the excuses for all the strife between people and nations and you will find Soul's desperate need for more freedom. So I'm not using you as my foil, O. I'm involving you in history's most exciting drama."

"History's most exciting drama?" I said, flabbergasted.

"The drama of spiritual evolution," Jesus explained. "Every few centuries the world produces a new crop of Souls ready to be harvested. Today we have the most bountiful crop of Souls that the world has ever known. This is why the Living Soul Master has come out into the open with the pure teachings of the Light and Sound of God. The world is ready for the secret teachings of the Way to be made public in this extraordinary drama."

"I'm flattered, J; but you know my position," I said, somewhat meekly.

"Yes, I know; as far as you're concerned the world can find its own way. I respect that. But that does not preclude the benefits the reader will get from our dialogue."

"True. I just want you to know that I respect the Great Law of God so much that I really don't give a damn how people live their lives!" I replied, reaffirming myself.

Jesus burst into laughter. *"Your humor amazes me!"*

"Didn't you say that those born of the Spirit are unpredictable? Or was that St. Paul?"

"I'm sure we both said it at one time or another," Jesus said, still laughing.

"If we can get down to business, then," I said, anxious for Jesus to explain himself. "I'd like the reader to know what it really means to be a savior of the world. I think it's time we begin the long and difficult task of taking you down off your cross, J."

"As much as I hate to admit it, I think you're right. The next stage of Soul's evolution has started; and if it is to go anywhere we have to awaken Christianity from its stupor that only through Jesus Christ can Soul be saved. Since you brought up the subject, I'll let you explain what it really means to be a savior of the world."

"I don't think I can do that unless I explain the most misunderstood of all your words," I replied, taken by surprise.

"Which are?" Jesus asked.

I flipped through my Bible to John's Gospel. I found the verse, which I had circled in red ink. "John. Chapter 14, verse 6. *I am the way, the truth, and the life; no man cometh unto the Father but by me.*"

"Fair enough. Those words have been responsible for fueling the Gospel conspiracy and keeping the illusion of Christianity alive, but it's time to demystify what I said."

"Let me!" I exclaimed, like an excited child.

"If you wish," Jesus said, smiling at me. "But don't you think it would be more credible if it came from me?"

"At this stage of the game the reader won't care because he probably can't make up his mind one way or the other about us," I said, with a mirthful chuckle.

"Perhaps. But just in case he hasn't, let me explain myself. I'm not speaking of Jesus when I said I am the way, the truth, and the life. I'm speaking for Holy Spirit. Spirit is the way, the truth, and the life. By this time in my mission I had become so imbued with Holy Spirit that I could speak for the Way, because I and my Father were one; but this only confused the world and distorted the premise of my teaching that Holy Spirit is the way, the truth, and the life. I did explain myself in my good shepherd parable. Why don't you turn to that for the reader to see the full context of what I meant?"

"Good idea. That should help to dispel the illusion that only through you can the world be saved," I said, happy to oblige; but I think I'm going to call upon my Muse to help open my reader's eyes—"

"You mean the Christian reader's eyes?" Jesus amplified.

"If you will," I said, and closed my eyes for a silent HU.

Jesus waited patiently. I called upon the Inner Master to let Soul speak with the clarity of the most pristine waters of living truth. *"But not too temple-throbbing,"* I said in my silent plea, and I heard the Inner Master chuckle. I laughed, and opened my eyes.

"What's so funny?" Jesus asked.

"Oh, just some comment I made to my Muse."

"Can you share it with me?" Jesus asked.

"Sure. The Inner Master loves my sense of humor also. I asked him to let the waters of living truth flow at their most pristine but not too temple-throbbing, and he got a chuckle over that."

Jesus gave me a warm, understanding smile. "You were saying?"

"Okay. I have to reveal what it means to be a savior of the world in the true sense of the word, and the first thing the reader has to fix in his mind is that karma and reincarnation govern Soul's evolution through the exoteric circle of life. That means from the inception of life on earth all the way to the dawning of spiritual consciousness when Soul becomes aware of karma and reincarnation and takes evolution out of the hands of nature and accepts responsibility for its own spiritual growth. It is here at the gateway to the mesoteric circle of life that the saviors of the world stand ready to open the door for Soul to enter into the mysteries of the Way; and by Way I mean what you metaphorically referred to as the kingdom of heaven. How am I doing so far?"

"Excellent," said Jesus. "You're leading up to my parable of the good shepherd very nicely. Please continue."

"The reader has to grasp that Soul grows and evolves through life experience. From lifetime to lifetime, Soul grows in self-consciousness with each new experience. When it grows enough to become aware of its divine essence it is ready for the next stage of evolution to spiritual self-realization consciousness. I should mention here that every atom of God is encoded to become spiritually self-realized and God-conscious, just as an acorn seed is encoded to become an oak tree. This is why Soul is driven to become spiritual self-realized. It has a conatus just as the acorn seed. The more Soul becomes aware of its divine essence, the greater the pull to God will be. This is why some Souls become so passionate in their search for God that they will go to extremes to satisfy their hunger for God. They can't help themselves, because their drive compels them to do whatever it takes to satisfy their hunger for God-realization consciousness. Just as you had to do what you did, J. You had to have more energy to nourish your hunger for God, so you indulged in sex. Not for pleasure *per se*, but for the abundance of sexual consciousness that you transformed with the secret teaching to nourish your need for more spiritual identity—"

"Please explain this transformation for the reader's sake," Jesus interrupted.

I thought for a moment. "It might be difficult for the reader to see, but in essence it has to do with the God force. The God force gives birth to life and sustains life. This God force is the un-individuated consciousness of God. I suppose we could just call it the consciousness of God, but what makes the God force in these lower worlds different from the God force of the higher worlds is the nature of its self-awareness. The God force of the lower worlds is not aware of its divine essence, whereas the God force of the higher worlds is aware of its divine essence. For the God force of the lower worlds to become aware of its divine essence it has to be individuated through life experience. This is what the purpose of life and natural evolution is all about. This is what the DPG is about — the individuation of the God force through the evolution of the atom of God; and man is the precious life form that is capable of processing the God force that individuates the 'I' of God."

I stopped for Jesus to comment, but he just smiled and motioned for me to continue.

"If I may just back up for a moment," I continued, reflecting on what I had just said. "The atom of God comes into these lower worlds from the Body of God. The atom of God has Soul consciousness but no self-consciousness. As the atom of God evolves through the life process from the inception of life on earth all the way to the dawning of self-consciousness in the life of primordial man, it is governed by collective karma. The moment the atom of God experiences the dawning of self-consciousness it creates individual karma, because the newly realized self now has some measure of personal choice; and with personal choice comes personal karma. Through the creation of personal karma Soul realizes its individuality. The newly realized self-consciousness in primordial man now begins to break free from its group consciousness, and the more it breaks free the more it will exercise self-expression. I experienced this in my fourth past-life regression, so I know this is how it works. And I should mention that during this same regression the Inner Master first took me back to the Ocean of Love and Mercy where I began my spiritual journey as an atom of God. This is how I was able to work

267

out the Divine Plan of God. So, the atom of God evolves through the process of natural evolution—"

"May I?"

"Yes."

"I sense a slight confusion in the reader's mind. If I may, let me just say that when you speak of the atom of God you mean an individual Soul; correct?"

"Yes; but a Soul seed not unlike an acorn seed or any other kind of seed," I explained. "The atom of God is an un-self-realized Soul seed, and the whole purpose of natural evolution is to individuate the atom of God. We can call the atom of God an individual Soul *in potentia,* just as an acorn seed is an oak tree *in potentia.* Then when the atom of God experiences the dawning of self-consciousness in the primordial life of man it experiences its own sense of individuality. I'll tell you, J; it's an indescribable experience when you realize for the very first time that you are a separate self. Try as I may, I have not been able to describe this experience. And the same thing happens again thousands of lifetimes later when Soul experiences its divine essence for the first time. Let me share the experience I had when I came to the realization that I was a separate Soul from my body—"

"Wonderful!" Jesus exclaimed. "This is like icing on the cake! Please, it will do our dialogue wonders to flesh in the metaphysics of Soul's individuation!"

I chuckled at Jesus' excitement. "This happened during my past lifetime as a black slave in southern Georgia. My name was Solomon, and I was known as Solomon the Good Slave. To make a long story short, I tried to run away from the plantation twice. I had an irrepressible desire for freedom, but I got caught both times. The second time I got caught the plantation master had me whipped every Sunday morning in front of all the slaves to set an example, but they could not break me. The master even had other slaves whip me. Still, I would not break .This incensed the plantation master. It was during one of my whippings that I had the realization that I was separate from my body. One lash of the whip set me free to realize that I was separate from my body, and that was the day I knew that in my Soul I was free. No one could take that freedom away from me unless I let them, and I became fixed in my desire to not be broken by the master's whip. That's how I became so passionate about my inner freedom. I realized that the master could possess my body but not my Soul, and from that one liberating lash of the whip I have never let anyone possess my Soul in all of my subsequent lives. I realized that if we let the world possess us we forfeit our spiritual freedom and become slaves to the world; and not until we evolve enough to sense our divine essence as distinctly as I did as Solomon the Good Slave will we ever be ready for the next stage of evolution in the Divine Plan of God!"

I paused. Jesus smiled, but said nothing.

I continued. "So the process of natural evolution through one's own karma determines Soul's experiences in life. I earned my lifetime as a black slave because in my previous lifetime I had blasphemed the Great Law of God. In my lifetime as the *Scoundrel of Paris* I sexually and morally depraved women; but that's another story. The point I want to make now is that Soul has to be aware of its own distinct identity before it is ready for the Way. This is where we are at now. We're introducing Soul to the gateway that leads to the mesoteric circle of life, which simply means that Soul can take evolution into its own hands and liberate itself from the recurring cycle of karma and reincarnation. At this point we can reveal the true meaning of savior of the world."

I paused to catch my breath. Jesus was delighted and waited patiently for me to continue. "A savior of the world is a spiritually conscious Soul that has chosen to introduce the Way to the world," I continued, with a silent plea for Spirit to flow freely. "You, Jesus Christ, are not only a spiritually conscious Soul; you are also God-realized. This is why you could say, 'I and my Father are one.' You either chose to introduce the Way to the world, or you were compelled by the reconciling power of Holy Spirit to do so; or perhaps the Spiritual Hierarchy asked you. Either way, this is how you became a savior of the world. But you are only a savior to those Souls ready to be introduced to the Way; Souls such as me who discovered the Way in your teaching. For all other Souls that are not ready for the Way you have become a curious mystery that only excites their imagination enough to open the door a crack so they can catch a glimpse of the kingdom of God."

Jesus chuckled. "This is what I tried to tell my disciples when they asked me why I spoke to the public in parables—"

"I know the verse," I interrupted. "Let me quote it for the reader's sake.

"By all means," Jesus said, smiling at my enthusiasm.

I flipped to Mathew, found the passage where the disciples asked Jesus, and he replied: *"'Because it is given unto you to know the mysteries of the kingdom of heaven, but to them it is not given. For whosever hath, to him shall be given, and he shall have more abundance; but whosever hath not from him shall be taken away even that he hath. Therefore I speak to them in parables; because they seeing see not; and hearing they hear not, neither do they understand.'*

"That's from Mathew 13:11-13. That's the distinction you make between Souls in the exoteric circle of life that are not ready for the Way and those that are ready to enter the mesoteric circle, which you call the kingdom of God. You even went further by introducing the Spiritual Law of Attraction. This law says that much gathers more. The more one has, the more he will attract of what he has. And the opposite is true also. The less one has, the Law of Attraction will take away even what he has because those who have more of what he has will pull what he has away from him. This is why the rich get richer and the poor get poorer. As cruel and unjust as it may seem, this is nothing more than the metaphysics of spiritual growth in action. But one will never understand this until he walks through that straight gate into the mesoteric circle of life where these spiritual laws that govern life are made clear. This is the logic behind your comment to your disciples. Now we can reveal the meaning of your good shepherd saying."

"Not quite," Jesus said. "You haven't explained the transformation of the God force that I took in with my sexual indulgences. Would you please do that for my sake?"

"Yes, of course. Okay, the alchemy of this transformation is so abstract that I completely understand why the world has failed to grasp the central dynamic of your teaching. You indulged in sexual pleasure because this is an extremely effective way to take in the God force. The God force is the consciousness of life not yet individuated. This is the creative life force that we all take in with every experience we have in life, and sex is one way to take in this God force in an extremely concentrated form because the sex act concentrates the God force to such intensity that quite often when a lover climaxes he will scream in rapturous joy, *'God I love you!'* I know I do, anyway."

"You too?" Jesus said, with the biggest smile on his face.

"Every time Cathy and I make love. So concentrated is the God force in my orgasms that I have to scream *'God I love you!'* But this is a digression. I no longer have to purify the sexual consciousness of my lovemaking because it goes straight to my spiritual self. This is the problem with every person who is not centered in their Soul self. All of this God force they take in through sex feeds the lower self, and the more ego gets the more ego wants. This is why people become addicted to sex. The seeker of God however has such a hunger for God that he is compelled to seek ways to satisfy his spiritual hunger, and one way is to transform the consciousness of his sexual energies. You indulged yourself sexually, and you abstracted the God force from all the selfish consciousness of your lower self. This remarkable technique satisfied your voracious hunger for God, and now this forbidden secret is going to be out in the open for the whole world to see."

"And I thank you for it," Jesus said, with an approving nod.

"You're welcome. Now the reader will have an explanation for your sexual forays in those houses of pleasure even if he can't grasp the logic. But what will this information do to all those Christians who are so blinded by your mythic stature that they can't see that you were once a man like the rest of us with an insatiable hunger for God?"

Jesus laughed. "That's a risk I'll have to take. I agree with you, O; it's time to be taken down off my cross. My symbol of self-sacrifice has been completely compromised, and there's no point hanging up there any longer. Besides, the modern world has called for a gentler, kinder method of self-transformation. This is why the Way has been revealed to the modern world in the new religion of the Light and Sound of God. But that's not for us to talk about. The reader can take his cue if he pleases. Our purpose is to demystify my sayings, and I'm tickled pink at our progress despite our digressions."

"Are you, really?" I asked, begging for validation.

271

"More than you realize, O. I knew that the dynamic of our relationship would reveal the mystery of my sayings, but I had no idea at the temple-throbbing clarity—"

I broke into laughter, and so did Jesus. "That's enough for today, O," he said. "We can take this into our next discourse. I'd like to delve as deeply as possible into the mysteries of my good shepherd parable, if that's okay with you?"

"Fair enough," I said, and Jesus faded to the Other Side and I changed into my work clothes and went to the new taping job I had just picked up.

51. *The Metaphysics of Karma*

When I did my morning HU a few days after our last talk, the theme of my next chapter came to me and I knew that we would have to explain the Great Law of God before we delved into his good shepherd parable; and when Jesus appeared, I said, "We have to talk about karma before we demystify your good shepherd parable."

"Excellent. Where would you like to start?" he replied, with an eagerness that took me by surprise. "Karma was central to my teaching two thousand years ago, but I could not convey the mystery of karma to the messianic culture of my time. The world cried out for a redeemer, and I sacrificed my life to give them one in my gospel; but I did not expect to be taken so literally. Perhaps we can take the mystery out of karma and convince the reader that the best way to live life is with one's eyes open to the Great Law of God."

"You're absolutely right, J; blindness to this Great Law is responsible for most of the suffering in the world. I think our entry point into the mystery of karma should be the fundamental purpose of life."

"That's a far stretch, don't you think?"

"Why?" I asked, puzzled.

"We don't want to be too abstract in our explanation of how karma works in life by expounding upon the DPG. We should stick to the Spiritual Law of Karma itself and simply explain the principle of cause and effect."

"Whatsoever ye sow so shall ye reap?"

"Yes," said Jesus.

"That's good in the context of your gospel teaching, but not in the context of our talks. Our talks are about taking the mystery out of your sayings and parables. Metaphor is good for a public that is not yet ready for the Way, but we're providing a road map for Soul. In all honesty, J; you can't imagine how frustrating it was for me in my own quest every time I came upon a new metaphor for the Way. Sufism has all the metaphors for the Way that any seeker could possibly ask for, which is why Rumi has become so popular today; but the time will come when Soul hungers for the meat of the last supper. The seeker will grow tired of metaphor, and I don't want my book to be just another one of those finger books."

"Finger books?" Jesus said, with a puzzled look. "What's a finger book?"

"A finger book points to the Way but never explains what the Way is, like the book I'm currently reading, *Sage-ing While Age-ing* by Shirley MacLaine. For my money, there are far too many finger books out there."

"And why do you think that is?" Jesus asked.

"Whenever someone catches a glimpse of the Way they get excited and want to shout it from the rooftops, and with every shout we have a new finger book. Finger books have become a cottage industry, like all those annoying *Chicken Soup for the Soul* books; and I don't want to fall into that category. I want my books to be about what the finger books point to. They can point **TO** the Way, but I want my books to be **ABOUT** the Way. I don't want this book to be anything like your teaching two thousand years ago where one has to spend the rest of his life trying to decode your message. I want this book to be about the Way, period. I want the reader to feast on the meat of the Way. Did you not say — give me a minute here," I said, and turned to my Bible.

I spent a few minutes looking through Mathew for the meat metaphor, and then Jesus said, "Check John's Gospel, Chapter 4."

I did, and I read what Jesus said about the Way: ***"I have meat to eat that ye know not of...My meat is to do the will of him that sent me out to finish his work.'"*** I turned to Jesus, and said, "And what is this meat that the world knows nothing about if not the secret teaching of the Way?"

"Exactly," replied Jesus. "But how else could I convey the secret teaching? Even today the undiluted truth of the Way would be too much for most people. I understand where you're coming from, O; but allegory, parable, and metaphor are necessary for the waking mind. Soul cannot be shocked awake. If it is shocked, it will do one of two things. It will recoil into itself, or it will defend its position with instinctive passion."

I laughed. "Exactly. That's how the people of my hometown reacted to my two novel memoirs. My truth was so undiluted that it shocked Soul awake. The people of St. Jude could not stand the burden of spiritual responsibility that their awakened conscience demanded of them, and they recoiled in horror; but not after a sufficient display of venom at the author for disturbing their precious sleep!"

"They crucified me!" Jesus exclaimed, and broke into delicious laughter. "So you see my point? Allegory, parable, and metaphor play their part in introducing the Way to the world, because most people cannot take the undiluted truth of the Way."

"Yes, of course they play a part; but not for me. I spent the best years of my life working my way to the esoteric circle of life, and what I have to say about the Way will not be clothed in mystifying language. I don't want my reader to be told that the Way is like unto this and like unto that — be it a grain of mustard seed, a treasure, a precious pearl, or whatever other metaphor the creative mind may conjure. You mystified the public with metaphor, J. I don't want to mystify my reader. I want my reader to see the Way for what it is. This is why I love the Way of the Eternal. This path tells it as it is; and that's what I want to do with this book. *Consciousness is our entry point into the mystery of karma!"*

"It's your book," Jesus calmly replied, and motioned for me to continue.

"The purpose of life is all about the evolution of consciousness," I continued, with a satisfied smile as I reconnected with my Muse. "We evolve through the process of natural evolution, and as we evolve we unfold in the consciousness of who we are. This is the mystery of the DPG. Only through the evolution of our individual self through karma and reincarnation can we unfold in the consciousness of what we all are, which is Soul. In short, the more we evolve in our individual identity the more Soul-conscious we become; and we evolve in our own identity through the metaphysics of karma."

Jesus smiled, nodding approval. "Quite frankly, O; I didn't think it was necessary to expound upon the inner dynamics of karma, but I agree with you. The reader must be made to see that his purpose in life is to grow in self-realization consciousness until he becomes aware that he is Soul; and it is this growing process that you wish to explore with the metaphysics of karma, is it not?"

"Precisely. The reader must be made to see that karma is life's way of waking Soul up to its divine nature. Through the metaphysics of karma a person grows in spiritual consciousness until he is mature enough to see the spiritual laws of life at play in the world; and then he can live his life accordingly. As you said, all of these laws of life stem from the one Great Law of God—"

"The Law of Spiritual Freedom," Jesus clarified.

"Yes. Soul has absolute freedom. Any violation of Soul's freedom is a violation of the Great Law of God, and karma ensues," I added, feeling very confident.

"All life strives to be in agreement with the Great Law of God," Jesus amplified. "This is what all the strife, turmoil, conflicts, and personal tragedies are about. They are life's way of bringing Soul into agreement with the Great Law of God."

"Exactly," I quickly agreed. "When a person suffers a personal tragedy — be it the loss of a loved one, a fatal illness, the birth of a handicapped child, a bitter divorce, the loss of a steady job, a devastating accident, a tragic house fire, whatever — these are all karmic consequences that help Soul synchronize with the Great Law of God."

"But why?" Jesus asked. "Do you not wonder what is going through the reader's mind when he is told that personal tragedy is karma's way of bringing him into agreement with the Great Law of God?"

I laughed. "Of course I do. That's the point of this discourse — *to dispel the mystery of the metaphysics of karma!*"

"Well, pardon me," said Jesus, putting a dumb expression on his face. "I'm sorry for being so—"

"Don't say it!" I exclaimed. "I'm sorry, J. I didn't mean to imply anything."

"If I may then, just to set the record straight of who is foil to whom here, let me explain the metaphysics of karma—"

"By all means," I said, laughing at Christ's rejoinder. "This will give you a chance to redeem yourself for mystifying the world with your cryptic sayings!"

"I'll never be able to do that," Jesus said, with that glint in his eyes. "But I might be able to snap a few Souls out of their stupor. If I may, let me say at the outset that the metaphysics of karma is all about the exchange and transformation of the God force. The God force is Holy Spirit, the life-giving energy that Soul needs to grow. This exchange of the precious life force takes place naturally through the process of evolution. The strong exploit the weak, but in their exploitation they violate the Great Law of God that respects the sanctity of Soul's absolute freedom. Anytime someone takes another person's life force — be it by way of theft, manipulation, deceit, guile, brute force, seduction, or whatever — unless there is an equal exchange of energy the exploiter will create a karmic debt with life, and the Great Law of God will demand spiritual recompense. As I said two thousand years ago, *'whatsoever ye sow so shall ye reap.'* Some time in a Soul's life, be it in the present or future life, it will have to pay back the life force that it has stolen from life."

Jesus paused, giving me a chance to respond. I knew exactly what to say: "This life force is responsible for all human experience. When a boss exploits an employee in his work place, whether it be in his factory, restaurant, office or whatever, he cheats his employee of his life force. This employer has violated the Great Law of God, and he will have to repay the life force that he has exploited from his employees. Life will demand that he pay it back. He may have to pay it back by being reborn into a life where he becomes the exploited Soul, and even though he won't be able to see it his suffering will have been born of his former life where he exploited the life force from others."

"An excellent example," Jesus said, his eyes sparkling with love. "But I would go even further. This life force, which is the currency of karma, can be reduced to what can simply be called the energy of spiritual freedom. **The life force is Spirit, and Spirit is pure spiritual freedom**. When someone exploits another person of their life force, he is stealing their spiritual freedom. This is a violation of the Great Law of God, and the exploiter will have to make recompense. This is usually by way of personal suffering, which I referred to metaphorically in my gospel as the weeping and gnashing of teeth."

"But why suffering, J? This is what the reader wants to know. And this, if I may be so bold, is what constitutes the metaphysics of karma."

"Why don't you explain it, then?" Jesus said, happy to give me the floor.

"I'll try," I said, and closed my eyes. I knew I would need help from the Inner Master to take the mystery out of the transformation of consciousness. I did a silent chant using my power word, and instantly I felt the tide surging. I opened my eyes. **"Suffering is nature's way of keeping Soul in agreement with the Great Law of God,"** I heard myself saying, and I just let go and let Soul speak: "On the whole, the suffering that we have to go through is brought about by our own karma. How we obtain and use the life force is responsible for our agreement or disagreement with the Great Law of God. If we obtain the life force without earning it, we will have to pay it back to life. We often do this unconsciously through suffering, because suffering is life's way of extracting the life force back from us; so the metaphysics of karma has to do with how suffering purifies the life force that is trapped in the consciousness of our lower self. The life force is un-individuated Soul consciousness. When Soul consciousness is individuated through experience, it nourishes the evolving 'I' of God. A person nourishes his evolving self-consciousness with every experience he has, because experience takes in the life force; but if one takes in the life force to nourish his lower self, his individuated self-consciousness will have to be purified in order to nourish his higher self because the higher self cannot be nourished on a life-force that is inherently selfish. The lower self is our human self, and our human self is by nature selfish; so the more selfish a person is the more he will have to purify his self-consciousness in order to realize his encoded spiritual destiny of total self-realization consciousness. This means that the values a person lives by will determine the nature of the life force that he takes in with every experience he has in life. The more selfish his values are, the more selfish the life force he takes in will be. If a person's greed makes him cheat people of their life force, or compels him to take it by force, guile, or manipulation, his individuated life force will be a selfish consciousness that will have to be transformed in what you so dramatically called the furnace of fire for him to be brought into agreement with the Great Law of God — *and he will be brought into agreement, because no-one can complete his destiny in life until he is in total agreement with the Great Law of God!"*

278

"Very good, O," Jesus calmly said, clapping his hands quietly with a big smile on his loveable face. "I could not have explained this better."

"If I may," I continued, because I got a sudden urge to flesh in the exploitation of the life force with examples taken from real life, and three relationships popped into my mind of women I knew in St. Jude that were exploited by their partners. Spirit wanted me to explain that when a man forces a woman to submit to his will he is violating the Great Law of God, because forcing another person to do your will is the greatest violation of Soul's freedom. "Let me just add this," I said to Jesus, to bring my point home. "Relationships are made or destroyed on the axis of free choice. Exploit your partner of their freedom, and you damage the relationship because you have stolen the precious life force that your partner needs for their own spiritual growth. A happy relationship rests precariously upon the axis of mutual respect of each other's freedom, be it a personal or professional relationship. This is how we can grow together in comfortable agreement with the Great Law of God."

"Excellent," said Jesus, with another round of quiet applause. "The metaphysics of karma is all about this mutual exchange of energies. This exchange should balance life. As the old saying goes, 'an honest day's work for an honest day's pay.'"

"Not today, J!" I rejoined, and burst into laughter. "I've never seen such shameless exploitation of the workforce in my entire life! The rich are getting richer and the poor are going nowhere fast! It's oppressive! But that's life, isn't it? It's not my place to save the world, J; but if only people could understand the metaphysics of karma the world would make sense of even monstrous tragedies like the holocaust—"

"STOP RIGHT THERE!" Jesus shouted, shooting his hand up like a traffic cop about to stop a fatal collision. "We don't want to go there, O! You will upset the applecart if you do, and I don't dare envision what this would unleash. Leave that alone. Let the world wake up on its own to the forbidden logic of God's ways!"

I wanted to laugh, but couldn't. Jesus was deadly serious in his glare. His piercing eyes were relentless. "You don't want me to tell the world?" I said, with a nervous chuckle.

"Definitely not. It's for your own good, O. I don't want to see you get hurt."

"Reluctantly, I agree with you," I said, with a thankful smile for Christ's concern. "But all the same, I'd sure love to explain the karmic logic for the holocaust. I know the reader would love to know why it happened. Everybody asks where God was—"

"DON'T GO THERE!" Jesus shouted again, jumping to his feet.

I was taken aback by his dramatics. "I guess the reader will have to find his own way to the shocking truths of life," I said, with a nervous smile. "All I can do is give him a road map back home to God."

"On that note, I bid you a nice day, O," Jesus abruptly said, and vanished before my eyes with a severe look on his face.

52. *The Incredible Technique of Letting Go and Letting God*

Had I not worked out the DPG I would not have been able to capture the metaphysics of karma. Once I did all the pieces fell into place. That's why tragedies like the holocaust no longer puzzled me. But Jesus did not want me to open that door. He knew the Jewish people would react fiercely to the karmic reason for the holocaust, but I had to make my point about racial karma and I opened our next conversation with the question: "If a person is responsible for the tragedy that befalls him by the bad karmic choices he has made, then it would follow logically that a group of people that continues to follow the same negative karmic pattern would inevitably invite a collective tragedy; don't you think?"

"You want to sneak into this through the back door, do you?" Jesus replied, shaking his head at my audacity.

"I do and I don't," I said, squirming in discomfort. "I just want the reader to appreciate that as elusive as karma may appear to be, it's the natural dynamic of spiritual growth. I don't want to upset the applecart, J; but can we pussyfoot around a subject as serious as Hurricane Katrina? If we look at a tragedy that befalls a group of people we should be able to make the same causal connection as we would with a person who smokes two packs of cigarettes a day for thirty years and gets lung cancer, shouldn't we?"

"True," Jesus agreed. "But if you will permit me, let's look at this from another angle. You must have read of people with lung cancer who sued the tobacco industry for millions of dollars to compensate for their disease. They blamed tobacco companies for their addiction to nicotine. I'm not saying that the tobacco industry is not culpable for the smoker's addiction. It has its own karma to pay for unleashing such a vile product onto the marketplace; but does this absolve the smoker of the responsibility that goes with his choice to smoke? What the world has trouble accepting is that with choice comes consequential responsibility. Soul is absolutely free, and man's destiny is to strive for this absolute spiritual freedom; but freedom comes with a price tag."

"Accountability. Yes, I know that. That's the point I'm trying to make."

"If I may be allowed to complete my thought," Jesus curtly said.

"I'm sorry. Please continue."

"The smoker who sues the tobacco industry for contracting lung cancer is in effect telling the world that his choice to smoke cigarettes is predicated upon his addiction to nicotine. That's like saying that the cart pulls the horse. This kind of perverse logic governs the behavior of the selfish little self of man when it is cornered."

"And your point is?" I said, challenging Jesus.

"When you corner the little self you can expect it to attack you with blind furry, because the last thing the little self will do is admit culpability. How many politicians have you seen admit to their mistakes? How many priests have you seen admit to their pedophilia? It is to the nature of the little self to never accept blame for its shameful behavior. Rather than admit culpability it will do the opposite and blame someone else; like the alcoholic husband who blames his wife for driving him to drink. This is the logic of the little self when it is faced with the harsh reality of its own karmic indiscretions. What would you expect the world to do if you shone the light of spiritual logic upon the holocaust? Would you expect a courageous *mea culpa* from those karmically responsible for this unspeakable tragedy, a people who may not even be aware of their karmic indiscretions; or would you expect a vociferous denial?"

"Denial, of course," I automatically agreed. "I'm very familiar with the shadow self of man, and I wouldn't expect the collective shadow of a race of people to respond with a remorseful *mea culpa.* Do you think the native people of this country want to accept karmic responsibility for their life on reservations when they can continue to ride the government gravy train? Of course not. That's the point, J; there are no free rides on the Great Train of Life. Karma spares no one. Man can shout and scream and plead and beg and justify all he wants, but he will be made to see the logic of karma one fine day — *after he has suffered enough tragedy that he cannot stand his life any longer and begs God for liberation from his misery!"*

Jesus laughed. "Aye, there's the rub that makes a fortune of so great a calamity," Jesus said, playing upon another one of Shakespeare's famous lines.

"Good one, J!" I said, and joined in his laughter. He never ceased to amaze me. "So we see eye to eye on this, then?" I asked, for personal confirmation.

"Absolutely," said Jesus, with the twinkle back in his eyes. "There are no free rides in life. As long as the indigenous people expect their government to pay their way through life they can expect to incur a karmic debt with life that will have to be paid back one day. The natural process of human suffering will exact this debt, because suffering is nature's way of transforming the selfish consciousness of the little self. Their problems won't go away on their own, despite how much money their government throws at them. Now that we got that tired old chestnut off your chest can we move on to my good shepherd parable?"

I was forced to laugh at how Jesus zeroed in on one of my most irritating pet peeves, which was born of my loss of thirty thousand dollars for a job I did on the native reserve just outside my hometown of St. Jude. "Not just yet," I said, smiling self-consciously. "We have to make it clear why the selfish consciousness of the little self has to be transformed in the furnace of fire. I do love your metaphor for the metaphysics of karma. It's too bad the world has taken this phrase to mean the fires of hell instead of the spiritual anguish of human suffering that the Living Soul Master calls 'the slow burning love of God.'"

"But it is hell!" Jesus exclaimed, to my astonishment. "It's the hell of one's own karmic resolution! This is the crux of my teaching, O. This is why I sacrificed my life on the cross to prove to the world that the little self must die for the spiritual self to be born. When will the world see through my metaphors and grasp the logic of the Way of Christ? How long must this charade of redemption go on? *There are no free rides in life, and I want the world to know this once and for all!"*

Jesus slumped back in the chair with a heavy sigh. I felt his disappointment, but I was taken aback by his show of emotion. I said nothing. We sat quietly for two or three minutes before I broke the silence. "Okay," I said, with a smile; "now that you got that chestnut off your chest can we talk about this mysterious door into the sheepfold?"

With a half smile, Jesus said, "I don't know if I have the heart for it now."

"It's your agenda, J. I'm just your foil, remember?"

"You may be my foil or I may be yours, but we are both foils of God, O. *And that's the truth!*" Jesus exclaimed, and broke into laughter.

He was back. "I don't disagree, J. The beauty of life is that we have free will, and it's the freedom to choose that throws a monkey wrench into the system. You convinced the world that it was your destiny to be crucified, but that was your choice. You had a point to make about self-sacrifice, and you made it; but the world has spun your choice to mean that God sacrificed you for the salvation of the world, and we both know that's a crock. You were responsible for your crucifixion. God had nothing to do with it; because if God demanded of you to be crucified, where would that leave the Great Law of God?"

"Exactly!" Jesus exploded. "Spiritual freedom would mean absolutely nothing if we blamed God for everything! You're right, O; I chose to be crucified to make my point about sacrificing one's life for the Way. But let's explain that for the reader. We can't continue our dialogue until we clear up this mystery."

"I agree. And if I may, I know just the entry point into this mystery of self-sacrifice." I said, excited by the insight and Christ's startling emotion.

"You do?" Jesus said, looking surprised.

"Yes. It's something you said. I believe it's in the Gospel of John." I flipped through my Bible to John, found the verse, and read his words back to him: *"'He that loveth his life shall lose it; and he that hateth his life shall keep it unto life eternal.'"*

"Excellent point of entry, O," Jesus said, with obvious delight. "Would you like to explain my saying or should I?"

"I'd love to explain it!" I said, chomping at the bit. "But I'd also love for the reader to hear how you would explain it in light of our dialogue," I quickly added.

"In light of our dialogue?" Jesus asked.

"Our dialogue is all about taking the muddle out of the puddle—"

Jesus burst into laughter. "Of course, spiritual clarity! That's what defines our dialogue! Yes, I certainly would like to take the muddle out of the puddle. But I would also like to hear how you managed to decode my saying. What do you say we flip on it, then?"

I took a coin out of my pocket, tossed it into the air, caught it, and slapped it onto my other wrist. "Heads you explain the mystery of self-sacrifice; tails I do."

"Let's see the coin?" Jesus said.

"It's heads," I said.

"Of course," said Jesus, and laughed. "It's only fitting that chance would give me the responsibility to explain my own saying, isn't it?"

Suddenly my mind went back in time and I felt an emotional flood of all the times I flipped a coin to make up my mind for me. "There's much more to this chance business than meets the eye," I said, as the memories kept flooding in. "At one point in my quest for the Way I had nowhere to turn. I hit another brick wall and I just didn't know where to turn. I was so desperate that I abandoned completely to God. You've heard the expression, 'let go and let God?'"

"Yes, of course," Jesus said, wondering what I was up to.

"Well, I decided to do just that. But I needed practical proof of my abandon to God, and you'll never guess what I came up with. I came up with the flip technique. Every time I had a difficult decision to make I flipped a coin and abandoned to God. I would say, 'Okay God, you decide what I should do: *heads I do, tails I don't.'* I did this for five or six months every time I had a big decision to make. You would not believe the result of this incredible technique! I lost a possible romance because of the flip, not to mention whatever else I lost; but believe it or not, out of this insane technique was born my unbelievable insight that God agreed with me whenever I felt that what I had to do was the right thing to do!"

"I don't follow that," Jesus said, with an amused look on his face.

"Every time I flipped the coin with a strong feeling that what I had to do should be done, the flip agreed with my feeling; and whenever I had doubts about what I should do, the flip proved my doubts. It was spooky, the number of times the flip confirmed what I felt I should or shouldn't do! It went so far beyond chance that I had to discard the technique because it had proven to me that the Light of God did in fact enlighten my own gut feelings, or intuition if you will, and I no longer needed God to decide for me! Believe it or not, I came away from this experience with the certain knowledge that **free will coincides with the will of God whenever what we choose to do is for our own good!** That's the conclusion I was forced to come to with the flip technique of letting go and letting God. That's how I resolved the dilemma of free will and personal destiny. **We are free to destine our own life**. God is not there to pre-destine our life, but to guide us in making the right choice for our own good! In short, J; **OUR GOOD IS GOD'S WILL!"**

Jesus was so astounded by my insane experiment that he stood up and clapped his hands. "BRAVO!" he exclaimed. "A THOUSAND TIMES BRAVO!"

I stood up, bowed to an imaginary audience, and with great aplomb I began my oration of gratitude: "First, I want to thank God, my Creator who made all of this possible. I want to thank my mother and father. I want to thank Gurdjieff. I want to thank Jesus, because he likes me. *He likes me! He likes me!* And I want to thank—"

53. *The Greatest Salesman in the World*

Cathy and I were having dinner at our little get-away restaurant in Bruce County when I stopped eating and said to her, "I can feel it happening."

"What?" she asked.

"Tomorrow's talk with Jesus. I can hear him whispering into my ear."

"Really?" Cathy said, not the least bit incredulous.

"Not verbal whispers. It's like feelings with words. I can feel Christ's presence. I just know Jesus is going to reveal something very important tomorrow morning."

"I wish I could be there. Why can't I meet Jesus?" she asked.

"I don't know. These Masters all have their own agenda," I said, with a snicker at the thought that flashed across my mind.

"What?" she asked.

"They have their own agenda, alright — *to do the will of God!"*

"You mean Divine Spirit," she said.

"Same thing," I said.

"So, can I meet Jesus tomorrow morning?"

"Sweetheart, I have no say in this matter."

"It doesn't really matter. It would just be nice, that's all," she said, and took a sip of wine to wash down her disappointment.

"You did meet him on the Inner," I said, to cheer her up.

"That doesn't count. I don't remember meeting him," she replied.

"Well you did meet the founder of the Way of the Eternal. I'd just as soon he came to me instead. He was the Light-giver of the world."

Cathy smiled. "I'll never forget that, either," she said.

Cathy met the man who brought the ancient teaching of total awareness to the modern world before she became a chela of his teaching. He manifested to her out of thin air just as she was going to sleep one night, and he said to her: *"You have found the Way. I am very pleased."* He gave her the most loving smile and disappeared before her eyes. I had just introduced Cathy to the Way of the Eternal, and his appearance removed all doubt about my spiritual path and Cathy enrolled in the teaching.

The next morning I was impatient for Jesus to appear, but he didn't show up; and neither did he come the following morning. In fact, I didn't see Jesus again for a whole week. His explanation was simple enough: "You needed time to process what you were given. We've come to the turning point in our dialogue, O. What we're going to reveal from here on in will take all the mystery out of my sayings."

His voice was different. Not more serious, which it was, but more exact and to the point; like the voice of a salesman who had come to the bottom line and all that remained was to sign the contract and close the deal. It made me uncomfortable.

I looked at Jesus, at his gray shirt, dark gray slacks, matching socks, and shiny black dress shoes. "There's something different going on here," I said, feeling uneasy.

"Yes, there is," Jesus replied, with a different look in his eyes.

"Can you tell me?" I asked, my mind racing to understand.

"Certainly," Jesus said, eager to explain. "I don't know if this will make sense to you, O; but what we've done so far has broken the psychic hold that Christianity has upon the world. This psychic hold was due to Kal's influence upon the Gospel writers. The time of the new harvest has come, and Soul must be set free from its psychic bondage. You were chosen by the Order of Spiritual Masters to help with this task, because you have found your way out of this psychic bondage. You know the way out, and we all agreed that you should show Soul the way to spiritual freedom."

"What Order?" I asked, puzzled by Christ's explanation.

"The High Order of Spiritual Masters. Masters from every tradition of the Way meet frequently to discuss the affairs of the world. It was decreed by the Order to reveal the DPG to you so that you could introduce the Way to the world, and I was asked to open up a dialogue with you to reveal the principles of the Way to your readers."

"Why me?" I asked, now feeling very uneasy.

"Because of your facility to connect the dots," said Jesus, in a flat, metallic voice that for some reason put me on edge. "Few people can connect the dots with such facility. Your readers need to see that the Way is the Way regardless which path they follow. This is why there is such fragmentation in the spiritual consciousness of the world. With your facility to connect the dots you bring all traditions of the Way to the hub of the Divine Wheel, and your readers will come out of *Jesus Wears Dockers* with respect for all spiritual traditions!"

I glanced at Christ's grey shirt and dark slacks. "So you're like an emissary for the Order?" I asked, suddenly feeling enormous pressure to sign on the dotted line.

"Yes," he replied.

"I don't know what to say. Do I have a choice?"

"You've already decided on the inner."

"And now the inner is coming to terms with the outer?"

"Yes," he flatly agreed.

"But I don't feel like I'm in agreement with myself," I said, with a nervous laugh.

"It's only natural that your little self would be taken aback by the reality of your spiritual commitment," he explained, with a steely-eyed assurance that unnerved me, "but our dialogue has prepared the way for the truth to be disclosed."

"You took me by surprise, J. I expected our talk this morning to be about the core of your teaching, using your power saying from the Gospel of John to open the door to the mystery of spiritual rebirth—"

"And it will," Jesus abruptly jumped in, not letting me complete my thought. "But we had to clear the air first."

"Does this mean *Jesus Wears Dockers* is going to become just another one of those titillating finger-pointing books?" I said, with another nervous laugh.

"It will be titillating, no doubt; but definitely not a finger book. What the reader will learn about the Way from our dialogue will satisfy that deep spiritual longing so many seekers are trying to satisfy with the finger book industry. But it doesn't matter how many *Chicken Soup for the Soul* books they read, these finger books will never satisfy their spiritual longing. As you have correctly discerned, the vast majority of seekers have trapped themselves in their ego

289

personality, and it is our purpose to reveal the limitations of the ego in Soul's journey home to God. We are not here to muddle the puddle, O; we are here to eviscerate the psychic hold that Kal has upon Soul!"

"And what the reader does with this information is entirely up to him," I instinctively responded, feeling terribly defensive now.

"Exactly," said Jesus, with a gleeful smile. "Once it's out there it will be one more gateway into the glorious mysteries of Soul's divine purpose in the Garden of Life. All it takes is for one Soul to be liberated with the information of our dialogue, because in this one liberation the angels in heaven will unite and blow their trumpets for all the heavens to hear, for such is the glory of Soul's emancipation from the lower worlds of God!"

"Let's settle down," I said, feeling so overwhelmed by Christ's fervor that it took my breath away. "Look, J," I said, my voice trembling; "I can appreciate being a player in liberating Soul from the psychic hold of life, but as I told you I couldn't care less what path people follow. The world can find its own way, and I'll tell you why—"

"Yes, please do," Jesus abruptly cut in, with an uneasy look in his eyes that I had never seen before. Something about Jesus' whole demeanor really made me wary.

"It's not my place to save Souls," I continued nervously in my defense. "It's Soul's place to save itself. That's the spiritual law. So if you don't mind, I'd like to call on the Inner Master now just to confirm what I suspect is going on here."

"You don't have to do that!" Jesus exclaimed.

"But I do," I said, staring Jesus in the eye. *"Z, please protect me,"* I pleaded, and three times in quick succession I shouted my spiritual power mantra (my personal word coupled with HU) that instantly summoned Divine Spirit's protection.

No sooner did I shout my power mantra and Jesus vaporized into nothingness leaving a faint noxious odor, and I knew that the greatest salesman in the world had just visited me in the form of the Archetypal Shadow Christ!

54. *Jesus Resolves the Paradox of His Teaching*

It took several days to come to terms with Jesus' last visit. What gave the Archetypal Shadow Christ away was the ego stroking. By making me feel like a special player in the drama of Soul's liberation he wanted me to lose my footing and slide into the abyss of false self-importance, but the Kal could not compromise me with flattery; so the next time Jesus appeared (with a big grin on his face) I said, "I've asked the Inner Master to be present during our talk today, and every talk from now on; if that's okay with you?"

"Of course. I wouldn't expect otherwise."

"You know about Kal's visit, then?"

"Of course," Jesus said, with a chuckle.

"And you think that's funny?" I said.

"Yes. Kal had to test you, O. That's what he does. How do you think all these gurus today have so much influence over people?"

"You tell me," I said.

"They have a great product to sell. They tell people exactly what they want to hear, not what they need to hear. That's why Kal could not sell you."

"And just what do people want to hear?" I had to ask.

"Think of the first person that comes to your mind, and then ask this person what it is they want to hear," Jesus said, with that playful twinkle in his eyes.

I did; and the first person that came to my mind was a contractor friend. His name was Doug; he had built his house the same time we built ours. He wanted to hear that he had not compromised himself to his wife, whose salary tripled his take home pay. He wanted to hear that he was still the man of the house. *"I still wear the pants in this house!"* I heard him shout in my mind, and I knew exactly what Jesus meant. "People want to hear the exact opposite of what they are. Is that what you're trying to tell me?" I said to Jesus.

"Yes," replied Jesus, and smiled his loving smile that convinced me he was present in my room and not the Archetypal

Shadow Christ. "And on this note, we can now reveal the hidden wisdom of my saying according to John," he added.

"Your Big Gun saying?"

"Yes."

"Well, J; you won the toss, so you can explain it for the reader."

"Yes, I know. Get yourself a cup of coffee first. This is going to take some time."

"Actually, I've cut back on coffee. I'll bring up a pot of herbal tea."

"Why did you cut back on coffee?" Jesus asked,

"I got a fright a few nights ago. My heart started racing so fast I thought I was going to have a heart attack, and I probably would have had I not done a spiritual technique to calm myself. That's when I decided to cut out the coffee. Would you like herbal tea?"

"What kind?" Jesus asked.

"I've been drinking detox tea for the last couple of days, but this morning I'll put on whatever you like. We have a good selection."

"How about Camomile? That's a nice calming tea."

"Good. Camomile it is, then."I made tea and brought up the pot covered with a cozy, and two cups. I placed everything on my desk first and then cleared a spot on the glass coffee table that functioned as my filing cabinet, and I placed the pot and cups there; then I looked at Jesus, and said, "What the Kal told me wasn't all lies, was it?"

"Not at all. Kal's a great salesman, O. And well he should be. He's been playing humanity since the day man gave birth to his reflective self."

"Should we explain to the reader why Kal pretended to be you?"

"Let me explain," Jesus said.

"Please," I said.

"Kal Niranjan's mandate as the God of these lower worlds is to teach Soul the lessons it needs for spiritual self-realization and God consciousness by setting up the dynamics of opposites that will have to be resolved for spiritual growth. Soul has to become a pure channel for Holy Spirit in order to become God-realized, and to be a pure channel it has to have a firm grip on its own ego. Ego must be made to realize that it is in the service of Soul and not the other way around. The only way to do that is to keep ego in check. The best way to keep ego in check is to stay spiritually centered; and the best way to stay spiritually centered is to keep in mind that the only reason we are in this world is to become co-creators with God. A co-creator with God serves God by serving life. A co-creator helps Soul to reconcile itself with God; and Kal's duty is to pump up the ego and keep Soul trapped by life until Soul learns the ultimate lesson in these lower worlds."

"What ultimate lesson?" I asked.

"Absolute humility," Jesus replied, with a big loving smile.

As Jesus smiled, I saw the face of the Living Soul Master and I *knew*. I smiled at Jesus, and then I broke into a chuckle because I could not contain the joy of the realization that Jesus had just given me by letting me see the face of the Living Soul Master, who was my Inner Master and Jesus' Father in Heaven; and Jesus gave me a little wink to confirm my realization. I wanted verbal confirmation, but I knew better; so I turned to my Bible and read Christ's power saying out loud for Jesus to explain: *"'He that loveth his life shall lose it; and he that hateth his life in this world shall keep it unto life eternal.'"*

"Good," said Jesus. "When I use the word 'life' I am referring to both the lower and higher self. The lower self is one's life born of the world, and one's higher self is one's life born of Spirit. Before I reveal the metaphysics of transformation that this saying refers to, it would be prudent to introduce the reader to the core of my teaching. Let's pour our tea and then I can tell the reader the real truth of my teaching."

I poured the tea. Jesus took a gentle sip. "Very nice," he said. I took a sip and said, "I can't wait to hear how you're going to explain the most paradoxical of all your sayings."

"It's only a paradox if we see the self as two selves," Jesus explained. "In reality, the self is one. And herein is the mystery of my teaching. At the core of my gospel lies the realization that the seed of the self was planted in the soil of these lower worlds of consciousness, which are the Physical, Astral, Causal, and Mental Planes. These planes exist below the Soul Plane, the first plane of the spiritual worlds of God. Let me give the reader a glimpse of the big picture. It's time we took the myth out of the Garden of Eden fable. This fable was created to give man a glimpse of the dual nature of the God force in the lower worlds, thereby planting the seeds of good and evil. Man must become familiar with the dual nature of the God force in order for Soul to negotiate its way through life. Soul cannot grow in life without the conflict created by the play of the negative and positive forces of life. This is the central dynamic of the DPG—"

"Of course!" I exclaimed. "How else can the seed of the self grow if not through the resolution of the conflict created by the lower and higher forces of life?"

"Exactly. These forces are forever at play in life, and the real mystery lies in the fact that the self of man must nourish itself on both of these forces in order for the spiritual self to be realized. The God force is the consciousness of Soul. It is the 'I' of God not yet self-realized, and the seed of man's self individuates the 'I' of God through life experience. This is the core of my teaching. The seed of man's self—"

"If I may," I interrupted. "Could you please amplify for the reader what you mean by the seed of man's self?"

"Yes, of course. Just as an acorn seed is not an oak tree, so the self is not a complete entity unto itself; or, if you will, the Soul of man is not a complete unit we can call an individual self. True, each self is an individual Soul; but it only becomes an individual Soul through the growing experience in life. Each Soul is an atom of God, and God's Plan is to grow in God-realization consciousness through the evolution of life. As the acorn grows to become an oak tree, so does the atom of God grow to become a Soul self. This is the core of my teaching, which is implied in all of my sayings and parables. Once this knowledge is revealed the reader should make sense of the confusing paradoxes of my sayings."

"Not until you reveal the conflict that exists in the self," I added.

"Yes, I'm getting to that. The seed of man's self is planted in the world, and as it grows from lifetime to lifetime it takes on more identity. Just as any seed in life becomes more of what it is, so does the seed of man's self become more of what it is, which is Soul. To put it succinctly, Soul becomes aware of itself as it individuates through the growing self of man. Does that make sense to you, O?"

"It does to me because I've worked out the DPG. I hope the reader can follow the logic of Soul's growth in life," I replied, unsure of my reader.

"I hope so too. I realize there are people who prefer to hold onto the mystery, because they don't want to assume the responsibility demanded by a conscious understanding of my teaching; but my explanation is for those Souls ready to be harvested."

"Please explain that for the reader, if you would?"

"What?" Jesus asked.

"This whole concept of harvesting Souls," I said.

"This should be obvious given my explanation of the seed of man's self," Jesus replied, and then winked at me; but I knew he was playing to the reader.

"I can appreciate your respect for the reader's intelligence by not talking down to him," I replied, smiling at Jesus; "but even the most intelligent reader can have a problem following the logic of our discourse. You know as well as I do that it's not intellect that solves the mysteries of the Way, but spiritual consciousness. Even so, I know that even seasoned Souls have to be awakened to the mysteries of the Way with the light of spiritual reason; so, please shine this light as brightly as possible."

Jesus laughed. "Of course. I was just having some fun. Okay; the point I have to make clear is that the seed of the self is like every other seed in the dominion of life. It is no different. The seeds of all life forms have to go through their individual stages. The acorn seed grows through the various stages until it becomes a mighty oak tree. In like manner, the seed of man's self grows through life experience to become a Soul self, and by Soul self I mean a spiritually self-realized Soul. This takes many lifetimes. For all those Christians that have been told that Soul only lives one lifetime — *hear ye, hear ye! Soul lives more than one life!* And it takes many lifetimes for the seed of man's self to give birth its own individual identity. Then as the self grows from one life to the next it grows more hungry for the God force, which satisfies its growing need for more identity just as a boy needs more food to satisfy his growing body's needs." Jesus paused and took a sip of tea. Looking at me, he said, "Would you like to add anything before I continue?"

"Yes. I'd just like to say that this need for the God force is real. I know, because it was my need for the God force that drove me to a solar cult teaching that promised nourishment with the Logos. This Christian solar cult teaching was introduced to the world by one of Kal's own, and I fell for this guru's sales pitch hook, line, and sinker. According to this teaching, the Logos, which we know to be the God force, is imbued with the rays of the sun. By ingesting the rays of the sun through the eyes with the solar techniques one ingests the Logos directly. This is how the spiritual self is created and nourished in this teaching. But for the sake of the reader, let me say that this is a dangerous teaching that can do irreparable damage to one's eyes. I have three solar burns in my eyes; two in my right retina and one in my left. So we have to let the reader know that this hunger for God is as real as a physical hunger for food. Just as a starving man will do anything to satisfy his hunger, so will Soul do anything to satisfy its hunger for God. This is why people fall for cult teachings. Their need for God can be so great that they will do anything to satisfy their hunger. This can be tragic. I managed to get out before I got lost in this teaching; but many seekers aren't so lucky. So I would stress that the safest way to satisfy this hunger for God is to simply be a good person and try to not be too selfish in everything you do. I can't stress this enough. I've been there, so I know from bitter experience what this hunger for God can do to a person."

"I agree," said Jesus, with a warm, commiserating smile. "All paths lead to the Way eventually; so don't panic. Thank you for sharing that, O. The reader will appreciate your experience with this cult teaching. I shared my experience of sexual indulgence to gather the God force; but that was also a dangerous and foolish thing to do. One can compromise himself by the pleasures of the flesh and completely lose his spiritual balance."

"As I did in my Sufi lifetime," I said, smiling wryly at the memory.

"You do have a good stock of personal experiences to make your points about the Way, don't you?" Jesus said, and took another sip of tea.

"A few," I said, thankful for my seven past-life regressions. "I've initiated myself into the mysteries of life with my own experiences, and now I can reveal the mysteries of the Way with spiritual clarity for my reader; but this is your show, J. Please, continue," I said, with a gesture of my hand.

"Thank you," Jesus said, putting down his cup. "As the child's appetite for food grows to nourish the growing child's body, so does the self hunger for the God force. Man's hunger for God is in reality a hunger for more self-realization consciousness, because as the self grows in its own identity the more it hungers for God."

"If I may, the self grows with life experience; right?"

"Absolutely," said Jesus.

"Can't we just say that the more the self grows, the more it needs to grow; and the more it needs to grow, the greater its hunger for God will be?"

"I don't see how that makes it any less confusing. As the self grows it needs more food to grow—"

"Or to be more specific; as the self grows so does its appetite for the God force."

"That's better yet. Okay; the self needs more spiritual energy to grow, but when it reaches a certain stage life cannot satisfy its enormous appetite for spiritual energy—"

"Exactly!" I exclaimed, instantly recalling my own voracious appetite for spiritual energy that I could not satisfy when I had come to that critical stage in my own journey. *"I was desperate, J! That's why I fell for that solar cult teaching!"*

Jesus smiled, his eyes bright with love. "That's why I went out into the world to plant the seeds of God's kingdom," he said, speaking softly to calm me down. "It was my mission to plant the seeds of the Way for all those Souls whose spiritual hunger could no longer be satisfied by experience alone. These Souls needed to nourish their hunger for God so badly that they came to me in droves because I offered them a way to satisfy this hunger. This is why I make references to food, meat, and drink in my sayings and parables. I was addressing Soul's need to be nourished. As metaphorical as I was, in reality I was not being metaphorical at all. I do hope that I have made this clear for your reader."

"I think you've made it abundantly clear," I said.

"Good. Now I have to explain the dynamic of my teaching."

"And by dynamic, you mean?"

"I mean the guts of my teaching," Jesus said, with emphasis in his voice. "I mean the mechanics of the self-transformation process. I mean the drive shaft that makes my teaching operate. Without understanding the drive shaft the reader will never grasp the core of my teaching. Perhaps you could explain what I mean by drive shaft?"

"Me? I'm a mechanical dunce, J! But I know what you mean. Let me see if I can express it differently." I took several sips of tea and appealed to the Inner Master. *"Please, Z,"* I said, in the quiet of my mind, *"give me the insight to express what Jesus would like the reader to hear."* I did a silent HU for a minute or so, and when I felt the tide surge I let Soul speak: "At the heart of your teaching lies the power to transform the negative consciousness of man into positive consciousness. All of your sayings make reference to the dual consciousness of man's nature. This dual consciousness is the key to decoding your sayings. We can't reveal the mystery unless we tell the reader how the self of man is created. The self of man is the seed of his Soul self. This divine seed cannot grow a Soul self unless it creates a human self first. As preposterous as this may sound, this seed of our Soul self must be born out of our human self, which we create through life experience. In the simplest terms possible, the seed of man's Soul self creates a human self first, and as we grow in the consciousness of life we nourish our spiritual self. Our human self collects the life force through the experiences we have in life, and this life force is made up of the positive and negative energies of life. Our spiritual self feeds on the positive energies and the negative energies have to be transformed for our spiritual self to grow. This is done naturally through the karmic resolution of our negative experiences. This is all very metaphysical and hard to digest, if I may be allowed a pun here; but this is where saviors like you stepped onto the stage to harvest Souls. How am I doing so far?"

"Very well. Please complete your thought," Jesus said.

"Thank you; but I'd rather you take over from here because we've come to the most difficult aspect of Soul's growth in life. This is the dynamic relationship of the lower and higher self. This is where your power saying in the Gospel of John comes into the picture. If you would, please explain this dynamic between the lower and higher selves of man."

"I guess there's just no getting around it, is there?" Jesus said, with a smile.

"Nope. You won the toss; you take the responsibility!"

"And so I will. Let's hope the good Christians of the world will forgive me for tearing down their illusion of spiritual salvation with my death on the cross. My crucifixion was a metaphor for the transformation of the lower self of man, and I hope to God that I will be able to convince the reader that's all my death was meant to symbolize."

Jesus fell silent. He closed his eyes and remained silent. I waited patiently.

When Jesus opened his eyes, he said: "I have to clarify something, because I would like the scholars of Christ's teaching to see the big picture as clearly as possible; then perhaps they will be able to piece together the central message of my teaching. This may shock your reader, but I came back into my same life from the future to harvest Souls and redirect the energies of the world. I came from a long line of Masters who taught the secret of God's Divine Plan, and I was perfect for the job. Master Zadok revealed the secret to me; but a secret is not yours until you have been initiated into the secret. The only way to initiate oneself into the secret is by living the Way. Knowledge is not enough. Knowledge is mental consciousness. Spiritual consciousness is different from mental consciousness. The secret of my teaching has to do with transforming the mental, emotional, and physical consciousness of the lower self. This is what my saying in John's Gospel refers to. To make this absolutely clear for the scholars, they have to understand the principle of Soul's growth. If they do not understand this principle, they will not grasp the core message of my teaching."

"And for clarity's sake, what is this core message?" I asked.

"Spiritual rebirth, of course," Jesus replied, and closed his eyes for another two or three minutes. When he opened his eyes he smiled, and said: "The Way of Christ is the core of this dynamic. The Way of Christ is only one of many aspects of the Way, but the Way of Christ is specific in the transformation of the consciousness of the lower self of man. It is this specifically that has boggled the minds of scholars."

"May I?" I said, on behalf of the reader.

"Yes, please," Jesus said.

"You keep referring to the scholars. May I ask why?"

"The scholars have concentrated their energies upon the life of Jesus, not the sayings of Jesus. This has distorted the reality of my teaching. If the scholars were to call me X, Y, or Z and focused on my sayings instead of X, Y, or Z they would do a lot more for my teaching than they could possibly imagine, because the real Jesus lives in his sayings more than he does in the undisclosed knowledge of my life. Capture the soul of my sayings and you capture the soul of Jesus Christ — which you did, O. I'm addressing the scholars because I would like them to shift their focus from Jesus the savior of the world to Jesus the messenger of the Word. I sowed the seeds of the Way, O. That's all I did."

I laughed. "That's perfect. You sowed the seeds of the Way and millions of people continue to nurture themselves on the seeds you have sown, but few Souls have nurtured themselves all the way to their spiritual birth. That's the tragedy of your teaching, J!"

"That's so true," Jesus sighed. "For every million Souls that take to the Way of Christ, perhaps one will give birth to their spiritual self in their lifetime; and that is not good enough. I have to explain my teaching for the reader to see that there are no shortcuts to the kingdom of God as the Gospel conspiracy has led the world to believe."

"But at least millions of Souls are introduced to the Way," I replied, to my surprise because I was defending Christ's message to the world.

Jesus saw the irony. "You do see the good in the bad, don't you?"

"Our talks have shifted my paradigm. Yes; I do see some good in all of this Gospel conspiracy nonsense. But when push comes to shove I still suspect the world would be better off if we took you down off your cross. I believe Christianity has run its course, J; and I don't think I can ever shake this conviction."

"Why?" Jesus asked.

"Because the spiritual impasse in the logic of Christianity continues to warp the psyche of man; that's why!" I heard myself say, and I knew that Soul had something that my reader had to hear: "This impasse is instant salvation through Jesus Christ. Life cannot transcend itself unless it resolves the dilemma of this impasse. This impasse is responsible for most of our problems in society today. The energies of life cannot be used for man's spiritual growth because of this impasse. All of this creative energy is being consumed by the lower self and bloating ego to such monstrous proportions that it's becoming impossible to keep ego's ravenous lust in check. Our social systems are crushing under the oppressive weight of ego's needs. The marketplace has gone insane trying to satisfy ego's needs. Our prisons are overcrowded because there's no more room for the unchecked ego's needs. And our entertainment industry has become schizophrenic because of ego's needs, not to mention ravaging our eco systems because of ego's lust for power and profit. Can ego gorge itself on life's energies and at the eleventh hour beg God's forgiveness? This impasse in the logic of Christianity has done more harm to social evolution than your teaching has done good, and unless the scales are balanced we're going to have more of the same mindless madness. There; I said it. I wanted to get that off my chest for years. Now I can sit back and let you finish your explanation of the most paradoxical of all your sayings."

I expected Jesus to rebuff everything I said, but instead he nodded in quiet assent. "I've been hanging up there too long, O. It's time to be taken down off my cross so the world can get on with the business of spiritual growth. Does not a good farmer pull the weeds out of his garden to keep them from choking his crop? It's time to weed my garden. I will begin by explaining my power saying, which I hope will help resolve this spiritual impasse created by the Gospel conspiracy. Before I do however, let me address the issue of Soul's growth. If what I'm going to say rings a familiar note, don't be surprised. I will be drawing upon your writing to give your reader a better understanding of spiritual growth."

Jesus stopped for me to comment, but I motioned for him to continue.

"The Soul of man comes from the Ocean of Love and Mercy," he began, speaking in his soft, healing voice. "It is an atom of God, or seed of God — call it what you will; it is not an individual Soul yet because it does not have a self. God plants its divine seeds in the soil of life, and as they grow through natural evolution they take in more and more life consciousness until they reach a critical mass and become aware of their essential nature. This is what you experienced in your regression. Now I have to make it clear that the seed of man's self grows in a consciousness of life that is both positive and negative. When it reaches critical mass and becomes aware of itself as a separate self, this self is both spiritual and human in essence. It is spiritual insomuch that it is made up of the positive aspect of the life force, and it is human insomuch that it is made up of the negative aspect of the life force. Does any of this sound familiar to you?"

"Yes. That's how I worked it out. But I like the way you're explaining it."

"Alright," Jesus said, and took a deep breath. "We have taken the seed of man's self all the way to critical mass where it experiences itself as a separate self in the primordial life of man. This separate self is both human and spiritual. In essence, it is all spiritual because the negative energy of life is no less spiritual than the positive energy of life. It just has to be transformed to be purely spiritual. This is where the DPG steps in to help the self of man grow. It is at this stage of Soul's growth in life that the spiritual law of individual karma takes over Soul's growth, and by Soul's growth I mean the individuation of the self. Until the dawning of self-consciousness the evolving self was governed by the collective karma of life, which biologically speaking we can simply call the process of natural selection. This unseen intelligence that governs natural selection is in reality Holy Spirit, the omniscient life force that guides the evolving seed of man's self to create the best possible biological traits for its survival. As it evolves through the various life forms it takes in the life force until it evolves into a species that can take in enough life force to reach critical mass and become aware of itself as a separate self, as you experienced in your regression. This suggests that other life forms may create this unit of consciousness that we call a self, but we won't go there now because we have our hands full as it is."

I laughed. "Dolphins with self-consciousness? *Why not?*"

Jesus smiled his all-knowing smile. "Like I said, we won't go there now. This unit of self-consciousness that we see in the primordial life of man creates its own personal karma, because personal karma is created by personal choice. As long as the separate self expresses itself it creates personal karma, and since karma is both positive and negative the self grows in the consciousness of the positive and negative energies of life. However, because the primordial self is so rudimentary it is fundamentally concerned with its own survival. This makes it very selfish and aggressive. So this rudimentary self grows in the consciousness of primordial self-interest in order to survive in the world. Clear so far?"

"Absolutely," I said.

"However, because other primordial selves also come into being at this time there will be karmic interaction between these higher primates; and with this karmic interaction the human drama of life begins. It is out of this drama of karmic interaction that the metaphysics of karma plays its role in the growth of the human self, and out of this exchange of karmic energies the spiritual self of man begins to form. In effect, it can be logically deduced with biological certainty that the spiritual self of man is created out of the consciousness of his human life. This is the central mystery of the DPG as I experienced it in my own journey through these lower worlds. This is why Master Zadok called life God's Garden and my Essene brethren the Gardeners of Life."

I smiled. "Yes, I remember. It was our duty to tend to the Garden of Life. The Great Book of Life contained all the secrets of Soul's growth in the Garden. It's coming back to me now. You did study the Great Book of Life, then?"

"Yes. I drew my inspiration from the Great Book of Life. Do not misunderstand me, O. Let's explain that the Great Book of Life was not only a record of the wisdom sayings that the Essenes collected from the world; it refers as well to the whole life experience. For the Essenses, life was the Great Book; and all the wisdom sayings that they recorded were keys that unlocked the mysteries of how the Way worked in life. The reader has to understand that in the Essene tradition life itself is the Way, and unlocking the mysteries of life is what their secret teaching was all about. This is why they called their teaching the Way of Life; and all of my sayings and parables were designed to unlock the secrets of the Way of Life. Once one learned how the Way of Life worked, he could then use life to grow in spiritual self-realization consciousness. That's the core of my teaching."

"Wow! I wish I had expressed it this clearly!"

"Thank you," Jesus said.

"Just one thing," I said. "We should make it abundantly clear that the life force is the un-self-realized 'I' of God; so when man consumes the life force with every experience he has, he is in effect feeding on the 'I' of God. This un-self-realized 'I' of God becomes self-realized as man consumes it through experience, and depending upon his values this life force either nourishes his lower or higher self—"

Jesus held up his hand. "You're correct, O; but I think we're getting ahead of ourselves. I don't want to introduce this dynamic of my teaching at this stage. I'd like to reserve this for some of my other sayings. If you don't mind, let me just explain my power saying in the Gospel of John to make the point about the transformation of one's lower self in order for one to realize his spiritual self. If you don't mind, that is?"

"I defer to your wisdom," I said.

"Thank you," Jesus said.

"I just wonder what all those Christian scientists will have to say about our discourse on the self," I said, thinking of the conflict that our dialogue would create when their belief in one life was shattered by the truth of man's Soul.

Jesus laughed. "It doesn't matter. It's time to throw their ill-conceived baby out with their dirty bath water!"

"Wow!" I exclaimed, and broke into laughter. Jesus joined me.

After a moment or so of laughter, he continued: "When I said **'he that loveth his life shall lose it,'** I meant that the self of man has chosen the spiritual life over the material life, or the inner self over ego if you will; and this means a radical change in one's priorities. Man now chooses to live by spiritual and not material values, because the energies of the life-experience grounded in spiritual values will nourish Soul and not ego. And when I said **'he that hateth his life in this world shall keep it unto life eternal,'** I meant that when man stops living by material values that feed the ego he will nourish his spiritual self to the point where he will reach critical mass and realize his divine nature. Or, as I said, he shall realize eternal life. Hating one's life means shifting one's priorities from feeding the ego self to nourishing the spiritual self, and loving one's life means that one prefers the spiritual life to the material life. It's as simple as that. And it all hinges upon the understanding that the two selves of man vie for the same life force that man takes in with each new experience that he has in life, because man needs this life force to grow in his own identity. The question we have to ask ourselves is this: *which self does man want to grow in — his ego or spiritual self?* This is why there is conflict in the heart of man, because the two aspects of the self vie for the same life force; and not until man has assumed enough spiritual consciousness to become aware of the Way will he be ready to live the Way. This is why I said that many are called and few are chosen. Clear enough for you, O?"

"Very clear," I replied, but not quite sure about my reader.

"Would you like to add anything?" Jesus asked.

"If anything, I would like to reiterate that life is a garden for Soul; and when Soul has grown enough individual identity to be harvested Way-showers like you step out into the world scene to teach the Way. On one level, your sayings and parables are not metaphors at all. They speak to the spiritual growth of Soul in the Garden of Life."

"Good. Thank you. Now I think we can end our talk and rest up for our next discourse on the Way of Christ."

"Which will be about?" I asked.

"Who knows? Holy Spirit is writing this script, O. You know that."

"Of course," I said, with a snigger. "But before you go, let me thank you for this discourse on the self. It was as enlightening for me as I'm sure it will be for the reader."

"You're welcome," Jesus said, and faded to the Other Side.

55. *The Secret of the Way*

Cathy and I attended a worship service in Carlton the day after Christ's last talk. It was the first service we had attended in quite a while. We had taken a break from spiritual functions to consolidate my energies, which were running high from my seven past-life regressions and all the energy that I had released with my Soul talk books. The facilitator at the service gave a talk on the quest for spiritual truth. During our HU song, we were to contemplate on the question, "What is truth?"

As we sang the Love Song to God the Inner Master gave me the answer to the question that has stumped truth seekers for centuries. *"Truth is,"* he revealed to me, in the quiet of my mind. When the subject came up for discussion, after the facilitator did a reading from the first volume of *The Way of the Eternal* and offered his own insights into truth, I gave my answer; but I had to explain it for our small group of chelas.

"Life, reality, and existence are synonymous," I said, paraphrasing the modern day founder of the ancient teachings of the Light and Sound of God. "Spirit is life; Spirit is existence; and that which is, is truth. In effect, Divine Spirit is truth; and one's level of consciousness determines one's perspective on truth. Truth is one, and the experience of truth is different for each person because no two people have the same level of consciousness. If a person wants to experience more truth he has to expand his consciousness; ergo, the quest for truth becomes a quest for one's true self, because the more one realizes his true self the more truth he will experience..."

On our drive home after the service I thought of how fortunate we were to be chelas of the ancient science of total awareness, because our spiritual exercises were the most effective way to realize one's true self. My talk with Jesus was still fresh in my mind, and I could not help but compare the Way of Christ with the teachings of the Light and Sound of God. "I'm glad Jesus and I are having these talks," I said, feeling genuinely blessed.

"Why?" Cathy asked, wondering where that had come from.

"I noticed something at the service this morning," I replied, my mind working frantically to put my thoughts together. "I don't quite know how to express it, but it's a characteristic that every chela I've met so far seems to have. It was obvious this morning, and for some reason I've connected this with my talks with Jesus."

"I'm not following you," Cathy said, with a puzzled look.

"I'm not surprised," I said, my mind still grinding out what I wanted to convey. "I haven't made my point yet. Let me back up. In our teaching we know that the more we practice the spiritual exercises the more we nourish our spiritual self, because the spiritual exercises tap Soul into the Creative Life Stream. In other words, the more we do the exercises the more we grow in spiritual consciousness because we're taking in the pure life force directly. Every time we sing HU we tap into the Sound Current, which is the pure energy of God."

"Yes," Cathy said. "So?"

"So the Light and Sound of God nourish Soul," I said, with Socratic clarity. "Soul becomes more spiritually self-realized with the pure life force, and the more self-realized Soul is the more it manifests the qualities of Soul, which are *Being, Knowing,* and *Seeing.* As I listened to the other chelas talking about truth this morning, I noticed that they did not have the consciousness of their knowledge. That's what my talks with Jesus are all about — making conscious what Soul already *knows*. Does that make sense to you?"

"Not at all," Cathy said, and laughed.

I laughed too, because my Socratic point was much too elusive. "Okay," I said, with a silent plea to my Higher Self for clarity. "Do you remember how we began our discussion this morning on the question, what is truth?"

"Yes."

"Each person gave their definition, and then I said: 'Truth *is*.'"

"Yes. So what's your point?"

"The point is that at the end of our talk Brian quoted the Living Soul Master and ended our discussion on truth by saying: 'Truth is Divine Spirit, and Spirit just *is*.'"

"So?" Cathy repeated.

"It took the whole talk to reveal what was implicit in that short definition of truth that I gave. Truth *is,* but it all depends upon one's level of spiritual consciousness to see what truth is. I'm saying that most chelas know that Divine Spirit is truth, but they don't have the spiritual consciousness of their own knowledge. To know mentally is one thing Cathy; but to have the spiritual consciousness of what one knows is another thing entirely, because spiritual consciousness is *being* what you know."

"Let me think about that for a minute," she said.

We drove in silence. Finally, she said, "You're spiritually conscious of what truth is, and you expressed it. That means that you *are* your knowledge of truth and they aren't?"

"Exactly. I've raised the level of my consciousness on the nature of truth. I've been a truth seeker my whole life, and I learned how to *become* my truth by living it. What I know implicitly about truth I've also learned to make explicit because I'm a creative writer. A writer seeks to make explicit what he knows implicitly. That's pure Socrates; and this is why I love my talks with Jesus. *We're making explicit the implicit truth of his teaching!"*

"What did you and Jesus talk about yesterday?" Cathy asked.

"Oh goodness. We talked about the seed of the self, how the self grows, and how the Way of Christ nourishes one's spiritual self. It was a fascinating talk, and I can't wait to work it into my book. I'm going to get to it as soon as we get home."

And when we got home I worked on it all afternoon while Cathy did housework, went for a long bike ride, and made dinner.

"Did you finish your chapter?" she asked, when I came downstairs for dinner.

"Yes. Good thing I'm taking notes as we talk. You know what, sweetheart? It really hit home working on this chapter that the Gospel writers must have made up much of what Jesus said and did. I think I understand now why the Inner Master would tell me that the Bible is mostly a work of dialectical fiction. I can't see how the Gospel writers could quote Jesus verbatim. It's not possible. The Gospels of Christ were written many years after Christ's crucifixion, so something's not right."

"Does it really matter?" Cathy asked.

"It does to the scholars. To me the Gospels are discourses on the Way of Life, and it doesn't matter if Jesus said what he is quoted as saying. The real question is this: *do people understand what Jesus is saying?* My answer is no, they do not. That's why Jesus and I are having this dialogue. We're explaining what he is supposed to have said. Like our talk at the worship service this morning. We know what truth is, but are we spiritually conscious of our knowledge of truth?"

"But isn't that what the spiritual life is supposed to be about, becoming more conscious?" Cathy asked, with disarming innocence.

"Exactly. The more conscious you become the more truth you experience. And this is the crisis that Christianity is faced with today. It's not making conscious the implicit truth of Christ's teaching, because it has come to an impasse with its misunderstanding of Christ's teaching. I'll have to ask Jesus about this the next time he shows up."

I did ask him the following morning after Cathy went to work, and he just smiled at me. "You do make a point, though," he said, after a moment's reflection. "The truth of the Way is implicit in all of my sayings and parables, but the only way to release this truth is by living the Way. This is why I stressed over and over again in my sayings—"

I interrupted Jesus with my hand. I turned to my Bible and found the passage he was referencing. I read it for Jesus, smiling at the thought of quoting Jesus to himself: *"'Whosoever heareth these sayings of mine, and doeth them, I will unto a wise man which built his house upon a rock...And every one that heareth these sayings of mine, and doeth them not, shall be likened unto a foolish man, which built his house upon sand.'* That's from Mathew. Chapter 7, verses 24 to 26."

"Exactly," said Jesus. "It's in the *doing* that one grows in Spirit, not in paying lip service to my teaching."

"Here's a question for you, then," I eagerly asked. "Why would anyone want to take up the Way of Christ now that we have the pure teaching of the Way in the teachings of the Light and Sound of God which can tap Soul directly into the Creative Life Stream? Does that make sense to you?"

"Of course it does. But not all Souls are ready for the pure teachings of the Light and Sound of God," Jesus replied. "They have to experience more life to make themselves ready. I know it sounds foolish to take a long and difficult road to one's true self when there is a much more direct path, but that's the way of karma. Some Souls have to play out the karma of their life before they can embrace the pure teachings of the Way. What I hope our dialogue will do is break up the karmic patterns that Souls cannot break up on their own."

"Like Christianity's spiritual impasse?" I said, and laughed.

"In effect, yes," Jesus said, unmoved by my laughter. "A great many Souls have trapped themselves in this paradigm of instant salvation, and they are forced by their own karma to play it out. Just as you had to. Had you not seduced those women of their faith to satisfy your lust for vengeance with God and the Roman Catholic Church you would not have had to pay for that karmic indiscretion in future lives."

Jesus was referring to my lifetime as Riel Laforchette, *le salaud de Paris* that still made me blush at the thought of what I did to those women. "You're absolutely right. That lifetime cost me a lot of unnecessary grief and suffering."

"It all depends upon how you look at it," Jesus said, with that all knowing smile. "You're the better man for it, I'm sure; but you could have realized yourself without having to play out that karmic pattern. That's why I want to explain the Way of Christ. I want to raise the consciousness of Christianity in the hope that this spiritual impasse can be resolved and set Soul free from a karmic pattern that is doomed to repeat itself."

"God, I hope this works," I said, letting out a big sigh of relief. "You can't imagine the anguish one suffers when he's trapped by his own faith! I was so trapped by my Roman Catholic faith that I did something so despicable it shocked my conscience awake! That's how I began my spiritual quest in this lifetime. But I can't talk about that. Suffice to say that I know what you're talking about, and I'll do everything I can to help you raise the reader's consciousness with my understanding of the Way."

"Thank you," Jesus said, mercifully not pursuing the subject of my shameful behavior that night long ago when I abandoned to the lustful spirit of my lower self, which I didn't learn until many years later was the shadow personality of my Parisian lifetime that popped out of the dark regions of my unconscious to satisfy its ravenous lust. "I think we've done a good job so far." Jesus added, his eyes bright with healing love. "In all fairness, O; this would not have been possible without you. Your experience with the Way offers the reader a new perspective on the spiritual life. Your understanding of my sayings has created a whole new thought pattern for my teaching, and I promise that readers will walk away from your book shaking their head in awe and wonder."

"I hope so," I said, silently thanking Jesus. "If our dialogue can jolt them enough to step outside their paradigm we will have done a wonderful service to the world."

"Yes, we will," Jesus confirmed. "So do you want to continue chit-chatting this morning, or would you like to explore my good shepherd parable?"

"Let's chit-chat. I like it when our talks find their own way."

"Me too," said Jesus, with an approving smile.

"If I may then, let me flesh in what you were just talking about with a personal experience I had," I said, eager to make my point.

"What was I talking about?" Jesus asked.

"Karmic patterns. As you know, I had a past life as a student of Pythagoras. Because of that lifetime I broke the karmic pattern that was to destine me to more of the same kind of selfish karma, which was a pattern of imposing my will on life. Pythagoras saw my future lives letting that karmic pattern play out, and it was to be more of the same old hard lessons; but because I studied the secret teachings of the Way with Pythagoras I broke that karmic pattern and began a whole new personal line of destiny."

"What karmic pattern did you break?" Jesus asked.

"I was karmically programmed to become a selfish leader in future lives because I loved power. I used life, and I wanted life to serve me; but I had a hollow in my Soul and I sought Pythagoras out to see if I could fill this hollow. I had heard whispers and rumors in Athens that possessed a secret knowledge and that he was a healer of Souls, but when I met him he told me that there was only one way to fill the hollow in my Soul, and that was to learn how to serve life instead of using life to satisfy my lust for power."

Jesus smiled. "Pythagoras was a wise teacher. You were fortunate to be his student. He certainly left his mark on you."

"Does it show?"

"Yes."

"In what way?"

"Because of Pythagoras you have finally earned the secret of the Way."

"That's intriguing," I said. "What's the secret of the Way?"

"You tell me. You have it in your eyes, in your smile, and especially in your laughter," Jesus said, his eyes just shining with a love that nourished me.

"I have it in my eyes, my smile, and my laughter?" I repeated, intrigued. "What do I have in my eyes?" I asked myself. "I have the light of Spirit," I answered. "People tell me that my eyes shine with light. And I have it in my smile, too. My smile brightens people up. And when I laugh the joy of life surges throughout my body. People enjoy my laughter. I've often been told how good people feel when I'm around. Given this, I'd have to say that the secret of the Way would be the light of Soul, the goodness of Soul, and the joy of Soul. How am I doing, J?"

"And if you put them all together what would you have?"

"A happy Soul!" I exclaimed, and burst into laughter.

"And that's the secret of the Way. HAPPINESS!" Jesus shouted, to my astonishment. "The spiritual life of Soul is a happy life, and your life is a fine example of what it means to be a happy Soul!"

I was flattered; but I could not help laughing at the thought that just flashed across my mind. "Would you like to hear something interesting?" I asked.

"What?" Jesus asked.

"I have never met one resolved Christian in my entire life!" I exclaimed.

Jesus burst into laughter, and the more he laughed the funnier it seemed to be, and I couldn't help myself and joined in his laughter.

"Not one resolved Christian!" I repeated. "That is funny, isn't it?"

"It certainly is," Jesus said, shaking his finger at me. "You would think that there would be at least one resolved Christian in the world; but that would be *ipso facto* impossible, wouldn't it?"

"Exactly. That's why I've never met one!"

"But will your reader understand why there are no resolved Christians in the world?"

"Probably not," I said. "Why don't we tell him, then?"

"Should I, or would you like to?" Jesus asked.

"I think it would be more appropriate if you did," I said, with a mischievous smile.

"Fair enough," Jesus said, and parted the veil. "If Soul's purpose is to realize total self-realization consciousness, how can it do so in a faith that will not allow it to transcend itself? Christianity does not believe in karma and reincarnation. But these spiritual laws are nature's way of nurturing Soul's growth, despite all the resistance it gets from Christianity's unbelief. Soul is anguished by Christianity's resistance, so it is good for Soul's growth; but the wheels of karma grind very slowly. There are many good Christians in the world today, but there is a world of difference between a good Christian and a resolved Christian."

"And on that note, I think we can call it a day," I said.

"Yes," said Jesus, and disappeared before my eyes.

56. *One of the Most Unholy Mysteries*

I took time to read Mathew, Mark, Luke, and John several times, and the idea struck me to pick out all the sayings and parables that most expressed the core of Christ's teaching; but I did not have time to do that before our next talk. I told Jesus my idea.

"By all means," he said. "That way we can cut to the chase. Our dialogue has taken on a life of its own, and we do have to reveal the secret of my teaching, don't we?"

"I can't help but wonder why so few people have penetrated the secret of your teaching" I said, hoping Jesus would offer an explanation besides the one I suspected.

"It's impossible to see clearly through a glass darkly," he replied.

"Are you saying that to learn the truth one must first unlearn what he believes to be the truth?" I asked, calling upon my Sufi wisdom.

"That's exactly what I'm saying. How can a Christian steeped in his faith shift his perspective enough to look at his faith differently? It's not likely. This is why life is so hard on these Souls. Karma demands spiritual growth, and Souls trapped by their own spiritual impasses will be given experiences that shock them awake enough to see their way through life more clearly. It is not a pleasant way to grow spiritually, but it is for Soul's own good."

"The hard knocks of life, you mean?"

"We could call it the school of hard spiritual knocks; but whatever we call it karma is the teacher, and no-one is immune. This is the DPG. Soul's destiny is to grow in its own identity until it becomes aware of its divine nature."

"We know this, and so does every initiate of the Way; but how do we get this point across to the reader?" I asked Jesus, genuinely intrigued by the challenge.

"You would be amazed at the power of the written word," Jesus replied, with that magic twinkle in his eyes. "Do you think the

Gospel writers were not aware of the power of the written word? Do you think I said and did everything they ascribed to me?"

"Now there's a question that keeps the Jesus Society scratching its collective head!" I said, and burst into laughter. "So, did you?"

"What?" Jesus asked, playing dumb.

"Did you say and do everything they said you did?"

"What do you think?" he asked, drawing me out for the reader.

"Quite frankly, I think the Gospel writers were initiates of the Way. I think they used your remarkable life to personalize the teachings of the Way with dramatic affect to win over the readers of their Gospels," I replied, with conviction.

"BINGO!" Jesus exclaimed.

"You mean I'm right?" I said, surprised by his confirmation.

"You could not be more right," Jesus said, his face glowing with satisfaction."An initiate of the Way speaks for the Way. It does not matter how the Way is packaged, it will always be the Way. This is what puzzles the Jesus Society and every scholar that studies my life and teaching. To understand me one has to understand the Way, but one cannot understand the Way until he becomes an initiate of the Way; and there are only two ways to become an initiate. One way is through the straight gate that my sayings open—"

"And the other?" I abruptly interjected, anticipating Jesus.

"You tell me," Jesus said, smiling at my enthusiasm.

"One has to find the Living Soul Master who will initiate Soul into the eternal stream of the Light and Sound of God, that's how," I eagerly responded. "And believe me, J; that's a thousand times easier than initiating oneself into the Life Stream with your sayings. *I did both, so I know of what I speak!"*

"Yes, you did," said Jesus, still smiling at my show of emotion. "This is why you have such a deep understanding of the Way. Each step of the Way was a conscious step for you. This is why we're having this dialogue. It is your consciousness of the Way—"

"And you have nothing to do with it?" I cut Jesus off.

"You're right. It takes two to tango," Jesus said, and we both laughed.

"Now I have to ask you a touchy question," I said, suddenly feeling very serious.

"What?" Jesus asked.

"If the Gospel writers took liberties with your life to give dramatic expression to the Way, do you think what they did was right?" I asked, feeling the enormous weight of that insight. "There's something rotten in the state of Denmark, J. *I know there is!"*

"I was wondering when you were going to get around to it. What do you think, O?" he asked, challenging me with a direct, piercing gaze.

"I wish you would stop doing that," I said, avoiding his gaze. "You sound just like a therapist by turning everything back on me with a question. Or is that just your Jewish nature coming out of you?" I quickly added, and broke into a nervous laugh.

Jesus said nothing. He just stared at me.

"I want to hear what you have to say about the liberties that Mathew, Mark, Luke, and John took with your life and teaching. Can you tell me?" I said, still very nervous.

"And Thomas," Jesus added, for the reader's benefit. "Of all the Gospel writers, Thomas was the most true to my life and teaching. John was the most creative. His Gospel was the lens by which the other Gospels were understood but which distorted the perspective on my life and teaching and combusted the Gospel conspiracy. Of course I can tell you, O. The reason I turn everything back on you is not because it's the Jewish thing to do, which I know can be quite annoying, but because it's common practice for a Master to let seekers come to their own understanding of truth."

"Maybe that's why Jews do it!" I instinctively retorted.

This time Jesus burst into laughter. He couldn't help himself.

"What a courageous sense of humor you have!"

"I have no idea where it comes from," I said.

"Alright; tell me what you think and I'll either confirm or deny it. Fair enough?"

"Fair enough," I said.

"Good. So, why do you think it was wrong for the Gospel writers to take liberties with my life and teaching? After all, they did introduce the Way to the world."

"I can't be sure if they did take liberties, but if they did I feel they violated the Great Law of God." I replied, to make myself perfectly clear.

"Please explain what you mean by that," Jesus said, for the reader.

"Soul has absolute spiritual freedom. This is the Great Law of God. And any violation of Soul's spiritual freedom is a violation of the Great Law of God."

"And just how do the Gospel writers violate Soul's spiritual freedom?"

"By deceiving Soul," I replied, and fell silent.

Jesus did not speak for a moment. Finally, he said, "You do know that you have just penetrated one of the most unholy mysteries?"

Astounded by Christ's comment, I said, "I know no such thing. As a creative writer, I have an intuitive feeling for what is right and what is wrong in a story. My writer's instincts tell me that the Gospel writers violated the most sacred law of the creative process when they wrote the narrative of your life, just as my instincts sensed that Castaneda was leading me down the garden path, and the leader of that Christian solar cult teaching; and I've just realized that the most sacred law of the creative process is the Great Law of God. Every writer worth his salt knows this. We have to be true to our work. We can't play with the reader's mind, J. That's like saying: *I will deceive you for your own good.* This is what Christianity has been doing for centuries, and look at the mess it has created with the spiritual impasse of its teaching. How can this be for Soul's own good when Soul's inherent capacity for free choice has been manipulated by deception? I don't believe it does Soul any good whatsoever to be misled by deception, honorable or not. This goes back to the Socratic question: can there be such a thing as a noble lie? I don't believe there can be. I believe it's much safer and honorable to come clean. Don't you think so, J?"

Jesus took a long sip of green tea that I had brought up for our talk. Finally, he said, "I think you're right. The honorable deception is no less a lie. Lies foster a consciousness of falseness, and false consciousness keeps Soul from realizing its divine nature."

"That's precisely what I feel!" I exclaimed.

"If I may, just how did you arrive at this observation?" Jesus asked.

"One devastating blow at a time," I said, with a wry snicker. "I bought into Castaneda's honorable deception, not to mention how many other teachings that wasted my precious time; but when I bought into the lie of the alleged Child Christ's solar cult teaching I paid a terrible price. *God, did I pay with that teaching!*"

"There was nothing honorable about that deception, O," Jesus said, with a commiserating smile. "The birth of a Child Christ was a deliberate deception to manipulate honest seekers. There was no honor in that whatsoever."

"Was it a deliberate deception?" I asked.

"Yes. The forces of darkness were at play there, and there was no honor whatsoever in that teaching. You were very fortunate to get out when you did."

"I know," I said, still feeling the warmth of Christ's smile. "But honorable or not, I still learned my lesson about deception; and regardless of its intention, deceiving Soul is a violation of the Great Law of God. I can feel this in the marrow of my bones!"

Jesus nodded his head, and his face lit up with a radiance I had not seen before. It was so bright I had to turn my head away. I waited a moment or two, and then turned back to Jesus. I wanted to say, *I love you*, but I couldn't; I just basked in his love.

"Shall we disclose this unholy mystery that you have just penetrated?" he asked.

"By all means," I said, realizing why Jesus had showered me with love. It was to wash away the pain I still felt from the occult forces of that offshoot Christian solar cult teaching that did irreparable damage to my eyesight and devastated me with such humiliation that to this day almost forty years later I still can't bear to think about it, let alone write about it. I smiled, thanking Jesus silently for his healing love, and then I continued. "What unholy mystery did I penetrate?"

"Christianity's spiritual impasse." Jesus said.

Instantly I was possessed with perfect clarity: "*False consciousness!*"

"Yes," Jesus affirmed. "You're absolutely correct, O. The lie fosters a consciousness of self-deception, and self-deception imprisons Soul in the lower worlds. The more false the consciousness, the more deeply Soul is incarcerated in the prison of life. You spoke of Socrates earlier. Socrates explored this spiritual impasse his entire life and concluded that Soul has to be purified to open the door of its prison. The false light of the cave, to refer to his famous allegory, imprisons Soul; and not until Soul is unshackled from the deceptions of the mind will it be free enough to climb out of the cave of life. This is what I hope to accomplish with our dialogue. The more we can cast the light of spiritual truth upon my teaching, the more we will free Soul from the shackles of the mind—"

"From self-deception," I clarified.

"Exactly. Self-deception keeps Soul from taking the initiative to seek the Way. False consciousness is responsible for the hard spiritual knocks of life, because karma demands the transformation of false consciousness. This is why Christians can never be resolved as long as they hold onto the belief that I died on the cross to save the world. This deception has fostered a consciousness of such impenetrable falseness that few Souls can break free of its hold. This is the heart of the Gospel conspiracy. And this is why the redemptive law of karma has to kick in to free Soul with experiences that wake Soul up from its own deceptions, like the father who loses a child to a senseless accident and gets no solace from his minister because his minister cannot see that life is governed by spiritual laws. The minister's faith will not allow him to see the truth of karmic justice. Do you see what I mean now when I say that you have penetrated one of the most unholy mysteries?"

"Of course. But just to clarify how life shocks Soul awake with personal tragedies, this bereaved father in your analogy loses his faith when his minister cannot comfort him and he goes elsewhere for answers. In effect, he becomes a seeker. I've witnessed this twice in my life with grieving parents, so I know that karma governs Soul's growth until it is mature enough to find the Way. It's sad that one has to experience a personal tragedy to be shocked out of their spiritual stupor, but that's just the way it is in the DPG. I can only hope that our dialogue will pry open the reader's mind enough to let in the light of God, and just maybe we can spare the reader a personal tragedy."

"Me too," said Jesus, and then laughed.

"What's so funny?" I asked.

"This was a pleasant surprise, wasn't it?"

"What, our foray into the consciousness of self-deception?"

319

"Yes. I'm sure we'll touch upon this subject again; but we certainly opened the door for the reader this morning. Do you think we may have opened it too much?"

"I have no idea, J. All I know is that I spent the best years of my life transforming the consciousness of my own false personality, and it all started one lonely night in my bedroom when the Inner Master asked me the question, *'Why do you lie?'"*

"So you too were forced to deal with the devil within?" Jesus said, and laughed.

"I wouldn't have put it like that; but yes, I was forced to transform the consciousness of my own false self," I replied, smiling at Christ's revelation. "It took well over twenty years to authenticate my life, but I don't want to talk about that anymore. I've written about that again in my last book and I hope never to go back to it. Besides, this dialogue is supposed to be about the Way of Christ, not the Way of O!"

Jesus burst into laughter, and I joined him; and after Jesus left I basked in sweet silence until it was time to go to work and earn my keep.

57. *The Good Shepherd Is Witness for the Prosecution*

"Okay, J," I said, feeling excited because I had read the four Gospels again and was full of questions, primarily the question of Christ's miracles; "I would like you to explain why the narrative of your short mission is so replete with miracles. Take the miracles out of your life and all we have left is a mystifying teaching couched in parable, and I don't believe it would have had the legs to make it to the twenty-first century. It was your miracles — casting out demons, healing the lame and blind, feeding the multitude, turning water into wine, raising the dead, and of course your resurrection miracle — that sold your incredible story to the world. I have to ask you, J; were you the miracle worker that the Gospel narrative of your life says you were?"

"You came loaded for bear this morning, didn't you?"

"Yes."

"Why?"

"I got a different feeling as I read the Gospels this week. I was overwhelmed by the miraculous power of Jesus Christ. This made me uncomfortable because I wanted to believe the whole narrative of your life, including your temptation. It occurred to me that the Gospel writers knew exactly what they were doing. They passed off the false coins with the real with such skill that no one was the wiser, and for centuries the world has bought into this narrative of your life. It was woven into the historic fabric of your life with such skill that no one but the most discerning reader will see the false coins from the real."

"And what are the false coins?" Jesus asked, with a twinkle in his eyes.

"Some of the miracles. Especially your resurrection," I replied.

"And why would you believe that?" Jesus asked.

"I was a scribe at Qumran. I heard of your mission to establish God's kingdom on earth, and I did see you before you went out to spread the Word of God."

"Yes, I remember," Jesus said, smiling at the memory.

"Well, as I read the Gospels this week I was so overwhelmed by your life that I was pulled back to my lifetime as Samuel, and I heard Jacob the Elder telling us about your mission to spread the Word of God. We were in the great library, and he told us that you cast out evil spirits from a few tortured Souls and that you did some healings here and there; but I don't think they were the great feats the Gospel writers made them out to be. Jacob explained how you did what you did. I have my notes right here."

I opened my notebook and read what Jacob revealed to us: *"The power of God flows through the messenger of God, and anything is possible; so do not discount the miracles of Jesus. But do not put too much stock into them either. They are what they are, and Jesus himself is no less surprised by the power of God that flows through him. The miracles of Jesus are signs that our Father in heaven sends to help him spread the Word of God, for people believe more in what they see than what they hear. This is his mission. But Jesus will suffer greatly for revealing the Word to the world."*

"Why?" asked Michael, my fellow scribe.

"It is a fact of history. The secret teaching offends those that are not ready to receive it. Jesus will offend more Souls than he will redeem with the Word of God."

"Why would Jesus put himself in harm's way?" I asked.

"Jesus is crazy with God. He must do what he must do for God."

"For God, or for Jesus?" Michael asked.

"Only Jesus can answer that," Jacob replied.

"So what do you have to say for yourself?" I asked Jesus, after I read my notes. Once again I felt like a prosecutor with Jesus in the witness box, and I felt uneasy again.

"Yes, I was crazy with God," he began, very thoughtfully. "I did cast out evil spirits, and I did witness the power of God heal some people; but what sold the narrative of my life was the miracle of my resurrection. My crucifixion was an honorable deception. As we discussed in our last talk, honorable or not a deception is still a deception; and my crucifixion created a fog that has blinded Soul. How can Soul find its way home to God when it is lost in this fog? It cannot. I hope to dispel this fog with our dialogue, and the only way to do that is to explain my sayings and dispel the Gospel conspiracy."

"Meaning?" I asked, surprised by Christ's naked frankness.

"We have to take the mystery out of my teaching. And we can begin with my parable of the good shepherd. Please read it, and then we can reveal the meaning."

I turned to John, Chapter 10, and read verses 7 to 18; and then I read verses 27 to 30, with the emphasis on verse 30 which revealed the deepest mystery of the Way of Christ: *"Verily, verily, I say unto you, I am the door of the sheep. All that ever came before me are thieves and robbers; but the sheep did not hear them. I am the door; by me if any man enter in, he shall be saved, and shall go in and out, and find pasture. The thief cometh not, but for to steal, and to kill, and to destroy: I am come that they might have life, and that they might have it more abundantly. I am the good shepherd; the good shepherd giveth his life for his sheep. But he that is an hireling, and not the shepherd, whose own the sheep are not, seeth the wolf coming, and leaveth the sheep, and fleeth; and the wolf catcheth them, and scattereth the sheep. The hireling fleeth, because he is an hireling, and careth not for the sheep. I am the good shepherd, and know my sheep, and am known of mine. As the Father knoweth me, even so know I the Father, and I lay down my life for the sheep. And other sheep I have which are not of this fold; them also I must bring, and they shall hear my voice; and there shall be one fold, and one shepherd. Therefore doth my Father love me, because I lay down my life, that I might take it again. No man taketh it from me, but I lay it down of myself. I have power to lay it down, and I have power to take it again. This commandment have I received of my Father."*

I paused, took a sip of tea, and waited for Jesus to comment. He smiled, and said, "Please complete the reading."

I picked up my Bible and read verses 27 to 30: *"My sheep hear my voice, and I know them, and they follow me. And I give unto them eternal life; and they shall never perish, neither shall any man pluck them out of my hand. My Father, which gave them me, is greater than all; and no man is able to pluck them out of my Father's hand. I and my Father are one."* I turned to Jesus. "The floor's yours," I said.

"First, I have to unpack the truth of my metaphors," Jesus began, without fanfare. "By sheep, I mean all those Souls that are

323

spiritually mature enough to begin the next stage of their journey home to God. Let's back up a moment and explain what we mean by the stages of Soul's journey back home to God."

"We've already done that," I said.

Jesus took another sip of tea. There was a slight tension in the air. "Yes; but we need to explain my parable in the context of your understanding for the modern world," Jesus said, and put his cup down. "If I may continue; the first stage of Soul's journey through life is the evolution of the seed of man's Soul. When it has evolved enough to become aware that it is a separate self it begins its growth proper, because now it creates personal karma that is responsible for the individuation of the self. This takes man to the second stage of evolution. The first stage was all about the acquisition of a self through natural evolution. The self evolves through the first stage until it has individuated enough consciousness to awaken to its spiritual nature, and it takes many lifetimes for this awareness of one's spiritual nature to evolve enough for Soul to want to free itself of its bondage to its human self. Let me explain this, for the reader's edification.

"The spiritual and human self are one and the same self, but the spiritual self cannot become spiritually self-realized without transforming the consciousness of its lower self. When I tell the multitude that I am the door of the sheep, what I am telling them is this: I have the secret teaching, and all you Souls that are ready can learn the secret of how to be saved. By saved I mean realize your own divine nature. If you live my teaching you can walk in and out of the rich pasture of life and grow and unfold in spiritual self-realization consciousness. This is what I mean by going in and out to find pasture. This was my way of saying that you can now use life consciously for your own spiritual growth, because life is the rich pasture of experience that generates the energy for your spiritual growth. And when I say that I have come that my sheep may have life more abundantly, I mean that with my teaching man can grow in spiritual self-realization consciousness, just as you used life to grow more consciously with Gurdjieff's teaching of 'work on oneself.' The spiritual life is the life everlasting of my gospel, and life more abundantly simply means to grow in spiritual consciousness. That's clear enough, don't you think?"

"For me, it is," I said, smiling at Christ's explanation.

"Good. When I say that I know my sheep, all I mean is that I am conscious of those Souls that are evolved enough to begin the next stage of their journey through life."

"The second stage of evolution?" I said, for clarity.

"Yes. Soul is now ready to leave the outer stage of life and enter the more spiritually conscious second stage of evolution. These Souls have ears to hear and eyes to see, because their spiritual senses have been awakened by life."

"That's clear," I said.

"Good," said Jesus.

"One more thing," I said. "When you say that you are the door to the sheepfold, you mean that with your teaching man can enter the second stage of evolution. Your teaching is the door to greater spiritual consciousness; right?"

"Precisely. As one lives my teaching he grows in spiritual consciousness. And if he grows enough he will realize his spiritual identity. Then he can also say my Father and I are one. But I've gotten ahead of myself. Let me back up, if you don't mind."

"Of course not. I'm sorry for interrupting the flow of your thoughts."

"It was necessary. I want the reader to know that a messenger of God — good shepherd, if you will — serves God by serving life. This is why the good shepherd will do what he must to serve God. I may have exaggerated when I said that the good shepherd would lay down his life for his fold. I just wanted to emphasize that the integrity of the messenger of God is beyond question, and he will do everything he can to help man understand the secret teaching of spiritual self-transformation."

"Spiritual self-transformation?" I queried.

"Yes. The Way of Christ is all about transforming the consciousness of the lower self of man so the spiritual self can grow and become aware of its divine nature. When Soul becomes aware of its divine nature it realizes that it is an 'I' of God. This is the mystery behind my words 'I and my Father are one.'"

"Like in the Sufi allegory of the thirty birds that looked into the Face of God and saw their own reflection?" I added, with a big smile.

"Exactly. But let's not confuse the reader. I believe he has enough to deal with as it is without bringing Sufi allegories into the picture."

"Sorry," I said, and motioned for Jesus to continue.

"When I talk about other sheep in my parable, I'm talking about Souls that are ready for the Way but are elsewhere, in other pastures; or paths, if you will. These Souls can also enter through the door of my teaching into the second stage of evolution and be initiated into the mysteries of spiritual self-realization consciousness. When I talk about the hireling, I am referring to people who think they are good shepherds but have not yet been initiated into the mysteries of the Way. They have neither the commitment nor spiritual awareness to help Soul find its way to the second stage of evolution. These are the pretenders of the Way. There are many pretenders, but we won't go there now. Suffice to say that good shepherds are far and few between. As I said, the Way is straight and narrow, and few there are who find it. You are one of the few. This is why we are talking."

I smiled, but said nothing.

"The next mystery that has to be cleared up is the mystery of my Father sending me to tend to his flock of sheep. As I said, these sheep are the Souls that are ready for the next stage of their journey to God. When I said that I would lay down my life for them and take it up again, I meant that I had learned the secret of dying to my lower self to nourish my spiritual self. I explained this secret in my power saying in the Gospel of John that we have already discussed. Briefly, all I am saying is that I had mastered the discipline of shifting my priorities from my lower to higher self; or of dying to my life to save my life. I referred to this discipline as the commandment that I received from God. By commandment, I meant the spiritual power of my saying to shift my priorities from my lower to higher self; and by God I meant the secret teaching, which is the Word of God. Clear enough?"

"Yes," I said, as I jotted down Christ's words in my notebook.

"Good. If necessary, just elaborate for the reader's edification when you include this in your book," Jesus said, trusting me to get it right.

"That's what I've been doing all along," I said, with a grateful smile.

"Good. Now, when I said that my Father gave me the sheep all I meant was that the natural process of spiritual growth in life made these Souls ready for the Way. My Father here refers to the DPG. It is the Divine Plan of God that readies Soul for the Way with the reconciling power of karma and reincarnation, and with my teaching I open the door to the next stage of evolution. *Door, shepherd,* and *Father* are the key words to my parable of the good shepherd," Jesus summed up; and then, in quiet voice full of more authority than I had heard before, he explained himself: **"By door, I mean secret teaching; by sheep, I mean Souls ready for the secret teaching; and by my Father, I mean Holy Spirit. The more spiritually self-realized man becomes as he lives the Way of Christ, the more he becomes one with Holy Spirit. Then one day he can say, as I did two thousand years ago, I and my Father are one."**

Jesus slumped in his chair and breathed a sigh of relief. I completed my notes, turned to him, and said, "Thank you, J."

"You're welcome," he said, and slowly faded to the Other Side.

58. *I Am Soul, Therefore I Am*

I was taping the drywall of a new house one week after Jesus expounded upon his good shepherd parable when he spoke to me. *"We have revealed the central mystery of my teaching,"* he said in my mind as distinctly as if he was standing beside me, *"and all we have to do now is correlate my most relevant sayings to the central mystery of the Way."*

"I got the feeling when I wrote my last chapter that our dialogue might be coming to an end," I replied, audibly. "Should I choose the most relevant sayings that relate to the central mystery of the Way and we can correlate them?"

"If you would," replied Jesus.

"I would like to include the Epistles of St. Paul in our dialogue. For my money, St. Paul captured the essence of your teaching better than the Gospel writers. Can we talk about St. Paul's wisdom on the Way of Christ as well?"

"If you like," said Jesus.

"When will I see you again?"

"Tomorrow morning," he said, and the following morning he was sitting in my reading chair dressed in tan Dockers and white polo shirt ready for a cup of tea.

I poured Jesus a cup. He picked it up, and before taking a sip said, "What have you gotten out of our dialogue so far?"

"I can't really say. I won't get a good feel for it until I transpose it to my computer and print it out. I've got it all here, in my notebooks; but my overall impression so far is still one of wonder and awe," I replied, smiling at his curiosity.

"Yes, of course; but what of our dialogue itself? What have you gotten out of our talks on my life and teaching?" Jesus asked, making me feel obligated to answer.

"I don't know what to say, J," I said, wondering what he was up to. "I guess, if anything, I would have to say it's refreshing to talk to you as a modern Master and not as the Jesus of history. It's exciting to hear you explain the Way of Christ. Maybe this will help change the minds of our Christian readers about Soul Masters."

"Why don't we talk about Soul Masters for a moment?"

"Sure. What would you like to tell me about them?"

"The world has always had Soul Masters. They come from the inner circle of life. This is the God-conscious domain. A Soul Master is a God-realized Soul, and his service to God is to help Soul find its way back to the God worlds."

"I sense confusion in the reader's mind, J. Can you explain the distinction between Soul and an individual Soul? I think the reader would appreciate this, because in our dialogue we use the two concepts indiscriminately."

"Good point. Soul is who we all are, both the self-realized and the un-self-realized atoms of God. The distinction between Soul and individual Soul is one of self-realization consciousness. The more self-realized the atom of God is the more conscious it is of being Soul. Soul then is one and many; or, to be precise, Soul is only one but forever in the process of becoming self-realized and God-conscious through the individuating self of man. When we speak of Soul, we mean both an individual atom of God and the collective consciousness of all spiritually self-realized atoms of God. Does that help?"

"I don't think we're quite there yet. Chelas always speak of themselves in terms of Soul. 'I am Soul,' says a fellow chela; but he also recognizes that Souls are individuals too. This causes some confusion. The readers of *Jesus Wears Dockers* won't be familiar with the language of the Way of the Eternal. I'm sure they would like to know what it means to be Soul and an individual Soul. Can you offer them a distinct explanation, please?"

Jesus smiled, and then chuckled.

"What's so funny?" I asked.

"I was just thinking of the famous Cartesian line, *'Je pense, donc je sui,'*"

"'I think, therefore I am,'" I said, translating Rene Descartes.

"Yes. We could say, *I am Soul, therefore I am.*"

"That's good, J. But wouldn't it be equally correct — perhaps more precise, in fact — if we said, *I am, therefore I am Soul?*"

"Yes, that's good too. In that, you have the whole presupposed drama of Soul's journey through life all the way to spiritual self-realization consciousness. But for simplicity's sake, I would stick with *I am Soul, therefore I am."*

"Why?" I asked.

"Soul is the consciousness of the self, and without the individuated consciousness of Soul there would be no self."

"Touché! So, the more a person grows in spiritual self-realization, the more conscious he will be of being Soul?"

"Precisely," said Jesus.

"That's an excellent point of entry into the transformative power of your cryptic sayings," I said. "Like your alms-giving saying. When doing alms let not your left hand know what your right hand is doing—"

"Excellent," said Jesus excitedly. "Would you like to explain the secret meaning of my alms-giving saying, or should I?"

"Let me," I said, grateful for the opportunity to share my insight on one of the most puzzling and spiritually rewarding sayings of Christ. "This saying has to do with the metaphysics of spiritual growth. Spirituality cannot be taught, it must be caught; but how does one catch Spirit? That's the mystery of your teaching, isn't it?"

"In essence, yes," said Jesus, his eyes beaming with love as they always do whenever the water of everlasting life starts to flow freely into our dialogue.

"Well, the only way to make sense of this mystery is to talk about the lower and higher self of man. Until the reader realizes that his self-consciousness is split in two, one lower and one higher, he will never fathom the secret of catching Holy Spirit, because that's what your alms-giving saying is all about; isn't it?"

"Precisely," said Jesus.

"The spiritual premise of your alms-giving saying is about catching Holy Spirit, or the creative life force, if you will; but for what purpose?"

"To nourish the higher self," replied Jesus.

"Spirit is the energy of life, and doing alms is one way to catch this precious life force; but the problem with catching this precious life force is that both the lower and the higher self want it because both have a need to be more self-realized. This is why the little self wants to take all the credit for one's alms giving. When the lower self takes credit for the charity one does, this precious life force is consumed instantly by the ego. On the other hand, when one does charity work and does not vaunt the good he has done, the precious life force of one's goodness bypasses ego and nourishes the higher self. The precious goodness of one's charity is pure Spirit. It has not been sullied by the selfish ego. Am I getting too metaphysical here?"

"I don't see how else you can explain the metaphysics of spiritual growth," Jesus said, and laughed.

"Well, in order for the reader to appreciate the true meaning of your alms-giving saying perhaps we can refer to your saying about storing one's treasures in heaven?"

"Excellent!" said Jesus, excited by the correlation.

"Before I look it up let me point out that you imply the two selves in the alms-giving saying with the left and right hand. You often use body parts to refer to the lower and higher self. We can expound upon this with the appropriate saying. The saying that comes to mind is the one where you admonish one to cut off his hand or pluck out his eye if they offend him; but for now let's explain the mystery of catching Spirit."

Jesus was smiling at me. His smile turned into a grin. And then he broke into a hearty chuckle. *"You really do understand my sayings, don't you?"*

"Of course I do. Once I came to the realization that we have two selves it all made sense to me. It was like dominos. Once one domino fell, they all fell eventually; and as each domino fell I understood your teaching all the more. The real issue we have with your teaching is to get that first domino to fall. This could happen with any one of your sayings. One saying may connect with one person better than another, and once that connection is made the dominos begin to fall one by one because each domino in the Way of Christ speaks for the whole teaching of the Way of Christ."

"And which domino would you like the reader to knock down?" Jesus asked.

"I can't say. One reader may connect with one of our talks, and another reader may connect with another one of our talks; it depends upon the reader's spiritual needs. Overall, I would like the reader to grasp the concept of the lower and higher self. Once he grasps this concept he should begin to make sense of your teaching, because your whole teaching has to do with liberating the spiritual self from the consciousness of its lower self."

"Absolutely. If we can do that we will accomplish my goal and dispel the Gospel conspiracy for good," replied Jesus, delighted by my answer.

"Your goal is to set the record straight; right?"

"Yes. But primarily to dispel the Gospel conspiracy."

"We may do that," I said, feeling a sudden urge to speak my mind; "but I don't think it will do any good. Christianity has always fed on the desperate and foolish, and it will never stop until the spiritual consciousness of the world has been raised."

"It is happening. The marketplace is flooded with new works of creative spirituality, and it will continue to be flooded. God has opened the floodgates of heaven and the world is awash with the creative consciousness of Holy Spirit. This is the time of the new harvest. Never in the history of the world has the harvest been as abundant as it is today. In the days of my mission on earth the harvest was plentiful, but it was a mere drop compared to the harvest today. It is inevitable for this harvest to take place. This is why there are so many shepherds collecting sheep today. Despite your attitude about letting the world find its own way, you are one of God's chosen shepherds. Why else do you suppose you were granted permission to receive the Golden Wisdom of the Way on the Ninth Heaven in your last past-life regression? Why else were you brought to the Ocean of Love and Mercy to experience the beginning of Soul's journey into life? Why else were you granted the experience of your first primordial human life on earth where you had the dawning of your own self-consciousness? And why else were you given the experience of the genesis of life on earth? The Inner Master decided that you should divine the DPG for the world to have a blueprint of Soul's journey through life so you could introduce it to the world through your writing; that's why you were given those experiences. No one has connected the dots from the alpha of Soul's journey in life to the omega of Soul's return to God like you have. Despite yourself, O — or rather, it is precisely because of what you are that your contribution to this new spiritual awakening will be deemed invaluable."

"Are you sure you're not speaking for our good friend Kal?" I said, and laughed.

"Not at all," Jesus said, in all seriousness. "Our good friend has lost his authority over you. Whatever you have to say about the Way can no longer be sullied by your ego. That is why you were chosen to help me dispel the Gospel conspiracy. Many Souls were called to help me, but none was able to connect the dots enough to see the big picture as you have. So be flattered if you must; you have certainly earned it."

"Curiously enough, I was just telling Cathy last night that I found it incredible that no one in history — at least that I am aware of, and I've read a lot of books on spiritual teachings — has ever explained the secret of your sayings. After I finished my day's work yesterday I read the Epistles of St. Paul again, and good lord the secret teaching jumped off the pages at me! I could not believe how clear it was this time around. Our talks have lifted the fog off your teaching enough for it to be seen for what it really is!"

"And what is that?" Jesus asked, smiling at my excitement.

"St. Paul makes it clear much more than you did in the Gospels that the secret teaching is all about transforming the consciousness of the lower self. But let me make my point before we get off topic. Why in God's name has no one else been able to lift the fog off your teaching? I can't fathom this mystery, and it puts a burden on me that I don't think I can support. *I can't, J!"*

Jesus smiled. "The responsibility that you feel is the same responsibility that all shepherds of God have for their sheep. As I said, you may have adopted the attitude of letting the world find its own way, but in this attitude lies the heart of the true lover of God. If I may allude to Paul's Epistles, you have been bought with a price, O; and the price that you paid to look into the Face of God was exceedingly great. This is why you are among the few Souls to have lifted the fog off my teaching."

"So others have, then?" I foolishly and instantly regretted asking.

"Yes, of course. They were not all writers, though. Your gift is creative writing, which will reverberate in the world when you work with the Ascended Master who bore my wounds. You have no idea how much you are appreciated on the inner, O."

333

"Yes," I sighed. "As you know, I had a conversation with Doctor Jung on the inner planes one night. We talked about one of my Soul talk books, which isn't even transcribed out here yet; so I know how much I'm read on the inner planes. But that's not doing me much good out here, is it? Believe me, J; I don't know how much longer my body can do the work that I have to do to earn my living. I don't want to admit this to Cathy because I don't want to worry her, but I'm getting concerned. I'm going to devote all the time I can this winter to look for a publisher. And I'll tell you this; I'm not above asking for help. If you can do anything to get this show on the road, you have my permission."

"I'll see what I can do for you," Jesus said. "So, are you satisfied now?"

"Yes, I got my answer. It puzzled me why few people have been able to penetrate the secret of your teaching. This is why the fog of your teaching continues to obfuscate. In yesterday's *Globe* they had a full page drawing of a tree. Each branch of the tree represented a world religion. On the Christian branch they quoted your grain of mustard seed parable. The irony of this quotation is that they had no idea what you meant by the metaphor of the mustard seed. They used it to make a point about saving the environment, which is a good thing; but your mustard seed parable is one of the most revealing of the secret teachings of the Way. If I may, now that I've brought it up, mustard seed refers to the tiniest of apertures that opens to the mighty spiritual consciousness of the Way, which you call kingdom of heaven. This tiny aperture could be any one of your sayings. Your alms-giving saying, for example. As one lives this saying with the wisdom to store one's treasures in heaven, which I'm going to explain, one will open the door for the consciousness of the Way to guide one's life. This tiny grain of mustard seed will grow in spiritual consciousness to become a tree of enormous stature in the consciousness of the Way. In effect, what you are saying with this parable is that any entry point into the secret teaching of the Way will allow for the magnificent consciousness of the Way to come into one's life, because any aspect of the Way speaks for the whole Way."

"That's the mystery of the mustard seed!" Jesus exclaimed, astonished by my explanation. "Thank you for that, O. I did not expect to have this parable explained so clearly. Thank you again,"

Jesus repeated, radiant with gratitude.

The love in Christ's eyes was so touching that I was compelled to say, from the very depths of my heart, *"You're welcome, J."*

"May we continue with storing one's treasures in heaven now?"

"Yes; but as we were talking I got a nudge to explain the mystery of the two selves again. I was nudged to reveal their distinct nature so your sayings can have more clarity. If you don't mind, can we just talk about the dual consciousness of the self before we reveal the secret of storing one's treasures in heaven?"

"By all means," said Jesus "Where would you like to begin?"

"Where to begin? Let me do a short HU to help open the door to this mystery. Give me a couple of minutes, please."

I closed my eyes and did a silent HU. My silent HU became an audible HU, and Jesus joined me in the Love Song to God. After two or three minutes we brought our HU to a gentle close, and we both said, "May the blessings be," which means quite simply that it is not for our will that we do what we do, but for the will of God.

During the HU I got the distinct impression that I had to open the door that Spirit wanted open to explain the two selves of man. There are an infinite number of doors that open up to the same mystery, but I knew that the door that Spirit chose to open would give contextual clarity to our whole dialogue on Christ's teaching, so I just blurted out, *"The selfish and unselfish nature of Soul!"*

"Pardon me?" Jesus said, surprised by my outburst.

"That's the entry point to the mystery of the two selves of man."

"Please explain that," Jesus said, his eyes still brimming with love.

"Yes, of course," I said, feeling myself being pulled by the powerful surge of the Holy Current of God. *The less evolved a Soul is, the more selfish it is; and the more evolved a Soul is, the less selfish it is.* It's a sliding scale of spiritual growth. The more selfish a Soul is, the more influence the lower self will have over its higher self; and the less selfish a Soul is, the more influence the higher self will have over its lower self. That's the dynamic of the two selves of man!"

335

"You do know what this implies, don't you?" Jesus said.

"Conflict, of course. It implies the battle that goes on in man's heart between his lower and higher self. It implies the constant tension of both selves fighting for the same precious life force to satisfy their hunger for more self-identity. It implies the never-ending war of the two selves in man's Soul!"

"That, you will have to explain," said Jesus.

"Why don't you explain it, J? After all, you did sacrifice ego on the cross—"

Jesus burst into laughter. *"Touché!"* he exclaimed. "For the reader to understand this tension between the lower and higher self he has to see what drives Soul. Soul is our essential self, an atom of God that comes from God for one purpose only: to grow in spiritual consciousness until it becomes God-realized. Spiritual self-identity is realized in the second stage of evolution through life by the reconciling power of Holy Spirit. Soul's DNA drives Soul to grow in its own identity, so despite the fact that all Souls are unique they are all genetically driven to grow in their own spiritual identity—"

"If I may cut in," I interjected. "I don't want to interrupt the flow of your thoughts, but I have to add that this need for self-identity is our most basic need in life, and it drives all of our other needs — physical, mental, and emotional."

"Good," said Jesus. "Soul's greatest need in life is self-identity. This is encoded in Soul's DNA. Just as the acorn seed is genetically encoded to become an oak tree, so is Soul encoded to realize the 'I' of God through its own distinct individual self, which it realizes through karma and reincarnation. Are we clear on this point so far?"

"I believe we are," I said, and paused to give my note-taking hand a rest.

"Soul's need for self-identity drives Soul through life," Jesus continued; "but Soul has created a dual consciousness as it evolved. This is Soul's lower and higher self. The higher self is the resolved consciousness of Soul's karmic energies, and the lower self is Soul's unresolved karmic energies. Since Soul is innately driven to grow in spiritual self-realization consciousness, it is forever trying to resolve the consciousness of its lower self; and this is where the tension of the two selves begins. The more Soul grows in spiritual consciousness, the more influence it will have over its lower self, or ego if you will. This gives ego more incentive to resist being resolved, because the more resolved the lower self becomes the more ego will cease to be."

"Wow! Please explain that or you will lose the reader completely!"

Jesus laughed. "Of course. Since Soul is driven by its DNA to grow in self-identity, it follows that the two selves would be driven to become more self-realized; but the lower self is driven to become egoically self-realized, not spiritually self-realized. The difference in the consciousness of the lower and higher self can be described in the simplest terms possible. As you said, the consciousness of the lower self is selfish, and the consciousness of higher self is unselfish; so the conflict in the heart of man is ego's desire to be more self-serving and the higher self's desire to be more giving, or life-serving."

"I like it. Please, continue," I said.

"It follows that when a person's need to do good possesses him and he goes out and does charity work to satisfy his higher self's need for more spiritual identity, like you did when you volunteered your time for Habitat for Humanity or picked blueberries for your elderly painting customers, then ego's selfish needs are denied and ego will pull out all stops to steal the precious energy of the goodness that Soul has realized by doing good works; so the conflict that ensues in the heart of man is the conflict over the precious life force that the two selves need to satisfy their appetite for greater identity—"

"This is the conflict of the selfish and unselfish nature of man?" I jumped in.

"Exactly," said Jesus.

"This is why there are few really good people out there then," I said, and laughed.

"Yes; because ego wins most of the battles," Jesus added, with a smile.

"And this poses a problem for Soul," I said.

"Which is?" Jesus asked.

My insight just poured out of my mouth, as the Word always does when it has been thoroughly individualized: "Now that Soul has evolved to the point where it needs to be more spiritually self-realized, how can a person ensure his spiritual growth in a consumerist society like ours where all the values are directed to satisfying man's selfish ego? It's a very materialistic world out there, and all the market forces are focused on satisfying man's ego — from food, to drink, to sex, to fashion and all the toys that man could possibly want to make his life heaven on earth. Do you see where I'm going with this?"

"I see your point exactly," said Jesus. "Man must learn to survive spiritually in these times no less than he had to learn how to survive spiritually in other times. The world is constantly changing, but the three stages of human evolution exist in all epochs."

"If I may quote Wordsworth," I said, smiling at the thought: *'The world is too much with us; late and soon /Getting and spending we lay waste our powers /little we see in nature that is ours; /We have given our hearts away; a sordid boon!'* Even in the eighteen hundreds the world was too much with him, and Wordsworth, who had an enormous appetite for spiritual consciousness, had to learn how to survive spiritually in his own way!"

"And how did he do that?" Jesus asked, for the reader's sake.

"Wordsworth didn't have the advantage we have with the spiritual exercises of the Way, so he had to survive spiritually the old-fashioned hard way — by spiritualizing his consciousness through conscious effort!"

"Please explain that," Jesus said, again for the reader's sake.

I went to my bookshelf and took out my volume on Wordsworth's poetry. I opened it to his poem *Character of the Happy Warrior*. I was just about to say something when Jesus spoke up. "If I may," he said. "I very much like how Holy Spirit has opened up this subject of spiritual survival in our modern times."

"You do?"

"Yes. I think this is a subject of vital importance for our reader."

"Our reader?" I said, and smiled at Jesus.

"Your reader, my reader, our reader; it doesn't matter. The important thing is that man has to learn spiritual survival skills. He cannot become spiritually self-realized unless he does, so I'm glad we have opened up this subject. It's off topic, but in the grand scheme of things it's all relevant. By all means, tell the reader what we can offer him for his spiritual survival in today's consumer society. You were going to tell me how Wordsworth managed to do this in his world."

"Wordsworth reveals his spiritual survival skills in *Character of the Happy Warrior*. He begins his poem by acknowledging that Holy Spirit is his strength, and the rest of the poem has to do with how to catch Spirit so he will have the strength to withstand the negative forces of life. Actually, for the reader's sake, I'd like to quote the whole poem because it shows how a poet's talent for connecting with the creative life force has allowed him to catch a glimpse of God. Wordsworth reveals his glimpse of God in his poem *Intimations of Immortality*. So at this point I'd quote the whole poem for the reader, but the first seven lines of the *Character of the Happy Warrior* will do for now. May I?"

"Please," Jesus said, with a gesture; and I put on my glasses and read:

> "Who is the happy Warrior? Who is he
> That every man in arms should wish to be?
> —It is the generous Spirit, who, when brought
> Among the tasks of real life, hath wrought
>   Upon the plan that pleased his boyish thought:
> Whose high endeavors are an inward light
> That makes the path before him always bright."

"I see what you mean," said Jesus. "In those few lines Wordsworth reveals that his path in life will always be bright as long as he is guided by Holy Spirit. I like that very much. That's what spiritual survival is all about, keeping one's path in life bright with the light of Holy Spirit. Please, continue with your thought."

"I don't have much to add. In the rest of his poem he reveals how to keep the path always bright by living life with the high values of the spiritual life."

"Which are?"

"The spiritual life is the ethical life. The spiritual life is the moral life. The spiritual life is the virtuous life. The more one is guided by the noble virtues of truth, goodness, forgiveness, kindness, humility and so on his path will always be bright with the light of Holy Spirit. My favorite lines in all of literature come from this poem. Let me quote them for you, J. They're my guide on how to survive spiritually in our time."

"Please. I'd love to hear your favorite lines in all of literature. I'm only sorry it's not something I said," Jesus said, feigning hurt feelings.

I laughed. "I'm sorry, J. For all of your genius for metaphor you did not possess the gift of poetry like Wordsworth, Keats, or Rumi; but you come very close," I said, just to rub a little phony salt into his feigned wound. "Some of your sayings do scintillate with the light of poetic genius, which opens up another door to the mystical teachings of the Way — the door of the creative process; but we can't go there now. I love Wordsworth because he reveals the character of the Happy Warrior. To be a spiritual survivor you have to be a Happy Warrior, and my favorite lines in all of literature are:

> 'He labors good on good to fix, and owes
> To virtue every triumph that he knows:
> —Who, if he rise to station of command,
> Rises by open means; and there will stand
> On honorable terms, or else retire,
> And in himself posses his own desire.'"

Jesus started to laugh. He laughed and laughed, to my complete perplexity. "What are you laughing at?" I asked, feeling like he was laughing at my expense.

"You said that these are your favorite lines in all of literature?"

"Yes," I said, wondering what he was getting at.

"Do you not see where your attitude of letting the world find its own way comes from?" Jesus said, with a grin like he had swallowed the canary.

"I don't follow you," I said, genuinely perplexed.

"'*And in himself posses his own desire,*'" Jesus explained, quoting the last line.

A light went on. "Of course," I said, feeling embarrassed. "I have always tried to live my life on honorable terms. And when I could not, I didn't care what the world thought of me. Whenever the world tried to compromise me I withdrew into myself and possessed my own desire and told the world to stick it in its ear!"

Jesus broke into another fit of laughter.

"What's so funny now?" I asked, feeling like I had just been check-mated.

"Do you understand now why I said that you were bought with a price?"

"Hey!" I instinctively lashed out at Jesus, *"I don't need you to tell me I've been bought with a price! I'm still paying the goddamn price, and it's not funny!* I won't tell you what happened with the owner of the house I just painted because I'm still reeling from my humiliation, but I can tell you this, Jesus of Nazareth: we may be bought with a price to enter the kingdom of heaven, but Old Whore Life never stops screwing us of our virtue! That's why we have to have spiritual survival skills in this goddamn selfish world! It's impossible to live the honorable life today without spiritual survival skills! That's why I made *Character of the Happy Warrior* my personal ideal! *I can't survive without it!"*

My beast was out, and dead silence fell into the room. I was so angry that my body was still trembling, and I just stared blankly at Jesus.

Jesus felt the anger of my humiliation and didn't say anything. I thought he might say something witty like, *get thee behind me, Satan*; but he was silent. When I finally calmed down, in a very soft voice he said, "I apologize. I took liberties that I should not have taken. We have all suffered humiliation, because this is what Holy Spirit does to burn away our vanity. Vanity is our greatest spiritual threat in life. It is not anger, lust, greed, or even attachment to the material life. Vanity can consume the ego. I sympathize with your feelings of humiliation. I experienced the fierce burning love of God many times, because I had more vanity to burn off than most. Do you not think it the height of arrogance to die on a cross to impress upon the world the symbol of self-sacrifice, which is the very core of my teaching? When I cried *My God, my God, why hast thou forsaken me?* do you think I was calling upon God? If my Father in heaven and I are one, who do you think had forsaken me? I had forsaken myself. I was vain enough to believe that I could save the world with my gospel of the Way, but the world did not need to be saved. By all means, let us inform the reader that even the most advanced Soul must be on guard against the negative forces of life; especially vanity. But let's not terrify him either," Jesus added, with a gentle smile. "As long as man

341

lives his life in good faith he will have nothing to worry about."

"Thank you, J," I said, moved by his compassion for my humiliating experience with the nit-picking homeowner whose new house I had to repaint because I did not meet his impossible expectations of professional standards. "Please don't feel bad about crossing the line. I should have been more attentive to my work. But I do want to make one point for the reader's sake. Spirit is the reconciling power of God. Man is only a channel for Holy Spirit. To survive spiritually we have to be a clear channel for Spirit's guidance. There are two sure ways to do this. One, by practicing the spiritual exercises of the Way daily, because they spiritualize the lower self; and two, by living the life of the Happy Warrior."

"Bravo," said Jesus, still in his soft gentle voice. "And I would emphasize that staying alert is vital to spiritual survival. I admonished my disciples to stay awake. To survive spiritually we have to be vigilant to the negative forces of life, because there is no guarantee that once one wakes up spiritually he will not fall asleep momentarily, as you have just proven with your humbling painting experience."

"Yes," I agreed, with a wry smile. "But aside from the spiritual exercises and the Happy Warrior ethic, what would you suggest we do to stay spiritually awake?"

"The goal of the spiritual life is to serve God by serving life. It would follow that the more one dedicates his daily activities to the service of God, the more he will stay conscious of what the spiritual life is all about. I would suggest that one do the best he can in whatever he is doing, and always in the name of God."

"I would reduce that even further," I said, as my humiliation washed over me again. "Even as one lives his life in good faith life will force him to stay alert, because Old Whore Life never stops trying to screw us of our virtue!"

"Isn't that the truth?" Jesus exclaimed, and broke into laughter.

"Now we should get back on topic," I said, with a big smirk at my dig at Old Whore Life. I flipped the pages of my Bible to Mathew's Gospel. "If I may, let me quote your metaphor for catching Spirit. This is from Chapter 6, verses 19 to 24*: `Lay not up for yourselves treasures upon earth, where moth and rust doth corrupt, and where thieves break through and steal: But lay up for* *yourselves treasures in heaven, where neither moth nor rust doth corrupt, and where thieves do not break through and steal. For where your treasure is, there your heart will be also. The light of the body is the eye: if therefore thine eye be single, thy whole body shall be full of light. But if thine eye be evil, thy whole body shall be full of darkness. If therefore the light that is in thee be darkness, how great is that darkness! No man can serve two masters: for either he will hate the one, and love the other; or else he will hold to the one, and despise the other. Ye cannot serve God and mammon.'"*

Jesus had his eyes closed. I waited patiently. When he opened his eyes, he said, "It is important that we reveal the hidden wisdom of this metaphor, because it will make an excellent point of entry for the reader into the mysteries of the kingdom of heaven."

"By kingdom of heaven, you mean the secret teachings of the Way?"

"Yes. The reader should know by now that kingdom of heaven is my metaphor for the Way. We could be more graphic in our description and call the kingdom of heaven the mesoteric circle of life, or those states of higher consciousness that Soul is destined to reach at some point in its journey through life—"

"If I may," I interrupted, "I think we should make it absolutely clear that Soul will complete its journey to total self-realization consciousness because it's written in the DPG. There is no such thing as failure in the DPG. We can remove all fear of failure, because the reconciling power of Holy Spirit will bring Soul into agreement with God eventually. It may take the rest of one's life or a hundred more lifetimes, but Soul will find its way to its true self. There is no such thing as eternal punishment. The metaphor of hell in your teaching has to be seen for what it is, a karmic cleansing experience; and until the world realizes that's all you meant by hell, people will always misunderstand your teaching."

"If I may repeat what you just said, so the reader can hear it straight from the horse's mouth: <u>THERE IS NO ETERNAL DAMNATION!</u>" Jesus shouted.

He pronounced each word distinctly and underscored them with his forefinger, and then I followed with: "<u>HELL IS A KARMIC CLEANSING!</u>"

Jesus laughed. "Do you think the reader will get it?"

"Some will and some won't. Those who get it are ready for the kingdom of heaven, and those who don't will just have to suffer the indignities of life a while longer until they are spiritually mature enough to get it," I replied, with an ironic chuckle.

"Having said that, let's reveal the secret of my treasures metaphor."

"Good. Let me," I said.

"By all means," Jesus said, gesturing with his hand.

"For spiritual clarity, I'm going to do a short HU," I said. After a couple of minutes of connecting with the Holy Current of God, I let Soul speak: "Treasures is your metaphor for the creative life force. The creative life force is Holy Spirit. The higher self needs the life force to grow, but the lower self needs it to grow also; so there is a constant battle in the heart of man for the creative life force. This is why you stressed in your saying that one's eye should be single. I'm going to simplify this metaphor by substituting the word eye with the personal pronoun 'I'. This will make all the difference in the explanation of your metaphor. If the reader can be made to see that the 'I' of the higher self and the 'I' of the lower self are one and the same 'I' then he might just grasp the central mystery of your saying, and quite possibly your whole teaching. Of course the reader will ask the question: how can the same 'I' occupy both the higher and lower self? And the best explanation would be that the 'I' of Soul's lower self is unconscious of its spiritual nature, whereas the 'I' of Soul's higher self is conscious of its spiritual nature, and the purpose of your teaching is to make spiritually conscious the spiritually unconscious 'I' of Soul's lower self. The more spiritually conscious the 'I' of the lower self becomes, the more the two become one conscious 'I'. This is why you stress that the 'I' of Soul should be single. This means that the lower and higher self should be in agreement with Soul's destiny of spiritual self-realization and God-consciousness. How am I doing so far?"

Jesus just shook his head. "I marvel at your perspicacity. I would never have thought to substitute eye with the personal pronoun 'I'. By doing so, you have lifted the fog off my teaching with so much clarity that it dazzles my mind. *I marvel at your gift for clarity!*"

"Not I, J; my Father in heaven," I said, and laughed. "Alright; having said this, let me explain the difference between treasures in heaven and treasures on earth. If man expends all of his energies to acquire material treasures, he is feeding the 'I' of his lower self; and when he dies he will leave this world rich in the consciousness of his lower self. And here we can explain your rich man parable—"

"By all means," Jesus said, his eyes sparkling with excitement.

"Let me find the passage," I said, and scanned the pages of Mathew's Gospel until I found the parable. "It's in Chapter 19, verses 21 to 24: *If thou wilt be perfect, go out and sell that thou hast and give to the poor, and thou shalt have treasures in heaven; and come and follow me. But when the young man heard that saying, he went away sorrowful, for he had great possessions. Then Jesus said unto his disciples, Verily I say unto you, That a rich man shall hardly enter into the kingdom of heaven. And again I say unto you, It is easier for a camel to go through the eye of a needle, than for a rich man to enter the kingdom of God.*"

I paused, took a drink of tea, and said, "To be clear then, by rich you don't mean earthly riches; you mean rich in the consciousness of the lower self. The rich man symbolizes the Soul that is blind to its spiritual nature. This means that the richer one is in the consciousness of his lower self, the less aware he will be of his spiritual nature. This is why you said that it is easier for a camel to pass through the eye of a needle than it is for a rich man to enter into the kingdom of heaven, because the lower self cannot enter the higher worlds of God until it is spiritualized. You tell the rich young man how to enter the kingdom of heaven by divesting himself of the rich consciousness of his lower self through generous acts of charity by giving his riches to the poor, because his charity will transform his lower self and allow him entry into the kingdom of heaven; but he took your words literally and feared the loss of all his worldly riches and walked away from your teaching because he wasn't ready to take up his cross of self-sacrifice and follow you. The rich man parable ties in beautifully with your treasures in heaven metaphor, because it explains how the consciousness of the lower self keeps man from entering the kingdom of heaven."

"This is why I said that man cannot serve both God and mammon, because if he does he will always be conflicted," Jesus amplified. "Yae yae, or nay nay," Jesus added.

"We can't have our cake and eat it too," I said, and laughed.

Jesus smiled at me. "I marvel at how you can make light of such a serious subject. You see the humor of man's spiritual obtuseness, and I love it. I cannot let myself go that far. After all, what would the world think of me?"

"Yes, you do have an image to uphold, don't you?" I said, with a chuckle.

"Let's get back to the topic," Jesus said, taking advantage of the incredible connection that we had with the spirit of his teaching. "Do you have anything else you would like to say about my treasures in heaven metaphor?"

I scanned the verses and was prompted to explain the concept of personal priorities. "You said that one's heart will be where one's treasures are. By this you meant that if one's priorities are to satisfy the needs of his lower self, that's where he will spend his time and energy; but these earthly treasures will pass away because they are of this temporal world. On the other hand, if one spends his time and energy nourishing his higher self then the treasures he stores in heaven — meaning the spiritual consciousness that he realizes through his efforts to live the spiritual life — will not pass away, because the consciousness of one's spiritual self is eternal. You know, J; this is so obvious to me now that I fear I won't be able to make it clear for the reader!"

"Just let Soul speak, O," Jesus said, with the warmest smile.

"Then let me say that this is why you admonish man to seek the kingdom of heaven first and everything else will follow, because by seeking the kingdom of heaven one is forced to bring the lower self into agreement with the higher self. The more the two selves agree, the less conflict one will have in his heart and the more in agreement Soul will be with life; and life being the Holy Current of God, it follows that the more Soul is in agreement with the Holy Current of God the more life will be in agreement with Soul. This is why you said, '*But seek ye first the kingdom of God, and his righteousness, and all these things shall be added unto you. Take therefore no thought for the morrow; for the morrow shall take thought for the things of itself. Sufficient unto the day is the evil thereof.*' That's from Mathew, Chapter 6, verses 33 and 34."

"Please explain what I meant by 'sufficient unto the day is the evil thereof.'"

346

"That does seem puzzling, doesn't it? But all you meant is that the riches of life are never ending, and Soul will never fear running out of experiences that provide Soul with the life force it needs to nourish itself. By evil thereof, you mean the unconscious karmic energies of life that Soul needs to grow. By living the spiritual life of the Way, the spiritually unconscious energies of life that Soul takes in through daily experience are transformed into the pure spiritually conscious energy that Soul needs to grow in spiritual self-realization consciousness. This is why you stressed that by seeking the kingdom of heaven first all the experiences we have in life will be used for Soul's spiritual growth."

"Good," Jesus said; "very good, indeed."

"Let me sum up by saying that Soul grows through human experience. If one's efforts in life are focused on satisfying his human self, he will starve his spiritual self; and this will make for a lot of future karmic reconciliation. On the other hand, if one makes his spiritual life his first priority, then all the experiences he has in life will nourish his higher self and bring his lower self into agreement with his higher self. The more he is in agreement with his higher self, the more in agreement he will be with the Holy Current of Life; and the more he is in agreement with life, the more he will be in agreement with God!"

"Excellent," said Jesus. "If I may, I would just add that one should avoid the danger of extremes. One should try to live a balanced life. One should not devote all of one's time to the spiritual life. As wonderful as this goal may be, it will throw one's life off balance. When one finds the Way he should not abandon to the spiritual life completely. As the old saying goes, make haste slowly."

"That's a far cry from your message two thousand years ago," I said, with a wry chuckle. "You were gung ho on telling the world it was one way or the other. You are either with me or against me, you said. *Talk about extremes!* Now you're telling the reader to make haste slowly. Why the change of heart, J?"

"I've had two thousand years to reflect on my mission — *and two thousand years on the cross of abject humiliation can do wonders for one's humility!*"

I burst into a fit of laughter, and Jesus joined me; and we laughed, and laughed, and then we called it a day. But I regretted lashing out at Jesus the way I did, and it took a long time to forgive myself...

59. *A Short Dialogue with the Inner Master*

Despite my sudden burst of anger, I enjoyed writing the chapter of our last talk because it revealed so much about Christ's teaching. But more enjoyable were the little side trips that we took. They offered precious insights that illuminated the sayings of Jesus and added new layers of meaning to the Way, not to mention how much they revealed about my own unpredictable nature. I couldn't get over how I took my anger out on Jesus.

But we covered a lot of ground in our talk. It seemed that the more we talked about Christ's sayings and parables, the easier it was for Soul to speak; and this began to scare me, because I was beginning to see what it meant to be a God-realized Soul.

If Soul can speak freely all the time one would be a Soul Master. Despite this being the goal of human life, this seems to be forever in the distance; and as it approaches one fears reaching this goal because it would mean the journey is coming to an end.

Of course, there is no end to Soul's perfection because there is no end to God-realization consciousness; so it's a false fear. Nonetheless, it's still a very real fear of letting go of the old and embracing the new.

I did not want to talk with Jesus about this. I preferred to talk with the Inner Master about Soul's fear of endless perfection. To prepare for my dialogue I did a contemplation using my secret spiritual word, which gave me a special connection with the Inner Master, and then I picked up my pen and wrote in my notebook:

O. Why do I fear coming to an end in my spiritual journey?

Z. *It is not the fear of coming to an end of your spiritual journey; it is the fear of your human consciousness coming to the realization that it now must be brought into total agreement with Soul. This is perfectly natural; so do not make more of it than it really is. This is the same fear that we all have in life when we come to those transition points where we are forced to let go of the old and embrace the new, like parents seeing their children off to college.*

O. Thank you. So my human consciousness is coming into greater agreement with Soul? That's good. Is this why I had to experience abject humiliation again, to burn off some more vanity?

Z. *Yes.*

O. Can we talk about this experience of burning off karma?

Z. *By all means.*

O. As I worked these last few days I could not get my humiliating experience out of my mind; especially after lashing out at Jesus the way I did. Try as I may, using all of my spiritual skills to keep from thinking about my experience, I could not succeed; and the anguish I suffered was unbearable. Then it occurred to me that all of my anguish was simply an excruciating experience of karmic cleansing, because my humiliation went to the core of my vanity; and as I anguished over the experience I knew that I was burning off the karma of my unconscious vanity. This is what you call the slow burning love of God. Am I correct in this realization? (I heard the Inner Master laughing.) I'm right about this, aren't I?

Z. *Yes. Anguish is an excruciating pain. In this case, you suffered the spiritual anguish of self-transformation, which is the merciful slow burning love of God. This is the natural process of karmic reconciliation, which every Soul experiences throughout life. Thank you for this insight, O. It will help your reader to understand how the natural process of spiritual growth works in one's life through the anguish of God's burning love.*

O. You're thanking me? I could be witty here, but I feel restrained. You're welcome. So, if I may, are you pleased with how my dialogue with Jesus is unfolding?

Z. *It is an extraordinary feat of creative expression. Please complete your dialogue and share it with the world. It will be your drop of water, which will grow into the mighty River of your dream experience; and like the River Nile it will nourish millions of Souls.*

O. My dream experience? Wow! Thank you.
(I had a dream many years ago of being a tiny drop of water that grew into a trickle, then a stream, then a creek, and finally a river as mighty as the River Nile.)

Z. *You're welcome.*

O. Now, my health?

Z. Do what you have to do to stay healthy. Drink plenty of water, eat nutritionally, pace yourself at work, and do some cardiovascular workouts and you will complete your life very satisfactorily. Okay?

O. Thank you. I guess besides the obvious then, I should do my spiritual exercises with a disciplined regularity, shouldn't I?

Z. It will certainly enhance your spiritual growth.

O. One more question. I've thought of writing you another series of letters, starting with what I called "My Karmic Body." No. I won't go there now. It's not relevant here. Thank you. I will end this dialogue with my deepest appreciation for your guidance.

Z. You're welcome. My love to you and Jesus. I am always with you, O. Don't ever forget that.

O. I know. That's my biggest problem. Had I been aware that you're always with me I wouldn't have suffered that insufferable humiliation.

Z. But you would still be packing those extra pounds of vanity, wouldn't you?

I broke into a fit of laughter. I heard the Inner Master laughing also, and I ended our short, but spiritually reassuring dialogue.

60. *Stupidity Is Not a Gift of God*

"The light of the body is the eye; therefore when thine eye is single, thy whole body also is full of light; but when thine eye is evil, thy body also is full of darkness," Jesus said, quoting himself. "That's from Luke, Chapter 11, verse 34. That's the topic of discussion this morning because it will round off our last talk very nicely."

"I think I know where you're going with this, but I'm not sure I'm up to plummeting the depths of the self this morning."

"Why not?" Jesus asked, looking surprised.

"I don't know. Perhaps we should take a break from our talks. Too much of the same thing takes the shine off, and for some reason I feel rather bored with this whole business. Please don't be offended, J. I feel so familiar with your teaching now that I just don't have the heart I had when we started our dialogue."

"I understand. But we started this project together, and we're going to finish it together; so can we get on with my light of the body saying?"

"Let's just chat for a while. Prime the pump, as it were. I have to connect with Soul before I plummet the depths of the self."

"Plummet the depths of the self?" Jesus repeated, with a reflective smile. "It's unfortunate the scholars didn't connect the spiritual dots of my teaching as you have. If they had, we wouldn't be having this dialogue."

"Let's talk about that, then," I said, challenged by the thought. "In our last talk we revealed why the rich man could not enter the kingdom of heaven. Do you think it will be any easier for the scholars to let go of their theories on your life and gospel? I don't think so. They're much too rich in intellect. I think on the whole most people reflect the same character flaw as that agnostic Christian minister I was telling you about; they all want their cake and eat it too. This is what's at the heart of the saying you just quoted. People don't want to look at life through a single eye, because that implies sacrificing one's precious little self, which you say is evil and full of darkness. You know what, J? It would take a miracle to undo the damage this metaphorical evil of yours has done to the world!"

"Wow!" Jesus exclaimed. *"Talk about instant connection!* Can you turn down the voltage just a bit, please?"

I laughed. "I didn't expect that. It just came out. But I'm not going to deny it. I think your metaphor for evil has warped the psyche of the world. You make so damn much of the lower self being evil that it completely obfuscates the spiritual purpose of the lower self. The body is the temple for Holy Spirit, which you acknowledged; but that doesn't mean that the consciousness of the lower self is evil simply because it obstructs the eye of man from being single, if I may play upon your metaphor."

"I thought you weren't up to plummeting the depths of the self?"

"I'm not going there deliberately. I'm just venting."

"Venting? Why?" Jesus asked, again with a look of surprise.

"I don't know. Things are coming to a head."

"What do you mean?"

"It's this damn humiliation that I experienced on my job. I can't bring myself to talk about it, but I've been anguishing over it for days; and it's brought back a lot of memories of past humiliations. I'm just tired of all this karmic cleansing. *Damn it, J; is there no bloody end to my goddamn vanity?"*

Jesus stared at me. I thought he would have objected to my language, but he didn't. "Perhaps I should come back when you're in a better mood," he said.

"I'm sorry. It's just the after-effects. I'm almost over my humiliation and I'm in that self-guilt frame of mind where I whip myself for my own stupidity. You know what, J? *Stupidity is not a gift of God. It's entirely man-made!"*

Jesus broke into laughter. "That's so true, isn't it?" he said, shaking his head at me and smiling. "But don't beat yourself up over it, O. It's in the past, and you can't change that. Get on with the present. Let the moment be your life. I told you; once you learn how to live in the present your life will never be the same."

"What's the trick to that? There has to be a way I can click into the moment. What's the trick, J?" I asked, not really believing this was possible.

"The trick is to realize that each moment of time is an entry point into eternity, and as you live for the moment you allow eternity to flood your consciousness and the moment ceases to be a moment and becomes eternal. Once you capture the gift of the Holy Now you will never again live your life in the past or the future; your mind will be anchored in the ever-present now of your life."

"I follow the logic, but I have problems executing it," I said, still incredulous.

"At first it's a question of mental effort. It has to be, because man is a thinking creature. Just think about what you are doing. Place all of your attention on what you are doing and do it with your whole being. Once you master the art of focusing all of your attention on the task at hand you will develop the skill of mindful presence. This will eventually become a habit and second nature to you. There is an apprenticeship to the spiritual skill of living in the moment, and like all skills it requires disciplined effort."

"Mindful presence?" I repeated. "I think I'll try that today."

"Why wait?" Jesus said. "Why don't you try it right now?"

"Now?"

"Yes. Just give in to the moment. Your heart is not into our talk this morning, so your eye is not single. Because your eye is not single, you are conflicted by the unresolved anger of your humiliating experience. This is the source of your agitation. Just abandon to the moment and let Soul speak."

"Yes; when Soul speaks my eye is single, isn't it?"

"Yes," Jesus confirmed.

"I never feel so whole and complete as when Soul is speaking. Are you saying that living in the moment is another way of letting Soul speak, as it were?"

"You do connect the dots quickly, don't you?" Jesus said.

"Perhaps. I'll try, then. But let me vent just a bit longer. It does my heart good to let out all of this angry energy. You're right, J. *'That which defileth a man proceedeth out of the mouth of man,'*" I said, quoting his words from the Gospels.

He laughed, and so did I. I continued. "I confess that I'm still feeling a little bored by all of this. I don't know how much more we can say to pry open the reader's mind."

"There's plenty more to say. You have to keep in mind that the reader comes from all walks of life. One reader's interests may connect him with one aspect of my teaching, and another reader's interests may connect him with another aspect—"

"But it's all the same bloody teaching!" I exclaimed in frustration.

"We know that," Jesus calmly replied; "but the reader does not know that. That is what we're trying to convey with our dialogue. We are trying to get the point across that the Way is the Way, and each one of my sayings opens the door to the Way."

"I know that. I'm just being stubborn. Perhaps this is why I've come to the conclusion that the world has to find its own way. I'd like to help, J; I really would. But in the end it's a personal journey. As Plotinus said, Soul's journey home to God is a flight of the alone to the Alone. In the final analysis Soul is a community of one. That's the sentiment that I tried to express at our worship service last Sunday."

"Can you share the experience?" Jesus asked.

"Sure; why not? A fellow High Initiate who strangely enough suffers from OCD was going on and on about how our spiritual community has become her family, and how she needs the love she gets from the community; but when Cathy and I joined the community down here we both needed this love badly because we had been traumatized by the publication of my books that so disturbed the people of my hometown we had to leave, and we also had the added trauma of relocating, building our new house, and starting my business over down here; so we could have used some of that love from our community that she was talking about, but it wasn't there. It was all talk, J. Cathy and I took a break from all our community functions to consolidate our energies and heal on our own. The worship service Sunday was our first in eight months. When this chela told me how much she needed the community, I said to her, 'Ultimately we're all a community of one.' I wanted her to know that I did not need the community like she did, but she was so caught up in her own neurosis that she missed my point entirely. I'm telling you this because I want you to appreciate that when I say the world can find its own way, my experience with life continues to affirm this. You can't count on the world to be there when you need it, J. All you can count on in the end is yourself. Do you see where I'm coming from?"

"Perfectly. So because you didn't get the support you needed from your spiritual community you stopped attending your spiritual functions?"

"No, it wasn't that at all really. That just brought the point home. Cathy and I needed to heal on our own. When we go to community functions now we don't go for the wrong reasons. Too many chelas use these functions for personal therapy. That's why they need the love they get from the community. Which is a good thing. But they too will learn one day that Soul is a community of one, and they will stop pretending and face the fact that Soul's journey home to God is a journey of the alone to the Alone. It's a tough truth to face, J; but we all have to face it one day."

"That sounds so cold, O," Jesus said, with a grimace. "Are you sure you want your reader to see this side of you?"

"I'm beyond caring what people think of me. This is what my experiences have led me to conclude, and until I experience life differently I'm not going to change the way I feel. I am a community of one, and that's the real bottom line of my life!"

"As I said, you have been bought with a price. Indeed, Soul is a community of one; and not until one comes to this realization will he be in complete agreement with the Alone. Now, have we licked our wounds enough to get on with our talk?"

"You stinker!" I burst out, taken aback by Christ's healing sarcasm.

Jesus laughed. "It's not like you didn't invite it. From the moment I arrived this morning you've done nothing but whine. Get over it and let's get on with my saying, shall we? The light of the body is the eye—"

"Let me!" I cut in, grabbing the reigns with both hands. "You're metaphor for the self is the eye. The eye sees the world. The eye sees out and lets the light into one's life. The eye is the self, but the self is not one but two. The self is made up of the higher self and the lower self. When the higher self looks out at the world, one's eye is single — meaning; one is one's true self, Soul. But when the lower self is looking at the world one's life is filled with the egoic consciousness of the unresolved lower self, which you call evil; so it

356

all comes down to a question of the consciousness of Holy Spirit, which you call the light of the body. If one is centered in his higher self his eye is single because he is his whole, true self; and being Soul he lets in the light of Holy Spirit into his life. But if one is centered in his lower self then his eye is not single, because the lower self is not in agreement with its higher self. Only when the lower self and the higher self are in agreement can one's eye be single. If one is centered in his lower self, the consciousness of his experiences will be evil, and by evil you simply mean the unresolved karmic energies of life; right?"

"In effect, yes," Jesus replied. "If a person does not align his priorities to coincide with his divine purpose, his eye will never be single. Only when the lower self is in agreement with the higher self can one's eye be single and his body full of the light of Holy Spirit; otherwise one will flood his consciousness with the impure energies of one's lower self, and these energies will have to be resolved in order for Soul to be whole."

"Let's make it absolutely clear then that what you refer to as evil is the impure, selfish energies of the lower self; right?"

"Absolutely," Jesus said, with the biggest smile. "There. Now we have plummeted the depths of the self and I can get on with my other duties."

"What other duties?" I asked.

"I have an appointment with the Lords of Karma."

"What is it this time, J?"

"Who knows? It's the same old story; Christians doing things in my name when I had absolutely nothing to do with their behavior. As you said, O; stupidity is not a gift of God."

I broke out. So did Jesus. Our laughter left me in such good spirits that I went to work with a song in my heart.

PART THREE

JESUS COMES CLEAN

61. *Sifting the Wisdom of God from the Wisdom of Man*

Once again, Jesus quoted himself. After I poured our tea, he said: *"The kingdom of God cometh not with observation. Neither shall they say, Lo here! or Lo there! for, behold the kingdom of God is within you."*

"I'm familiar, and I understand the implicit meaning; but can you tell me the chapter and verse. I'd like to read that in context," I said, and took a sip of tea.

"Luke. Chapter 17, verses 20 and 21," Jesus replied. "Yes, by all means look it up. I do set the stage here for what you have called the Big Gun of my sayings."

I read the entire chapter, and said, "It could not be any clearer here that you reveal the mystery of the two selves of man. Just after you blast the world with your Big Gun saying — *'Whosoever shall seek to save his life shall lose it; and whosoever shall lose his life shall preserve it'* — you said something I'd better quote to give the reader the contextual clarity of the two selves. In verses 34 to 36 you said: *'I tell you, in that night there shall be two men in one bed; the one shall be taken, and the other left. Two women shall be grinding together; the one shall be taken, the other left. Two men shall be in the field; the one shall be taken, and the other left.'"* I stopped and took a sip of tea, and so did Jesus, and as we drank our tea I reflected on the exact moment when my two selves became one self while I was standing in the doorway of my mother's kitchen as she was kneading bread dough on the kitchen table. "Do you like it?" I asked Jesus, referring to the tea.

"Yes," Jesus said. "What kind is it this morning?"

"Cranberry."

"Excellent. Now that you have the full context, what can you say about it?"

"The first thing we have to make absolutely clear is that by kingdom of God you do not mean a place, as such. You do not mean a celestial paradise; you mean the Holy Current of God that flows through life. This Holy Current is the creative life force, which is Holy Spirit. Holy Spirit is the Word of God; the Word of God is the Way; and the Way is what you call the kingdom of God. When you say that the kingdom of God is within you, you are simply pointing man to the Holy Current of God that flows through life. Good so far?"

"Perfectly," said Jesus.

"Alright. Having established that the kingdom of God within is the Holy Current of the creative life force, which is the Word of God, then it follows logically that the real mystery would be how to connect with this Holy Current. This you do with your Big Gun saying. In this saying you have the entire dynamic of the Way of Christ. In the effort to die to one's lower self one will automatically connect with the Holy Current of God. In other words, one inches his way into the kingdom of God within with each sacrifice that he makes of his lower self. This is what St. Paul called 'dying daily.' How am I doing so far?"

"Perfectly. Please, continue," Jesus said.

"So, the more one seeks to die daily to his lower self—"

"May I?" Jesus cut in.

"Yes."

"Perhaps we should explain what we mean by dying daily?"

"Let's give the *Reader's Digest* version for now," I said, with a smile. "We can go into more detail when we talk about St. Paul's perspective on your teaching, because he has a better conceptual understanding of the two selves of man than you give expression to in the four Gospels of Christ."

"By all means, let's hear the *Reader's Digest* version," Jesus said.

"Dying to one's lower self simply means shifting one's priorities in life from material interests to spiritual interests," I explained, feeling absolutely confident in the gnostic wisdom of my own experience with Christ's teaching. "It means to stop indulging the lower self. It means to not let the body appetites control one's life. It means becoming less selfish and more unselfish, because the less selfish one is the more one dies to one's lower self. The consciousness of the lower self is a consciousness of selfishness, and it forever seeks to satisfy its appetite for food, drink, sex, money, possessions, and especially personal attention; so, the more one sacrifices his egoic needs the more he dies to his lower self. This is what it means to die daily in St. Paul's famous dictum."

"Understood," said Jesus, with a grateful smile. "As one disciplines himself to die daily he begins to see the nature of the two selves more clearly. This is what I refer to as the two men in one bed, the two women grinding together, and the two men in the field. By this I mean that wherever man is, there shall be two selves in that man, and these two selves will be in constant conflict because the lower self does not want to die to its higher self; and the more the lower self resists being sacrificed, the greater the conflict will be—"

"Until one is bought with a price!" I exclaimed.

Jesus laughed. "Yes, there will be one final price to pay in the sacrifice of the lower self. That is inevitable."

"And like a thief in the night one will experience the birth of his spiritual self and know that he is immortal!" I erupted, as my own experience in my mother's kitchen possessed me, because from that moment on I knew that I was immortal.

"Precisely," said Jesus, with a big satisfied smile.

"My God," I said, bursting with emotion, *"it couldn't be any clearer what your teaching is about! Why in God's name has no one ever put it all together before? Why, J?"*

"It is a puzzle," Jesus calmly replied. "Many servants of the Way of Christ have pieced it no less brilliantly; but the Light of God shines in your understanding. Your explanation makes me feel ashamed for concealing the meaning so hermetically; but what choice did I have? The world was not evolved enough for the undiluted truth. Hearing, they heard not. But they understood on a Soul level. That was my purpose; to plant the seeds of God's kingdom in the soil of man's consciousness. Then one day they would take root and quicken Soul for God's harvest."

"One day?" I said, with a snicker. "How about ten, twenty, a hundred lifetimes? You did not only come to harvest Souls that were ready for the kingdom of God; you came to sow the seeds for generations to come!"

"Absolutely," said Jesus, with a big grin.

"But it backfired on you, J," I said, to his astonishment. "The seeds you sowed have sprouted a crop of such bizarre mutations that no one can tell the Word of God from the word of man. That's the tragedy of your teaching today. It's this strange crop of mutated wisdom that has choked the spiritual life out of the Christian Soul!"

"Mutated wisdom?" Jesus said, with a bemused smile. "But this is why we're having this dialogue, O; to sift the wisdom of God from the wisdom of man," he calmly said, and reached for his cup of tea.

"We are doing that. But I'm afraid it will take no less time to undo the damage done by the misunderstanding of your teaching than it will for the world to see the distinction between the wisdom of God and the wisdom of man. You did express this nicely when you said, 'what shall it profit a man if he gain the whole world but lose his own soul?' or something like that. I'll look it up later. It doesn't matter what generation we live in, the consciousness of the world grows so slowly that it will take generations for the wisdom of God to be sifted from the wisdom of man in the religion of Christianity!"

"Do you really think so?"

"Yes, I do."

"Why?"

"Christians have too much invested in their faith, that's why," I replied, with absolute conviction. "Like the agnostic Christian minister who outgrew his faith but rationalized it to hold onto the financial security that his faith provided, so do all Christians in one way or another compromise themselves for their faith. People go into denial the moment the ground of their being is threatened. Believe me, J; I experienced this with the publication of my novel memoirs. Not one person in St. Jude acknowledged the sifting that I had done in those two books. I sifted the wisdom of God from the wisdom of man with such narrative imperative that I shocked the psyche of my hometown, and those good Christians turned on Cathy and me like wild beasts defending their lair. I would never have believed Christians could behave with such blind fury to defend the ground of their being that my books threatened. I'm sorry to say this, J; but I don't think our dialogue will make much difference to the Christian psyche. It may make a difference to the tired Souls that are so fatigued from the burden of the Christian lie that they can stand the pressure no longer and walk away, but on the whole, no; Christianity will have to go the full course and die a slow death as Christians leave the fold one by one. Then one day it will dawn on Christianity that it is so out of step with the spiritual consciousness of life that it will be forced to change or die — as John Shelby Spong predicted with his book *Why Christianity Must Change or Die.*"

"I agree," replied Jesus, with surprising calm. "And with our dialogue we can help to bring this change about. Let's get back on topic, if you would."

"What's there more to say? We've explained the mystery of the lower and higher self of man. What's left to say?"

"The mystery lies in the resolution of the lower self," Jesus replied. "I wanted my sacrifice on the cross to impress upon the world the Big Gun of my sayings, as you call it. We have to make it clear that until Soul resolves the consciousness of its lower self it will never break the cycle of life and death. Like I said, **I did not die to life; I died to death.** That's the core of my message to the world. I don't think we have quite finished yet. We should reveal the secret meaning of my other sayings and parables to give the reader more reason to believe in the underlying mystery of the Way of Christ."

"But why?" I said, feeling justified in my defiance. "Why bother when the Way has been revealed in the new religion of the Light and Sound of God that addresses man's spiritual needs today? Your teaching was for another time and a much lower level of consciousness than exists in the world today. This is why people have problems with their Christian faith. It's not giving them the answers they need. But they can't leave their faith. They're afraid to let go of you, J. Fear keeps them trapped in their faith—"

"But that's the point, O," Jesus cut in. "We have to alleviate this fear with spiritual clarity. We have to sift the wisdom of God from the wisdom of man with our dialogue so the reader can step outside the box and embrace Soul's real purpose in life."

"I guess you're not going to let me off the hook, are you?"

"No," Jesus said, and smiled. "You made a commitment to help me set the record straight, and I'm holding you to it."

I laughed. "Okay. I promise, no more trying to wriggle out of it. Where do we go from here, then?"

"I like your suggestion. Go through the Gospels carefully and take all of my sayings that you feel will help us to sift the wisdom of God from the wisdom of man, and we will reveal the truth of my teaching one saying at a time. Fair enough?"

"Certainly. But you know that they will only be entry points. When the spirit of our dialogue takes over, we have no choice but to follow —*wherever it takes us!*"

Jesus laughed. "I know, O. That's what makes our talks so much fun. Until the next time then," he said, and again vanished into thin air.

62. *The Parable of Christ's Temptation*

When Jesus did not show up for a few days I got the feeling I knew why, so I began to single out all the sayings I felt most relevant to the core of his teaching. It took three days to go through the Gospels (and St. Paul's Epistles), and Jesus appeared in my bonus room the morning after I had completed my notes. I wasn't surprised to see him.

"Good," said Jesus, when I told him we could begin with his temptation by Satan. "That should set the stage very nicely to demarcate the two selves of man."

I had my Bible ready. "You said: ***'It is written, man shall not live by bread alone, but by every word that proceedeth out of the mouth of God.'***"

"Yes," Jesus sighed.

"Why the heavy sigh?" I asked.

"I'm not so sure I'm happy with this — what can I call it; a parable? Little did Mathew realize that this scene would be taken so literally. Right from the get-go the Gospels seduce the world with the narrative power of the Way of Christ."

I knew exactly what Jesus meant. "Let's call it the parable of Christ's temptation, then," I said, with an ironic chuckle. "I can see why you would sigh, J. This little scenario does make a compelling introduction to the narrative of your mission — *but it's nothing more than an imaginative piece of dialectical fiction!"*

"We better explain this before we disclose the meaning of my saying," Jesus said, not reacting to my emotional outburst.

I looked at Jesus; and with a mischievous smile, said: "Would you like to explain Mathew's little scene with you and Satan, or should I?"

"Let me," Jesus quickly responded. "After all, it's only fitting that I undo the damage done by this dramatic piece of creative writing."

"By all means," I said, delighted by his enthusiasm.

"Mathew's heart was in the right place," Jesus began, with a look on his face like the little boy who got caught with his hand in the cookie jar. "After all, at the heart of my teaching lies the truth of the two selves of man; so why not introduce the reader to the two most complete expressions of these two selves — the Christ figure and Satan? Mathew represented my higher self as the spiritually self-realized Christ, and my lower self in the image of Satan, the archetypal consciousness of the lower self of man. Satan's name is legion because he is the unresolved lower self of man, and with this scene Mathew sets the stage for the drama that is to unfold in my mission to save the world."

I smiled at Jesus' uncompromising candor. I did not expect him to be so revealing, and I did not want to say anything for fear of not hearing the whole story. I waited patiently for him to continue while he slowly and thoughtfully sipped his tea.

"You see, O," he continued, in his quiet voice of authority now; "what Mathew and the Gospel writers wanted to do with my life story was to personify in dramatic narrative form the secret teachings of the Way. The Gospel writers were initiates of the Way who drew primarily upon the ancient Gnostic wisdom of the Essenes, and they saw in me a golden opportunity to manifest in gospel form the whole drama of Soul's journey through life. They used my life to write large the little drama of every Soul's journey through the different stages of man's growth to spiritual self-realization consciousness. This is why the narrative of my life is so compelling. The truth is much simpler. This narrative magnifies my life and mission to such proportions that it dazzles the mind of man. Satan is the archetypal lower self of man, and Christ is the archetypal higher self of man; and the drama of my life is played out as I go about my mission to liberate Soul from the consciousness of its lower self. That's what the parable of Christ's temptation is all about. It sets the stage for the liberation of Soul from its lower self, culminating with my death upon the cross."

"Yes, I can see that. So the whole dialectic of the Gospels is a play of these two archetypal figures — Satan and Jesus Christ?"

"In effect, yes. The Gospel writers took liberties with my life to personify the Way of Life; and as my mission was to establish the kingdom of God on earth they had the perfect model in my life for their dialectical narrative."

"Let's explain what you mean by dialectical narrative," I said.

"They took the ball and ran with it," Jesus said, and laughed.

"So how much truth is there in the story of Jesus Christ's life and mission?"

"I did exist. I did study the Essene teachings. I did travel to foreign lands. I did become an initiate of various mystery schools in Egypt, Persia, and India. I did study the pure teachings of the Way in the Golden Wisdom Temple at the Katsupari Monastery in northern Tibet, and I was initiated into the Creative Life Stream. I did become so crazy with God that I was compelled by Holy Spirit to establish God's kingdom on earth. I was crucified. My appearance after my crucifixion was intended to confirm the central motif of my teaching, which is spiritual rebirth through the death of the lower self. My resurrection was both spiritual and literal. My uncle Joseph of Arimathea and my Essene brethren arranged for my escape from the cave. It was all pre-arranged. They had tunneled an escape route out of the back of the cave, which they had dug before my crucifixion; and after they took me to safety they filled in the tunnel so no one would be the wiser. The Gospel writers took creative liberties with my life and made me the Begotten Son of God who sacrificed his life on the cross to save the world; and the rest, as they say, is history."

I should have been surprised by this information, but I wasn't. It felt like I already knew the whole story. "I gather they took liberties with your healing powers as well?" I replied, not questioning Jesus on the most astonishing details of his life.

"Yes," he said. "I was a healer, and I did heal the sick according to the law of redemptive karma; but the Gospel writers dramatized my healings for narrative effect."

"May I ask why they took liberties with your life?"

"As I said, they meant well," Jesus replied, without a trace of judgment. "They saw in my life a window of opportunity to introduce the world to the Way, believing that the secret teaching would raise the consciousness of the world which was steeped deep in materialism and the suffocating letter of God's Law. As I said, they took the ball and ran with it."

I didn't know what to say. I was astonished by Christ's frankness. I took a drink of tea, set my cup down, and looked at Jesus.

"What?" he asked.

"I've said this already, but it's worth repeating," I heard myself saying. I felt strange as I spoke, as though I was more myself than I had been throughout our dialogue, and every word that I spoke came from a depth I had not experienced before. "For all the good that your life and teaching has done the world, I'm still in doubt whether the world would not have been better off without you," I said, and paused for thought. "I don't say this lightly, J. I have my reasons for believing this. Soul's struggle to realize its divine nature is the struggle to transform the consciousness of its lower self, and I believe that however noble the intentions of the Gospel writers were to introduce the world to the secret teachings of the Way through the narrative of your life and teachings, they created an illusion so alluring that it seduces Soul into believing it can short-circuit the natural process of spiritual self-realization consciousness. Soul cannot bypass this entire mesoteric stage of spiritual growth and go straight to the higher worlds of God. Soul can't go to heaven on a free pass from Jesus. That's just not in the cards. That's the illusion that the Gospel writers have created with their conspiracy, which was reinforced by St. Paul. The world has failed to see the metaphysics of spiritual growth that your whole teaching is about. This is why I feel the world might have been better off without this free pass to heaven."

"I agree," said Jesus, again to my astonishment. "But how do we break the spell of this illusion? Can we do it by revealing the truth of the secret teaching?"

I snickered. "It's not like the secret teaching is hidden in some inaccessible region of the world like the Katsupari Monastery in northern Tibet. After all, you yourself tell us that the Way, which you call the kingdom of heaven, is not a secret at all. It's out in the open for all those that have eyes to see. We don't have to make any special effort, do we? It's all a question of Soul's maturity. As each Soul evolves through life it gravitates more and more to the mesoteric consciousness of life where it can see the secret teaching much more clearly. Personally I think the Gospel writers tried to force-feed Soul with the Way of Christ, and the world has been suffering spiritual indigestion ever since!"

Jesus laughed. "I'm glad you can see the humor, O. For myself, I feel an obligation to set the record straight. Should we get to my saying, then?"

"If you like," I said, smiling at Christ's equanimity.

"Would you like to reveal the truth of the Way in this saying, or would you prefer that I do so?" Jesus asked.

"You're all business again. Alright, let me. I want to do a HU first because I need all the help I can get. I want the best possible explanation for this saying, because this is how St. Mathew begins the incredible narrative of your mission."

I closed my eyes and chanted the Love Song to God. I expected Jesus to join me, but he didn't. After a few minutes of feeling the sweet bliss of God flowing into every pour of my being, I said to the Inner Master: *"I really would appreciate a free flow of Spirit for this discourse on Christ' saying. I believe this saying is pivotal to his whole teaching."*

To my surprise, the Inner Master replied, via the inner channel. *"Don't forget the God-eaters,"* he said, and I could feel him smiling at me.

I opened my eyes. "What on earth did he mean by that?"

"What?" Jesus asked, staring at me.

"The Inner Master just told me not to forget the God-eaters."

"Oh, the Eshwar-Khanewale," Jesus said, with a big smile on his face. "These are the spiritual adepts who live in the spiritual city of Agem Des. They are God-eaters who take in the cosmic energy instead of material food. They live to great ages, far beyond the life span of man. Yes, I can see his reason for reminding you of the God-eaters. But I'll let you connect the dots. Please, let's hear your explanation for my saying that man shall not live by bread alone but by every word that proceedeth out of the mouth of God."

I was taken aback by the Inner Master's comment, and Jesus' explanation didn't enlighten me. I had read about the God-eaters, but I was challenged to connect the dots of Christ's saying and the cosmic energy of life. But no sooner did I think about how to go about it and a line was drawn so quickly between the two dots that a sonic boom of spiritual consciousness exploded in my mind, and I knew exactly what to say!

Bursting with excitement, I exclaimed, *"Your saying is all about the food that the two selves of man need to survive!* The body houses the two selves of man," I explained, the words pouring out of my mouth as from a fountain of spiritual wisdom. "The lower self is nourished with the food that the body needs to grow — what you refer to in your saying as bread — and the higher self needs the food that comes from the Word of God. Satan tempts you further, trying to seduce you with all the things of this world that would feed the selfish consciousness of your ego self, but you have already made your decision to live by the Word of God. If I may, you said, *'Get thee hence, Satan; for it is written. Thou shalt worship the lord thy God, and him only shalt thou serve.'* You tell Satan that even he is in the service of the Divine Plan of God, and Satan is forced to leave because he could not seduce you with the tempting pleasures of life. You made your choice to shift your priorities from your lower to higher self, and thus the whole drama of the conflict between the two selves of man is revealed in this parable of your temptation! How am I doing so far?"

"Excellent," Jesus replied, with a Cheshire grin on his face.

"Now it gets tricky," I said, and reached for my tea. I took a sip, then another. "It's all a question of food," I began, as I placed my cup down. "Food for the lower self and food for the higher self. The lower self feeds on the energies of selfish indulgence, and the higher self feeds on the energies of unselfish living. The more selfish the lower self is, the more it grows in ego consciousness; and the less selfish the lower self is, the more it grows in spiritual consciousness. By 'bread alone' you meant the energies of life, all the food that the lower self needs to grow in ego consciousness. This can be expanded to include food for all the appetites of man. Food for the pleasure of eating, drinking, sex, money, and all those other pleasures that the ego loves to indulge in. These are what you called bread of life for the lower self. And the Word of God is food for the higher self. As one lives by the Word of God he fulfills his destiny in life, which is spiritual self-realization consciousness. The Word of God is not food *per se.* It is the experience of living by the Word of God, which catches the cosmic energies that nourish the spiritual self. Now I see what the Inner Master wanted me to see; but I have to explain this for the reader's sake. Do you mind, J?"

"By all means, please do," Jesus said, still grinning.

"This involves the metaphysics of spiritual growth," I began, as the thoughts rushed into my mind. "Experience is what Soul uses to catch the life force, or the cosmic energies of life. With every

369

experience we have we take in this life force. This is how the atom of God grows. The atom of God experiences life, and as it experiences life it takes in the creative life force, which is the consciousness of God—"

"Please explain that," Jesus cut in.

"The creative life force is the consciousness of God; but this consciousness of God is not God-conscious, if one can imagine such a paradox. It only becomes conscious of its divine nature as it is individuated through life experience. The first dawning that the atom of God has individuated the consciousness of God occurs in the primordial life of man, when it has individuated enough life force to reach critical mass and the consciousness of God becomes aware of itself for the very first time as a new 'I' of God. This is the birth of self-consciousness, which I experienced during my fourth past-life regression. If I may, let me take a moment here."

"By all means," said Jesus.

After a moment's pause, I said, "To be honest with you, I had no idea just how miraculous this experience was. The wonder of realizing that I was an individual 'I' cannot be expressed. I'm sure I spent the rest of that life in a state of confusion. It wasn't until I had worked out the DPG in my current life that it occurred to me what I had actually experienced with the dawning of my own reflective self-consciousness. I had no idea just how momentous that experience was until I connected all the dots!"

Jesus laughed. "Yes," he said, with a smile that glowed like the sun, "you experienced the wonder and mystery of God's birth. Few Souls have been granted such a privilege. Many people have been regressed to their physical birth in life, but few have experienced their own birth as Soul. This is what you experienced, O; the birth of a new 'I' of God. This is why you were in a state of wondrous confusion."

I looked at Jesus, and said, "Do you have any idea what this information will do to the religions of the world, not to mention the scientific community?"

"Yes," Jesus said, and laughed. "It will give them food for thought, if I may be allowed to pun here—"

I burst into laughter. "It certainly will give them food for thought! My God, we've brought religion and science to the starting point of life! It's here that science meets religion and religion meets science — in the dawning of man's reflective self-consciousness! God, the ground of all being, becoming aware of itself in man! Am I right?"

"Perfectly. As you have written, the self is the greatest mystery of life; and you reveal this mystery in the DPG with the birth of a new 'I' of God. This is why man is said to be made in the image of God. If man only knew how much truth there is to this he wouldn't be so confused about who he is. Yes, science and religion come together here. This is the starting point of man's life on earth as a self-conscious 'I' of God, and the evolution of the 'I' of God to spiritual self-realization and God-consciousness is what the DPG is all about!"

"And the metaphysics of spiritual growth is all about taking in the creative life force to individuate the 'I' of God," I emphasized.

"Exactly. So if you would, continue with my saying."

"There's nothing more to say? You tell man to live by the Word of God, because this is how Soul catches the life force. That's the sum of and substance of your saying!"

"Let's make it absolutely clear then that in the context of my gospel the Word of God is not in itself the food of God until one *lives* by the Word of God and catches the energy of Holy Spirit. This is why I stress in my teaching that it is in the *doing* of my sayings that one will profit by them. Do I make myself clear on this point?"

"That's clear enough for me," I said, suddenly feeling a wave of exhaustion possess me, as it often does when the Holy Current flows through with such intensity. "This took a lot out of me, J. We should call it a day. I still have to go to work yet. I have to take a power nap to regenerate myself. Would you mind if we end our talk now?"

"Not at all," Jesus said. "Go ahead. Rest before you go to work. We did well today, O. We did well indeed!"

63. *The House that Jesus Built*

"You know, Cathy," I said to her a couple of days after my last discourse with Jesus (we were out on a leisurely drive to the Muskokas to catch the last of the autumn colors), "the more Jesus and I talk, the more convinced I am that the Gospels are a blend of fact and fiction. I can't prove it, but I'm more convinced now than I ever was."

"What do you mean?" she asked.

"The other day Jesus and I talked about his temptation by Satan. Stop and think for a moment. Try to imagine a person walking up to you and offering you your most secret pleasures in exchange for your Soul. Can you imagine such a scenario?"

Cathy thought for a moment, and then said, "How can this person give me my most secret pleasures in exchange for my Soul?"

"He has the power to do so. Or does he? Can you imagine a person having the power to buy your Soul with your most secret pleasures?"

Again, Cathy thought. "No, I can't. Soul can't be bought. We are Soul, and Soul just *is*. That means no one can buy Soul. If Soul chooses to experience its most secret pleasures, that's the experience Soul chooses to have; and whatever karma it has for experiencing these pleasures, that's the price it has to pay. I don't believe any person can buy another person's Soul. I suppose a person can sell out their principles. I know people who have sold out, but that's only temporary. They'll pay for it down the road because that's how karma works. Maybe they'll have to pay in a future life, but they will pay for selling out."

"By selling out you mean forfeiting their spiritual freedom? But let's just call it their integrity for simplicity's sake. They compromise their integrity for the pleasures of life, the security of their career, the glamour of fame, or the glory of success — whatever; what you mean by selling out is the exchange of one's integrity for personal gain, right?"

"Yes," Cathy said.

"But that's not forever. No one can sell his Soul to the Devil forever, because it's not in the Divine Plan of God. Soul must return to life to work out its karma and continue its journey back to the Higher Worlds of God."

"So what's your point?" Cathy asked.

"In St. Mathew's Gospel Satan tempts Jesus, and the world has bought into this temptation as though it actually happened. Jesus tells Satan to get lost because he's not interested in compromising his integrity. I think this whole scenario is a parable for the temptations of life. Let's say you work for the government, which you did. You know how easy it is be seduced by the security of a government position. You experienced the abuse of employees that took advantage of the system. They compromised their integrity for the material benefits they got from the system, as civil servants often do. Let's say that the system is a metaphor for Satan, the archetypal manifestation of all the selfish consciousness of life. So, did you see any person come up to one of the employees in the office and make them an offer they couldn't refuse?"

"Yes," Cathy said, and laughed. "You wouldn't believe how quickly the girls in the office jumped at a free lunch from our boss. *A free lunch!* It was a joke. He worked us like slaves and expected a free lunch once or twice a year to make up for it! I refused to be bought with a free lunch. I don't know how people can live with themselves."

"But they do, sweetheart. They repress their guilt and in the process feed their shadow personality; but I don't want to go back there now. Let's go back to the employer who buys his employee's loyalty with a free lunch. Would you call him Satan?"

"Yes," Cathy said, and laughed again.

"You're right. He is Satan. But not Satan *per se*. He speaks for Satan insomuch that he has compromised his integrity to the system and now speaks for the system."

"He is the system!" Cathy exclaimed.

I laughed at Cathy's acuity. "Yes, he would be the system; as would all 'we' people. A 'we' person is someone who doesn't take responsibility for his decisions. 'We' decided this, and 'we' decided that says the 'we' person. This amorphous non-existent 'we' is responsible for individual decisions. A 'we' person has compromised himself to the system and ceases to be an individual. He's become a civil servant!"

I broke into laughter. I couldn't help myself. "That's why they're all the same!" Cathy said, excited by my insight.

"Your powers of intuition have been magnificently amplified," I said, and laughed some more. I couldn't repress the irony of exposing the Archetypal Shadow.

"But it's true," Cathy said, reassuring herself. "I saw it dozens of times. These people all speak the same language. It's like they have a secret code or something."

She made me laugh. "Like gays who can tell other gays. They pick up on the gay vibe, as it were. You're absolutely right, sweetheart; a compromised Soul can tell another compromised Soul. They all have the same vibe."

"I wonder what kind of vibe that would be?" she asked, genuinely curious.

"Whatever it is, it's hollow at the core," I said, with an ironic chuckle.

Cathy didn't laugh, but she knew what I meant. "I would call it a selfish vibe," she said. "These people take care of themselves first and then they worry about others."

"There's more to this selfish vibe than meets the eye. They take care of themselves at the expense of others. There's a primal quality to this vibe that makes these people predatory and totally untrustworthy."

"*Exactly!*" Cathy exclaimed. "I couldn't believe how the office staff turned on me after your books were published! Karen even spit in my face in the copy room! I would never have believed people could be so cruel, but I experienced it—"

I felt the hurt in Cathy's voice. I waited before replying. "When push comes to shove people show their true colors. Believe me; a compromised Soul can be dangerous when it's been exposed to the light of day."

"I'm still not over the way they treated me for the books you wrote. Don't get me wrong, O; I love your books, and I'm proud that you wrote them, but to treat me the way they did for something I didn't do—"

Cathy stopped in mid sentence. She took a breath, and said, "I don't want to talk about it anymore. It's spoiling our drive, and I won't let them do that to me. It's their life and their karma, so may the blessings be," she added, and dropped the subject.

We continued our drive to Huntsville, doing a long HU to clear the air of all the bad feelings we had released recalling the difficult times we had with the people of St. Jude when my books were published, and before long we were enjoying the late fall splendor of the Muskoka colors; but in the back of my mind I couldn't help but smile at my own experience with the capricious God of these lower worlds.

I hadn't told Cathy that he had appeared to me as the Archetypal Shadow Christ, because that would have cast the wrong light on my dialogue with Jesus; so I knew that St. Mathew's temptation of Jesus might have been possible. But the writer in me told me that he had created the scene out of whole cloth for dramatic effect, and if Divine Spirit wanted that information out we would be given the opportunity to reveal it.

The next morning Jesus was in my bonus room waiting for me. I was downstairs seeing Cathy off to work. Smiling, he said, "I feel it's going to be a good talk today."

"Why do you say that?" I asked.

"I just do. After all, I am Jesus Christ," he said, with that playful twinkle.

"Yes, you are Jesus Christ; but just what does that mean; that you can see into the future?" I asked, happy to explore the subject.

"We don't operate like that, O. We try to stay in tune with the present and let tomorrow take care of itself," he replied, again with that playful twinkle.

"If we live in the moment we don't have to worry about future?" I said.

"Precisely!" Jesus exclaimed.

I smiled at his emotion. "You're in good spirits this morning. How come?"

"I'm overjoyed with our last talk. We broke some pretty tough ground by decoding the parable of my temptation. Mathew introduces me to the world with my temptation, and one would think the astute reader would have picked up on his stratagem; but very few people have. The world has taken my temptation to be an actual encounter with the Devil; but Satan is not as obvious as Mathew makes him out to be. As you know, O; Satan is real, but not in the way the Gospel writers have portrayed him. Satan is the archetypal collective consciousness of the unresolved lower self of man, and the more compromised the lower self of man is the more evil a person will be; and the more evil one is, the more he speaks for the archetypal negative forces of life — hence, Satan. Is that clear enough?"

I burst into laughter. "Loud and clear," I said, marveling at how the omniscient guiding force of life guided our dialogue. "This speaks to the dark side of the personality. Are you up to talking about the dark side of the personality this morning?"

"No. Not yet. Let's just talk about the right kind of personality that Soul needs to complete its journey through life," Jesus said, playing it safe for the time being.

"Fair enough. We'll talk about the personality first, and then we can reveal the deeper secrets of the human personality — that cesspool of unresolved consciousness that you called unclean spirits?" I said, with a deliberate smile.

"Let's not open that door yet, O. We have a long way to go before we reveal the truth about personal demons," Jesus said, with what sounded like self-recrimination.

I had to laugh. I wanted to open that door, but I knew we had to talk about the human personality to set the stage first. I said to Jesus, "I know the perfect saying to pry open the mystery of the right kind of personality that your whole teaching strives to create."

"What saying would that be?" Jesus eagerly asked.

"'*Be ye therefore perfect even as your Father which is in heaven is perfect,*'" I replied, and then I turned to my Bible and found chapter and verse. "I'm going to read what you said first that led to this saying. We have to see it in context. This is from Mathew's Gospel, Chapter 5, verses 41 to 48: '*And whosoever shall compel thee to go a mile, go with him twain. Give to him that asketh thee, and from him that would borrow of thee turn not thou away. Ye have heard that it hath been said, Thou shalt love thy neighbor, and hate thine enemy. But I say unto you, Love your enemies, bless them that curse you, do good to them that hate you, and pray for them which despitefully use you and persecute you. That ye may be the*

children of your Father which is in heaven, for he maketh his sun
rise on the evil and on the good, and sendeth rain on the just and
the unjust. For if ye love them which love you, what reward have
ye? Do not even the publicans the same? And if ye salute your
brethren only, what do yet more than others? Do not even the
publicans do so? Be ye therefore perfect even as your Father which
is in heaven is perfect.'"

"That's an excellent point of entry into the mystery of the spiritual personality," Jesus said, with glee in his voice. "Would you like to reveal the consciousness of the Way in these verses, or would you like me to?"

"No," I sighed. "I'd like to reveal the mystery. It's still fresh in my mind. I've still got scars from Old Whore Life that aren't quite healed yet. It's been one tough battle, J. Few Souls pass through this straight gate of yours, but I did; and I don't regret for one moment the price that I had to pay to tell Satan to stick it where the sun don't shine!"

Jesus laughed. "Good for you, O!"

"Before we begin, let me say something first about what I got from your teaching," I said, and took a deep breath to embolden myself.

"Good. The reader can absorb the truth of my teaching through your experiences. Please, let's hear what you have to say," Jesus said, with eager anticipation.

"With all due respect to your teaching, J; it was Gurdjieff's system that opened up the door to the mystery of the spiritual personality that your teaching strives to create. Had I not lived G's teaching of 'work on oneself' I would not have resolved the paradoxes of your impenetrable teaching, especially your Big Gun saying."

"Why is that?" Jesus asked.

"Because the more I 'worked' on myself the more I was able to discern my lower self from my higher self. In fact I became acutely conscious of my lower self. That's how I finally managed to penetrate the mystery of your paradoxical sayings."

"I can see that. Life is the training ground for Soul. My disciples were all made ready by their own life experience, and they heard the Word of God in my teaching. It appears that all you did was speed up your spiritual growth with Gurdjieff's teaching."

"I certainly did," I said, smiling at Christ's understanding of my life. "A person has to sense his own lower self to be attracted to your teaching."

"That's not necessarily true, O," Jesus replied, surprising me. "More often than not people are so trapped by their lower self that they turn to me out of sheer desperation. Take the alcoholic who praises me to high heaven for saving him. He was trapped by his lower self and his faith in me saved him from his alcoholic demons—"

"Yes," I said, cutting Jesus off, "and what does he do? *He rushes out to save the whole bloody world!* He's the worst kind of Christian! He's replaced his addiction to alcohol with an addiction to you! I've known alcoholics who found Jesus Christ and you can have every last one of them! All they do is perpetuate the myth that you're the savior of the whole goddamn world, and you're no more savior than that chipmunk that's making all that racket outside my window!"

I didn't expect to be so emotional, but Jesus struck another raw nerve. "Of course, you're right," he said, with an understanding smile. "All I'm saying is that Soul cries out for freedom when it is so trapped by its lower self that it can't live with itself. After all, isn't this why you fled to France to look for the Way?"

I burst into laughter. *"There's just no getting around it, is there?"*

"What?" Jesus asked, pretending ignorance.

"You pull out all stops to make your point, don't you?" I said, now wise to his tactic.

"Of course I do. I want to set the record straight. Why pussyfoot around the bush, as you would say?" Jesus replied, his eyes smiling at me.

"Good," I said, re-establishing my balance. "I prefer the no-nonsense approach too. You're right. I did begin my quest because I could no longer suffer myself for what I did that godforsaken night. I was trapped by my own shadow personality, and I had to find a way out. I fled to France to look for my true self. I've written about this already, so I won't go there now. Suffice to say that unless one creates the right kind of personality he will never experience spiritual freedom, despite what new-born Christians believe!"

"You've really got it in for newborn Christians, don't you?" Jesus said.

"Yes, I do," I replied.

"May I ask why?"

"They're dangerous fools, that's why! Newborn Christians want to convert the whole bloody world! They go to all manner of extremes to convince the world that you're the savior of the world. Well here you are Jesus. Tell me, what powers of salvation do you really have? What can you tell me about salvation that will convince me to give up my path of the Light and Sound of God and become a newborn Christian?"

"So it's come to this, has it? I thought we had a beautiful friendship, O," Jesus replied in a different voice and that playful twinkle in his love-filled eyes.

Jesus took me by surprise again, and I bent over with laugher at his Humphrey Bogart impersonation. "Sorry, J," I said. "I didn't mean to put you on the spot."

"I accept your apology," he said, with the biggest grin. "I also accept your challenge," he quickly added. "The reader should know where we stand. To answer your question about my powers of salvation, the answer is much more obvious than you would expect. As you have said repeatedly, there are many entry points into the kingdom of heaven, and faith is one of the best. Faith will open any door in life if it is strong enough. The alcoholic's faith in me opens the door for the healing power of Holy Spirit to come into his life and cure him of his addiction. Unfortunately, there are side effects to this miraculous cure. The cured alcoholic's personality is now awash with the reconciling power of Holy Spirit, which he attributes to me, and he wants to tell the world about my powers of salvation; but I had nothing to do with it. It was Holy Spirit. I was merely the focal point of this man's faith which opened the door to the healing powers of Holy Spirit. *Capisce?"*

"Fair enough," I said, smiling at his use of the American slang *capisce*. There was something final and absolute about it, and I smiled because that's how I often ended a point I no longer had the patience to discuss; and I knew that Jesus knew that, which is why he used the word. "It's the side-effects of this cure that turns the newborn

Christian into a fool; that's all I'm saying, J," I said, feeling like I had to justify myself to him.

"I don't disagree with you; but lay off the newborn Christian, will you please? As you say, let him find his own way," Jesus said, in the same *capisce* tone of voice.

"But what about the damage they leave in their wake?" I responded, desperately holding onto my stubborn conviction "What about shooting doctors who perform abortions or bombing clinics because they believe they're soldiers in the army of Christ? Aren't these people dangerous fools?"

"Of course they are," Jesus agreed. "That's what I had to account for in my last appearance before the Lords of Karma. And before you ask, I do not have an army of soldiers. These people are deluded. That's what happens when people refuse to see the play of karma in life and why I have to set the record straight. You're right, O; the world has come to believe that I am a free pass to the kingdom of heaven, but the Spiritual Law of Karma dictates otherwise. Soul must earn its own way into heaven. I simply gave man the tools that he needs to catch a ride to heaven; that's all I did."

"Tools to create a spiritual personality, you mean?" I said, for clarity.

"Yes. I gave the world a teaching to help man create the right kind of personality to free his Soul from the cycle of karma and reincarnation. But this spiritual personality comes with a price tag. That's what makes my teaching so hard to live by. For the life of me, I cannot fathom why the world refuses to see the simple clarity of my teaching."

"Simple clarity? Your teaching is so abstruse it has spawned a global industry! More books have been written about your life than any other person in history, and one more is about to be added to the list! Don't tell me that your teaching is simple, J. It's only simple to those on the inside, not to those who cannot penetrate the mystery of your sayings — *which is the vast majority of the Christian world!"*

Jesus was forced to laugh. "You're right, of course. It's so obvious from the inside that I forget myself sometimes. I'm sorry, O. I guess the moral here is not to take oneself too much for granted."

"Tell me about it!" I exclaimed. That's how my self-confidence got shattered with that paint job from hell last month! But

I don't want to talk about that. I've finally come to terms with my humiliation and I don't want to revisit those emotions. Can we get on with the secret of creating one's spiritual personality?"

"By all means," Jesus said, with a sweet smile. "Let me kick-start your explanation with this saying: *Whosoever heareth these sayings of mine, and doeth them, I will liken him unto a wise man which built his house upon a rock. And the rain descended, and the floods came, and the winds blew, and beat upon that house; and it fell not: for it was founded upon a rock. And every one that heareth these sayings of mine and doeth them not, shall be likened unto a foolish man, which built his house upon sand: And the rain descended, and the floods came, and the winds blew, and beat upon that house; and it fell: and great was the fall of it."* That's taken from Mathew 7, verses 24 to 27."

"Thank you," I said, smiling to myself. As you were speaking I was reminded of a poem by Shelly. I'll quote it just to make your point about building one's house on sand. By house on sand, you mean the wrong type of personality; and by wrong type of personality, you mean a personality that will not let Soul become aware of its divine nature. Give me a moment, please..." Jesus waited patiently. I found my book *Immortal Poems of the English Language,* which was earmarked to Shelly's *Ozymandias,* and I read the poem:

> I met a traveler from an antique land
> Who said: Two vast and trunkless legs of stone
> Stand in the desert...Near them, on the sand,
> Half sunk, a shattered visage lies, whose frown,
> And wrinkled lip, and sneer of cold command,
> Tell that its sculptor well those passions read
> Which yet survive, stamped on these lifeless things,
> The hand that mocked them, and the heart that fed:
> And on the pedestal these words appear:
> "My name is Ozymandias, king of kings:
> Look on my works, ye Mighty, and despair!"
> Nothing beside remains. Round the decay
> Of the colossal wreck, boundless and bare
> The lone and level sands stretch far away.

"A perfect example for the house built upon sand," Jesus said, with an ironic twinkle in his eyes. "Thank you, O. It's a wonderful symbol for the wrong kind of personality. The mighty Ozymandias built his house upon sand, and all that remains are the broken pieces of an inflated ego in the deserted sands of life. Yes; that's a perfect illustration of what I meant by my saying. Do you have an example in poetry for the right type of personality?"

"Of course I do," I said, with a proud smile.

"Would you share it?" Jesus asked.

"I already have. It's Wordsworth's *Character of the Happy Warrior.*"

"Of course," Jesus said, with that playful smile that let me know he was asking on behalf of the reader. "You can go on with your explanation. Your reader now has literary reference points whenever he needs to remind himself of my saying."

"Okay," I said, laughing to myself at how Jesus directed the flow of our dialogue without interfering with my free will. It was magical. I thought for a moment, and when I had my thoughts in order said: "Just to make it easier for the reader to get a fix on your metaphor for creating the right kind of personality to free Soul from the confines it its lower self, let's just call a house built on stone the Happy Warrior personality, and the house built on sand the Ozymandian personality. Is that okay with you, J?"

"That's excellent. This will take the metaphor out of my saying and make explicit the hidden truth of the Way of Christ. By all means, let's do that."

I broke into a gentle laugh.

"Did I say something funny?"

"I was just thinking of Doctor Jung's words to describe personality types; you know, *introvert, extrovert.* We've just augmented his typology with a spiritual perspective. Now we have the Happy Warrior personality, which represents the right kind of personality that Soul needs to liberate itself from the cycle of karma and reincarnation; and the Ozymandian personality, which fetters Soul to the cycle of karma and reincarnation. I was laughing because I caught a glimpse of these words down the road in the language of everyday life. Do you think this perspective will ever find its way into the vernacular?"

"Why not?" Jesus said, as if it was a foregone conclusion. "If the logic of our discourse is convincing enough, there's no reason why these personality types cannot work their way into life like the Jekyll and Hyde personality. And when they do we will know that the spiritual consciousness of society will have been raised considerably."

I laughed as my Essene lifetime rushed into my mind. Jesus stared at me, waiting for an explanation. "That's what we did at Qumran," I explained. "We gauged the spiritual consciousness of life by recording the sayings of life in the Great Book when our brethren brought them back from the outside world. But you know that, don't you?"

"Yes," Jesus said. "I pondered the sayings of the Great Book every day during my silent years. Of course I could not carry the Great Book with me. As you know, there were scrolls and scrolls of wisdom sayings, all categorized for different levels of life. Master Zadok had an Elder scribe the sayings most suited for my mission—"

"Pardon me? This is new information. Are you telling me that Master Zadok knew what your spiritual mission was and helped you to prepare for it?"

"This will come as a revelation to your reader, but the Living Soul Master of the times helped to prepare me for my spiritual destiny."

"This I have to hear! What exactly was your spiritual destiny?"

"To die for the sins of the world." Jesus said, with a sly chuckle.

"That's nonsense!" I burst out. "What's the real reason for your crucifixion?"

Again, Jesus smiled at me. "To wake the world up by whatever means I could devise," he explained, in his serious voice. "I was charged with the mission to spread the Word of God. I returned to my Nazarene lifetime from the future to change the outcome of my life and reveal the Way to the World. I was not crucified the first time I lived my life, but I chose to be crucified the second time because Soul cannot complete its destiny without helping to raise the spiritual consciousness of the world. If you look at history you will see that all the people that have made a lasting contribution to life were great Souls. Socrates, Buddha, Gandhi, Mozart, Einstein, Michelangelo,

Shakespeare, Lincoln; it doesn't matter what field you look into — science, religion, politics, the arts, whatever — great Souls will often return to help lift up the consciousness of the world. My destiny was to become a savior of the world. Savior of the world is a metaphor for an enlightened Soul whose destiny is to introduce the Way to the world. The Way saves the world, not the messengers of the Way; and I had to devise the most effective way to introduce the Way to the world. Master Zadok knew that it was my mission to introduce the Way to the world, and when it was time to leave the community he selected some of the most powerful reconciliation sayings from the Great Book of Life to quicken my spiritual growth; but it was my duty to work out my own destiny, and I conjured up the idea of my own crucifixion so I could reveal the central metaphor of my *individuation process,* if I may borrow a phrase from Dr. Jung."

"You mean the metaphor of self-sacrifice?" I asked.

"Precisely," said Jesus.

"So most of your sayings in the Gospels come from the Great Book of Life, then?" I asked, still pinging from the shocking new information on his life.

"Yes. I picked up many wisdom sayings along the way, of course; but I came up with many of my own sayings also as I caught the spirit of the Way, just as you have; but on the whole I quoted from the Great Book of Life."

"And here I thought you had this genius for metaphor!" I exclaimed, and laughed.

Jesus laughed with me. "To be an original thinker one has to tap into the Creative Life Stream. Most people tap into the consciousness of the Mental Plane, and all they do is rehash the same old thoughts. A true original thinker has to step outside the box of the Mental Plane of Consciousness and tap into the Soul Plane—"

"Sat Purusha!" I interjected, again astounded by Christ's revelation.

"Pardon me?" Jesus said, playing dumb.

"I don't know why I said that. It just came out. I'm not even sure what it means. Let me get my spiritual dictionary..." I looked up the phrase *Sat Purusha,* read the definition, and broke into a gentle laugh.

"What?" Jesus asked.

"Here's what *Sat Purusha* means — as if you didn't know. 'True being; true CREATIVE ENERGY; the predominating and presiding Lord; the source of creative energy; SAT NAM.'"

"And for the reader's benefit, please explain SAT NAM," Jesus said.

I looked it up on the same page and read the definition for SAT NAM: "True name; the ruler of the ATMA LOK, the fifth plane (Soul Plane), and the first manifestation of God; the lord of all above and below; the power, the light, flowing down and out into all CREATION, to create, govern, and sustain all regions, like a gigantic stream of water."

"As I was saying, then," Jesus said, in his serious voice, "the true creative thinker draws his inspiration from the Soul Plane of Consciousness. He has tapped into what you have just described as *Sat Purusha,* the pure creative energy. This is why the intellectual never really has anything new to offer the world. All the intellectual has to offer is a rehash of the same old same old, but dressed up in his own words of course."

"That's the feeling I got when I was studying philosophy at university," I said, all excited by where our talk had taken us. "As much as I learned from the philosophers, I never really learned anything new. It was only those few philosophers like Socrates who had tapped into the Soul Plane that had something new to say!"

"Exactly," said Jesus. "And at the risk of giving you a big head, this is what you have been blessed with. You have the gift of *Sat Purusha,* O."

"Gift?" I said, and snickered. *"Not on your life!* There are no free gifts, J. We earn the privilege and then the gift comes. 'We poets in our youth begin in gladness, /But thereof come in the end despondency and madness,' said Wordsworth in his poem *Resolution and Independence.* A writer has to write through all the nonsense before he gets to the good stuff, and I spent years writing through the nonsense of my mind before I got to the good stuff; so don't tell me it's a gift. *We earn God's favor!"*

Jesus did not respond. I did not know how to read his silence. A minute or so later, he said, "Let's get back to the personality. What do you have to say about creating the right kind of personality for Soul to liberate itself from the Mental Plane?"

"You're not going to tell me, are you?"

"What?" Jesus said, with a straight face.

"Don't play dumb. You know what I'm referring to."

"Yes, I do. And no, I'm not going to tell you. You have your take on it and I have mine, and I think we should leave it at that."

"I'm only taking the logic of your path to its conclusion. That's why I feel as I do about earning God's favor."

"Good. If you're comfortable with the spiritual logic of my path, then so be it. It's true for you as long as your logic lets you into the Heart of God. That's the most that I can say on the subject."

"That's enough. I'm not uncomfortable with my relationship with God, so I'll stick with what I said. Now we can get back to the house that Jesus built."

"The house that Jesus built? What do you mean by that?"

"The personality that you created for yourself was the house that you built upon the solid rock of the Way, which you drew extensively from the Great Book of Life. All I meant by the house that you built is that it's an extreme Happy Warrior personality."

"Extreme?" Jesus said, pretending to be surprised.

"Of course. You took this personality all the way to the cross. You died to your human self to give birth to your spiritual self, and if that's not extreme—"

"Okay," Jesus said, raising his hands in mock surrender. "Please, continue."

"This extreme Happy Warrior personality has been bought with a great price. It is a personality that has died to its lower self completely. This Soul now has free access to the resolved consciousness of its human self but is not bound by it. In other words, the human self is now in total agreement with its spiritual self. Or, to put it differently; the spiritual self and the human self are now effectively one individuated self. This is what you tried to tell the world with your crucifixion. You wanted the world to see your whole teaching in the symbol of your self-sacrifice. By sacrificing your life on the cross you told the world in symbolic imagery that self-sacrifice for the Way is one's admission into the kingdom of God. Since we know that the kingdom of God is the Way, then self-sacrifice is the price that one must pay to be initiated into the mysteries of the Way.

This is what your Big Gun saying is all about. We have to die to our life to save our life; right?"

Jesus did not reply. He stared at me, and then he said: *"you truly do possess the gift of creative thought, don't you?"*

"But am I right?" I asked, deflecting his flattery.

"Yes," he replied.

"So all of your sayings then are directed to creating the extreme Happy Warrior type of personality? For example, blessing one's enemies instead of cursing them; walking the extra mile with a person; giving to someone in need; doing good to them that hate you; praying for them that use and abuse you, and so on and so on and which you conclude by telling us to be as perfect as our Father in heaven; right?"

"Exactly," said Jesus, with a grin from ear to ear. "Would you please explain what the spiritual logic behind all of my sayings is? Unless the reader grasps the logic he won't penetrate the mystery, nor will he ever manage to catch the spirit of the Way."

Not quite sure what Jesus was asking, I thought for a moment; and in a sudden flash it came to me with a saying I had created that perfectly summed up the Way of Christ. Once that came to mind I knew what I had to say to pry open the reader's mind to Christ's secret teaching of the Way: *"The more you give of yourself, the more of yourself you will have to give; and the less you give of yourself, the less or yourself will have to give!"*

Jesus laughed until he had his fill of laughter. I waited patiently, watching him relish in the joy of laughter. He looked at me, and in his most serious voice said, *"That is a million times better than my Big Gun saying!"*

"Do you think so?" I said, not knowing whether to believe him or not.

"I certainly do! You do not threaten the lower self with death as I do in my Big Gun saying. You tell the lower self to stop being selfish. That way it's up to the lower self to see that it is the author of its own demise. It takes the sting out of my teaching. *I love it, O!"*

"Good," I said, finally giving in to the flattery. "The whole point of my saying has to do with the two types of consciousness. The Happy Warrior personality is unselfish, and the Ozymandian personality is selfish. So the more selfish a person is, the more he feeds his Ozymandian personality; and the less selfish a person is, the more he feeds his Happy Warrior personality. And the whole thrust of your teaching is to create a Happy Warrior personality at the expense of the Ozymandian personality — which means that there will be inevitable conflict in the heart of man when he seeks to create a Happy Warrior personality, because his lower self will not be sacrificed willingly. And here we can introduce the reader to the most troubling of all your sayings, because out of the gnostic context of your Big Gun saying this paradoxical saying boggles the mind!"

"I can't wait to hear this," Jesus said, still grinning like a kid in a candy store.

I flipped the pages of my Bible. "This is in Mathew, Chapter 10, verses 34 to 39. I'll read it for you: *"Think not that I am come to send peace on earth; I come not to send peace, but a sword. For I am come to set a man at variance against his father, and the daughter against her mother, and the daughter in law against her mother in law. And a man's foes shall be they of his own household. He that loveth father and mother more than me is not worthy of me; and he that loveth son or daughter more than me is not worthy of me. And he that taketh not his cross and followeth me, is not worthy of me. He that findeth his life shall lose it, and he that loseth his life for my sake shall find it."*

"Bravo!" Jesus exclaimed, clapping his hands. "Now we can finally set the record straight on the most troubling of all my sayings! *Thank you, O!* For centuries the world has puzzled over how the Prince of Peace could say such a thing, and now the world can see what I meant in the real gnostic context of my teaching!"

Taken aback by his excitement, I just stared at Jesus; but I couldn't contain myself and broke into laughter. I reached over and poured us another cup of tea and took a sip. Jesus also took a satisfying drink, his eyes seeming to gloat in the fact that he was finally being vindicated for the most troubling of all his sayings.

"The Prince of Peace came into the world to teach people how to create a spiritual personality," I began, feeling the floodgates open; "and since the spiritual personality has to be created out of the context of one's life, it follows that creating a spiritual personality in the context of one's life will pose a threat to all the people around him. The Happy Warrior has to extricate his consciousness from those around him in order to create his spiritual personality, and as he pulls back from the material values that those around him live by he's going to threaten the ground of their being. In symbolic terms, the Happy Warrior has waged war on the Ozymandian personality. This is the meaning behind your saying that you came not to bring peace but a sword. Your sword is the truth of the Way. With this sacred sword you slash your deliverance from those around you who live by values that nourish the Ozymandian personality. This is why you set father against son and daughter against mother, because the uncompromising sword of the Way cuts the lower self off from the spiritual self and liberates Soul from the material consciousness of life. There, J; I can't do any more than that to explain the saying that has plagued theologians ever since the world made you the Prince of Peace!"

Jesus got up and kissed me on the top of my head and sat down and took a sip of tea and looked at me smiling.

"You're welcome," I said, my heart swelling with pride. I took a sip of tea to break the spell because I was beginning to feel embarrassed with all the love that Jesus poured into me. "I know that this saying is true," I spoke up, my voice full of emotion. "I unsheathed the mighty sword of the Way and slashed my own deliverance from my family's shadow personality. You cannot believe the rancor, resentment, and ill feelings that I set free in my family with my deliverance. My sword slashed so deeply that to this day most of my siblings will have nothing to do with me. The wounds that I inflicted with my sword cut so deep that they will not heal in this lifetime. It will take another life or two before they heal, because the sword of the Way cuts to the marrow of the spiritual bone. So, Jesus of Nazareth; with all the love, respect, and admiration that I have for you, I have to tell you that your teaching, for all of its efficacy in liberating Soul from the material consciousness of life, is a very dangerous teaching to live by, and I don't believe it's suited for the modern world. It was a teaching brought into the world by an extreme Warrior of the Way because your times were extremely hard and cruel. The Roman occupation was a conquering consciousness of the material life, and you had to match this with an equally conquering spiritual consciousness; that's why you did what you did. Your teaching was born out of the womb of its times, and it was appropriate then; but not today. We live in a free society now. The Way has revealed itself today in a way that does not set man apart from man but embraces him in a fellowship of growth and understanding. That's what I think, anyway; and if this offends you, I'm sorry."

"I'm not offended," Jesus said, his eyes just brimming with love. "I welcome the opportunity to deliver Soul from my misunderstood teaching."

"The Gospel conspiracy, you mean?"

"Precisely!" Jesus exclaimed, and dramatically vanished before my eyes; but his gratitude lingered for days in my writing room.

64. *The Real Cost of Being a Christian*

I needed time to compose myself from our last talk. It was the most powerful and rewarding talk to date. We had penetrated to the core of Christ's teaching, and the more I thought about it the more certain I felt that the New Testament Gospel writers had done the world a great disservice.

It took a whole week to work our last talk into my book, so I had plenty of time to reflect on it; but what kept coming back to me was the fact that Christ's secret teaching was revealed by Holy Spirit to address the spiritual needs of Jesus Christ's times.

The Romans were a civilized but brutally conquering race. They exacted loyalty from their conquered subjects. In like manner, the teaching of Christ was a spiritually conquering teaching and it exacted loyalty from its followers. *"He that is not with me is against me,"* said Jesus, in Mathew Chapter 12, verse 30; *"and he that gathereth not with me scattereth abroad."* And he went further to reveal in verse 32 the exacting demands of his teaching: *"And whosoever speaketh a word against the Son of man, it shall be forgiven him; but whosoever speaketh against the Holy Ghost, it shall not be forgiven him, neither in this world, neither in the world to come."*

One was either for or against the Word of God. Holy Spirit was the Word of God, and Jesus laid the spiritual law down by telling man that he had a choice to follow the Word of God and be rewarded with admission into the kingdom of God, or to follow the way of the world and not be admitted into the kingdom of God. What Jesus and/or the Gospel writers failed to make clear was that deliverance from the consciousness of life was not limited to one lifetime alone. That made Christ's teaching no less cruel than the exacting demands of loyalty by the conquering Romans!

"Render therefore unto Caesar the things which are Caesar's, and unto God the things that are God's," said Jesus in Mathew, Chapter 22, verse 21, demonstrating the extreme consciousness of the spiritual warrior that Jesus had become. It was

one or the other for the Romans and it was one or the other for Jesus also, and taking this extreme teaching out of the context of its times would do the world a great disservice. It would only perpetuate an either/or spirituality, and in the DPG there are no extremes of either/or. Soul has forever to realize its divine nature, because God's love is infinite in its mercy.

The DPG is implicit in Christ's teaching, because any part of the Way speaks for the whole Way; but few people realize this. Only an initiate of the inner circle of life can see that the Way is one, regardless how it is expressed. For the Gospel writers to imply that one is either for or against Jesus Christ has perpetrated a consciousness of extreme spirituality. This is the core of Christianity's conceit that only through Jesus can one be saved, and this is the premise of the Gospel conspiracy that Jesus wanted to dispel.

Man's purpose in life is to realize his divine nature, but he cannot realize it in a consciousness of self-deception. This is why I'm convinced that the Gospel writers, for all their good intentions to introduce Christ's teaching to the world, created conditions for Soul to trap itself in a consciousness of self-deception that will take lifetimes to resolve.

"I have to believe it," I said to Jesus, when he came for our next talk. I explained my feelings about the Gospel writers. He listened politely, but said nothing. "This is why I wrote in one of my books that self-deception is our greatest threat to personal growth, wholeness, and happiness," I continued, feeling good for getting that off my chest. "Christianity fosters a consciousness of false spirituality, and rather than liberate Soul as your teaching intended it does the exact opposite; it traps Soul in the life cycle, because man cannot liberate himself until he resolves the false consciousness of his lower self. That's why I'm convinced that the Gospel writers did the world a great disservice; and if not the Gospel writers, the bishops at the First Council of Nicaea who may have doctored the Gospels to satisfy Constantine who wanted to unite all the Christian factions."

Jesus did not respond, but his silence confirmed my feelings. He reached over and took the tea cozy off the pot and poured us a cup of tea. He picked up his cup, took a sip, and placed it gently onto the coffee table. I waited for him to say something.

"This speaks to the wrong type of personality," he began, speaking softly, but with a tone that told me I had struck a nerve. "Since Soul cannot exist in these lower worlds without a self born of these lower worlds, it takes many lifetimes to create the right kind of personality for Soul to grow in spiritual consciousness. I do not disagree with you in principle, O; but is this not a case of six of one and half a dozen of the other?"

"I'd like to believe that," I replied, smiling at his use of the expression. "But no; I'm afraid I can't buy that explanation. I can see the good that your teaching has brought into the world, but so dense is the fog of deception created by Christianity that it has become virtually impossible for the good Christian to liberate himself from the false understanding fostered by the Gospel conspiracy. For example, last Sunday Cathy and I drove to Bruce County to buy some fresh-picked apples, and on the way we listened to one of my favorite programs on CBC. Mary Hynes, the host of *Tapestry*, was interviewing John Shelby Spong, a retired Anglican Bishop who wrote the controversial book *Why Christianity Must Change or Die*. This man has outgrown his faith because he sees through most of Christianity's deceptions, but as liberated as he may be from the false consciousness of Christianity he's still trapped by the great lie of Christianity that we only live one lifetime that you came into the world to save. In all fairness, I love the man's courage to speak out the way he does against the deceptions of Christianity; but despite my love for him, until he sees through the big lie of Christianity he's no less free than the fundamentalist who's bought into the whole package of lies. Do you see my point?"

"Of course I do. But is not Bishop Spong helping to bring Christianity into the twenty-first century?" Jesus asked.

"Yes, he is; and all the more power to him. But a lie is a lie, and until the great lie of Christianity is dispelled Christianity cannot help but foster this false consciousness of extreme spirituality. What do you think was responsible for the conquering mentality of all those missionaries that went abroad to convert the heathen world? The blood that has been spilled in your name continues to flow to the present day. Doesn't this convince you that this extreme spirituality is out of context with our times? To hold onto the great lie of Christianity — despite the good Bishop's overwhelming feelings of being in the transcended presence of God — is to be no less trapped by one's lower self than King Ozymandias was. This is not to take anything away from this courageous man, because he's working his way out of the lower worlds the best way he knows how; but does the Way have to be made so difficult for him? That's the question at the heart of my tirade."

"Is this why you say that stupidity is not a gift of God?" Jesus asked, with that twinkle in his eyes that for some reason annoyed me today.

"*Yes!*" I exclaimed, and burst into nervous laughter.

"*And you think my teaching is hard?*" Jesus replied. "You should look in a mirror, O. You're no less severe than I ever was!"

"Are you serious?" I asked, surprised by Christ's comment.

"No, not really; but you do come across that way sometimes. True, the extreme consciousness of my teaching has been responsible for a great deal of blood spilled in my name; but that's why I'm here now. I want to set the record straight. If we may then, why don't we talk about the false personality of man this morning?"

I was just about to say something, but I was nudged to stop and reflect before speaking. I picked up my tea and took a sip. "If we do we'll have to get into the metaphysics of spiritual growth, and I'm not so sure I want to go there this morning."

"Why not?" Jesus asked.

"It doesn't feel quite right yet to introduce the reader to the deeper issues of spiritual growth. We can't talk about the false personality without talking about the dark side of the lower self of man, and I just don't feel like going there today; so if you don't mind, why don't we address some of your other sayings this morning?"

"You don't think the reader is ready yet to take a look at his false self?"

I laughed. "*Is one ever ready to see his own falseness?*"

"No; I suppose not," Jesus replied, smiling at me. "Alright; let's talk about some of my other sayings. Which one did you have in mind?"

"How about revealing the Spiritual Law of Attraction?"

"Good. Which saying in particular?" Jesus asked.

I turned to my notes and then read from Mathew, Chapter 25, verse 29: **"*For unto every one that hath shall be given, and he shall*** *have abundance; but from him that hath not shall be taken away even that which he hath."*

"The rich get richer and the poor get poorer," Jesus amplified.

Jesus was definitely in a no-nonsense mood this morning, despite how he tried to mask it. "Did I bring out your hard side this morning?" I asked.

"You think?" Jesus said. "Your comment about all that blood spilled in my name has hit home, and I don't know what to say now but to call a spade a spade."

"Then how about much gathers more? That's a little softer; don't you think?"

"It is. And the obverse would be equally true. Less gathers less," Jesus replied.

"Alright," I said, feeling a surge of energy. "I guess we can't avoid it, so let's talk about how the Law of Attraction is responsible for the type of personality man creates. It seems like this information is busting to come out. Let me do a short HU. I'd like the clearest exposition on the false consciousness of man for my reader."

"I was hoping you would come around," Jesus said, smiling at me. "I think we can use that saying to open the door to the mystery of the false personality. Would you like me to open this door for the reader?"

"Since you're so gung-ho on holding the mirror for man to see his false self, by all means; go ahead. I'll just sit back and hear what the savior of the world has to say about the false consciousness of life!"

"False personality of man," Jesus corrected. "The false consciousness of life is a whole other matter. It goes to the issue of evil, and I'm not in the mood this morning to call the God of these lower worlds up to the Docket of Truth!"

"The Docket of Truth?" I repeated, and laughed. *"As if Kal would come willingly!"*

"He has no choice when summoned by Christ," Jesus said, with unimpeachable authority. "After all, it's in my name that he spilled all of that blood; so when I wish to address the issue he has no choice but to come. But not now. Now we're going to talk about the false consciousness of Soul, and by this I mean the false personality of man."

395

"Fair enough. Where would you like to begin?"

"With the Spiritual Law of Attraction. If as you say much gathers more, then it follows that the more false one is in his behavior the more false the consciousness of his personality will be; and the more false the consciousness of his personality is, the more it will attract the false consciousness of life. In effect, the false personality type will gravitate to that level of human consciousness that reflects his personal values that are responsible for the false consciousness of his personality. Do you follow the logic so far?"

"Yes, of course," I said, smiling at Christ's teacher role. "But I just had a thought while you were talking that revealed something I did not know before."

"What?" Jesus asked.

"The consciousness of life is stratified," I replied.

"Yes, it is. And just how did you come to perceive this?"

"It just occurred to me that the consciousness of life is one dimension in which all dimensions of reality exist, and these dimensions are made up of various compositions of being and non-being. The more false one is, the more he gravitates to that dimension of consciousness that is similar to the composition of his own non-being. In effect, the more false one is the more he is pulled into the heart of non-being, which is the deepest and darkest consciousness that Soul can descend to. Of course the opposite would be true as well. The truer one is, the more he gravitates to the heart of being, which is Soul's true spiritual nature. Along the way there are all these various dimensions of reality that Souls with a similar level of consciousness will gravitate to — *and that's what I think the guiding force of Holy Spirit wants to reveal about the metaphysics of spiritual growth!*"

"This is what the three levels of consciousness in life speak to," Jesus replied, unmoved by my outburst of emotion. "What Spirit allowed you to catch a glimpse of was the various levels within the three circles of life; and I'm glad you were given this insight because now you have a firm grasp of the metaphysics of spiritual growth. You are correct, O; Soul gravitates to its own level of consciousness in life. This is what the everyday consciousness of life speaks to with sayings like, 'it takes money to make money,' 'it takes one to know one,' 'misery loves company,' 'nothing succeeds like success,' 'birds of a feather flock together,' and so on. These sayings speak to the various dimensions of reality that exist within the three levels of consciousness. The real question is how to break the karmic patterns of life that keep one bound to his level of consciousness; or, better still, how can one gravitate to a higher level of consciousness?"

I laughed as memories of my own struggle to liberate myself from my own false consciousness flooded my mind. "You must be kidding?" I said.

"Why?" Jesus asked, intrigued by my laughter.

"Because it's impossible for man to look at himself with such honesty!" I replied, overwhelmed by memories of my own confrontation with the unconscious. "If this were possible the world would not be what it is. Many great men have lived their whole life in the belief that they were true to themselves, but so thoroughly duped were they by their own life-lie that only an experience of tragic dimensions could wake them up to their own false consciousness. I know this for a fact, because I experienced a shock to my psyche that so traumatized me I could not live with myself and fled to France; and even then I still could not see the real depths of my false self. The Inner Master had to bring this to my attention with his question, *'Why do you lie?'* I spent the best years of my life coming to terms with my own falseness, so if you think the reader is going to take our word that he has a false self you would be sadly mistaken, because no-one wants to see their life-lie!"

"You're very emotional about this, aren't you?"

"Yes, I am."

"May I ask why?"

"Because I paid such a dear price to authenticate my life that it sends shivers up my spine to think what people will have to go through to find their true self; especially Christians that have been so thoroughly cuckolded by Christianity that it will take an experience no less traumatizing than mine to shock their conscience awake! But that's the only way man can wake up to his true nature. Man has to be so sensitive in conscience that he will be forced to refine his ethics until his every thought, word, and deed are brought into agreement with the spiritual laws of life. I know this because that's what I had to do!"

"So you do care after all," Jesus said, with a jocular laugh.

"You can make light of my feelings all you want, J; but I'm telling you, it doesn't matter what we say about the metaphysics of spiritual growth man will not give up his life-lie for the asking. *And that's a truth our readers can take all the way to the bank!"*

"What would you propose, then?" Jesus very calmly asked.

"I'll tell you," I replied, speaking from the depths of my own painful experience. "Man can avoid the cruel experiences he would need to be shocked awake to his life-lie by finding a teaching more merciful than yours. *Your teaching is brutal, J!"*

"I see where you are going with this," Jesus said, "and I agree. The Way of Christ is too extreme for most people. It will only brutalize one's psyche if lived as I admonished; but that's not the point of our dialogue, is it? I want to reveal the mystery of self-transformation that lies at the heart of my sayings. I don't expect anyone to follow my teaching today when the pure teachings of the Way have been revealed to the world, but it is always man's choice which path to follow; isn't it?"

"It is," I agreed. "But experience has taught me that despite the best advice in the world people always end up doing exactly what they want. Do you think Bishop Spong would abandon his core belief in Christianity to embrace the Way of the Eternal? I doubt that very much. He has too much invested in his own life-lie despite the fact that he tells us he is as true to himself as he can possibly be. It doesn't matter how true one is to himself, if there exists one vestige of self-deception at the core of one's being that blinds Soul from seeing itself the Kal will not forfeit that self-deception for the asking. There is one final price that one must pay to forfeit that last deception, and that price comes with a cost most people are not willing to pay — *and you and I both know what that cost is, don't we?"*

Jesus laughed. "Yes, my Big Gun saying. There you have it, then. That's the real cost of being a Christian," Jesus concluded, and sat back in the chair and stretched his legs and put his hands behind his head. "Now how do you feel?" he asked, with a big smirk.

"Pardon me?" I said, puzzled by his question.

"Doesn't it feel good to get all that off your chest?" he said.

"You knew all along, didn't you?"

"Yes," he said, still smirking.

"You played me right to the end, didn't you?"

"You played yourself, O. All I did was let you vent. It does feel good, doesn't it?" Jesus said, rubbing it in; but I refused to reply. *"Come on, O! It feels good to get that load off your chest, doesn't it?"*

"Yes, it does," I reluctantly agreed. "And I hope this translates into relieving this sore chest I've been suffering from lately!"

"As within, so without," Jesus said, as he stood up. "That's another one of those laws that we will have to talk about; but not today. I think we've done enough damage to the Christian psyche for one day, don't you?"

I burst into laughter, and I laughed to myself all day long as I thought about how Jesus had played me to get out what he wanted the reader to hear!

65. *Journey into the Heart of God*

My life changed after I had my seven past-life regressions. I understood things about myself that I would never have understood without my regressions. My self-centered personality from my former life was responsible for the way I felt growing up in my current life. As the Earl of Wellington Manor, I fostered a personality in high society London, England that so disgusted me when an incident with Lady Beatrice Waverly revealed my hypocrisy that I fled to the new land of the Americas and became a trapper to repent for the unpardonable sin that I had committed against myself.

I had become what I most despised, and for eight long years in the American wilderness I wrestled with my conscience to "dismantle" the false personality I had cultivated in my self-appointed role as the *bête noire* of London's aristocracy, and I would have succeeded; but one spring day while checking my beaver traps a black bear cut my life short and I had to take up my spiritual quest in my current life where I had left off.

The irony of my role as the conscience of London's aristocracy was that I unwittingly became one of *them* — a foul blend of honor and deceit; and had I not experienced the incident with Lady Waverly that shocked my conscience awake I would have gone to my grave a blind, egocentric fool. Instead I died in the throes of my single-minded struggle to resolve the consciousness of my own hypocrisy, so I came into my current life with both feet on the ground running to find my true self.

I was a born seeker. I created the momentum in my former life as I struggled to transform the false consciousness of my aristocratic personality. As the penitent trapper I created enough consciousness of self-transformation wrestling with my demons to gravitate to Christ's teaching of spiritual rebirth at an early age in my current life, so I knew the interior journey of self-discovery well; that's why Jesus and I had a meeting of minds.

"If you walk in another man's shoes long enough you will see the world through his eyes," Jesus philosophized, when I told him about my former life. "It was courageous of you to sail to the Americas and live the life of a trapper. How many men do you know that would leave the security of their home and family, not to mention the privilege of your position, to live a life of hardship in the untamed wilderness of a foreign land because they had come face to face with their own hypocrisy and could not live with themselves?"

"None that I've ever met," I replied, smiling at Jesus' new look. He was wearing faded blue jeans, scuffed loafers, a plaid yellow shirt frayed at the collar, and a tired brown tweed sports jacket with cracked leather elbow patches, and he had bifocals resting low on his nose with a chain around his neck; and his unkempt hair looked oily, like it hadn't been washed in weeks, and he hadn't shaved either. He looked worn.

"Exactly," said Jesus. "Few Souls are ready for the kingdom of heaven, despite how many are called. Life is cruel; but man is the author of his own cruelty," he continued, in that same vein that came across as a bored professor giving a lecture that he had delivered one time too many. "Why? Because he panders to his own selfish needs, that's why. If he only knew how much his selfish needs contribute to his problems he wouldn't be so foolish; but such is life. From vanity to humility, the consciousness of man unfolds; and there is nothing we can do about it but accept the will of God."

"I know," I said, bemused by his new persona. Jesus really did look like a tired, bored professor of the humanities. "It just seems so unnecessary, though," I added.

"What?" Jesus asked, with a tortured expression on his whiskered face.

I smiled, wondering what he was up to. "All this anguish," I replied, refusing to confront him on his new persona. "Don't you think that if it were spelled out to man that our purpose in life is to realize the consciousness of God the quality of life on earth would be entirely different?" I said, waxing philosophical myself.

"That's a speculation I've never allowed myself to indulge in," Jesus responded, as though it wasn't worthy of his consideration. "Unlike you, O; I did not come into this world to find myself, but to realize who I already am. That was my purpose for assembling my message from all the mystery teachings that I ferreted out in my travels. I put together the most effective gospel that I could to quicken

401

man's spiritual growth, and my sayings brought Soul to the gateway of God's kingdom. That was my destiny. Your destiny was to liberate yourself from the consciousness of your own falseness. In my journey I was destined to travel through the consciousness of being, and in your journey you were destined to travel through the consciousness of non-being; and as vastly different as our journeys were, they both brought us to the heart of God. It all depends upon Soul's need. Until man is ready for total identity he will not step upon the path to the heart of God."

"But what makes man ready?" I asked, feeling very much now like his student.

"Two things," Jesus replied, with professorial gravitas. "One: the insufferable burden of false consciousness; and two: the insufferable burden of true consciousness."

"I beg your pardon?" I said, puzzled by his answer.

"Yes, I know; it does sound odd that one can suffer the burden of being too much himself. The truth is, one can become so true in life that it becomes too much to bear; and this burden of authenticity will compel him to look for a way to liberate himself from who he has become. Soul's journey to the heart of God can begin from the unbearable burden of one's true being, or the insufferable burden of one's false being. In either case, the destination is the same. All paths lead to the heart of God."

I chuckled at the thought of what St. Paul had written in his Second Letter to the Corinthians about the greatest false being of all: *"And no marvel, for even Satan himself is transformed into an angel of light."* I couldn't believe the door that Jesus had just opened, and I was forced to just stare at him and smile in awe at his gnostic genius.

He gave me a quizzical look. "Did you connect with something?"

"Yes. Believe it or not, I understand exactly where you're coming from. I'm afraid however that this is so far outside the box it won't fly with our reader. Thanks to the ancient Gnostic teachings and the Way of the Eternal, I also came to the realization that the Supreme Deity is beyond the being and non-being of the God of these lower worlds. Soul is pure Spirit, and Spirit is totally selfless. It's ironic that to become totally self-realized we have to create a self that is totally selfless. This is why your teaching boggles the mind. It's inconceivable for man to deny himself to find himself. And yet the journey into the heart of God lies in the art of denying oneself totally for God. Is that not so?"

"Love is the path into the heart of God," Jesus commented, in his new philosopher's voice that sounded so bored it downplayed everything we said. "We can talk of service to God by serving life, as many great humanitarians have done; but at the heart of this service you will always find one's love for God. Why not start there, then?"

"You want to talk about love this morning?"

"Yes," Jesus replied.

"Then it's one's love for God that motivates all great Souls to serve life?"

"Obviously," Jesus said, with a nonchalant shrug. "This is why I made love central to my teaching. Ultimately, love is the Way; and that's that."

"But the tragedy of your teaching is that it's so militant in its love!" I responded, with instinctive fearlessness. "I can just see all those little Christian soldiers marching out to the four corners of the world to save humanity from itself with all this love for their savior Jesus Christ. Don't you see the irony?"

"Certainly; and I regret that very much. You're correct to feel as you do about Christianity. You have been initiated into the mysteries of the DPG, so you know that the world does not need to be saved. I am responsible for this impression that the world must be saved, and I have to live with that. The Gospel writers took liberties with my life, and the world has been led down the proverbial path because of their desire to convert the world to my teaching; but as Pete Seeger once sang, *'the times, they are a 'changing.'"*

"Jesus Christ quoting Pete Seeger?" I said, and laughed. "What's going on here, J?"

Jesus smiled, but avoided my question. "There are as many Souls whose journey into the heart of God is through the consciousness of being as there are Souls whose journey into the heart of God is through the consciousness of non-being. It is the generous contributions of the former that inspire the lost Souls of the latter to find their way out of their own nothingness and into the heart of God," Jesus expounded, sounding like a New Age Christian existentialist. "You have found your way into the heart of God

403

through the darkness of your non-being, and your contribution to the living *Shariyat* —"

"*Stop!*" I interrupted. "What do you mean, living *Shariyat?*"

"The living Way," Jesus replied, with a casual indifference. "You're contribution to the living Way is of inestimable value, because there are few Souls in the world that have penetrated the darkness of the non-being dimension of life."

"*The shortest way to God is through hell!*" I exclaimed, summing up my life.

"I can see why you would say that," Jesus said, with such an air of indifference that it made me want to either laugh or slap him, but I did neither. "Let me complete my thought, if I may," Jesus continued, tilting his head to look at me over the top of his bifocals as if to provoke me even further. "The lost Soul resolves the consciousness of its own falseness through the natural process of karmic reconciliation, which entails suffering because suffering is nature's way of burning off karma. What you have done by quickening your liberation from the consciousness of your own falseness will shed light into the darkness of Soul's journey into the heart of God, and you should be commended."

"Thank you," I said, feeling both humbled and proud but perplexed by Christ's new persona. "As a writer, I need all the confirmation I can get," I added, with a sudden impulse to justify myself to Professor Jesus Christ, "because I've received many rejections over the years; but that's neither here nor there now," I quickly added, as I scrambled to center myself. "What matters now is telling the story of my journey into the heart of God. I have solved the mystery of the self, and I don't want to leave this life until I get my story out there. The DPG is too precious not to share with a spiritually famished world."

"Precisely," said Jesus, with a nod of professorial approval. "This is why I was delegated to talk with you on the correct interpretation of my sayings—"

"*Delegated?*" I interrupted.

"Yes. You don't think I did this on my own, do you?"

"Yes and no, leaning more to the yes," I replied, taken aback by his admission.

"We've gone through this already," Jesus said, with a curtness that reminded me of my old professor of Metaphysics who "cloaked" me one day in his class when I challenged his intellectual authority and never acknowledged me again. "Let's talk about love now. What have you learned about love that will shed new light on the living Way?"

"The living Way again," I repeated, with a self-conscious smile. "Alright, what have I learned about love that can help man find his way out of the darkness of his false consciousness?" I asked myself, and then closed my eyes to ask the Inner Master to pull out all stops because I knew that my love for God was aching to come out. *"Please, Z,"* I pleaded, after repeating my power mantra for a quick connection, and an overwhelming feeling of goodness shot through me and I knew precisely what to say. "I walk the extra mile with a person. That's how I give love to the world. But I only walk with people as far as their integrity will allow them to walk into the heart of God, and I leave the rest to find their own way. I've learned that love is best expressed through everyday experiences, not in grand gestures. Soul is never lost, never apart from God. God realizes itself through Soul's growth, and by giving love Soul becomes God-realized; so changing the world is entirely off the mark in God's Plan — because the world *is* the mark of God's Divine Plan!"

"What on earth do you mean by that?" Jesus asked, again with a tortured look.

I laughed. "It's through the individuation process of life that the Divine Plan of God unfolds," I replied, playing the game all the way with Jesus. "And to think the world can be changed to better serve God's purpose would be to reflect the same unforgiveable arrogance as the Gospel writers who felt they knew what was best for the world!"

"That's a rather mundane attitude about love, wouldn't you say?" Jesus replied, with a bemused look on his whiskered face. "No eloquent phrases? No profoundly moving insights? No bliss? No ecstatic joy? Just the realization that living the simple spiritual life is what loving God is all about. That's rather blasé, wouldn't you say?"

Jesus' new persona made me laugh now, and I snickered; but I refused to step off the stage until the final act. "My whole life has been one indefatigable effort to find my way into the heart of God," I

said, with a straight face; "so it's no wonder I have this work-horse attitude about love. I love my life, J. Since the values upon which I have built my life are spiritual, how I live my life reflects these values; and they all boil down to love. This is why I maintain that the fundamental purpose of life is to be a good person — *because no greater love can we have for our fellow man than to simply be a good person!"*

"BRAVO!" Jesus exploded, and took off his bifocals and let them hang around his neck and looked deep into my eyes and stared long and hard at me. "The most efficient vehicle for love is goodness, and one does not have to belong to any religion to be a good person. It all comes down to personal values. How would you sum up your love for God, then?" he asked me, in his normal, non-professorial voice.

"I don't know," I said, smiling at his instant metamorphosis. "God *is*, I *am*, and love is forever; that's what I would say. I would never talk like this in public, though," I added, with a chuckle. "To be honest with you, J; I think love loses its magic when you talk about it. It's like writing. Hemingway believed that if you talk about a story before you write it, it's like taking the dust off a butterfly's wings and your story loses its magic; the same thing with love. Love should be implied in our life, not worn on our sleeve; but the only way we can do that is to *become* love, and therein lies the problem."

"So true," Jesus said, with that familiar joyful twinkle in his loving eyes. "Love comes from a generous heart, and the journey into the heart of God is realized by learning how to be generous in thought, word, and deed. The more one opens his heart to the world, the more he will inch his way into the heart of God."

"From the heart of man into the heart of God, is that it?" I summed up.

"Precisely!" said Jesus, and stood up and gave me his hand to shake for the first time since we began our talks in the little park in the heart of Southlake.

We shook hands, both smiling contentedly at each other. Suddenly Jesus disappeared, and I felt rather foolish standing there with my hand in the air!

66. *The Living Way*

I opened my notebook and read to Jesus the saying I wanted to talk about: "'***And no man putteth new wine into old bottles: else the new wine doth burst the bottles, and the wine is spilled, and the bottles will be marred; but new wine must be put into new bottles.'*** That's from St. Mark's Gospel. Chapter 2, verse 22. I'd like to talk about this saying because of something you said when you played the role of the bored professor."

"What did I say?" Jesus asked, not reacting to my comment.

"You used the phrase 'the living Way.' As I worked our talk into my chapter—"

"If I may, what did you call your chapter?" Jesus interrupted.

With a proud smile, I said, "Journey into the Heart of God."

"Excellent. That should balance out Conrad's despairing journey into the heart of darkness," Jesus commented, with an ironic twinkle in his eyes.

"Now you're quoting Joseph Conrad?" I said, wondering if the professor was back; but I took up the challenge. "Do you know Conrad thought that too much consciousness was insufferable?" I said. "He called this malaise 'the curse of consciousness.'"

"What can you expect from a man who wrote *The Heart of Darkness*?" Jesus offered, with professorial gravitas in his voice. "The consciousness of man's inhumanity to man can be insufferable even for the most stalwart Soul. The only escape from the heart of darkness is the Light of God, and the Light of God comes with man's humanity to man. The more one opens his heart to life, the more he inches his way into the heart of God."

Memories of my relationship with that solar cult rushed to my mind. "If I may, J; I'm going to reveal something very personal. I have a very strong urge to tell you this. When I was studying that offshoot Christian solar cult teaching allegedly brought into the world by a Child Christ, I remember something that one of the followers said during one of the so-called Master's talks that sent a chill up my spine. This man stood up, full of nervous excitement, and told us that as he was meditating on the Child Christ's teaching he experienced what he called 'the ecstasy of darkness.' He said he knew what the teaching was all about now, and he could not believe how satisfying the ecstasy of darkness was. He sent such a chill up my spine that it snapped me out of the hypnotic hold the teaching had on me, and I dropped it instantly. The point I want to make is that the lure of the dark side of life can seduce one's Soul without one being aware of it; and it often takes a tragedy to snap one out of that hypnotic spell. Is this the polar tension that exists in the world; this lure of the ecstatic dark side of life and Soul's encoded need to return to the true Light of God?"

"You tell me. You were seduced by the ecstasy of darkness in your lifetime as Riel Laforchette. What was the attraction for you to turn on God as you did?"

Jesus took me by surprise with my lifetime as the infamous *Scoundrel of Paris*. I felt like I got my leg caught in a steel trap and wanted to squeal in mortal agony.

"You're right," I said, unable to deny the horrifying truth of my morally repugnant past life. "I was lured by the ecstasy of darkness. It gave me unbounded pleasure to seduce those high society women of their faith in you. The more they forfeited their Soul to me, the sweeter the ecstasy of darkness was. If you want me to describe this ecstasy, I will. It was the ecstasy they gave me as I sucked out the last vestiges of their virtue. I had the power to make my whores renounce you for the sexual pleasure that I gave them. It wasn't sex that satisfied my lust; it was the sweet satisfaction of taking those Souls away from you. Sexual pleasure opened the door for my whores to experience the ecstasy of darkness that devoured me, and the more women I seduced the more consumed I became by the spirit of my own nothingness. When I died in that rat infested dungeon under the streets of Paris after the secret tribunal of the Roman Catholic Church condemned me for sowing the Devil's seed, I died a complete and utter fool; but my death was not in vain. My horrifying death revealed the secret that lies in the heart of every Soul that compromises itself to its own ego."

"Please," said Jesus, motioning with his hand, "share this with your reader."

"I will," I said, deciding to walk the extra mile with Jesus. "What Joseph Conrad and every writer that has to write his way through the darkness of his own Soul reveal to the world is the utter hopelessness of their own nothingness. This is the heart of darkness. This is the lure of the dark side. The Big Empty, as Cathy called it the other day—"

Jesus laughed. "The Big Empty," he said. "The heart of darkness *is* the Big Empty. Did Cathy know how revealing that was?"

"Not consciously. She saw through the inanities of the good life on Facebook one day and called it the Big Empty, but I don't think she realized the metaphysics of the allure. The good life may be wonderful, but it can be very dangerous to one's Soul."

With a sad look, Jesus said, "The more one compromises his integrity for the good life, the more he will be pulled into the heart of darkness."

"The Big Empty," I said, with a snicker. "This black hole is the consciousness of one's own nothingness. 'I am no-one,' said Charles Manson at his trial.' No-one is the 'I' of one's non-self. As paradoxical as this may sound, one's non-self is a reality that one does not want to experience. I did in my Parisian lifetime, and I would not wish this experience upon anybody. And yet, this is where Hollywood gets some of its best material!"

Jesus smiled. "But why does Soul experience this ecstasy of darkness?" he asked me, again pushing the envelope. "Can you explain this for the reader?"

I didn't want to go there, but I felt compelled. "I can only speak from my own experience," I said, as the haunting memories flooded my mind. "When I abandoned all hope of going to heaven and embraced my eternal damnation in hell to avenge the honor of my love for Claudine, I experienced the ecstasy of darkness for the first time. I can only describe this experience as absolute freedom. I ceased to be who I was and became totally devoid of self. In this experience of my own nothingness I had the freedom to do anything I wanted with impunity. I feared nothing, because I did not exist as a self. Like Charles Manson, I was no-one. I ravaged the women in the high court of Paris because I lusted to fill the emptiness of my life with the virtue of their faith in you and the Holy Mother Church. Once I seduced them of their virtue, they became my whores; and I lusted for more virtue to fill the void of my insatiable non-self. That's why I had to have the purest Catholic virgin in all of Paris. I lusted for the virtue of pure innocence, and that became my undoing. I seduced a young noble virgin of her faith and she let it slip out to her mother that I had become her lord and savior and her horrified mother rushed her to their parish priest and her confessor found me out and reported me to the Cardinal of Paris, and I was tried by the secret tribunal of the Church and condemned to the rat infested dungeons under the streets of Paris for sowing the Devil's seed. I know the heart of darkness well, J; because I journeyed into the heart of darkness in my infamous Parisian lifetime!"

"Yes," Jesus said, with a heavy sigh. "May I ask; what would you draw from this experience to help the reader understand the behavior of man? Can you distill the wisdom of your experience as the lost Soul of Paris?"

"Lost Soul of Paris?" I repeated, and snickered. "I prefer *Scoundrel of Paris.* That sounds a little more romantic," I said, trying to make light of my horrifying life.

"It may sound more romantic, but it did not make you any less of a lost Soul. So what can you tell your reader about this experience that he can take to the bank?"

I had no choice but to go the distance with Jesus, so I acquiesced. "For one thing, it has given me the wisdom to see how sex can open the door into the heart of darkness," I began, as sexual memories flooded my mind. "What people will learn in their own time and way is that sex introduces the God-force into their life. I fancied myself a poet in my Parisian lifetime and I called this mysterious life force 'virtue,' and I craved this energy because it was the only thing that could fill the void in my life; but I could never get enough to fill the void. It was too deep, too all-consuming; so I lusted for more and more of this natural virtue. That's how I became insatiable in my lust for sex. There wasn't one woman that I could not satisfy with my sexual prowess, but she had to forfeit her virtue to me for the mindless pleasure that I gave her. This established my reputation as *le salaud de Paris*; and the wisdom that I can distill from my lifetime of sexual depravity is that sex can be a doorway to both heaven and hell; it all depends upon where one's 'I' is centered."

"Can you please explain that?" Jesus said, without a trace of judgment.

"For the reader's sake?" I asked, with a touch of sarcasm because I honestly did not want to relive my life of sexual depravity; it made me nauseous.

"Yes," Jesus curtly said.

"Why not?" I said, surrendering to the spirit of our talk. "One's values center his I-consciousness in his lower or higher self," I explained, realizing just how difficult it was to talk about. I called on the Inner Master for help, and the words just poured out: *"The more selfish a person is, the more he gravitates to the black hole of his own nothingness; and the less selfish a person is, the more he gravitates to the Light of God."*

Jesus said nothing. He motioned with his hand for me to continue. I took a deep breath, hoping this would be the last word on the subject.

"This is all very abstract and an affront to the rational mind," I continued; "but the metaphysics of spiritual growth cuts through all planes of consciousness, so it is by its very nature a complete logical system unto itself. Soul needs the God-force just as man needs air to survive, and if Soul is pulled deeper into the consciousness of its lower self it will desperately crave the God-force because Soul has to fill the void of its non-being. This is why the more selfish a person becomes the more insatiable he will be. Since sex is one way to get the God-force quickly, selfish people will go to sexual extremes to satisfy their lust for the God-force. In effect, sexual predators lust for God; but they have chosen the dark path to God, and this path will take them through the heart of their own darkness."

"But not forever," Jesus replied, with a smile on his face that told me we had finally come to the end of this terrifying road. "Soul does not stay in the heart of darkness. It experiences the heart of darkness as the end of its selfish karmic road, and then it must take another path home to the higher worlds, thanks to the merciful love of God."

"Yes," I sighed; "just as I did in my next incarnation. I had to start paying life back for all that virtue that I had stolen from my whores to satisfy my sexual lust for self-consciousness, so I came back as a black slave in southern Georgia to begin my climb out of the heart of my own darkness."

Jesus' face was glowing with love. "This has been extremely enlightening," he said. "Perhaps we can talk about my saying now?"

I grimaced. I could not see the relevance of our talk to his saying of not putting new wine into old bottles, but I knew it was there. Jesus had pulled that harrowing experience out of me, but I could not see the relevance yet; so I had to ask: "What is the relevance of your saying to our talk on man's journey into the heart of darkness?"

"The Way is the same regardless when it is revealed in history," Jesus began, eager to explain himself. "I revealed the Way to meet the desperate needs of my times. As you said, I was militant in my revelation of the Way. I came not to bring peace but a sword, and the purpose of the Way of Christ was to reveal the dual nature of man's self. Unless the reader understands that the consciousness of the self is split in two, one lower and one higher, he will never grasp the logic of spiritual growth. We cannot stress this fact enough that the self needs energy to grow; but because of this split in consciousness it all depends upon which self will be nourished by the God-force that one collects with his experiences. The lower self constitutes the consciousness of one's non-being, and the more one nourishes his non-being with the God-force the more his 'I' will gravitate to the center of his own nothingness; and eventually he will end up like you did in your lifetime as the lost Soul of Paris, totally disillusioned by God. On the other hand, if one chooses to live by what you have called inherently self-transcending values, then the God-force that one takes in as he experiences life will nourish his higher self; and the more one grows in his higher self, the more he will gravitate to the heart of God. I don't think I can make this any simpler."

But I still could not see the relevance of his saying. "So the point of my experience as the lost Soul of Paris was?" I asked, with a blank expression on my face.

Jesus laughed. "Oh, yes; I didn't make the point, did I?"

"Not explicitly," I said, feeling foolish for not making the connection.

Again Jesus smiled, his eyes twinkling with joy at what the omniscient Spirit of our talk had brought out. Taking a breath, he explained himself: "I wanted the reader to have a visual experience of what can happen to Soul when one chooses to nourish his lower self with the life-giving energy of God. What happened to you as the lost Soul of Paris is the destiny of all egoists that devour the virtue of life to satisfy the lust of their non-being. The relevance of your experience to my saying of not putting new wine into old bottles lies in your explanation of it: because you worked your way out of the heart of your own darkness, you shed the light of spiritual reason onto this impenetrable mystery; and in doing so you revealed the Way to the world, thereby making it a living reality."

"Let me see if I understand you correctly," I said, finally catching a faint glimpse of what Jesus was getting at. "I took the teaching of the Way, which you revealed in your sayings, and by living your teaching I captured the God-force and nourished my higher self. Your teaching here would be the old wine of your sayings; right?"

"Yes," Jesus said, with an encouraging smile.

"So I took the old wine of your teaching and drank it, and by drinking it I mean that I lived your sayings. As I lived your sayings, I liberated myself from the heart of my own darkness, because that's what your sayings will do if they are lived with passionate commitment. Am I on the right track?"

"Yes," Jesus said, with a triumphant smile.

"But because I live in the modern world now and the consciousness of life is much more evolved than it was two thousand years ago when you gave the Way to the world, I have conceptualized the Way of Christ in a language more suited to life today. This is what you would call putting the old wine into new bottles; right?"

Jesus laughed. "Please continue."

"So the relevance of my experience as the lost Soul of Paris has to do with how I conceptualized my spiritual liberation from that dark period of my life," I reflected thoughtfully, slowly grasping the logic of Christ's extraordinary insight. "Is this why I felt compelled to talk about my morally depraved past life this morning?"

Jesus said nothing, so I continued to press my point.

"What you meant by your old and new wine saying then was that you brought the secret teaching of the Way into the open and made it a living reality for your times, and you're saying that this is what I'm doing by conceptualizing the Way for our times?"

"BINGO!" Jesus exclaimed, and laughed to relieve the joy of my explanation. "Truth is one," he expanded. "It is always the same in every period in history. It is man's consciousness that differs. As man's consciousness evolves, his perception of truth changes; but it is the same truth. It is always one. Truth *is* the Way, O; but this is too far beyond the grasp of man's understanding, regardless which epoch he lives in. The point is that the Way is the living truth, but it only becomes the living truth when one lives it in his own times as you are doing. As you live the Way in your own times you make of the eternal truth of the Way a vibrant, contemporary spiritual path. Does this make sense now?"

"It makes sense to me," I said, finally grasping the essence of Christ's thought. "But I'm not quite sure we have expressed clearly enough what you mean by the living Way. I see more in this phrase than we have explained. This old wine that you talk about in your saying is your metaphor for the eternal truth of the Way, and the old bottles are your metaphor for the conceptual containers of the eternal truth of the Way. By providing contemporary conceptual containers for the eternal truth of the Way, I have provided new bottles for the old wine of the Way. I know this; but I think there is more to the living Way than this. The living Way tells me that every thought and deed of creative expression releases the spiritually liberating energy of the Way. This is what the living Way means to me. It is more than a contemporary conceptual expression of the eternal truth of the Way; it is the spiritual liberation that comes with every creative act of man!"

"Not quite, O. I see your point perfectly, and it is valid; but it does not address the central theme of our dialogue, which is the gnostic power of the Way. The Way of Christ is the path that I assembled from ancient secret teachings of the Way specifically to liberate Soul from its lower self. You have expressed the essential nature of the Way. Holy Spirit is the Way. You see the manifestation of Holy Spirit in every act of creative expression, but not every act of creative expression liberates Soul from its lower self. For example, the artist who releases the creative life force through his art more often than not will nourish his ego rather than his higher self with the energy of his art. Do you follow?"

"To the letter," I said, as the grizzled image of my literary mentor came to mind. "I know a writer who did just that. He collected the God-force with his vast life experiences, and then he poured his experiences into his novels and short stories; but so centered was this Nobel Laureate in his own massive ego that he devoured the virtue of his art and became an insufferable human being. His name was Ernest Hemingway, and as much as I loved his writing he was the total opposite of what I aspired to become in my own life."

"He was an egoist, you mean?" Jesus said, for simple clarity.

"Not just any egoist; he was unbearable. Hemingway used everyone in his life to serve his literary ambitions and desires. His third wife Martha Gellhorn called him a pathological liar, but ironically he was true to his art. That's what made him so conflicted. He had to live life on his own selfish terms or not at all. That's why he shot himself when he could no longer satisfy the desires of his massive ego, which were writing, sex, deep sea fishing, hunting, and drinking. The insufferable egoist imploded, because he could not compromise his selfish needs to the reality of his physically wasting life. Hemingway was responsible for the karmic disaster of his own life, J; and he died a tragic death."

"He speaks for a lot of people, O," Jesus said, with a commiserating smile. "Such is the way of unchecked egoism. But then, from the perspective of the DPG look at all the spiritual gold that the egoist will have to mine in future lives."

I burst into laughter. *"You'd better explain that for the reader!"*

"No," Jesus said, with that playful smile. "Let him figure it out. After all, we can't do all the work for him; can we?"

"Sorry, J," I said. "As much as I would like to agree with you, I can't. That was your attitude two thousand years ago, and look at the mess your teaching has left us in? It continues to mystify the world. I think I'll explain this for the reader."

"Then please do," Jesus said, with a wave of his hand.

"Gladly," I said, and silently called upon my Muse. "Ego is the biologically evolved instinct that Soul uses to collect the God-force of life. The egoist devours experiences, because the very nature of egoism is its insatiable desire to be more itself. The more the egoist gets from life, the more the egoist wants from life because it simply cannot be satisfied. This is the metaphysical reality of the non-being of the lower self, so experience after experience the egoist takes in the God-force, which you call the spiritual gold of life; but because this spiritual gold is devoured by one's ego it is not pure enough for the higher self, and it must be transformed karmically of its selfish content. This can only be done by future life experiences, such as my experience as a black slave in Georgia. The more I suffered in that lifetime, the more I resolved the selfish consciousness of my past lifetime as the lost Soul of Paris. This is what you mean by mining the spiritual gold of one's egoism. There, I think that should satisfy the reader's need to know."

"Not quite," Jesus said, with an eager look in his eyes. "If we're going to satisfy his need to know, let's explain again just what this spiritual gold is. The egoist consumes life because he has a need to become more himself. This is what drives the egoist — his insatiable hunger to be more himself. Hemingway was driven by his ego to be more Hemingway, which explains his excessive passion for life; Picasso was driven by his ego to be more Picasso; and Catherine Hepburn was driven by her ego to be more Catherine Hepburn. *'That's me, unstoppable ego!'* she said in an interview late in her life. These talented people were consumed by their wanton egoic need for more identity because the metaphysical nature of egoism is its own insatiability. All the life force that egoists consume with their voracious appetite for more self-identity is the precious spiritual gold of the consciousness of God, but this God-force that egoists consume imprisons the 'I' of God in the lower self of man, and all of this I-consciousness has to be transmuted of its selfish content in order to nourish the higher self and liberate Soul from the cycle of karma and reincarnation. The spiritual gold of life is the I-consciousness of God, but if it is trapped by ego it will have to be transmuted with karmically reconciling future life experiences—"

"Smelted, you mean!" I cut in. "Smelted in what you so dramatically called 'the furnace of fire,'" I explained, with a wry snicker.

"Yes; but let's not confuse the reader. This furnace of fire is my metaphor for the natural suffering of life that burns the consciousness of selfishness out of the 'I' of God that is trapped in one's lower self; my gospel burns it off consciously," Jesus clarified.

"Talk about new bottles for old wine!" I exclaimed.

"Indeed," said Jesus, smiling with satisfaction.

"So do you think we did your saying justice?" I asked.

"Yes," said Jesus; "unless you have something else to add."

"I do," I said, feeling a very strong nudge from the Inner Master to clear up a growing confusion in the reader's mind. "I don't want the reader to think that in my efforts to demystify the Way that I'm promoting my own path; I'm not. I'm an initiate of the Way, but I'm also a writer. The Way is an individual path, so I can only speak for myself; not for the Way, as such. That's what I mean by the living Way. I am my own Way, and I just want to make this clear for the reader; okay?"

"Fair enough," said Jesus. "And neither do I speak for the Way, despite the saying that confirms the Gospel conspiracy that I am the way, the truth, and the life and no man cometh unto the Father but by me. I am my own way also; and I hope our dialogue can provide new bottles for the Way of Christ. The old and new wine come from the same vineyard, and all that changes is the containers; and at the risk of offending some readers, it's time to replace the old bottles of Christianity with some new bottles of the Way that we are providing with this dialogue, and hopefully we can dispel the Gospel conspiracy—"

"You're dreaming again!" I burst out, unable to contain myself.

"I know," Jesus sighed. "But I have to spell it out, don't I?"

We laughed. Jesus left and I went to sand the new house I had just finished taping, thinking all day long about how Jesus had gotten his way with me again.

67. *A Bone to Pick with St. Paul*

Sanding the drywall of a new house is hard physical work. After a day of sanding I am totally exhausted, physically and mentally, and I have very little energy left even for thought. This feels so good that I cannot describe the feeling, except by comparison with a long distance run. After a run of ten or twelve miles my mind would be emptied of all "monkey" thought, and all that remained would be a quiet calm like the stillness of an inland lake on the calmest day of the year. This feeling of mental calm felt so good that I often went for a long distance run just to experience this calm.

I also experienced something else after a long distance run that is much more pronounced after a hard day of sanding drywall. This was a noticeable change of temperament from one of an easy-going, live and let live disposition to a forthright, shoot from the hip, tell it as it is, no-nonsense attitude. This was my temperament when I met St. Paul on the afternoon of my third day of sanding the drywall of the new house.

I thought the house was empty because I had not heard anyone come in, but I heard voices in the great room, which I had already sanded. I went to see who it was. I expected to see other tradesmen, but it was Jesus and another man, both dressed in casual wear. Jesus had on his tan Dockers and a yellow polo golf shirt, and the other man had dark trousers, not Dockers, and a flower patterned short sleeve shirt. Both had loafers.

Surprised to see Jesus, I took off my dust mask and said, "What are you doing here, J? Did we forget something in our last talk?"

"No. I want to introduce you to someone," Jesus said.

"Oh," I said, wondering who the other man was.

"I'd like you to meet Paul of Tarsus, whom the world knows as St. Paul," Jesus said. "Paul, this is my good friend O from Georgian Bay."

St. Paul gave me his hand. It was a firm, confident handshake. He looked me in the eye and said, "It is a real pleasure to meet a companion in Spirit."

"Companion in Spirit?" I said, and smiled. "I suppose by that you mean a fellow traveler in the science of spiritual growth?"

St. Paul laughed. "Yes; that's exactly what I mean."

"Well I'm glad you're here because I have a real bone to pick with you," I said, rather bluntly. I surprised myself, but not Jesus and St. Paul.

"I know. That's why we're here," St. Paul replied, and both he and Jesus broke into a private chuckle.

"This isn't fair," I said, instantly picking up on the spirit of their humor; "two Masters and one lowly drywall taper! *What chance do I have?"*

"Ours is a world of equal opportunities," St. Paul said, and smiled.

"Soul equals Soul, is that it?" I responded.

"Exactly," he said, and turned to Jesus. "You're right; he is a good catch."

"So now I'm a good catch, am I?" I responded, feeling very much like a trophy brook trout on the end of a fly-fishing line.

"So what's this bone you want to pick with me?" St. Paul asked.

I opened my mouth and the words just tumbled out as if they had been waiting for years to be heard, which they were. I looked at St. Paul and let him have it right between the eyes: "Faith is the cornerstone of your gospel of Christ, faith in the law of Spirit; but because of man's inability to penetrate the mystery of the law of Spirit this blind faith of yours has morphed into an uncompromising faith that Jesus Christ is the sole savior of the world, and this faith in a misunderstood teaching has spawned the grotesque spiritual illusion that passes for the infallible law of the Christianity that you're largely responsible for bringing into the world. This illusion that our friend Jesus here is the sole savior of the world has retarded the spiritual consciousness of the world. That's the bone I have to pick with you, and I'm glad you're here so I can tell you this in person!"

St. Paul looked at me and without batting an eye, said, *"For I am not ashamed of the gospel of Christ; for it is the power of God unto salvation to everyone that believeth. The just shall live by faith."* That's from my epistle to the Romans. Chapter 1, verses 16 and 17. Yes, I do make faith the cornerstone of my teaching of what you so aptly call the science of spiritual growth and which we called the kingdom of heaven in our day; but I went to great lengths to spell out the law of Spirit and the law of sin so man could distinguish the properties of the dual self that I called selfsame thing in my letters. After all, how is man to know sin if he is not first acquainted with the law of Spirit? That was my purpose in spreading the gospel of our Lord Jesus Christ—"

"Our Lord?" I cut in, with a quick glance at Jesus who had a big smirk on his face. "Let's back off here. We're not in ancient Judea now. This is the twenty-first century, and no one is Lord in this century but the almighty consumer!"

Jesus and St. Paul broke into laughter, but I didn't join them. I just smiled at the two spiritual giants who, curiously enough, were not very big physically. Jesus was just over five feet and St. Paul a couple of inches taller, but with a beard he seemed shorter; and he was balding, which didn't do much for his stature.

"If I may," I said, in reply to St. Paul's comment, "what good did it do the world for you to spread a gospel that no one but the most evolved Soul could even begin to understand? Do you realize the havoc that your gospel of Christ has wrought upon the world? You opened the door to a fantasy that now possesses the very soul of society, and I don't believe anything but time will ever destroy this delusion of spiritual salvation through our Lord Jesus Christ here. You may have spelled out the science of spiritual growth better than Mathew, Mark, Luke, and John; but the point eludes the good Christians of the world. It has eluded them for centuries, and it will continue to elude them; and that falls squarely upon your shoulders, Paul of Tarsus!"

"And for argument's sake, what about free choice?" St. Paul asked.

"Free choice?" I shot back, straight from the hip. "Can a sleeping Soul make a free choice? When a person is brought up from birth believing in all this nonsense about original sin, baptism in Christ, forgiveness of sins, and eternal damnation, can this person make a free choice? *I don't think so!* A free choice presupposes a free

mind, and a mind clouded by all of this Christian nonsense is not capable of free choice!"

"And that's the bone you have to pick with me?"

"Yes," I curtly replied.

"I don't know what to say, except that you must have your reasons for feeling as you do," St. Paul replied, with a nonchalant shrug.

"I do. What I would like to know is this: why the presumption?"

"What presumption?" St. Paul asked, with a puzzled look.

"The presumption that man must choose between the law of Spirit and the law of sin? In the Divine Plan of God there is no such thing as sin. There is only experience. And when Soul has had enough experience to reconcile its lower self with its higher self and can hear the Word of God it will choose to live the spiritual life consciously. Why this presumption that the world must be saved from itself? This insufferable worm of Christian conceit has devoured the spirit of Christ's true gospel; that's why I ask!"

"And you think the world would have been better off without the gospel of Jesus Christ, is that it?" St. Paul asked, sounding, and with good reason, a bit defensive.

"Given my understanding of the science of spiritual growth, yes," I replied, so matter-of-factly that it sounded like a blunt axe falling upon a dry piece of hard oak.

"I see," St. Paul said. "If you would then, could you spell this out for me, please; because I just don't see why you feel as you do, and I would like to know."

"*I doubt that very much!*" I said, with a sarcastic snicker. "Nonetheless I will spell it out for you. It's the impasse that this Christian fantasy has created. This spiritual impasse so frustrates Soul that it takes untold lifetimes to resolve the consciousness of falseness that this blind faith in our savior Jesus here fosters. I know this from personal experience, and every time I look around I see Christians walking through life in this deep stupor of spiritual idiocy. I don't say this to disparage Christians, because fundamental to spiritual growth is waking up to our own false consciousness; but how in God's name can Soul wake up from this stupefying fantasy when Christians hang onto the false premises of their faith? Soul cannot wake up. Soul must go on collecting as much of this karmic idiocy as it can before it can stand the pressure of spiritual ignorance no longer and out of desperation cry for a way out of the hold that this monstrous creature has upon it!"

"Monstrous creature?" St. Paul said, with a tortured grimace.

"Yes. What you called 'putting off the old man,' which we know to be the karmic body of man's unresolved consciousness. I know it's not my responsibility how the world unfolds, but it annoys me to no end to see so many good Christians frustrate themselves trying to reconcile their conflicted self within the constricted paradigm of blind Christian faith. I've seen too many good Christians at their wit's end trying to rationalize their belief in the Gospels of Christ, and I see this spiritual impasse as a travesty of cosmic proportions that no one dares to address — including Soul Masters! Well I have two of the world's most famous Masters right here in front of me, so can you please tell me why the world has been kept in the dark about this illusion that the Gospels of Christ have fostered?"

"I'll field this one," said Jesus, holding his hand up for St. Paul to not speak. "It's not like we have boardroom meetings to discuss the affairs of the world," Jesus began, in a tone of voice that was both friendly but uncompromising. "We do get together every so often, but generally we let the spiritual laws of life unfold as they would. Sometimes we're called upon to intervene, and we do; but on an individual basis. As you say, the journey of Soul is a flight of the alone to the Alone, and sometimes the alone needs all the help it can get. The point is that the world is what it is, and the spiritual laws of life govern the science of spiritual growth; so it does no good to shout 'as flies to wanton boys are we to the gods, they kill us for their sport.' That rant is not suited to one so wise in the Way."

"Shakespeare again?" I said, with a snicker. I wasn't in the mood for play. "It won't do you any good to flatter me, J. Had you two not presumed to save the world we wouldn't have this spiritual impasse to contend with today. I'm convinced that most of this karmic suffering that Christians buy for themselves with their blind reliance upon this Christian fantasy is unnecessary. This does nothing but give birth to more stupid suffering. However it's dressed up, Christianity makes a fool of man. Let me give you an example, if I may?"

"By all means," St. Paul said, welcoming an explanation.

"This is true. I'm not making this up," I continued. "I know a writer who has gone the full gamut, from blind faith in the gospel of Christ when he was an Anglican Church minister who believed in the literal resurrection of the body of Jesus, then to doubting the bodily resurrection of Jesus, then to a wonderful awakening to the Spirit of Christ's teaching; and then to the conviction that Jesus here did not even exist as a historical person, that you are a myth created by the Gospel writers. The pendulum has swung to both extremes for this Christian writer, and I doubt that he will ever extricate himself from his foolish conviction that you are nothing more than a myth like the Osiris-Horus myth."

"So what harm is there in his belief?" St. Paul asked, with conviction in his voice. "He may not believe that Jesus was a real man, but if he believes in the Spirit of Christ's teaching he has caught the essence of Christ's gospel. I don't see your point."

"He misses the point of Jesus' life and mission, which was to exemplify the science of spiritual growth in the Way of Christ. Jesus here was a real man who found the Way, lived the Way, and realized his spiritual destiny — which is the point of the science of spiritual growth! This is what your whole teaching is about — *putting to practice the science of spiritual growth!* What value is there to the gospel of Christ if Jesus himself does not embody the science of the Way? Jesus does. This is why he said, 'I and my Father are one.' This is not metaphor made up by the Gospel writers to prove the point of a mythical Christ. It's a reality, which I see standing right here in front of me!"

Jesus laughed, but St. Paul just smiled at my rant. I continued. "Do you see my point now? This Christian writer has become his own fool because he cannot step outside the box of his faith to see that the secret teaching spells out the spiritual laws of life, of which karma and reincarnation are governing factors in Soul's growth. This man cannot bring himself to believe in reincarnation because his Christian faith won't let him, however enlightened it may be for him now. *Regardless whether Jesus exists for him or not, his faith in Christ continues to keep him trapped in his own idiocy!*"

St. Paul gave me a reluctant nod, while Jesus just stood there taking it all in.

"That's why I feel as I do about the spiritual impasse that the cornerstone of your gospel of Christ embodies," I continued. I still had much to say. "It is this blind faith in Jesus Christ, whether he's a myth or a man, that's responsible for the idiotic behavior in man's search for meaning! And I think it's high time for this blind faith to be seen for what it is — *a stupid lazy approach to spiritual growth!* But don't get me wrong. I don't diminish the spiritual insights that you offer in your Epistles, especially in your letters to the Corinthians; I just think that unless the science of spiritual growth is seen in the light of the Divine Plan of God it will always be subject to misunderstanding in your gospel of Christ!"

"Spell it out, then," St. Paul said. "If that's what you feel needs to be done, then do it; you don't need our permission. Make this your contribution to the living Way."

"The living Way again? This is really something, you know that!"

Jesus laughed. St. Paul put his hand on my shoulder, and said, "We'll talk again, O. We have much to talk about."

"What else is there to say?" I bluntly asked, by body still trembling.

"I would like you to do for my Epistles what you are doing with the sayings of Jesus. Can you do that for me, please?" St. Paul asked, his eyes pleading with me.

"That'll take a whole new book," I said.

"So?" St. Paul said, as though writing a book was like making flapjacks.

"So we'll see," I said. "I have my Jesus book to finish first."

"After you do we'll talk some more. It's been a real treat talking with you, O," St. Paul said, and gave me his hand to shake.

I shook his hand, then Jesus' hand, and they turned and walked out the front door and down Tiny Beaches Road like a couple of little Jewish businessmen out for a nice summer stroll down the sand-swept street overlooking beautiful Georgian Bay.

68. *The Word Behind the Words of Jesus*

There were two sayings that I particularly wanted to talk about, both cryptic in their own right but together they offered an insight that I felt would help unravel the mystery of Christ's Way; but I didn't know when Jesus would show up again, if at all.

I had crossed the line. But I could not help myself. I was in the grips of my no-nonsense personality, which meant that all bets were off; so I spoke my mind in a way that led me to wonder if there was something wrong with me.

I need not have worried, though. Jesus came five days after our last talk, and the first thing he said to me was, "You certainly won St. Paul's heart with your point of view."

"Pardon me?" I said, surprised. "You mean he wasn't offended?"

"Not at all, He found your perspective so refreshing that he's still chuckling over it."

"I thought I came at him like a steam roller," I said.

"You did. That's what he found so refreshing," Jesus said.

"I guess Masters aren't used to being spoken to with such bluntness," I said.

"You're right," Jesus said, with another chuckle.

"Well, J; I even talked to the Inner Master like that. 'Must you be so bold?' he asked me in a dream one night; and I defensively replied, 'I'm not bold. I'm forthright.' But I was only justifying myself. Gurdjieff called this *self-justification*, and it refers to one of the many ways that the false self uses to protect itself from being found out. So I do regret saying what I did. He was right, of course. I just couldn't suffer a frontal blow to my ego. I was bold, and I'm still bold; and I can only attribute this to my former line of destiny when I lusted for power. But ever since Pythagoras helped me change my line of destiny from power to service I had to cultivate an awareness that made me conscious of my lower self. I guess there are remnants of my former line of destiny lingering in my spiritual personality, so if I offended St. Paul please tell him I'm sorry for being so forthright."

"I'll pass that on to him. But you can tell him yourself when you work on your book with him," Jesus replied, with a Cheshire smile on his face.

"Are you're sure that's going to happen?" I asked, challenging Jesus.

"Not absolutely, because life is not written in stone; but reasonably sure. After you finish this book you will be inspired to follow it up with a more nuanced exploration of the science of spiritual growth, and Paul's Epistles will be a perfect entry into the deeper mysteries of the Way. For now, let's explore this concept that you just brought up. I'm intrigued by it, because it cuts to the quick of my gospel teaching."

"Which concept?" I asked, not following Jesus.

"You called it *self-justification*. Please explain what this means in the context of spiritual self-realization consciousness," Jesus said, all business again.

"Before we get into this, let me tell you that I've selected two more sayings I want to decode this morning; your *narrow way saying*, and your *innocent children saying*."

"Good. But first we should explore this survival skill that the lower self uses to protect itself from being seen for what it really is."

I smiled at Christ's persistence. "Yes, it is a survival skill; isn't it? Well, if the spiritual self has to protect itself from the negative forces of life then why not the lower self from the positive forces of life? After all, it has its own identity to protect; doesn't it?"

"Precisely," said Jesus. "And that's the point of this whole dialogue, to reveal the secret lives of the two selves of man—"

"What St. Paul called *selfsame thing*," I interjected.

"Exactly. The self of man is made up of the lower and higher self, and these two selves are virtually indistinguishable; that's why Paul called them *selfsame thing*. But they are as different as night and day. This constitutes the first stage of the secret teaching: raising one's consciousness enough to distinguish the lower from higher self."

"This is what St. Paul did better than the Gospel writers when he spelled out the law of Spirit and the law of sin; but I'll leave that for my talks with him, if and when they happen. For now, yes; I agree with you, J. I think we should spell out how the two selves protect themselves from the world. As a matter of fact, last Sunday Cathy and I attended a worship service in Carlton and the cleric spoke about spiritual survival in our times. She went on and on about how easy it is to get caught up in the world today, which makes us vulnerable to the negative forces of life; but aside from the spiritual exercises of the Light and Sound of God she really didn't have much to offer. Which isn't to diminish the protection that we get from our spiritual exercises, especially the HU; but what this cleric failed to offer was a perspective on the lower self that seeks to protect itself from the influence of its higher nature. It's only logical to assume that the stronger the higher self is, the more its lower self will do to protect itself from being transformed. That's why I offered the Wordsworthian approach to spiritual protection in our times."

"The Wordsworthian approach?" Jesus said, drawing me out for the reader.

"Yes. You see, J; what this H. I., and most chelas for that matter, failed to see was that to survive spiritually we have to be conscious of our lower self, because it's not only the negative forces of life that we have to protect ourselves from but the resistance we get from our own lower self that refuses to be transformed into an angel of light, if I may be so dramatic about it."

Jesus laughed. "I understand perfectly. Please, continue."

"The whole premise of spiritual survival has to do with protecting the higher self from the negative forces of life, but this includes our lower self also; so any effort to survive spiritually in life has to include survival skills that transform our lower self."

"But that's what the spiritual exercises do," Jesus said.

"Of course they do; and I'm not excluding them. In fact I put them front and center in one's effort to survive spiritually in this world; but the Wordsworthian approach to spiritual survival has to do with a conscious awareness of the negative influence that our lower self can have on our life. Our lower self has its own agenda, its own needs and desires which can be spelled out by the five deadly passions of the mind — anger, lust, greed, vanity, and attachment. Wordsworth's approach addresses these passions with his poem *Character of the Happy Warrior*. The point I wanted to make at the worship service was that it's not enough to do the spiritual exercises; one has to be conscious of his lower self's survival skills, like the deadly habit of *self-justification*."

Jesus laughed. "I was wondering how you were going to tie that in. I see perfectly what you are getting at. What did your fellow chelas say when you introduced the Wordsworthian approach to spiritual survival?"

"Nothing. It seems that whatever I have to say about the Way goes straight to the heart of an issue and my fellow chelas get overwhelmed and say nothing."

"Perhaps they cannot stand to see their own reflection in the mirror that you hold up for them," Jesus said, and winked to let me know that I was right in my intuition.

"To see their own false self, you mean?" I asked, just to be sure.

"Exactly," Jesus replied. "That part of a person's nature that has to be resolved for one to grow in spiritual consciousness will always justify itself to keep from being transformed into an angel of light; but that's life."

I laughed. "I know. But can't you just see the lower self squirming to justify itself? I squirmed so many times to protect my false self from being found out that it still makes me sick to think about it. How about you, J? Did you — *of course you did!* You could not have avoided confronting your own shadow on your journey to wholeness, could you?"

"Of course not. I justified myself with the best of them," Jesus said, smiling at my insight into the life process. "So let's spell out this technique of *self-justification* that the lower self uses to protect itself from being transformed into an angel of light."

"Maybe we should tell the reader what we mean by an angel of light?"

"Yes, of course," Jesus said, happy to shed light on St. Paul's puzzling comment about Satan. "Paul said in his Second Letter to the Corinthians that even Satan would be transformed into an angel of light. Satan is the archetypal lower self of man. As one grows in spiritual consciousness he transforms his lower self into an angel of light, which is simply a metaphor for spiritualizing one's unresolved self. Is that clear?"

"Clear enough," I said. "Now we can define what we mean by *self-justification*."

"You explain it," Jesus said, with a wave of his hand.

"I'd love to. I've used this *self-justification* defense to protect my ego so often in my life that the mere thought of it makes me cringe, and I'll give you the simplest explanation possible with one humiliating illustration."

"By all means, I'd love to hear it," Jesus said.

"And so would the reader," I said, and summoned my courage to confess one of my most embarrassing character flaws. "Most people have been caught in a lie, and if they haven't they will be one day because I doubt that anyone can go through life without getting caught in a lie. Well, I got caught many times in a lie before I became conscious of how my shadow kept me blind to myself. Even after I became conscious of my false self I still persisted in justifying myself when I was pressured by my shadow to lie. To justify oneself is to protect one's false self from being revealed for what it is. But we have to make it absolutely clear that this false self is not simply an aspect of one's persona. It is that, certainly; but it's also an autonomous self in its own right, and it will do whatever it can to keep from being resolved. So it justifies itself. It does this by defending its false nature, however absurd and foolish it may appear in light of the cold reality of the truth. That's what I meant by squirming. The false self squirms as it scratches for ground to stand on once it has been found out; and I blush at the number of times that I got caught in a lie and made a fool of myself trying to justify my false self. So the whole point of this explanation is to reveal the dual nature of the self, because without understanding that we have a lower and a higher self we will never be initiated into the science of spiritual growth."

"Excellent," said Jesus. "And I would further add that the false self can be very aggressive, rude, and dangerous when it has been found out. One can become so trapped by their false self that they will do anything to hold onto their control, like the abusive husband who blames his wife for making him strike her. This type can become so extreme in their efforts to stay in control that they often become criminals and social deviants. *Self-justification* is not for them, because they choose not to justify their falseness; rather, they assert themselves with conscious intent. And the more they assert themselves, the more real their false self feels to them; and this satisfies their ego's greatest need to be."

"Wow! Where did that come from? You're absolutely right! I never thought of the aggressive liar, the social deviant, the clever cheat, and charming deceiver, the wife abuser; but that's what the person hell-bent on control would be, wouldn't he? Rather than justify himself he asserts himself with conscious intent. *What an incredible insight, J!"*

"Yes," Jesus said, smiling at my outburst. "He or she does not feel that they have to justify what they are. They have the power to foist what they are upon the world; and if not foist, they manipulate the world to their own ends because they have to be in control."

I chuckled as a thought came to mind. "May I be allowed an observation here?"

"By all means," Jesus said.

"This speaks to the logic of the self-deceiver," I said, still laughing.

"Why are you laughing?" Jesus asked.

"I'm laughing at the thought of how self-serving the logic of self-deceivers can be even when they are forced to confront their cognitive dissonance with the cold hard facts of life," I replied, and laughed some more at the absurdity. "Watching self-deceivers use logic to serve their own selfish needs has to be one of the most pathetic comedies in the theater of life; and I know, because I was a star player many times in this tragic comedy. But let me give you another example from life at large. Canada was in the throes of a political crisis a few years ago. The province of Quebec wanted to separate from Canada, so they held a referendum in Quebec to see what the people wanted. Quebec lost the referendum, but for the Quebec separatist party that only meant they had lost that particular referendum. There would be future referendums, and when they got the vote they wanted they would separate. So if the logic of the vote did not satisfy their desire to separate, it was not honored; but if it satisfied their desire to separate then Canada would have to honor the referendum and let Quebec separate. That's self-serving logic at its best; and the lower self of man can become a slave to this impulse to reason falsely. It's like saying: *if I get what I want, it's logical and right; but if I don't get what I want, it's not logical and wrong.* And I'll tell you, J; trying to get a self-deceiver to see that they use logic to serve their own selfish ends is like trying to fit a square peg into a round hole. *It can't be done!"*

Jesus laughed. "Life will teach them in good time. Alright, O; which two sayings did you have in mind for discussion this morning?"

"Let me say just one more thing about this self-serving logic to make it absolutely clear for the reader how the false self reasons," I said, still chomping at the bit.

"Certainly," Jesus said.

"Self-serving logic is wanting your cake and eating it too!"

"Exactly," said Jesus, grinning at my insight.

"Alright, let's get to your sayings now. The first saying I want to decode is your cryptic narrow way saying." I picked up my Bible and read from Mathew, Chapter 7, verses 13 and 14: ***"Enter ye in at the strait gate: for wide is the gate, and broad is the way, that leadeth to destruction, and many there be which go in thereat; Because straight is the gate, and narrow is the way, which leadeth unto life, and few there be that find it."***

"Wonderful," said Jesus. "This should give the reader a good glimpse of just how difficult it is to be initiated into the secret teaching with this saying."

"Hold on. I want to couple this saying with your saying about little children, because these two sayings work hand in hand," I said, and turned to Chapter 18, verses 3, 4, and 5: ***"Verily I say unto you, Except ye be converted and become as little children, ye shall not enter the kingdom of heaven. Whosoever therefore shall humble himself as this little child, the same is greatest in the kingdom of heaven. And whoso shall receive one such little child in my name receiveth me."***

"I can see why you would couple these sayings," Jesus said, nodding approval. "One has to be as an innocent child to enter the narrow way. That's an excellent point of entry into the Way of Christ—"

"What you call the kingdom of heaven," I interpreted.

"Yes, of course. Alright; since you coupled these two sayings, why don't you tell the reader what I meant to say to the world?"

"But you did say it! The world just didn't hear you, that's all!"

431

OREST STOCCO

"Yes, I did say it; didn't I? So how are you going to get the reader to hear the Word behind the words of Jesus?"

"Wow!" I exclaimed again. "That's precisely what we're trying to do with our whole dialogue — *get the reader to hear the Word behind the words of Jesus!"*

Smiling at my emotional outburst, Jesus said, "I think that would make an excellent chapter title for our talk this morning."

"It would," I agreed, and jotted the title in my notebook. "Alright; to decode these sayings I think we have to paint a bigger picture. We've already painted the picture of Soul's journey through life in the *Reader's Digest* version of the DPG, but we need a clear context of Soul's growth to decode your sayings this morning."

"By all means. Metaphor can only reveal so much, and no more. Please explain what I meant by my metaphors of the narrow way and innocence of a child."

"Let's start by reminding the reader of the three levels of human consciousness — the outer, middle, and inner levels. Soul's journey through life begins in the exoteric outer stage, and it evolves all the way to the mesoteric middle stage where the straight gate of your sayings can be found. For the reader's understanding, let me repeat that Soul's journey from the first stage to the second stage is governed by karma. Soul is an atom of God, but it does not have an individual identity until it experiences the dawning of self-consciousness in the primordial life of man, as I did in my lifetime as Grunt; and then the atom of God evolves in self-identity from lifetime to lifetime. Through karmic growth Soul finally evolves enough to want to be more spiritually self-realized, and this happens when Soul gravitates to the mesoteric stage of evolution. How am I doing so far?"

Jesus did not reply. He motioned for me to continue.

"Okay. It's worth mentioning here that just as the acorn seed is encoded to become an oak tree, so is the atom of God encoded to become a spiritually self-realized, God-conscious Soul; so every Soul is driven by this divine conatus for total self-identity. And by total self-identity I mean spiritual self-realization and God-consciousness. It doesn't really matter whether people believe in God or not, all Souls are driven by this inner drive for God-realization consciousness. Is that clear enough?"

432

"Yes," said Jesus. "Please, continue."

"It doesn't matter how many lifetimes it takes for karma to make Soul ready for the Way, it will be made ready by the natural process of evolution. When Soul has resolved enough of the lower energies of life to gravitate to the mesoteric stage it will sense the mystery of its own spiritual nature, and one will become a seeker in spite of himself. This was the theme of my first novel memoir."

"Yes, I read it," Jesus said; "and it was an excellent introduction to the narrow way of my teaching. Please, continue."

"Thank you. Okay. I want to remind the reader that spiritual growth in the first stage is a natural process. Through trial and error, Soul learns its karmic lessons. When Soul has resolved enough of its lower self to sense its spiritual nature, it will seek answers to life's purpose. Soul will do this in spite of itself, because it has no control over its inner drive for total self-realization consciousness. And it's at this point of Soul's journey through the exoteric stage that I'm concerned with when I rant about Christianity's hold upon Soul. There are many Souls out there that are ready to enter the narrow way of your teaching, but they can't because they're constrained by their idiotic Christian faith—"

"Enough already!" Jesus shouted, cutting me off. "We've heard enough of your rant, O. Let's get on with your interpretation of my sayings."

I smiled self-consciously. "It bothers you, doesn't it?" I said, justifying my rant.

"Yes, it does. How many times do I have to be reminded of Christianity's blunder? So the Gospel writers blew it. Can we set the record straight now?"

I laughed, and Jesus couldn't help himself and joined me. "I'm just being humorous," he said, justifying his emotional response to my rant.

"Good," I said, appreciating his playfulness. "The reader will appreciate that. This godly image of Jesus Christ obfuscates the fact that you were very much a man before you became one with your Father in heaven. If I may continue?"

"Please do," Jesus said, with that mystic smile that teased me.

"Okay. Life makes Soul ready for the Way through the natural evolutionary process of karma and reincarnation, but to be initiated

433

into the Way one has to find this straight gate of yours; and the only way to find it is by transforming the consciousness of one's lower self enough for Soul to be as pure in heart as an innocent child."

"Good," said Jesus. "But that's still too vague. Can you be more specific?"

"The only way I can do that would be to give an example of what it means to be as innocent as a child. If I may, in your saying you go on to talk about how one can become as an innocent child. You talk about how the lower self tries to keep the higher self from entering the straight gate of the Way. Let me quote the passage. This is from Mathew Chapter 18, verses 6 to 11: *`But whoso shall offend one of these little ones which believe in me, it were better for him that a millstone were hanged about his neck, and that he were drowned in the depth of the sea. Woe unto the world because of offences! for it must needs be that offences come; but woe to that man by whom the offence cometh! Wherefore if thy hand or thy foot offend thee, cut them off, and cast them from thee: it is better for thee to enter into life halt or maimed, rather than having two hands or two feet to be cast into everlasting fire. And if thine eye offend thee, pluck it out, and cast it from thee: it is better for thee to enter into life with one eye, rather than having two eyes to be cast into hell fire. Take heed that ye despise not one of these little ones; for I say unto you, That in heaven their angels do always behold the face of my Father which is in heaven. For the Son of man is come to save that which is lost.* " I stopped reading and put the Bible down.

Jesus nodded several times, and then motioned for me to continue.

"And then you go on about the lost sheep and rejoicing when the Son of man finds it, and so on," I continued. "The point of all this dramatic — and I do think you overplayed your hand here with all that hellfire nonsense, because your metaphor for the natural process of karmic reconciliation has given the evangelists all the ammunition they need to scare people into holding onto the illusion of instant salvation through Jesus Christ. I wish you wouldn't have used that metaphor of hellfire, J. It's impossible now to undo all the damage it has done to the psyche of man."

"As you said," Jesus calmly replied, "those were militant times. I had to be no less confrontational with the negative forces of life than they were with Soul. I had no choice but to demarcate the distinction between the lower and higher self of man the way I did. I had to get the world to see that there is a price to pay to enter the narrow way of my teaching. So if the lower self did something that kept Soul from entering the narrow way, like stealing a loaf of bread, the hand that stole the bread would be the hand of one's lower self. When I say that it would be better to cut it off than suffer eternal damnation, all I'm saying is that the consciousness of the lower self that has the impulse to steal has to be transformed in order for Soul to enter the narrow way. It's the consciousness of the lower self that I'm referring to when I talk about getting rid of one's hand, foot, or eye; not the literal hand, foot, or eye. This should have been obvious, but apparently it wasn't. But I did make the distinction between the lower and higher self; and I'm delighted that you coupled these sayings, because only by transforming the consciousness of the lower self can one become as an innocent child and enter the narrow way."

As happy as I was for Christ's explanation, I held fast to my conviction. "I understand why you did what you did to get the Word out there, but I still wish you hadn't been so dramatic. Evangelists intoxicate themselves with their false interpretation of your teaching, and they perpetuate this myth of eternal damnation to the point where it becomes virtually impossible to get through to these fools—"

Jesus shot up his hand again, but deliberately said nothing.

"I know, I'm ranting again; but I can't help myself. It makes me sick to see these righteous fools trying to save the world. They're even in the White House now. But I'll stop. Let's get back to the point. What you meant for one to be as an innocent child to enter the kingdom of heaven was to spiritualize the consciousness of one's lower self enough to gravitate to the mesoteric stage of evolution; and one becomes as an innocent child by becoming pure in heart. This can only be done one way, and that's to stop being selfish. I say this because this is how I entered the straight gate of Christ's Way. There you have it, J. Did I do your sayings justice?"

"Yes; but I would like to hear more about how you entered the straight gate of my teaching. However, before you answer that let's explain that this gate is the same in all spiritual teachings. This gate can be found in every person, because only through the transformation of one's lower self can Soul enter into the higher consciousness of life, which you call the mesoteric stage of evolution and I called kingdom of heaven."

"The passkey to the straight gate then is the secret knowledge of the transformation of consciousness. The more one resolves the consciousness of his lower self, the more he turns the lock and is allowed entry into the mesoteric stage of evolution. One enters the narrow way by not being selfish, because selfishness characterizes the consciousness of the lower self and keeps one blind to his higher self. Is that clear enough now?"

"Yes; but just how did you go about transforming the consciousness of your selfish nature?" Jesus asked. "I'd like to know, and so would the reader."

"With great indignity," I said, and laughed. "The abuse that I suffered for all of my conscious efforts to be a good person cost me my relationship with my family and friends. As you implied in your teaching, when one lives the Way consciously he brings a sword into his life and severs himself from the world. The sword that I chose to sever myself from the world was the two-edged sword of truth and goodness. I made it my personal ethic to be as truthful and good as I could be, and with my Wordsworthian ideal I went out into the world and hacked away at the consciousness of my own selfish nature by laboring good on good to fix with uncompromising honesty; and the more I hacked away the more I severed myself from the consciousness of my family, friends, and the world at large!"

Jesus smiled, but remained silent. I continued: "That's how I gave birth to my saying, *the more you give of yourself, the more of yourself you will have to give; and the less you give of yourself, the less of yourself you will have to give.* But lest we confuse the reader here, like you did with your Big Gun saying of dying to your life to save your life, let me explain that the self that I gave away was my lower self, and the self that I had more to give of was my higher self, because I grew in my higher self as I gave away my lower self. In fact, I can make this even more clear by expressing it this way: **the more selfish you are, the less your real self you will be; and the less selfish you are, the more your real self you will be.** This is why good people in society are fair and just in their relationships with life, and why self-serving people can never be trusted!"

Jesus had a grin from ear to ear. "So by being a good and truthful person you created enough virtue to work your way through the straight gate of my teaching; is that the gnostic wisdom of your experience?"

"To the surprise of the world!" I exclaimed.

"Why surprise?" Jesus asked, with a puzzled look.

"Because the world doesn't expect anyone to enter the narrow way of your teaching, that's why! The world knows it's there, and they all pretend to seek it; but when it comes to paying the price to enter few Souls will pay it. And I can tell you from experience that the world knows if you have paid the final price or not. From the moment you enter the narrow way the world will never again treat you as one of its own. It doesn't matter what you do, the world will always sense that you're no longer one of them, and you will be resented for reasons that the world will never be able to explain but which you and I both know to be one's mastery over the appetites of his lower self. And if I'm not mistaken, you said this in St. John's Gospel. Let me look it up…. It's in John 15, verse 19: `*If ye were of the world, the world would love his own: but because ye are not of the world, but I have chosen you out of the world, therefore the world hateth you.*' This is why you said that to enter into the kingdom of heaven one must be in the world but not of the world. 'Assume the virtue and it shall be yours,' as Shakespeare expressed it."

"BINGO!" Jesus exclaimed, shooting his finger into the air like an excited bingo player who just won the monthly jackpot. "Once you enter the narrow way you are no longer of the world because you are no longer a slave to your selfish needs. Soul is in charge of its destiny now, and the cycle of karma and reincarnation can finally be broken. The world senses this and resents you for it because it feels threatened. *Excellent, O! I'm delighted by the progress we made this morning!*"

"Good," I said, laughing at Jesus' burst of emotion. "I can only hope that you're this excited when we get to your next saying."

"Which saying would that be?" Jesus asked.

"I'll tell you when we meet again," I said, teasing Jesus.

"As you wish. Until our next talk, then," Jesus said, and took his leave.

69. *The Psychology of Christ's Teaching*

"Now we come to the most disturbing of all your sayings, J," I said, as I poured us a cup of green tea. "And to be honest with you, I don't even know how to broach the subject; so if you don't mind I'd like to do a short HU before we begin. Would you mind?"

"Not at all. I welcome the opportunity to HU with you, O."

"Thank you," I said, and closed my eyes. After a few deep breaths I started chanting the most beautiful Love Song to God, and Jesus joined me.

After a few minutes of singing HU I felt myself leaving my body. Slowly at first, and then much more swiftly I felt myself being pulled back through time, and before long I found myself in the time of Jesus' life on Earth. I was with Jesus and his disciples. They were gathered in the cool shade of a thick grove of trees out of the hot afternoon sun. I heard Jesus talking to his disciples about his plan to be crucified, how it was going to unfold because he had been called by God to reveal the secret teaching to the world through the sacrifice of his life on the cross. He told them that he would incur the wrath of the rabbis at the temple in Jerusalem who would condemn him as a heretic, and that he would be betrayed by one of his disciples, and this would set into motion the vehicle of his teaching to the world; and he promised his disciples that he would come back to them after his crucifixion, and with a look of disbelief on their face as they listened to Jesus I felt myself being pulled back to my body, and I opened my eyes and saw Jesus smiling at me.

"Do you understand now?" he said, to my astonishment.

"I don't know. Are you referring to my Soul travel experience?"

"Yes," replied Jesus.

"You know where I went?"

"Yes."

"Why was I given this experience?" I asked, still in awe.

"To reveal the truth of my saying *'I am the way, the truth, and the life.'*"

"But Spirit is the way, the truth, and the life; not Jesus Christ, as such," I replied, feeling a little disoriented by my Soul travel experience.

"Yes, Holy Spirit is the way, the truth, and the life; but when I became one with my Father in heaven Spirit and I became one. There is no distinction between the man Jesus and the Word of God," replied Jesus, his eyes alight with love.

"If you don't mind, I'd like a moment," I said, and closed my eyes and silently called upon the Inner Master. *"I'm in some pretty deep waters here. I need your assistance. Please Z, guide my every thought."* I opened my eyes, and Jesus was staring at me.

"You need not fear, O," he said, with a radiant smile. "There are as many paths to divine truth as there are Souls, and yours is one of the most direct. Just relax and let Soul speak as we explore the secret meaning of my sayings."

"To be honest with you, J; I don't know how to broach the truth of the saying that I had planned to talk about this morning."

"Which saying did you have in mind?" Jesus asked.

I turned to my Bible and looked at the passage. I had underlined and circled it in red ink. I read it again, silently. I had read it half a dozen times before Jesus appeared, and I still did not know how to broach the secret meaning of his saying; but I knew that I had to because this was the saying that made of Jesus the savior of the world.

"Would you read it for me, please?" Jesus asked.

"I hesitate to do so. I have to tell you, J; of all your sayings, this is the one I feel most uncomfortable talking about."

"Why?" he asked, deeply curious.

"I honestly don't know. Maybe because it's the saying that gave birth to centuries of symbolic meaning, and I feel a psychic resistance from the spirit of Christianity that wants to keep me from revealing the truth of this saying."

"Why? Because it will despoil the sanctity of the symbolic meaning that the Church has conferred upon my saying?" Jesus said, so matter-of-factly that it made me take notice.

"You know what saying I want to talk about, don't you?" I asked.

"Of course I do. So why don't you read it for the record," Jesus replied.

I turned to my Bible and in a nervous voice read from St. John's Gospel, Chapter 6, verses 47 to 51, and 53 to 58: *"Verily, verily I say unto you, He that believeth on me hath everlasting life. I am that bread of life. Your fathers did eat manna in the wilderness, and are dead. This is the bread which cometh down from heaven, that a man may eat thereof, and not die. I am the living bread which came down from heaven: if any man eat of this bread, he shall live forever: and the bread that I will give is my flesh, which I will give for the life of the world...Verily, verily, I say unto you, Except ye eat the flesh of the Son of man, and drinketh his blood, ye have no life in you. Whoso eateth my flesh and drinketh my blood, hath eternal life; and I will raise him up at the last day. For my flesh is meat indeed, and my blood is drink indeed. He that eateth my flesh and drinketh my blood dwelleth in me, and I in him. As the living Father hath sent me, and I live by the Father: so he that eateth me, even he shall live by me. This is that bread which came down from heaven: not as your fathers did eat manna, and are dead: he that eateth of this bread shall live forever."*

I stopped reading and turned to Jesus. He smiled and said, "Now why don't you read what I said next. That will explain everything you have just read."

I put my glasses on again and read, *"Doth this offend you? What and if ye shall see the Son of man ascend up where he was before? It is the spirit that quickeneth: the flesh profiteth nothing: the words that I speak to you, they are spirit and they are life. But there are some of you that believeth not."*

"Now do you understand why you were allowed to witness my private talk with my disciples about my crucifixion?" Jesus asked.

"No," I said, still feeling the deadly seriousness of Christ's saying. Even his disciples felt it to be a hard saying and had trouble accepting it. And one disciple didn't.

Suddenly, I remembered Jesus telling me why Judas had betrayed him, and there it was — *in Christ's saying!*

I looked at Jesus and said, "So Judas did betray you because he couldn't penetrate the mystery of your teaching? He resented the other disciples because they understood you and he didn't, and he turned on you because he couldn't suffer his own lack of sight!"

Jesus smiled. "In essence, yes. Judas was chosen but he was not called. I let Judas stay with my disciples because he served my purpose."

"For your crucifixion plot?" I asked, just to be certain.

"Yes. I knew that he would betray me because that was his nature. The unbeliever will never admit his inability to penetrate the mysteries of life, and to protect his own vanity he cloaks himself in unbelief. I was not absolutely certain that Judas would betray me, of course. After all, he did have free will. He was free to walk away altogether, but he didn't; and so the plot for my crucifixion was set into motion."

"But why, J? Why did you put yourself through that horrible fate? Were you so convinced that the sacrifice of your life on the cross would have such a powerful effect upon the world?" I asked, with a desperate need to understand his crucifixion.

"Yes," Jesus replied. "I had to take the logic of the Way of Christ all the way to my sacrificial death upon the cross. I had to be living proof that lest one die to his life he will never be born in Spirit. That was the pathology of my teaching, and I could not help myself. I know now that I was crazy with God, but I had to do what I felt compelled by Holy Spirit to do. It came to me in a revelation that I had to die on the cross to tell the world that the way into the kingdom of heaven was through the death of the lower self of man. That's why I did it. And if I had to do it over again—" Jesus stopped in mid sentence. I waited. He stared at me, and then completed his sentence — "I would not have been crucified. I would not have used Judas the way I did. I would have let the karma of the world unfold according to its own causes. *I was crazy with God, O. I was crazy with God...."*

Dead silence. I couldn't believe what I had just heard. "Are you saying that because of your crucifixion — *of course that's what you're saying!* You created a new cause with your crucifixion for the historical effects that followed! Was that your intention, to set the world on a new course of destiny?"

Jesus did not reply. He just looked at me, his eyes seeming to look back in time. Then very softly he said, "I revealed the truth of my saying in what I said later. *'The words that I speak, they are spirit, and they are life.'* But the world failed to make the connection and opened the door to the inscrutable mystery that followed." Jesus stopped, took a sip of tea, and said, "As this green tea will help to remove the toxins from one's body, so do I hope to remove the toxins of misunderstanding from my teaching. The world needs to hear that by flesh and blood I meant the eternal life-giving energy of Holy Spirit. As one eats of my flesh and drinks of my blood he feeds his spiritual self and grows in spiritual consciousness. For the world to make of my flesh and blood the symbol that it has become is to miss the whole point of my teaching. I was talking about the living Word, not my flesh and blood. I am the way, the truth, and the life of the living Word; and as one *lives* the living Word of my teaching he feeds his spiritual body and grows in the consciousness of his eternal nature. This is what I meant with my hard saying. I am the flesh and blood of the living Word of God, because I am one with the Word of God. To eat my flesh and drink my blood man has to live by the Word of God. *My God, could anything be clearer than that?"*

Jesus stopped talking. I was stunned. I just sat there overwhelmed. I felt the enormity of the consequences of Christ's revelation fill every pore of my being until I could stand it no longer and said, *"I can't believe what I've just heard!"*

Jesus smiled, but said nothing.

"I just can't think of anything to say. Why did you reveal this to me?"

"To detoxify the body of the Church," Jesus answered.

"Then the Pope should start drinking green tea," I said, and burst into laughter.

Jesus laughed also. "That's good, O. So, do you feel better now?"

"I needed that relief. *Good God, you laid a heavy on me!"*

"I know," said Jesus. "But we are coming to the end of our dialogue, and we have to tell your reader the truth about the Way of Christ. Once again, let me reiterate. By flesh and blood of Jesus Christ I mean the living Word of God. The living Word of God is the secret teaching of spiritual transformation. I did not die for the sins of the world. I died and resurrected to reveal Soul's power over the death of one's lower self. As I said, I died to death, not to life. The kingdom of heaven is my metaphor for the secret teaching of how to sacrifice one's lower self for spiritual liberation from the endless cycle of life and death. I am only a messenger of the Way. The Way is the living Word of God, and the Word of God is Holy Spirit. There, is that clear enough for your reader?"

Jesus spoke slowly for me to catch his every word on paper. When he stopped I put my pen down and said, "We're not done yet. I still have a few more sayings I want to decode. I have to tell you, J; I did not look forward to this morning's talk. I had no idea what Spirit was going to reveal. I'm sure glad we had it. This talk has opened a door to such spiritual clarity that just maybe some of the toxins in the body of your Church may be flushed out. I certainly hope so, anyway."

"Despite the fact that the world has to find its own way," Jesus said, with a snicker.

"Don't get smart! I do care, you know. I just don't want to get caught up in world karma, that's all!"

"Oh, so that's it; is it?" Jesus said, with that playful twinkle in his eyes. "You want to wash your hands of the whole thing, do you?"

"Yeah, right! I care for the world, J; but I will not be bound by my care. That's all I meant. After all, what's spiritual freedom if not the freedom to let Soul find its own way to God? If the Spiritual Law of Karma means anything at all, the more freedom you give to the world to find its own way the more freedom the world will have to give to you — *and that, to borrow a phrase from Jesus Christ, is the pathology of my teaching!"*

Jesus laughed, and laughed, and laughed.

443

70. *A Foretelling Dream*

The Sunday after my talk with Jesus Cathy and I went for the last of our fall leafing excursions. There was still plenty of color on the trees, and the various shades of red, orange, and russet were stunning; but as majestic as nature was in our favorite season my mind was still on Christ's revelation, and especially my Soul travel experience.

"I can't believe that no one has broken the code of Christ's sayings," I said to Cathy as we drove the scenic Horseshow Valley Road. "Someone else must have, but I've never read a record of it anywhere. Gurdjieff taught the same principles, and he did call his teaching 'esoteric Christianity,' but aside from him and what some Christian mystics wrote that's all I've read of anyone living the interior life of Christ's sayings; and to be honest with you sweetheart, my Jesus book is starting to scare me."

"Why? It can't be any more powerful than your last book. Why should it scare you?"

"I don't know. My last talk with Jesus was different. I know we crossed the point of no return with our talk because of the dream I had two nights ago; but—"

"What dream?" Cathy interrupted me.

"I dreamt of Father Meyer, my old parish priest," I said, bringing my disturbing dream back to mind. "I was an altar boy in my youth, and in my dream I was in his church; but he told me to get out of his church because he didn't want me there."

"Why?" Cathy asked.

"He said he had read what I wrote about Jesus and didn't want me in his church, so he kicked me out."

"Really?" Cathy said, with a quizzical look.

"Yes. So, what does that tell you?" I asked, anxious to hear what she thought.

"I don't know," she said. "What does it tell you?"

"It tells me that *Jesus Wears Dockers* must be published on the inner planes already, and the effects are being felt," I said, unable to think of any other reason.

"If it's published on the inner then it means it will be published out here, won't it?" Cathy said, with a big smile on her face.

"It will eventually. To be honest, I think my dream tells me that I've gone beyond the tipping point with this book. It can't be stopped now. The truth about Christ's sayings is revealed, and it doesn't matter if I stop these talks today the die has been cast."

"That's good," Cathy said, with a triumphant tone in her voice. "It's about time someone shed light on Christ's teaching. I've never read the Bible, but I just think that what the Church teaches is wrong. Jesus did not die for our sins. We have to resolve our own karma, and I think it's time Christians woke up to that; don' you?"

"That and much more," I said.

"What did the priest say about your book?" Cathy asked.

"Nothing. All he said was that he read it and didn't want me in his church."

"It must have been too much for him," Cathy said.

"My book shocked him into denial. I think the Dream Master has forewarned me of the denial that Christianity is going to go into when *Jesus Wears Dockers* gets published out here. That's what I think the dream means."

"Do you really think so?" Cathy asked, with concern in her voice.

"Yes. Christianity has too much invested in the great lie of Jesus Christ's life and death on the cross. It will never admit to the truth. As Jesus said, the unbeliever protects his vanity by cloaking himself in unbelief. Christianity has an enormous amount of vanity to protect. Its conceit that Jesus died for the sins of the world defines Christianity, so it has to go into denial once this book comes out. That's what my dream is telling me."

"That's the Church. I don't think every Christian who reads your book will go into denial. I think your book will open a lot of eyes."

"I hope so."

"How much more do you have to write?"

445

"We have a few more sayings to decode and then I can bring it home. I have my closing chapter already sketched out in my mind."

"You do? What's the title?" she asked.

I chuckled at the irony of my closing chapter. "I can't reveal that yet."

"Why not?" she asked, in her pleading voice.

"Sweetheart, you know I never talk about my writing until I get it on paper. Once it's on paper it's safe to talk about, but not before. Hemingway taught me that."

"I know; but I had to ask," she said, and laughed.

"So what do you make of my dream?" I asked, anxious for her impression.

"I've heard most of the chapters you've written, and if your old parish priest denies the truth of Christ's teaching then he's just a big fool. Can we enjoy our drive now?"

"Okay," I said, and dropped the subject.

71. *Be a Good Person, and Let the Universe Unfold as It Should*

Cathy was off to work and I had the day off. If Jesus wanted, we could have a long talk. I had coupled two more sayings, and it was possible we could bring closure to our dialogue; so I was both excited and apprehensive. "What kind of tea would you like this morning?" I asked, after bidding Jesus good morning.

"Surprise me," he said.

"Okay," I said, and went downstairs to put the kettle on. I selected a healing tea and poured the boiling water into the teapot, got two cups, and returned upstairs. "I have Echinacea Elderberry," I said, as I placed the pot and cups on the coffee table strewn with books, papers on literary agencies that Cathy had downloaded from the Internet, and a newspaper article on Bishop John Shelby Spong's new book *The Sins of Scripture* that was resting on the top of half a dozen other books on the coffee table.

"Why Echinacea?" Jesus asked.

"I'm low on energy from my last job, so I'm just fortifying my immune system," I said. "Besides, it's a very pleasant tasting tea."

Jesus poured our tea, took a careful sip, and said, "Yes, it is pleasant. Don't you find it strange that people don't do that for their spiritual life?"

"What? Fortify their spiritual immune system?" I said, sensing a door opening.

"Yes. If people only knew how vital it is to have a healthy spiritual immune system they wouldn't fall prey to all those nasty little negative viruses out there," Jesus said, as though foreseeing our whole talk. "That's where your spiritual community has the advantage over other spiritual paths. Your path has the sacred HU and the spiritual exercises of the Light and Sound of God to fortify your spiritual immune system."

"I know, and I thank my lucky stars for finding this path; but the concept of a spiritual immune system eludes most people. It takes a certain amount of spiritual maturity to see the metaphysics of the spiritual life. And yet your gospel speaks to this issue. That's the irony of Christianity. As coincidence would have it, the two sayings that I've coupled for our talk this morning address this very question of the spiritual life of man."

I turned to my desk and flipped the pages of my Bible and read the Gospel of John, Chapter 3, verses 3 through 8: *"Verily, verily, I say unto thee, Except a man be born again, he cannot see the kingdom of God.* Nicodemus said unto him, How can a man be born when he is old? Can he enter the second time into his mother's womb, and be born? *Verily, verily, I say unto thee, Except a man be born of water and of the Spirit, he cannot enter into the kingdom of God. That which is born of the flesh is flesh; and that which is born of the Spirit, is spirit. Marvel not that I said unto thee, Ye must be born again. The wind bloweth where it listeth, and thou hearest the sound thereof, but canst not tell whence it cometh, and whither it goeth: so is every one that is born of the Spirit."*

I stopped reading, flipped the pages, and read from St. John again, Chapter 4, verses 13 and 14: *"Whosoever drinketh of this water shall thirst again. But whosoever drinketh of the water that I shall give him shall never thirst; but the water that I shall give him shall be in man a water springing up into everlasting life."* I turned to Jesus, and said, "I think we can bring our dialogue to closure with these two sayings."

"Spirit willing," Jesus replied, with a twinkle in his eyes.

"We could drag this dialogue on forever if we wanted to, such is the breadth of the Word of God; but this book has its own mind, and it's telling me it's time to bring closure," I said, and gave Jesus a big smile to emphasize my feelings.

"Yes, of course. A writer knows when his book is coming to closure. If that's what you feel, then so be it. We'll just let Soul speak and see what comes out. So what is it you wish to say about these two sayings?"

"The thought came to me while I was reading them that we should tie these sayings in with what we were just talking about. What do you think?"

"The spiritual immune system?"

"Yes."

"By all means. It's all related. A healthy spiritual immune system needs the water of everlasting life to stay healthy; so please, tie it all in for the reader."

"I'd like to, because the spiritual rebirth that you talk about here can't happen unless one has a healthy spiritual immune system. Your whole teaching has to do with nourishing the spiritual self. But we should explain what your sayings imply here. I've given this a lot of thought the last couple of days, and I came up with a simple analogy to create an image that I hope will help the reader get a fix on the basic premise of your teaching."

"Please," said Jesus, with a little snicker; "I'd love to hear how you capture the basic premise of spiritual transformation with a simple analogy."

I smiled at the sarcastic tone in Jesus' voice. "I didn't mean to sound so vain," I said, as I quickly centered myself. "The image just came to me, so I'm going with it. After all, that's how the spiritual imagination works, doesn't it? It creates images for us to see reality more clearly, doesn't it?"

"You're quite right, O; Soul thinks in images, and imagination is man's salvation from the limitations of the mind," Jesus replied, and took another sip of tea.

"So there is a distinction between the mind and Soul?" I asked.

"Soul uses the intellect to think, but the less spiritual one is the less the light of Holy Spirit shines through the mind. The intellect uses the energy of the Mental Plane to think and reason. Soul uses the energy of the Soul Plane to think and reason. The difference between the Mental and Soul Planes is that the energy of the Mental Plane is impure. It is the positive-negative energy of the lower worlds, while the energy of the Soul Plane is pure Spirit; so the more one reasons from the Soul Plane the truer his reason will be."

I stared at Jesus in awe. He waited a moment or two, and continued. "This ties in with my saying of the water of everlasting life. This water comes from the Soul Plane of Consciousness. All I am referring to in this saying is the spiritual life force of Soul Consciousness. Lest your reader be confused, the water of everlasting life refers more specifically to the Word of God *lived*, because it is only in the *living* of the Word of God that one can tap into the boundless river of Soul Consciousness. This is what you have learned to do, O. This is why the *Shabda Dhun* flows so freely through you. You have learned the secret of tapping into the Soul Plane of Consciousness—"

"If I may," I said, interrupting Jesus. "I'm not quite sure I know what you mean by *Shabda Dhun.* I've heard of it. As a matter of fact, that phrase came to me one day while I was writing, and I did look it up; but I forgot what it means."

"Look it up again," Jesus said.

I went to my bookshelf and got my spiritual lexicon that had been assembled for our spiritual community by the Living Soul Master and found *Shabda Dhun.* I read the definition out loud: "One of the names of the Voice that is the ESSENCE, the Holy Ghost, the Comforter, the Divine Spirit that gives life to all."

"Good," said Jesus. "You can see what I mean by water of everlasting life, then. It is the water of the *Shabda Dhun,* the source of all life, the eternal life force of Holy Spirit; but as I have said, one has to *live* by the Word of God to tap into the water of everlasting life. Now, you were saying something about a simple analogy?"

"Yes," I said, trying to think of the best way to express my thought. "I don't think the world has a clear picture of what you meant by spiritual rebirth. If it did, there wouldn't be so many Christian fools running around out there asking people if they are born again. These people have no idea what it takes to be born in Spirit. It doesn't happen with baptism, or by simply embracing you as their savior. Instant spiritual rebirth is a con, and it deceives the Christian even more than he already is. Spiritual rebirth as you meant it in your sayings has to do with what St. Paul called dying daily to one's lower self. Soul cannot come out of the womb of its human self until the Word of God has purified the consciousness of the lower self, and that doesn't happen for the asking. Spiritual rebirth can take one a lifetime of effort to realize, as well I should know. The image that popped into my mind was of the self of man divided into two halves, one white and one black. The white half symbolizes the spiritual self and the black half symbolizes the human self; and the whole concept of spiritual rebirth has to do with transforming the impure consciousness of the black half into the pure consciousness of the white half, and this can only happen by *living* the Word of God. Am I clear enough on that?"

Jesus nodded agreement, and motioned for me to continue.

"In other words, one has to live the spiritual life to purify the consciousness of his human self," I continued, letting Soul speak. "When the human self is pure enough for the spiritual self to come out in full conscious awareness into the human self, this is what you refer to as spiritual rebirth. And as glorious as it is to become conscious of our own immortal nature, it is also the beginning of a lot of heartache because the spiritual self is now out in the open and vulnerable to all the negative forces of life."

Jesus vigorously nodded agreement, and again motioned for me to continue.

I completed my thought: "After I came out of the womb of my human self that day in my mother's kitchen I was so sensitive to the negative forces of life that I began to suffer excruciating anguish, and I scrambled for spiritual energy to grow stronger in Spirit so I could survive as an awakened Soul. That's when I fell prey to that offshoot Christian solar cult teaching that promised me instant spiritual energy with their solar techniques — an experience I will regret to the day I die, but one which I had to have to resolve the karma of my past lifetime as Salaam, the mad Sufi."

Jesus took a sip of tea and put his cup down. "That explains my saying very nicely," he said, in his soft, non-judgmental voice. "I would stress that spiritual rebirth is an actual birth of the inner self; not a metaphorical birth. For emphasis, let's reiterate that man has only one self that is split in two, one spiritual and one human; but the spiritual self can only experience life through its human self. This is why it is so important to live by spiritual values. The more one lives the spiritual life, the more he nourishes his spiritual self; and the more the spiritual self grows the more whole Soul becomes. Being born again in Spirit simply means that the spiritual self has come out of the womb of its human self. This is why one should have a healthy spiritual immune system, because the spiritual self is very vulnerable to the negative forces of life when it is born into life, as you well know."

"Yes," I said, with a proud smile. "That should cover it, then," I added, delighted by how Christ's sayings had been revealed. "But before we move on we should stress that spiritual growth is not metaphorical; it is very real. The self is like the acorn seed growing into the oak tree of its potential. Just as the sapling oak needs sunlight, water, and nutrients to grow into a mighty oak tree, so does the sapling spiritual self need the water of everlasting life to grow into a God-conscious Soul; and by water of everlasting life I mean the life force of Holy Spirit. And your teaching is all about collecting this precious life force until Soul has grown enough in spiritual consciousness to seek total self-identity, which we can only do by transforming the consciousness of our lower human self. There, do you think we've done your sayings justice?"

"It all depends upon whether the reader accepts the essential premise of spiritual growth," Jesus said, not quite convinced of my explanation.

"What do you mean by essential premise?" I asked.

"That the spiritual self needs the energy of the creative life force to grow, and that my teaching is all about collecting this spiritual energy," Jesus replied.

"Yes, it is; and of all your techniques to collect this spiritual energy, self-sacrifice is your most intimidating because few Souls are willing to die to their lower self to be born in Spirit. I'm afraid to say this, J; but I doubt there are many Christians out there who have taken your teaching all the way to the birth of their spiritual self. The most they can do with your teaching is to build up enough good karma to gravitate to the Way; so at the risk of offending you, I have to tell you again that your teaching is out of context with the times because it's much too extreme. This is why the Way has been revealed to the modern world in the much kinder and gentler teachings of the Light and Sound of God."

Jesus did not respond. He just smiled and took another sip of tea.

"What, no comment?" I said, genuinely surprised.

"What's the point? You've obviously made up your mind about my teaching; so why don't we just leave it at that?" Jesus curtly replied.

"But I'd like to know if you agree with me or not," I insisted.

"I do and I don't. You have to keep in mind that Soul has to evolve through all the stages of the exoteric stage of life before it finds the straight gate of the Way, so it's only logical that many Souls will have to work their way through their Christian karma before they find the narrow path of the Way. As extreme as my teaching may be, it is still a big part of social consciousness. This is why I want to set the record straight and dispel the Gospel conspiracy. All those Christians out there who feel they have outgrown their faith," Jesus said, with a deliberate glance at Bishop Spong's new book *The Sins of Scripture*, "can revisit their faith with the clarity that our dialogue will offer them. Then they can choose to live by blind faith or the true meaning of my teaching."

"Touché!" I exclaimed, excited by Jesus' unbelievable candor. Then, smiling with embarrassment, I said, "I apologize for my spiritual arrogance."

"Apology accepted. Are we done now?" he said, and reached for his tea.

"Not quite," I said, repositioning myself in my chair. "I just got a nudge to clear up a serious point about our two sayings this morning. You said that unless one is born again in Spirit he would never enter the kingdom of heaven. This implies the either/or extremes of your teaching. In light of the Divine Plan of God these extremes do not exist, because Soul has all of eternity to find the narrow path of the Way. Let's remind the reader not to panic, because there's no need to fear not finding the Way in this lifetime. I would say to the reader to just concentrate on being a good person and let the universe unfold as it should."

"Well said!" Jesus exclaimed, taking me by surprise again. "So do you feel closure now? We've covered a lot of ground. There are a few more sayings we could talk about, but I feel the reader has all he needs to work them out on his own."

"I agree; except for one more saying that the Inner Master just now reminded me of, so I don't feel we have closure just yet. Would you please come again after I've worked this morning's talk into my book?"

"Of course," Jesus said, and gracefully took his leave.

72. *Out of the Abundance of the Heart of Man*

I didn't want to open that door, but I had to. Christ's saying revealed the dark side of the personality, and our dialogue would not be complete if we did not include the shadow side of life. Because the Inner Master wanted me to decode this saying, I decided to ask him for spiritual guidance. I did a short contemplation, using my secret word to make the best possible connection, and then I dialogued with the Inner Master:

O. I need guidance for my next talk with Jesus. We're going to talk about the dark side of the human personality, and I don't want our talk to pull us down too deeply into that morass of unresolved karma. Can we make the point about his saying without getting too involved?

Z. *You cannot avoid the unconscious when you talk about the self of man. Jesus addresses the issue when he speaks of the human heart. Heart for Jesus, as for all spiritual paths, symbolizes the consciousness of Soul. Do not concern yourself. Let Spirit guide you. Divine Spirit will reveal what can be said in the context of your dialogue.*

O. But we'll have to talk about the shadow self, won't we?

Z. *Yes. Jesus did not have the psychological concepts that we have today to speak of the human psyche, so he will find it refreshing to put his old wine into new bottles.*

O. If I have to go where you know I don't want to go for the good of our talk, will you please see me through without those terrible after-effects I always get after one of my creative forays into the unconscious? I don't want to suffer those lingering moods after one of my forays into the shadow side of life. It's not fair to Cathy.

Z. *Yes, of course. Just do what you have to do to reveal the truth of Christ's sayings.*

O. Thank you.

Z. *You're welcome.*

Jesus knew I had worked our last talk into my book, and he was eager to get on with our dialogue. Without preamble I read Christ's saying from St. Mark's Gospel, Chapter 7, verses 15 and 16: *"There is nothing from without a man, that entering him can defile him; but the things which come out of him, those are they that defile the man. If any man have ears to hear, let him hear."*

"If I'm not mistaken," Jesus said, upon hearing his Gospel saying, "my disciples didn't quite grasp the significance of my saying. Please read what I replied to their questions."

I read verses 18 to 23 to clarify Christ's saying: *"Are ye so without understanding also? Do ye not perceive that whatsoever thing from without entereth into the man, it cannot defile him? Because it entereth not into his heart, but into the belly, and goeth out into the draught, purging all meats? That which cometh out of the man, that defileth the man. For from within, out of the heart of men, proceed evil thoughts, adulteries, fornications, murders, thefts, covetousness, wickedness, deceit, lasciviousness, an evil eye, blasphemy, pride, foolishness; All these evil things come from within, and defile the man."*

"We should make it clear for the reader here also that `out of the abundance of the heart the mouth speaketh,'" Jesus added. "`A good man out of the good treasure of the heart bringeth forth good things; and an evil man out of the treasure bringeth forth evil things.'* And I went on to say that `every idle word that men shall speak, they shall give account thereof in the day of judgment. For by thy words thou shalt be justified, and by thy words thou shalt be condemned.'* Those words can be found in St. Mathew, Chapter 12, verses 34 to 37 if the reader wants to see them in their full context."

I put my pen down and turned to Jesus. "The first thing we should clear up here is what you meant by final judgment. This has caused a lot of heartache for many people because of the false context given to your teaching. Let's reveal the true context and clear up this confusion about final judgment."

"Excellent point of entry," Jesus said. "By all means, I welcome the opportunity to take the muddle out of this ugly puddle."

"It certainly is an ugly puddle," I said. "The Christian world is terrified by this Day of Judgment, but all you were talking about is karma. Karma is the final judge of man's behavior. Soul is governed by karma in its journey through life. Soul has no choice but to be judged for its behavior in life, because the self grows through life experience, and every experience is karmic in one form or another. If an experience collects negative karma, then that karma will have to be resolved; and this karmic resolution is what you refer to as the Day of Judgment. This is why God is never mocked, because no Soul can cheat karma. The only way to avoid the Day of Judgment is to not create negative karma. This takes spiritual discipline, which you refer to when you admonish man to be perfect as our Father in heaven. In other words, if you are a good person you won't have to stand before the Lords of Karma with fear and trembling because you won't fear being condemned to resolving the karma that evil people are condemned to resolve. If you don't mind, J; I'd like you to confirm what I just said so the reader can hear it from the horse's mouth."

"Yes, of course," Jesus said, with an approving nod. "The false context of my teaching is founded upon the premise of eternal damnation, but there is no eternal damnation. That was my metaphor for the evil karma that man has to burn off in the furnace of fire. This furnace of fire is human suffering, because suffering burns off karma naturally. Just to make this absolutely clear; a man who sexually abuses children may be assigned by the Lords of Karma to take up the life of an abused child in his next incarnation to redress the suffering that he inflicted upon children. Soul cannot circumvent its misdeeds in life, so the final Day of Judgment refers to the Court of Karma where the Lords of Karma dole out the just rewards for one's behavior in life. Good karma reaps good life experiences, and evil karma reaps evil life experiences. It's that simple. The true context of my teaching reveals how karma works in life. This is why we reap what we sow. Is that clear enough for your reader?"

"I hope so," I said, smiling at Jesus.

"Why the smile?" he asked.

"I can see it gives you pleasure to take the muddle out of this puddle," I said.

"It certainly does," Jesus said, with a snicker.

"Alright; if we're going to take the muddle out of this puddle let's jump right into the dark side of the human personality and talk about the shadow side of life," I said, mustering all the courage I could for the leap into the abyss of spiritual darkness.

The smile left Christ's face. "This is not going to be pleasant, but how can we avoid talking about the dark side of life? Would you like me to open that door for us?"

"If you would," I replied, thankful for Christ's offer.

"Fair enough. In my gospel I speak of the heart being the center of man's consciousness, so whatever lies in the heart of man defines the man. We can dispense with the metaphor for our talk. The consciousness of the self of man is fractured. It is not one complete, unified, harmonious whole. The object of the evolutionary process of life is to make man's self-consciousness whole. This is what spiritual rebirth speaks to. It is about giving birth to this unified consciousness of the self, and my gospel is fundamental to spiritual rebirth because the premise of the Way of Christ is to make man whole. To do this I had to spell out the fractured elements of the self. Once I spelled them out I had to assign specific sayings to address the fractured elements individually so they could be reconciled with Soul. In effect, my gospel was one of revelation and reconciliation. I revealed the truth about the self of man, and I reconciled the self with my sayings; but what did I reconcile? I reconciled that aspect of the self that traps Soul in the darkness of its own unresolved consciousness, which I called evil. Now, this is a mystery that needs to be explained—"

"May I take this one?" I jumped in, chomping at the bit.

Jesus laughed at my enthusiasm. "Why would you want to do that?"

"Because I know exactly what this experience of being trapped in one's dark side is all about. My whole spiritual life has been one relentless effort to liberate myself from my own dark side ever since I fell from the Grace of God!"

"I was wondering when you would reveal this," Jesus said. "By all means, the best revelation of a truth is by way of personal experience. Please, explain what we mean by the reconciling power of the spiritual life."

I took a deep breath, silently asked the Inner Master for guidance, and jumped right into the story of my fall from the Grace of God. "What I'm going to reveal will give the reader pause for thought," I began slowly, thoughtfully. "But I have to reveal this to put the majesty of God's Plan into perspective. So if I may, in the Divine Plan of God Soul has to create the right kind of personality that will allow it into the Higher Worlds of God. In other words, any aspect of Soul's personality — and Soul's personality is made up of all the individual personalities of its past lives — that inhibits Soul's journey to spiritual self-realization and God-consciousness will have to be resolved; and it's resolved by the natural process of karmic reconciliation through life experience. This is the furnace of fire that you talk about. This is the spiritual purpose of human suffering. This karmic reconciliation through natural suffering is the true hell of all spiritual teachings, whether one wants to believe this or not; but it is not for eternity. Soul must transform that aspect of its spiritual personality that keeps it from realizing its destiny to total self-realization consciousness.

"Well, I fell from the Grace of God because — you guessed it, hubris. Most Souls fall from the Grace of God because of pride, but mine was extreme. This is why I had such a depraved lifetime as the *Scoundrel of Paris.* This was my fall from the Grace of God. I had reconciled myself in my new spiritual line of destiny, which Pythagoras helped me to begin by initiating me into the secret teachings of the Way; but I was unable to completely resolve the false pride of my former line of spiritual destiny that comes with power. Pythagoras made me see that to travel to the worlds beyond the worlds I would have to stop making life serve me and learn how to serve life; so in my lifetime as Phaedrus the Fair, as I was called, I began my new line of spiritual destiny by serving life. I had studied the Way under Pythagoras for eight years in Italy, and I taught his secret teaching for thirty years while serving Athens in the political arena, and I continued to serve life in future incarnations. This life of service to my fellow man was my new line of spiritual destiny.

"Then I came to my incarnation in Persia in the 15th Century where I tried once more to travel to the Higher Worlds of God by studying the secret teaching. My name was Salaam, and I was a member of the Sufi Order of the White Tiger. I failed to be initiated into the Order because I could not pass the test of initiation. I tried three times to pass the test, but I could not master my 'tiger of desire,' so I was banished from the Order. My life came to a sad end. I died of starvation babbling nonsense. That's when I decided on the Other Side to take up a life of sexual abandon in my next incarnation so I could face my demons of sexual desire once and for all. In my incarnation as Riel Laforchette in 17th Century Paris I let my beast of sexual lust devour me whole. I fell from the Grace of God by the choice I made to be consumed by my beast of desire, and I fell and fell into the abyss of my own nothingness. This was my archetypal non-self, the I-consciousness of all the unresolved karma of my past lives; and I would never experience spiritual freedom until I liberated myself from the shadow side of my spiritual personality.

"The shadow side of Soul's personality is the unresolved consciousness of all one's past-lives, and in my current life I managed to face the demon of my collective shadow self and reconcile myself with God. Because I redeemed myself, like one of the thirty birds in the Sufi allegory I was granted the privilege of looking into the Face of God. For the reader's sake, let's just say that I redeemed my dark side by being a good person, because out of the heart of a good person only good can come, and the more good one does the more goodness one will receive because this is how karma works. Knowing that the Law of Karma had to work for me, I maximized my good karma by doing the right-good-fair-just and noble thing every chance I got. If I could live my life true to this ethic, I knew I would redeem myself with God; and I did. This is why you're talking with me now."

"Yes; but let's not confuse the reader," Jesus said, with a big grin. "You're talking with me, not God. I am one with God, but I am not God. There's a big difference!"

I laughed. "Sorry, J; I didn't mean to imply that I'm sitting here with God. But we should clear up this misconception the world has of you being God, shouldn't we?"

"We should, because that goes straight to the Gospel conspiracy," Jesus said.

"Would you like me to give it a shot?" I asked.

"No, let me. After all, I'm responsible for this misconception. Soul is an atom of God, and when Soul realizes its destiny of God-realization consciousness it becomes one with God; but God is more than the sum of its atoms. God is all atoms, un-self-realized and self-realized, but so much more that it is beyond the mind to conceive. I am a God-realized Soul, so I am one with my Father in heaven; but my Father is more than Jesus Christ. I do hope the reader can make sense of this, because it's beyond me to make it any simpler."

"It makes perfect sense to me," I said.

"Yes, but you have looked into the Face of God."

"Yes, I have; but that didn't absolve me of all the karma I still had to burn off in the furnace of my life. And believe me; I suffered like hell ever since I looked into the Face of God! It was not fun, J; especially these past few years!"

"Would you like a hero cookie?" Jesus said, and smiled at me.

"Don't get smart! We can't get away with anything in life, that's all I mean. If we have a flaw in our spiritual personality we have to resolve it to complete our journey through life, and my flaw was vanity. I developed such an overweening spiritual pride after I looked into the Face of God that I thought I was above the Law of Karma; but no one is above karma in this world. Even Masters have fallen from the Grace of God."

"Indeed," said Jesus. "With some exceptions, Soul cannot exist in these lower worlds without the bodies of these lower worlds; and these bodies — physical, astral, causal, and mental bodies — are subject to karma. Even Masters who reside in these lower worlds are subject to the temptations of their lower bodies and can fall from grace."

"This is why the Living Soul Master said that heaven must be won anew each day," I said, happy to quote the Outer Master in our dialogue.

"Yes," Jesus sighed, as if reminded of his own spiritual misdeeds.

I glanced at the clock on my book shelf. "Sorry, J; I hate to cut our talk short, but I have to finish painting the house I'm working on. They want to start laying the hardwood floor on Friday, and I'd like to have all my painting done before they start. Can we pick this up tomorrow morning?"

Jesus respected my trade. "Of course," he said. "Take care of your life responsibilities first, O; that's what the spiritual life is all about. Until tomorrow, then."

73. The Unholy Children of God

"Where we're we?" Jesus asked, as I poured our tea.

For symbolic reasons I had selected a BIJA Deep Cleanse tea for part two of our discourse. I covered the pot with the cozy, and said, "We were talking about the dark side of the personality, which in today's psychology we call the shadow self."

"Yes," said Jesus. "Your conversation with Doctor Jung in your last book went a long way to explaining the shadow. Do you think we can add to that understanding?"

"It's not whether we can add to it or not. What's important for our dialogue is to see the dark side of the personality in the context of your teaching. After all, your gospel is all about revelation and reconciliation. Let's reveal what has to be revealed so the reader can grasp the fundamental principles of reconciliation in the Way of Christ."

"Indeed. Then the first thing I would say is that the dark side of the self of man can be compared to delinquent children that must be brought to their senses for their own good."

"What makes a child delinquent?" I asked, on behalf of the reader.

"The five poisonous passions of the mind," Jesus said. "Lust, anger, greed, vanity, and attachment. Whenever man indulges in the five passions of the mind he creates his own delinquent children. He will create a delinquent *lust child*; he will create a delinquent *anger child*; he will create a delinquent *greed child*; he will create a delinquent *vanity child*; and he will create a delinquent *possessive child* that cannot let go of its attachments; and the consciousness of these delinquent children coalesce into the dark side of his personality, which we know today as the shadow self. This shadow self is the culprit responsible for all those unclean spirits that the world believes I cast out of the heart of man."

Jesus snickered at the memory of his exorcisms. I smiled also because it instantly brought to mind my own exorcism. I had to tell Jesus. "Believe it or not, J — *of course you would!"* I exclaimed, and

OREST STOCCO

broke into a nervous smile. "I called upon you for help when I had to face the Unclean One that possessed my father. And now that I have the opportunity to thank you in person, thank you. I don't know what I would have done had you not blessed me with the power of the Holy Ghost. God, I dread to think about that experience! *I still can't believe I did that!"*

The memory of my experience with the Unclean One flooded my mind and I was visibly shaken. I reached for my tea to calm myself. I took one sip, then another.

Jesus felt my agitation. "First things first," he said, with a loving smile. "You're welcome. I was only too glad to help, and I'm happy that everything worked out in the end. That was a very courageous thing you did, O. Not many people would do what you did for your father. By taking his unclean spirit into your own heart you incurred the wrath of Satan. And by transforming the consciousness of your father's unclean spirit you forced entry into the darkest of life's mysteries, which you have brought to light in your writing; and for this the world will one day thank you."

I was living Gurdjieff's teaching of "work on oneself," as well as Christ's sayings, and in the course of time I did resolve my father's unclean spirit; but it cost me. I was tempted every moment of every day for years, until one by one the delinquent children that my father had fostered in his heart were transformed by my "work self," which I had forged out of Gurdjieff's teaching and Christ's sayings, and my father was free of his demons and peace came to our home for several years; and then my father's drinking got the best of him again, and before long he fell into the pattern of creating more delinquent children.

Soon my father was possessed again by his archetypal demons, and his shadow became unbearable in its efforts to resist resolution. It was like a malignant virus that had grown immune to the antibiotic, and my father's shadow-afflicted personality became insufferable. To further mock me for having the courage to exorcise my father's unclean spirit once, the Archetypal Shadow came and possessed my father's shadow. That's when I knelt and prayed to Jesus for help. Jesus came to me. I felt his presence. I felt the Holy Ghost fill me with the strength that I needed to cast the Evil One out of my father's heart. I looked at Jesus in my reading chair and smiled

462

nervously again. The memory of my experience had awakened all those powerful emotions, and I didn't want to go there. That was the most trying period of my entire life, and I paid dearly for what I did for my father; but it was because of this unbelievable experience that I could write in my journal: "The shortest way to God is through hell!"

I had found the shortcut to heaven, but Satan did not want me to reveal this because it brought to light the secret of evil. As unbearable as my experience with my father was, because of our relationship I was initiated into the unholy mystery of evil. I would never have solved the mystery of Satan had I not taken my father's unclean spirit into my own heart to resolve. As I struggled with my father's unclean spirit every single day I became more and more conscious of what my own shadow was; and the more conscious I became as I processed my father's unclean spirit through my "work self" the more I transformed my own shadow self, until one day I saw that these delinquent children were the individuated I-consciousness of God trapped in a matrix of negative karmic energy!

These offspring of the five passions of the mind were the unholy children of God, and as I *lived* the Way every moment of every day I slowly but surely reconciled them with Soul. I purified them of their unclean, selfish content and redeemed them from their depths of spiritual darkness. No wonder Satan came to mock me when my father took to his habit of closet drinking again. And the more my father drank, the more he nurtured his archetypal demons again until they were big enough, bold enough, and fierce enough to take over his personality and wreak havoc once more in our family home.

When Satan came that day — which I knew to be the Evil One because my spiritual sight had been awakened by the intensity of my efforts to live the sayings of Jesus — I knew I had to have help to cast him out of my father's heart. I went up to my study, knelt down, and begged Jesus for help. To my surprise, Jesus came. His presence was so palpable that I could almost touch him. Then it happened. I became infused with an energy that magnified my courage, my strength, and my confidence. I felt it flow into me through the top of my head until it filled my whole being. I got up, went downstairs, and wrestled with my father's demons in the dining room until the Evil One was forced to leave my father's heart. Apart from putting my father in the hospital with a brain aneurism and coming a hairsbreadth from committing patricide, I cannot reveal what happened; so I thanked Jesus again, and said: "The world will one day have a much more enlightened understanding of what these delinquent children are. I praise Doctor Jung for his insights into the unconscious, but not until we had our conversation in my dream that night did he have any idea that the shadow self of man is the I-consciousness of God trapped in a matrix of unresolved karma. This is the mystery of evil that the God of these lower worlds whom the world knows as Satan did not want me to reveal. I did reveal it to Doctor Jung in my last book, and now we're revealing the mystery of evil in the context of your teaching."

"And for this I will be forever grateful," said Jesus, patting me on the knee. "Now that this dark mystery has been revealed the fear of hell and eternal damnation can be seen in the light of spiritual clarity, and perhaps the course of Christianity can be changed. In all honesty, I would hate to see this great religion go by way of the dinosaur."

I couldn't help but laugh at Christ's foolish hope for Christianity. Jesus knew what I was laughing at, and said, "I know, I'm dreaming again; but one can hope, can't one?"

"Now, there's a revelation—*Jesus Christ hoping!*"

"Yes, hope," Jesus repeated, with a big smile. "All we can do is offer choices. It's up to the world to choose its own direction. By offering the world the spiritual clarity of my sayings it will be free to choose the conscious spiritual life of the Way over a life of blind faith. Conscious free choice, that's what the spiritual life boils down to; and all I can do is hope that the world will choose spiritual clarity over the muddle of the Gospel conspiracy."

"And by Gospel conspiracy, you mean?" I asked, for absolute clarity.

"I am not the only Begotten Son of God. I am not the savior of the world. I did not die upon the cross to atone for the sins of the world. Salvation is a personal responsibility. The Gospel writers imply otherwise. *That's the Gospel conspiracy!*" Jesus replied.

"Perhaps now you can appreciate why I'm so predisposed to letting the world find its own way," I said, and laughed.

"Of course I do. But I have to show leadership, don't I? After all, the world has made me its savior. What else can I do but continue to point the way home to God?"

Jesus' sense of irony forced me to laugh again. After a moment or two I asked him, "What else can we say about your saying?"

"Perhaps we should reiterate," he replied.

"Let me. I'll put it all into the context of the DPG for the reader."

"Excellent," said Jesus, and poured another cup of tea. He took a sip, then another, and with a playful smile, added, "This is truly a deep cleansing experience, is it not?"

Again, I laughed. "I'm sure our reader will get a chuckle over our sense of irony. I certainly do. After all, how much deeper can we go to cleanse the consciousness of man of his spiritual impurities?"

"We can't. It is no longer a question of *wonder* and *mystery*. It has now become a question of *knowing* and *doing*. We have made of life a conscious choice; and once again I can only hope that one will make the choice to live the life of spiritual clarity."

"That remains to be seen," I said, not wanting to burst Christ's bubble. "Let's make it absolutely clear for the reader what this choice for spiritual clarity really is. As I was saying, I'm going to put our discourse on the unholy children of God into the context of the Divine Plan of God. That way the reader will see the role that these delinquent children play in Soul's evolution through life."

"Good," said Jesus, and stretched out his legs to listen in comfort.

"Alright. We know that Soul comes from the Ocean of Love and Mercy as an un-self-realized atom of God, and the purpose of the evolutionary process of life is to create an individual Soul self. To do this, the atom of God needs the energy of life, which is Holy Spirit, or what we can simply call the God-force. This God-force is the I-consciousness of God that is not yet individuated. It is pure I-consciousness, and we gather and collect this life force with every experience we have. As we experience life, we individuate the I-consciousness of God. In other words, the self of man grows in self-consciousness as it experiences life. Because the self is made up of its higher and lower self, when one experiences life he nourishes both his higher or lower self with the energy of life depending upon the values that he lives by. If a person is selfish, he nourishes his lower self and grows in his human self-consciousness; and if a person is not so selfish, he nourishes his lower and higher self. The logic of spiritual growth rests upon the values we live by. If we choose to feed our ego, then our ego will grow and grow; and if we choose to feed out spiritual self, then our spiritual self will grow and grow. That's simple enough, wouldn't you say?"

"Yes. Please continue," Jesus said, smiling gleefully.

"Well, the point here is that the atom of God is driven by its own spiritual DNA to become God-realized; so in the self of man there is always this need for more self-realization consciousness. This pre-scripted need for more self-identity drives both the higher and lower self. This is the source of the conflict in the heart of man."

"But why?" Jesus jumped in, eager for total clarity. "Why should there be this conflict if the drive for more self-identity is the same in both the higher and lower self? Please explain this for the reader's sake."

"Because the higher self cannot grow on the unresolved energy of the lower self, that's why," I responded. "The lower self is our human self; and Soul, our higher self, can only experience life through its human self. This is why it's so important to create the right kind of personality for Soul to grow. In the simplest terms possible, if we create a selfish, self-centered, egotistical personality we make it impossible for the higher self to grow because all the I-consciousness of God that we take in will nourish the lower self and will have to be karmically resolved with future experiences. And this is not theory, because I was one of these selfish, egotistical personalities in my lifetime as Riel Laforchette. I had to resolve all of that selfish consciousness in future lives, starting with my incarnation as Solomon the Good Slave in southern Georgia. I suffered as Solomon, because this lifetime was my furnace of fire that burned off the selfish consciousness I had created as the *Scoundrel of Paris*. Does that answer your question?"

"Yes," said Jesus. "I just wanted the reader to get a clear picture, that's all."

"I know. So, where was I? Oh, yes. I was getting to the delinquent children of the mind. These unholy children are the spurious offspring of the five deadly passions that the ego gives birth to, because ego is insatiable in its appetite for self-identity. Ego indulges itself to excesses in these five passions and gives birth to its own demons. These egoic demons are the unholy children of God. They are the individuated consciousness of the God-force trapped in the unconscious lower self of man, which Doctor Jung called the shadow; and the more self-indulgent one becomes the more he feeds his shadow demons until they are powerful enough to take over his personality, which happens with many people. These people become shadow-afflicted, and eventually they become shadow-possessed. Their demons take over their personality and they have no more control over their passions — just as Mr. Hyde took over Dr. Jekyll's personality. These shadow possessed people become hopeless alcoholics, drug addicts, sexual perverts, violent husbands, child molesters, insatiable materialists, and possessive paranoids who have to control everyone and everything. They are at the mercy of the shadow side of their personality. In every sense of the word, they are their own worst enemy."

"Excellent," said Jesus, nodding his head in approval. "And it all starts with the values that one lives by. This is why it's important that we spell out the consequences of one's choices. The karma that one creates is the result of the values one lives by. If one chooses to feed his lower self, he will create karma that will have to be resolved to nourish his spiritual self's inherent need for total consciousness; and if one chooses to live by values that create positive karma, then he can grow spiritually without all the hassle of having to resolve the negative consciousness of his lower self."

"Well said, J!" I exclaimed, delighted by his explanation. "So it all comes down to one's individual choice. We should also make it clear then that most people are not conscious of the choices they make, because more often than not people create negative karma despite themselves!"

"Give us an example," Jesus said, for absolute clarity.

"Sure. How about Christians who believe they are doing the right thing by imposing their values upon the rest of society? Christians who seek to take a woman's choice away from her because they believe abortion is a sin against God? Free choice is supreme in the Divine Plan of God, and when one denies another person the freedom to choose their own life he is violating the Spiritual Law of Non-interference. It's all a balancing act, J; and man has no choice but to walk this spiritual tight rope."

"Can you explain that metaphor, please?" Jesus asked.

"Yes, of course. We have to be respectful of other people's choices, but we all have to live together in society; so finding the right balance of rights and freedoms is what this spiritual tight rope is all about. At least now we can make our choices with some spiritual clarity. Most people make choices in spiritual darkness because they have little awareness of the karmic consequences of their choices. With spiritual clarity, they will see these karmic consequences and hopefully choose more wisely."

"Bravo!" Jesus exploded, and clapped his hands. "As I told my disciples, out of the abundance of one's heart the mouth will speak. Fill your heart with love and you will speak love. Fill it with prejudice and blind desires and your heart will speak the five poisonous passions of the mind. The choice was clear then, and it is even clearer today. And that's the most that we can say about this saying. Unless you have something else to add, that is?"

"If I may borrow a line form a detergent commercial I saw on TV the other night," I said, with a wry chuckle, *"You can't get cleaner than clean!"*

Jesus loved the irony and broke into a hearty laugh. He took another sip of tea, and another to finish his cup, and said, "You certainly chose the right tea for our talk this morning. This has truly been a deep cleansing experience for the self of man! So; does this bring closure to your book, O?"

"Not quite. I got word from the Dream Master last night to talk about your Sermon on the Mount, so that'll be the theme of our next talk; and then I can bring my book home with one more talk where you and I can come clean with our reader."

"Come clean?" Jesus said, with a puzzled look on his loveable face. *"What on earth do you mean by that?"*

"You'll see," I said, with an ironic chuckle…

74. *The Beatitudes Revealed*

I read Christ's Sermon on the Mount half a dozen times before the conflicting metaphors of his beatitudes made sense to me.

When Jesus said that his Father in heaven *"maketh his sun to rise on the evil and on the good,"* and that he *"sendeth rain on the just and unjust,"* I finally saw through the confusion of his beatitudes, because implicit to God's fairness for all Souls was the mercy of God for those Souls not yet ready for the kingdom of heaven.

"When you said, `*Blessed are the poor in spirit,*' I said to Jesus in our next talk a couple of days later, `*for theirs is the kingdom of heaven,*' you were telling these Souls not yet ready for the kingdom of heaven that God's mercy will in the fullness of time reconcile them enough to be ready for the kingdom of heaven; that's why they are blessed."

"Yes," replied Jesus, with that twinkle of love in his eyes. "They are not ready yet for the kingdom of heaven because they are poor in Spirit, but they are blessed by God's mercy because in the Divine Plan of God all Souls will in good time grow in Spirit and be ready for the kingdom of heaven. It is God's mercy that blesses the Soul that is not ready for the kingdom of heaven. God's love for Soul is not limited to the rich in Spirit alone. God's love for Soul is equal, regardless at what stage of spiritual growth Soul is at."

"I'm glad you cleared that up," I said, with some relief. "Let's go to the next beatitude. `*Blessed are they that mourn, for they shall be comforted.*' By this, you mean?"

"Just that," Jesus replied. "Holy Spirit, the Comforter, is ever-present in Soul's life. In time of desperate need, such as the loss of a loved one, God provides comfort for the bereaved to see them through their time of grief. So they that mourn are blessed by the love of God, which is always with them to help Soul in its journey home to the Higher Worlds. All they have to do is be open to God's infinite, comforting love."

As Jesus spoke the memory of one of my painting customers came to mind. "I have an example of God's comforting love for a woman who mourned the loss of her husband," I said to Jesus, excited that I had the perfect example to illustrate this beatitude.

"Good," said Jesus. "As I said, the best explanation of the secret teaching is by way of experience. By all means, tell us how this woman was comforted by God."

"She loved her husband dearly, and they looked forward to his retirement so they could enjoy more time together, but he died shortly after he retired. It broke her heart. So grief-stricken was she that she could not bear the pain of her loss, and the Holy Comforter wrapped a blanket of love around her. For three days she felt no pain from the loss of her husband. For three days this woman lived her life in this blanket of God's love. She said she felt it around her body like an actual blanket. When she sat down, this blanket of love adjusted to her sitting position. She called it an invisible cloak of love. For three days she felt so blessed with God's love that her heart healed enough for her to bear the pain of her husband's death. So, yes, J; those who mourn are blessed, for God's love is there for every Soul in need of comfort."

Jesus smiled. "Go on," he said. "Read the next beatitude."

I turned to my Bible. "*`Blessed are the meek, for they shall inherit the earth.*`" Then I turned to Jesus, and said, "Indeed, the meek shall inherit the earth. They certainly won't inherit the kingdom of heaven! As the Living Soul Master said, only the most courageous Souls will find their way to God. By earth here, you're talking about the natural process of spiritual growth, aren't you? You're referring to the natural process of karmic resolution; about experiencing more life to grow in Spirit until they are ready to inherit the kingdom of heaven, right?"

Jesus laughed. "Do you realize how few people have discerned the truth of this beatitude? Yes, of course you are right; the meek must inherit the earth because they are not strong enough in Spirit yet to inherit the kingdom of heaven. The meek are blessed by God's infinite mercy, because God provides the experience for Soul to grow. The meek Soul must experience more life to grow strong in Spirit, because this is God's Plan. What the world will never understand is just how merciful the Spiritual Law of Karma really is.

It is God's love in action. Karma is so merciful, fair, kind, compassionate, and spiritually rewarding that Soul cannot help but be blessed with the opportunity to grow in the consciousness of its own divine nature. Indeed, the meek are truly blessed to inherit the experience of more life on earth, because this is how Soul grows and makes itself ready for the kingdom of heaven."

I turned to the Bible and read the next beatitude. *"`Blessed are they which do hunger and thirst after righteousness, for they shall be filled.'"*

Jesus smiled. "Here I'm talking about the Soul that begins to hear the Word of God and is called to the higher spiritual life of ethics and morality. The more Soul grows through the natural karmic reconciliation process of life, the more spiritually conscious it becomes; and with spiritual consciousness comes an awakening to the spiritual laws of life. It is inevitable that Soul seeks to be righteous in life, because it is now compelled by its own higher spiritual consciousness to live by the spiritual laws of life. As Soul struggles with the negative forces of life to be ethical and moral in its behavior, it is rewarded for its righteousness. And this reward is?"

"The transformed consciousness of one's lower self," I replied, completely certain of my answer. "I know this for a fact, because this is how I grew in Spirit. The more honest, good, kind and fair I was the more I transformed the consciousness of my lower self and filled myself with the God-force that I needed to grow in Spirit. Indeed, Souls that hunger after righteousness are filled with the God-force of their own reconciled karma, because the righteous life transforms the impure energies of one's lower self. That's clear enough for me, but I wonder if the reader can make sense of this?"

"Why don't we simplify it for the reader, then?"

"I give the floor to you, J."

"Alright. I would say that the ethical and moral life nourishes the higher self of man, and the unethical and immoral life nourishes the lower self of man. So those that hunger for the righteous life crave to grow in Spirit. As they live the righteous life, they fill themselves with the God-force that comes with living the spiritual life of ethics and morality."

"That should be clear enough," I said, and turned to Christ's next beatitude. ***"'Blessed are the merciful, for they shall obtain mercy.'"***

"And which spiritual law does this reflect?" Jesus asked.

"The Law of Attraction. You get back what you put out. This is reflected in sayings like, 'if you live by the sword, you will die by the sword.' 'Love begets love,' and hate begets hate.' Like attracts like. Souls that are merciful with life will invoke the Law of Attraction and be treated mercifully by life. Ironically, this spiritual law turns an old saying on its head. People who cannot see the Law of Attraction at play in life are always complaining that life is not fair. They are led to believe that life is cruel, and that you have to be on guard all the time because life is out to get us. But the Law of Attraction says differently. If you are fair with life, life will be fair with you; if you are cruel with life, life will be cruel with you; if you are forgiving with life, life will be forgiving with you; if you are understanding, kind, and merciful with life, then life will be understanding, kind, and merciful with you. It may not be obvious at first, but the more understanding, kind, and merciful one is with life the more one grows in the consciousness of understanding, kindness, and mercy; and by the sheer force of the Law of Attraction this consciousness will have to attract into your life the consciousness of understanding, kindness, and mercy. It is so precise that one could even call it mathematical!"

Jesus broke into a chuckle. "Indeed, the spiritual laws of life are mathematical in their exactitude. I need not add to your explanation, except that we must look at the spiritual laws of life from Soul's perspective. These laws have many lifetimes to work with, not just one life. This is why these laws are not so obvious. For example; one's kindness, goodness, and understanding behavior may be rewarded in his next lifetime. Do you see how the Law of Attraction and karma work hand in hand here?"

"Yes. That's why people think life as unfair. They can't see the big picture."

"Precisely. So what's the next beatitude?"

"'Blessed are the pure in heart, for they shall see God,'" I read.

Jesus grinned. "That should be an easy one for you to explain."

"Yes, it is," I said, with a big smile. "I looked into the Face of God. I filled myself with so much God-force by living the Way that I reached the tipping point and was pulled by the Law of Attraction to the source of the God-force. Like attracts like, J. So if one wants to look into the Face of God all they have to do is fill their heart with the God-force enough to reach critical mass and the Law of Attraction will pull them home to God!"

"To simplify then," Jesus said, still grinning, "the more one lives the spiritual life of the Way, the more one grows in Spirit. The more one grows in Spirit, the more pure his heart will be. This is why I said that the pure in heart are blessed and will see God. Clear enough?"

"I hope so," I said.

"To play upon that saying of yours, you can't get more clear than clear."

I laughed. "Okay, the next beatitude. *'Blessed are the peacemakers, for they shall be called the children of God.'* Now, this one's a little tricky to decode because it seems like it contradicts itself."

"How so?" Jesus asked.

"Because by children of God you mean initiates of the Way. An initiate of the Way brings the Sword of the Way into the world, because the inherent power of the Way severs Soul from the material consciousness of life. It's not peace that the initiate of the Way brings into the world, but the reconciling power of Holy Spirit that creates havoc in life because it threatens the lower self of man; so I don't quite see what you mean when you say that the peacemakers shall be called the children of God."

"What do you call a person who brings two contentious factions into agreement?" Jesus asked.

"An arbitrator," I answered.

"And does not an arbitrator bring peace to two contentious factions?"

"He arbitrates an agreement," I replied. "If by agreement you mean peace, then yes; he brings peace."

"Now apply this analogy to the self of man. The higher self is never in agreement with the lower self, because the higher self wants to go back home to God and the lower self wants to stay and indulge itself in life's pleasures. What would you call one who brings his lower self into agreement with his higher self?"

"A peacemaker," I said, and laughed.

"And what did I call peacemakers in my beatitude?"

I turned to my Bible. "'Children of God,'" I read, and laughed.

"So Souls that bring their lower self into agreement with their higher self are the peacemakers of the world, and they are blessed because this is how they become children of God. Now do you see what the secret meaning of this beatitude is?"

"Thank you," I said, with a grateful smile. "I honestly did not see this. I guess it's because I didn't make the connection with the lower and higher self. But it's clear now."

"Souls that bring their two selves into agreement have the same effect upon those around them. They are the true peacemakers of the world, because unless one has peace in his own heart how can he bring peace to others?"

"Excellent!" I said, excited by Christ's explanation. I glanced at the next beatitude. "Alright. The next beatitude is self-explanatory. But only in the context of the true meaning of your teaching."

"Please read it for the record," Jesus said.

"Of course. `***Blessed are they which are persecuted for righteousness sake, for theirs is the kingdom of heaven.'***"

Very thoughtfully, in a gentle voice filled with the emotion of someone who had the experience of this beatitude, Jesus said, "When a person is persecuted by life for being honest, ethical, and moral he will be rewarded by God for his righteousness, because only the righteous are allowed to enter the straight gate of the Way. The dishonest, unethical, and immoral are rewarded on earth for their behavior because the Kal looks after his own kind. The rewards born of one's unrighteous behavior are of this earth, and Soul must return to pay them back. This is the Law of Karma. Karma demands that everything be paid for in kind. Doing good rewards one with more goodness, and theft rewards one with loss. To put it simply, if you steal from life then life will steal from you. It's mathematical."

I couldn't help myself and snickered. "So it would be appropriate to say that one's sins cannot be forgiven with confession and/or a perfect act of contrition, because the Law of Karma does not recognize the concept of forgiveness of sin; right?"

"Exactly." Jesus replied, with an ironic smile. "This may shock your Christian readers, but this is the cold yet merciful reality of Soul's experience in life. There are no free rides on this train, O."

"Yeah," I replied, with a heavy sigh. "It costs to do the right thing, doesn't it? The world is oblivious to the Law of Karma. That's why people get disheartened by life and compromise their integrity to the spiritually complacent status quo. It takes courage to do the right thing, because the forces of the status quo are so powerful. Take whistleblowers, for example. Movies have been made of how they were persecuted for blowing the whistle on wrongdoers. So yes, J; I can see why those persecuted for righteousness sake are rewarded with the kingdom of heaven. They may not enter the narrow way completely, but their righteousness unlocks the gate for them, and in the fullness of time they will be initiated into the mysteries of the kingdom of God."

Jesus nodded in agreement. Then he stood up, picked up my Bible, and read the last beatitude in its entirety: *"'Blessed are ye, when men shall revile you, and persecute you, and shall say all manner of evil against you falsely, for my sake. Rejoice, and be exceeding glad: for great is your reward in heaven: for so persecuted they the prophets which were before you. Ye are the salt of the earth: but if the salt have lost his savor, wherewtith shall it be salted? It is thenceforth good for nothing, but to be cast out, and be trodden under foot of men. Ye are the light of the world. A city that is set on a hill cannot be hid. Neither do men light a candle, and put it under a bushel, but on a candlestick; and it giveth light unto all that are in the house. Let your light so shine before men, that they may see your good works, and glorify your Father which is in heaven.'"*

Jesus placed the Bible back on my desk and sat down. I looked it up, and wrote Mathew, Chapter 5, verses 11-16, in my notebook. I turned to Jesus. "This beatitude means more to me than all of your other beatitudes," I said, with a big smile.

"Why?" Jesus asked.

"I stuck my neck out when I introduced the Way to mainstream literature with my two novel memoirs, that's why. You cannot imagine the anguish this caused Cathy and me. So great was this anguish that God rewarded me with a glimpse of the Divine Plan of God when we left St. Jude and moved to Georgian Bay. I dared to be seen openly in my books for what I am. I let my light shine before men, and God rewarded me greatly. I know now what the purpose of life is, how God uses man to expand its consciousness, and how the atom of God grows to become a God-realized Soul. *That's the reward that I received for letting my light shine for the whole world to see!"*

Jesus' face was radiant. "Great was your suffering for the Way and great was your reward, and the world will one day profit from your experience. Shall we continue with the rest of my Sermon on the Mount? We've discussed most of the sayings, all adding up to the final saying which I think would bring nice closure to our talk this morning."

"Which saying is that?" I asked.

"Be ye therefore perfect even as your Father which is in heaven is perfect," replied Jesus, with a satisfied look on his radiant face.

I nodded in agreement. "In essence then, all you meant with your Sermon on the Mount was to instruct your followers in the Way of Christ, because only by living the spiritual life can one be initiated into the kingdom of heaven," I summed up.

"Precisely," said Jesus. "Now if I may, I think the reader has all the tools he needs to work out the rest of my gospel as I intended it for the world. As noble as their intentions were, the writers of my life and teaching have led the world astray, and I am grateful for this opportunity to set the record straight. The Gospel writers — and I include St. Paul in this conspiracy — meant well; but now that our dialogue has come to closure I can tell you that you were right to trust your intuition. They did conspire to establish the kingdom of God on earth by making me the only Begotten Son of God who sacrificed his life for the sins of the world, and only through me could one enter into the kingdom of God; but we have established that this cannot be. The Gospel conspiracy, however it came to be — by noble intention or willful manipulation — has been revealed, and in time the world will appreciate the true meaning of my gospel. I have you to thank, O. Our next talk will bring closure to our dialogue, and I understand you have a surprise for me."

"Yes," I said, taken aback by Christ's unexpected disclosure.

"Good. I like surprises," Jesus said, with that playful twinkle in his eyes.

"Can you give me a few days to work this talk into my book?" I asked, feeling very strange from the peremptory stop to the momentum of our dialogue.

"Of course," Jesus said. "I'll see you Sunday morning. That should give you plenty of time. Have a nice day, O," he added, with a goodbye wave.

Jesus faded to the Other Side, and I sat in my bonus room for a good hour before I went to work. I needed time to think...

75. *Coming Clean*

I finished painting the house Friday morning, just as the flooring crew came in to start laying the hardwood floor, so I had the rest of the day off. Cathy only worked till one o'clock, so we decided to go for a leisurely drive to Orillia and have dinner out.

Two curious coincidences happened that afternoon, telling me that the omniscient guiding force of life wanted me to address the issue of Christianity's militant spirituality, which is so out of sync with society today that it affronts the dignity of free will.

Spiritual growth is all about free will. Unless Soul is free to choose its own destiny it cannot complete its journey home to God. Free will is the essential nature of the spiritually self-realized life, and the only way to realize our wholeness is by exercising free will.

The more we exercise free will the more we grow in spiritual consciousness, until one day we will have realized enough spiritual consciousness to be set free from the confines of our human self; but free will costs, and that cost is karmic responsibility.

The final goal of life is responsible spiritual freedom. We cannot be spiritually free unless we accept responsibility for our freedom, so spiritual freedom means that we are karmically accountable for all the choices we make in life. This is what my two remarkable coincidences spoke to Friday afternoon.

Coincidences speak the Golden-tongued Wisdom of the Way, which is the omniscient guiding voice of Divine Spirit. I knew with the second coincidence that Spirit wanted me to address the issue of freedom and responsibility to thoroughly dispel the Gospel conspiracy, so I decided to talk with Jesus about free will in the final talk of our dialogue.

As he promised, Jesus showed up Sunday morning. He was in my bonus room waiting for me to see Cathy off to work. She did not work weekends, but she got a phone call Saturday evening and was asked to fill in for a co-worker on Sunday and I wondered if that wasn't also a coincidence arranged by the omniscient guiding force of life.

I expected Jesus Sunday morning, so I had tea steeping. I chose a blend of two herbal teas; both of which spoke to my body's needs and which I also felt would bring symbolic closure to our dialogue. I chose Echinacea and Breath Easy tea; Echinacea for the immune system, and Breath Easy for decongestion. "You do speak the language of symbols eloquently," Jesus said and laughed, when I told him my selection.

"Speaking of symbols," I said, excited by the opening Jesus had just given me for our final talk, *"the Golden-tongue spoke to me on Friday! Spirit wants me to address the issue of spiritual freedom and responsibility, since both coincidences were Christian-related!"*

Jesus smiled at my unbridled enthusiasm. "What coincidences?" he asked.

"Cathy and I went to Orillia Friday afternoon," I began, anxious to tell my story. "As I waited for her to change her clothes I turned on the TV. I was watching a program that didn't interest me, so I flicked my remote to the Biography channel; but instead of going to the Biography channel it unexpectedly landed on a Christian channel. A man and woman were praying over a bowl of prayer-requests. The man went on and on about being a soldier in the army of his Lord Jesus Christ, and the woman kept babbling 'Praise the Lord.' I listened for a few minutes, but I couldn't stomach all of that manic Christian nonsense so I switched to the Biography channel. What I experienced watching that Christian program was an assault upon my psyche. Its sole purpose was to win me over to the army of Jesus Christ, their Lord and savior. That was the first coincidence. I know I didn't make a mistake on my remote control. I selected the right number for the Biography channel, but I believe Spirit chose the Christian channel to set the stage for my second coincidence which would lead me to dialogue with you on spiritual freedom and responsibility for our final talk."

Jesus smiled his all-knowing mystical smile, but said nothing.

"Cathy and I drove to the Orillia Square Mall to browse, because we were too early for dinner. When we walked back to our vehicle I spotted a small booklet on the ground just in front of my car door. I picked it up. It was a three by four inch white booklet with a bright yellow happy face on the cover, and the words SMILE on top of the happy face and JESUS LOVES YOU on the bottom of the happy face. I looked to see if any other vehicles in the parking lot had a booklet on the windshield, but none did; so I found it strange that this Little Bible Ministry, as it was called, should be right there on the ground by my door where I couldn't miss it. It certainly wasn't there when I got out of the car. I took the booklet with me because I knew Spirit was trying to tell me something.

"Over dinner, I read the Little Bible Ministry. It spoke to the militant nature of Christianity's efforts to convert the world, quoting your famous saying, *'He that is not with me is against me.'* I've read the booklet three or four times since. This is it right here," I said, and handed it to Jesus. He smiled and waited for me to complete my thought. I continued. "As I read it I knew we would have to address this issue of Christianity's assault upon free will; and I knew that we would have to make every effort possible to dispel this Christian conceit that you are the sole savior of the world by stressing one final time the central theme of your gospel message."

"Which is?" Jesus asked, on behalf of the reader.

"Every person is responsible for his own salvation through the spiritualization of his own consciousness. There is no instant salvation. That's an illusion."

Jesus looked at the booklet in his hand, and said, "In what way does this booklet assault the dignity of free will? After all, you are free to discard it; aren't you?"

"True. But that's not the issue here. The issue is the fundamental premise of Christianity's militant spirituality. Open the booklet and you will see passages I've underlined that speak to the confrontational consciousness of Christian spirituality. The premise of this fundamentalist Christian belief is the direct opposite of Soul's purpose in life. This Little Bible Ministry speaks of the wages of sin being eternal damnation. *'For all have sinned and come short of the glory of God,'* they quote St. Paul — with whom I believe I'm going to talk again because he's largely responsible for this militant spirituality that assaults the dignity of free will today. If I may, let me see the booklet. They quote St. Paul again, for which I'm certain he will have to answer to the Lords of Karma if he hasn't already done so!"

Jesus laughed as he handed me the booklet. "Yes," he said, still chuckling, "Paul has been called to the High Court a few times. He has no less explaining to do than Mathew, Mark, Luke, and especially John. Which saying are you holding him to this time?"

I found the quotation. "*'For the wages of sin is death; but the gift of God is eternal life through Jesus Christ our Lord.'* This is the saying that has led the Christian world down the proverbial path, because this saying justifies the most abominable thought ever to come out of the mouth of man—"

"What?" Jesus interrupted me, with a look of surprise on his face. *"What could possibly be so abominable?"*

I found the page. I had underlined the entire passage. I read it for Jesus*:* "'If we die in our sins, we are eternally lost and forever separated from God. But God offers another way. If we are willing to turn from our sins, we can have eternal life free as a gift. This means we can't earn it by being good, or going to church, or by baptism, or anything else. We simply receive it as a gift through Jesus Christ, God's Son.'"

I stopped reading, took a drink of tea, looked at Jesus, and stared at him long and hard "This is the spawn of the Gospel conspiracy," I said, waving the Little Bible ministry. "Do you see how clearly it's spelled out here? This is why Divine Spirit placed this booklet there for me to read. It spells out the whole Gospel conspiracy in one seductive sentence. **We receive eternal life as a free gift from Jesus Christ, the Son of God!** This is what Mathew, Mark, Luke, and John wanted to achieve with their Gospels of your life and teaching, and they succeeded brilliantly! *This is the Gospel conspiracy in a nutshell!"*

"Yes. Ironic, isn't it?" Jesus replied, with obvious sadness in his voice.

"And St. Paul!" I exclaimed, now completely possessed by the spirit of my final talk with Jesus. *"He's just as much responsible for this nonsense as the Gospel writers!"*

"Yes," Jesus sighed. And then he smiled and said, "So, tell me; what is this most abominable thought ever to come out of the mouth of man?"

I snickered in disgust. *"Can you imagine saying that eternal life can't be earned by being good?* That implies that the good we do

481

is all for naught unless we accept you as our savior! That has to be the most abominable thought ever to come out of the mouth of man, because there is no other way for Soul to complete its destiny than by realizing the consciousness of goodness! Socrates made goodness the noblest virtue. He knew that goodness opens the gate of the narrow Way. Pythagoras taught the same teaching. And these Christians dismiss goodness as though it means nothing at all for our salvation! How in God's name can these people be so warped in their understanding of what the spiritual life is about? *No, don't answer that!* It's St. Paul's free gift of eternal life through Jesus Christ that has warped the psyche of the Christian world! I really do have a bone to pick with that man, and I feel compelled now to write a sequel to my book! In fact I know I'm going to write a sequel, and I'm going to call it *St. Paul's Conceit!*"

Jesus had a smirk on his face from ear to ear. "You will," he said, and broke into a hearty chuckle. "You still have too much anger left in you from your lifetime as the lost Soul of Paris. You're right, though; it is an abomination to dismiss goodness so cavalierly. Let me say it for the record: eternal salvation is not a free gift from me. It has to be earned through one's choice to live the spiritual life. If one chooses to live the Way of Christ, he can realize liberation from the cycle of life and death; but there are many paths to spiritual freedom aside from my teaching. So salvation is not a gift of God, as such; it is an earned gift. To enter the narrow way requires a life of spiritual accountability. This Little Bible Ministry purports that I died for the sins of the world, and accepting me as savior grants one eternal life in the kingdom of heaven. This is counter-intuitive to Soul's purpose in life. Soul cannot realize its divine nature without accepting responsibility for the choices it makes. All sins are karmically accountable and must be redressed in the natural order of life. This idea of a free ticket to salvation is the tragic result of the Gospel conspiracy that makes me the sole savior of the world and bane of every Christian who has been spiritually victimized by the Gospel writers. I agree; this is an assault upon the dignity of free will. To be perfectly frank with you, O; I do not believe Christianity will ever change until it accepts the true message of my gospel."

"Spell it out again, please," I said, for categorical clarity.

"My gospel to the world then was as it is today: personal salvation through the self-transformation of one's consciousness. There, does that make you happy?"

Jesus spoke slowly so I could record every word. I looked up, and smiling said to him, "Yes, it does. I had to hear it from the horse's mouth that these Christians are caught in a fantasy of spiritual nonsense. Their faith in you goes so contrary to the logic of spiritual growth that it actually makes my stomach turn whenever I hear them preach the Word of God. They have no idea what they're talking about. *Absolutely no idea whatsoever!*"

"And this bothers you?" Jesus said, with a bemused smile.

"Yes and no," I said. "It bothers me because this logic drove me to a lifetime of sexual depravity for which I am still not yet completely resolved; and no because every Soul has its own karma to work out. But I am a writer. This makes me a voice for all those Christians that have outgrown their faith but remain trapped by their faith. This is the reason for my tirade against Christianity's perverse logic. And if I may, this is probably why I consented to these talks in the first place. But now it's time to come clean, J."

"Come clean?" Jesus said, feigning surprise. "What do you mean?"

"You know very well what I mean. Before we come clean though, I wonder if you would sum up all of our talks so far. Speak directly to the reader and tell him why you want to set straight the record of your life and teaching. Can you do that for me, please?"

"Of course," Jesus said, and reached for his tea. He took several long sips and replaced his cup. "I love this tea," he said, with an ironic smile. "I hope that what I'm going to say will decongest the Christian Soul and help it to breathe easy in the consciousness of my true gospel, and that the true message of my gospel will build up Soul's immune system and ward off the infectious virus of the Gospel conspiracy."

I laughed at Jesus' sense of play and also took a drink of tea; but I was very anxious about coming clean with our talks because I honestly did not know what to expect now that we had to place all our cards on the table.

Jesus continued, slowly and with authority in his voice. "The Way just *is*. There is no other description for the Way. The Way is life, and Soul must live life to experience the Way. Soul grows through life experience. Soul creates karma and resolves karma, and through the creation and resolution of karma Soul grows in self-realization and God consciousness. The purpose of life is to create God-realized Souls. I was sent to quicken Soul's spiritual growth and harvest Souls that were ready for the kingdom of heaven. I came from the inner circle of life, and my purpose in my Nazarene lifetime was to introduce the outer circle of life to the secret teachings of the kingdom of heaven.

"It has been said that the world is a school for Soul, but that is not entirely true. The world is a womb for Soul to gestate and grow. Once it is ready to be born, Soul must come out of the womb of its human life consciousness and accept its responsibility as a Child of God. This responsibility is to become a God-realized Soul. Soul cannot become God-realized without assistance. It cannot do this alone. Soul needs help from a Soul Master, as we needed help from our own Masters. Soul Masters are God-realized Souls that have been initiated into the mysteries of the Divine Plan of God, and their mandate is to help initiate Soul into this mystery of spiritual self-realization and God-consciousness.

"I introduced the world to the secret teaching with my gospel of the Way. I received the essential precepts of my gospel from the Essenes, but it was my mission to gather the secret teachings of the Way scattered throughout the world and put them into one teaching, which became my gospel of self-sacrifice; very much like the modern day founder of the ancient secret teachings of the Light and Sound of God gathered the fragmented teachings of the Way and assembled them into the Way of the Eternal for the modern world. I made myself central to my teaching, because I wanted the world to see the Way incarnate in my person. I wanted to impress upon the world the symbol of spiritual self-realization consciousness through a living human gospel. I regret that this symbol was taken so literally by the Gospel writers, especially by John whom Holy Spirit dangerously possessed. Let me say once again for the record: it is only by living the spiritual life of the Way that one can enter the kingdom of God. It is not by turning one's life blindly over to me that will save one, but by accepting responsibility for one's own salvation. I hope that's clear, because I did not die for the sins of the world. I died to show the world that only through the death of the lower consciousness of the human self can Soul be liberated from life. When I said, 'I am the way, the truth, and the life I meant it to be a revelation of the living Way. It is only by *living* the Way that one can say, 'I am the way, the truth, and the life.'

"It is not the Christ in man that must be awakened, as these Christians of cosmic spirituality propose, but Holy Spirit, which is the Way. I, as the Christ, am the way of Jesus the man who lived the Way to realize my own God consciousness self. Each Soul must realize the Way through the consciousness of its own unique individuality. It is not the Christ Consciousness that must be awakened, but the unique spiritual identity of each Soul; that unique God self that has taken millions of years to evolve. Each Soul must awaken to Soul Consciousness, not Christ Consciousness. The two are distinct.

"The reason for God's Divine Plan is to create a new 'I' of God with each divine atom that God sends into these lower worlds. Let me say once again; it is not the Christ Consciousness that must be awakened in man, but the unique spiritual identity of each atom of God. It is the God self of Soul that must be awakened. The God self can only be awakened by living the Way, which I reveal in my gospel teaching. Once again, let me emphasize that the Christ Consciousness is the awakened universal self of the Mental Plane of Consciousness, not the individuated self of the Soul Plane of Consciousness. This is the central mystery of the Way that very few Souls penetrate, and that is all I have to say on the subject. The rest can be left for the reader to work out on his own, if he so desires."

Jesus fell back into his chair, seemingly exhausted.

"That took a lot out of you, didn't it?" I asked.

"Yes. But it had to be said," he replied.

"Now it's my turn, J," I said, and reached for my tea. I took one, two, three gulps and emptied my cup. I took a deep breath, closed my eyes, and let the air out of my lungs. *"Z,"* I said, in the quiet of my mind, *"this is it. I have to come clean. I cannot leave my reader with a false impression. This is a presumption that I could never support. How the Gospel writers were able to do it is beyond me. For all of Christ's revelations in our dialogue, I have to come clean. Please, Z; give me the guidance to reveal the truth in the most satisfying way for Soul to grow in the consciousness of its own individuality."*

To my surprise, the Inner Master replied. *"Soul is the subject in question here,"* he said, in the quiet of my mind. *"Whatever you have to say to come clean with your reader will come from Soul. Just keep in mind that there are many entry points into the divine mystery of God, and quite often by indirection Soul finds direction out."*

I chuckled. I opened my eyes, and saw Jesus staring at me.

"What's so funny?" he asked.

"'By indirections find directions out,'" I replied, quoting from *Hamlet.* "The Inner Master also likes Shakespeare," I said, and laughed at how the Inner Master had summed up my relationship with Jesus by playing upon a famous line from Shakespeare.

Jesus' eyes twinkled, but he said nothing. After a moment's pause, I took a deep breath and bit the bullet. "This is very difficult for me to do, J; but I have to do it for my own conscience."

"This sounds ominous," Jesus said, in his serious voice.

"It is. I'm astounded that the Gospel writers of the New Testament could have had such outrageous presumption, and I don't want to do the same."

"What presumption?" Jesus asked, with a look of blank surprise.

Quickly realizing that he had asked on behalf of the unsuspecting reader, I said, *"The presumption that they knew what was best for Soul!* This presumption has morphed into the insufferable Christian conceit that assaults the consciousness of life today. I could accuse you of this presumption also, but hearing what you just said I know that you were only living out your spiritual destiny; but I don't know if I can ever forgive St. Paul for his arrogant presumption. As insightful as he was, his Epistles have led the world down the garden path. St. Paul's Epistles confirm with clarion audacity the Gospel writer's message of instant salvation through you, Jesus Christ; and to be perfectly frank with you, I could never live with that skunk on my conscience!"

"The skunk of presumption?" Jesus asked, feigning surprise again.

"Yes. It's an arrogant presumption to believe that one knows better than God what's best for Soul; and couching the secret teaching of the Way in the literary conceit of your death upon the cross to atone for the sins of the world is just that kind of presumption. Making you the Son of God and sole savior of the world to accomplish their agenda of establishing God's kingdom on earth was such an outrageous presumption that I'm certain they're hauled up on the carpet regularly by the implacable Lords of Karma!"

Jesus burst into laughter. *"Indeed, they are!"*

"And a lot of writers over the centuries have followed suite," I added. "So I'm going to ask you now to tell the reader just exactly what the true nature of our relationship really is. Can you please do that for me, J?" I asked, with a lump in my throat.

"You want to let the cat out of the bag, do you?" Jesus said, and smiled.

"I have no choice. If I don't come clean I'll have hell to pay down the road!"

"Why don't we give the reader some options and let him choose which one he's most comfortable with?" Jesus said, and reached over and poured us another cup of tea.

"What kind of options?" I asked, suspicious of his intentions.

"You're a creative writer, aren't you?" Jesus asked, straight-faced.

"Yes," I said, now more suspicious.

"And as a creative writer, you have disciplined yourself to tap into the Creative Life Stream; have you not?" Jesus asked, and took a sip of tea.

"Yes. The Inner Master confirmed this for me. When I asked him where all my spiritual insights came from he gave me the word *Sat Purusha,* which as you know is true being and source of all creative energy; but I've known this ever since I initiated myself into the Creative Life Stream with your sayings. They tapped me into the well inside me, so I know what you mean by the waters of eternal life. I've experienced the flow from the creative well of my true being thousands of times, so what's your point?"

"When you tap into the Creative Life Stream, which for clarity's sake is the Word, you speak for Soul. When Soul speaks, it speaks from the Soul Plane of Consciousness and not the Mental Plane. What does it matter what the nature of our relationship is then if what you write comes straight from the Soul Plane? Truth is truth, however it is revealed."

"Nice try, J!" I exclaimed. "This is precisely the kind of logic that the Gospel writers must have used to justify the ways of man to God! *'In the beginning was the Word,'* said St. John, thereby setting the stage for the Gospel conspiracy that followed. Well, I refuse to buy into it! I have to come clean! I don't want my reader to labor under the illusion—"

"Hold on a minute!" Jesus exclaimed, shooting up his hand. "Let me offer another option before you come clean. May I, please?"

"Yes, of course. It won't do any good; but I'm curious," I replied, genuinely intrigued by Christ's insistence but also terrified of capitulating to his new option.

Jesus smiled, his eyes twinkling. "As you wrote in your last novel, an artist ensouls his work with the creative life force, which is the 'I' of God. This defines an artist's work. The more he ensouls his work with the 'I' of the creative life force, the more identity his work has. A Van Gogh is a Van Gogh, because it has been ensouled with the unique I-consciousness of Van Gogh's individuality; and a Picaso is a Picaso; and a DaVinci a DaVinci; and so on. Well, creative writers ensoul their works also; do they not?"

"I know where you're going with this, J; and I'm going to cut you off at the pass," I replied, calling upon every ounce of courage that I had in me. "As much as I find your argument credible, I don't believe it would be strong enough to remove the stench from my conscience. *It won't!"*

"But wouldn't it be prudent to spell it out for the reader?" Jesus asked. "After all, even Doctor Jung had his Philemon."

Jesus was right, but so was I; and I had to stand my ground. "Alright, if you want me to spell it out I will; but I think you're just playing for time," I boldly replied.

"I may be. All the same please spell it out for me," Jesus said.

"Alright. Your argument boils down to this. A creative writer ensouls his characters with enough of the I-consciousness of the creative life force for his characters to give birth to their own identity in the story. Once they have given birth to their own identity, the writer has no more control over his characters. They now have a life of their own. And for a writer to direct the life of his characters would be to commit the same kind of presumption as the Gospel writers and our esteemed friend St. Paul did with your life, because it would be a violation of the Spiritual Law of Non-interference. Soul has the right to choose its own destiny in life, and a character in a novel has the same right to choose his own destiny in the imagined reality of the novel. This makes for the most aesthetically satisfying novels, because the author is not intruding in his characters lives; but the reader knows that a novel's reality is a reality unto itself. It's a parallel fictional world, if you will; and the reader knows the difference between the world of fiction and the world that he lives in. Is that the option you want the reader to consider?"

"I want the reader to see that the truth of fiction can often be truer than the truth out here in the real world," Jesus said, emphasizing his words with all the authority he could muster just to intimidate me. "This is why writers write fiction. They have an intuitive ability to ferret out truth with the creative process, which is precisely why your novel memoirs shocked the people of St. Jude. The truth was too much for them. Don't you think then that the reader should have the option to choose the truth of fiction over the truth of life if the truth of fiction satisfies his spiritual need to know?"

I broke into a fit of laughter. The brilliance of Christ's argument was too much for me, and I had to release the pressure of the pure joy of his genius. *"That's exactly the same argument that the Gospel writers made, wasn't it?"* I said, smiling with pride for seeing through Christ's impeccable logic. "I know that the truth of fiction can be truer than the truth of real life. I learned that from Hemingway. He experimented with the creative process and concluded that the writer needs the power of imagination to give the truth of his story more reality, and I did the same with my novel memoirs that shocked the people of my hometown; but you will notice that I called them novel memoirs and not fiction. *Unlike the Gospel writers I came clean with my reader then, and I'm going to come clean now—"*

"MAY I?" Jesus shouted, shooting up his hand like a traffic cop about to stop a fatal collision and staring at me with what looked like desperation in his eyes.

"Yes," I said, sensing the inevitable collision of our two worlds.

"Let's offer the reader another option," Jesus said, his voice shaky. "Let's explore the possibility that with your talent you have tapped into the archetype that speaks the Way of Christ with even more clarity than the Gospel writers. That's a possibility, is it not?"

"It certainly is," I said, smiling to myself at his effort to win me over. "I honestly believe in what you're implying, because I agree with Plato in his theory of Perfect Forms; but as true as that may be, I have to tell you in all good conscience that I can't bring myself to deceive my reader. *I will not have that skunk on my conscience!"*

"I've run out of options then," Jesus said, and slumped into his chair.

"Then all we have left is the truth," I said, with unexpected tears in my voice.

"Yes," Jesus said, with a long and heavy sigh.

"Then please tell the reader the exact nature of our relationship," I said, as an ocean of emotion welled up inside me. I could not avoid the collision.

Jesus sat up in my reading chair. He waited a moment or two, and then looked me straight in the eye and held my gaze as if for the last time as our worlds collided. **"The exact nature of our relationship is that I am only as real as your reader's imagination will allow me to be,"** he answered, with that twinkle in his unfathomable, loving eyes.

"With that we can bring closure to our dialogue," I said, the tears just streaming down my cheeks now. "I want to thank you, J. This has been an unbelievable experience—" My voice cracked completely. I could not stop the tears from flowing.

"For me as well," said Jesus, and stood up. I stood up also. Jesus had the most beatific smile on his face. He raised his arms and placed them around me and held me tight for the longest time. *"Thank you, O,"* he whispered softly into my ear.

"You're welcome," I said, and Jesus faded to the Other Side with a grateful smile on his face that will stay in my heart forever, and ever.

♥

OTHER BOOKS BY OREST STOCCO

Old Whore Life
Exploring the Shadow Side of Karma

Healing with Padre Pio

Why Bother?
The Riddle of the Good Samaritan

Just Going With the Flow
And Other Spiritual Musings

Keeper of the Flame

My Unborn Child

What Would I Say Today If I Were to Die Tomorrow?

On the Wings of Habitat
A Volunteer's Story

COMING WORKS

Letters to Padre Pio

The Summoning of Noman
The True Story of My Parallel Life

The Beauty of Suffering
Reflections on Jung's Red Book

Saint Paul's Conceit

About the Author

Orest Stocco was born in Panettieri, Calabria, Italy. He emigrated to Canada and studied philosophy at university. A student of Gurdjieff's teaching for many years which opened him up to the Way, his passion for writing inspired such innovative works as *Keeper of the Flame* and *Healing with Padre Pio*. He lives in Georgian Bay, Ontario with his life mate Penny Lynn Cates. His personal dictum is: *life is an individual journey*.
Visit him at: http://www.oreststocco.com
Spiritual Musings Blog:
http://www.spiritualmusingsbyoreststocco.blogspot.com

ME AND MY SISPYHEAN ROCK